KINGFISHER
SEVEN

OTHER TITLES BY SHAWN KLOMPARENS

Jessica Z.

Two Years, No Rain

The Banks of Certain Rivers (written as Jon Harrison)

KINGFISHER SEVEN

A THRILLER

SHAWN KLOMPARENS

Published by Thomas & Mercer, Seattle

www.apub.com

EU product safety contact:
Amazon Media EU S. à r.l.
38, avenue John F. Kennedy, L-1855 Luxembourg
amazonpublishing-gpsr@amazon.com

ISBN-13: 9781662532382 (paperback)
ISBN-13: 9781662532399 (digital)

Cover design by Damon Freeman
Cover image: © Silas Manhood / ArcAngel Images; © SumanBhaumik, © Paopano, © Nature Peaceful, © lib Shabashnyi / Shutterstock

Printed in the United States of America

For Birch and Axel

A NOTE TO THE READER

As Shawn's spouse of twenty-six years, I'd like to express my gratitude to those who helped encourage his writing career.

With the goal to become a published author, Shawn began writing before our daughter was born. Over the years that followed, Shawn completed seven novels, worked on collaborative projects, and wrote short stories and poetry while managing a full-time job and house projects and caring for a family. Writing is an inward solitary journey. It is an expression of one's thoughts, emotions, and imagination that ultimately becomes open to public dissection and judgment. Shawn conflated his self-esteem with the commercial success of his books, which, as readers, we know is not the true value of a work of art.

Shawn's dream was to be a writer, and he was afflicted by the creative process. Living with that force, even when he swore he would never write again, we would always find a way to make space in our life for his writing—late nights, early mornings, or writing binges away from the family.

Journals found after Shawn's death made clear that he had more stories to share with the world. Shawn received the offer to publish this book on the day before he learned his treatment options for his terminal cancer were ending. He knew he would not be able to enjoy the publication of this book; I hope he feels the love and care that went into making this a reality.

—Julie Klomparens, November 2024

CHAPTER ONE

Thirty miles south of Galveston in the placid Gulf of Mexico, plumes of supercooled vapor swirled about the base of the massive seaborne launch platform. Once a state-of-the-art drilling rig, converted after thirteen years of service to the oil industry, it floated almost perfectly still beneath a cloudless sky. No human beings were within a three-mile blast zone; the only signs of life were seagulls swarming and wheeling above the scene and a droning, almost robotic voice emanating from loudspeakers mounted around the structure.

"Passing through the T-minus three-minute mark on the terminal countdown, fuel loading is complete; telemetry from the vehicle is looking nominal. This is Kingfisher Aerospace launch control . . ."

Towering twenty stories above it all, surrounded at its base by a churning mist, was the *Kingfisher Seven* rocket, the satellite-carrying workhorse of the upstart launch company Kingfisher Aerospace. Driven by seven powerful liquid-oxygen-and-methane-fueled engines, the reusable vehicle had proved itself with a string of thirty-two consecutive successful payload deliveries to low earth and geostationary-transfer orbit at a fraction of the cost charged by old incumbents like Boeing and Lockheed Martin. Like so many other industries, aerospace had been disrupted by new thinkers with venture capital backing, and it would never be the same again.

"We're just passing through T-minus two minutes on the count, and the flight director is taking a final poll from the control consoles . . ."

Three miles to the south, on another converted oil rig, the launch-control team worked in a fortified windowless room. Dimly lit, containing three rows of desks and a wall-spanning digital display at the front with a map of the world and multiple camera angles from the launch site, the control center was staffed by young recruits from the nation's top engineering schools. Each projected steely confidence as they were queried over their headsets by the flight director pacing at the back. At thirty-six, he was the oldest person in the room.

"Payload?"

"Go."

"Weather?"

"Go."

"Launch platform?"

"We're go, flight."

"Telemetry?"

There was a pause. At the telem console, flanked by two massive flat-screen monitors, a laptop, a tablet, and a three-ring binder, twenty-nine-year-old MIT graduate Tricia Cruz stared at the data on her screen. This was her first mission "on the rig" since being promoted up from a support position on the mainland, and something didn't look right.

"Telemetry, what's your status?"

"Hold, flight." Tricia leaned closer to the screen. Normally the neat columns of data flickered with changing information as the encrypted signal came in from the launch platform, but now the numbers were static. Without good data for the controllers, there was no way the rocket—or its $200 million communications payload—could be allowed to lift off.

"Telemetry?"

Tricia blinked, and the numbers began to stream steadily again. Just a momentary glitch.

"We're good, flight. We're go."

There was a pause, and Tricia felt the flight director's hard stare on the back of her neck. She didn't turn around or reconsider. The data looked good now, and she'd made her call to proceed. The flight director resumed his poll.

"Guidance?"

"Go!"

"Range safety?"

"You're go, Kingfisher," a staticky voice reported over the communication net. The range-safety officer, or RSO, was a US Space Force official based in Florida who could remotely destroy the vehicle with explosive charges if it veered off course.

"We're go for launch," the flight director said with a nod.

The public affairs announcer continued talking; all the controllers had learned to tune out the ongoing commentary provided for the thousands of people worldwide following Kingfisher's webcast of the launch and the bigwigs watching from the VIP lounge on site.

"Thirty seconds on the clock, flight control tells us everything looks good for Kingfisher Seven*'s launch of the TransAmerican CommSat payload along with three high school microsat experiments hitching a ride up to space. T-minus twenty seconds and* Kingfisher Seven*'s onboard computers have assumed autonomous control of the vehicle. T-minus ten . . . nine . . . eight . . ."*

On the launch platform, a torrent of water sprayed from three holding tanks to protect the area from the heat of combustion. A crack sounded, and a bright flash appeared beneath the rocket as its engines ignited in a controlled sequence within milliseconds of each other. The gulls scattered at the sudden roar, and a torch-like plume of thrust shot through the aperture in the platform toward the roiling sea below. With two seconds left on the count, the *Kingfisher Seven*'s computers determined that each of its motors was running flawlessly, and they sent the command for the platform's hold-down bolts to separate.

"Ignition and . . . liftoff! Liftoff of Kingfisher Seven *and TransAmerican CommSat Twelve, on a mission to provide enhanced voice and data services to western North America and the Pacific Ocean . . ."*

The platform shook with barely contained violence as the rocket climbed away. The *Kingfisher Seven* crept skyward at first, shuddering, its gimballed motors pivoting in concert to keep the stack upright through small gusts of wind. The vehicle picked up speed, faster and faster still, and the vibrations eased to nearly nothing as the noise settled into a distant, crackling growl.

"We've got a beautiful launch, just beautiful! Kingfisher Seven *is rising into the clear Gulf sky and tracking right down the center line on its ascent . . ."*

Back at launch control, the technicians remained glued to their readouts, mostly ignoring the images projected on the wall before them. The display looked good for the cameras, though, and it gave the VIPs up above something to watch through the glass separating the observation gallery from the control room. The controllers worked from a well-rehearsed script now, calling out milestones over the communication net.

"Propulsion nominal, all seven engines operating at one hundred and two percent rated thrust."

"Propellant pressures nominal."

"Vehicle velocity thirteen hundred kilometers per second. *Kingfisher Seven* is supersonic."

On the wall display, video showed a bow shock of compressed vapor spreading from the rocket's payload fairing, trailing a V through the air like the wake behind a ship.

"We've just heard flight control report that Kingfisher Seven *is moving faster than the speed of sound. This means we're approaching Max Q, the period of maximum aerodynamic pressure on the vehicle as it makes its climb out of the denser part of Earth's lower atmosphere . . ."*

Up on the display, anyone watching closely might have noticed the slightest wobble as the rocket sped upward, flying faster now than a rifle bullet. A call came from the guidance console with measured urgency.

"Flight, we're seeing a series of oscillations on the—"

At Tricia Cruz's telemetry console, the blur of data flashed, momentarily displaying nonsense before abruptly showing zeroes or blank spaces. All eyes in the room turned up to the wall display just in time to see the rocket come apart in a brilliant explosion. It glowed orange in the center for an instant before it was nothing but a white burst of showering, tumbling, smoking debris.

The camera operator panned out to show a wider view. The remnant of the explosion was the only cloud in the sky, and wisps of smoke trailed below it like dangling tentacles.

"It appears the Kingfisher Seven *has experienced some sort of in-flight malfunction . . . we're waiting here for word from launch control . . . obviously they're working now to determine what exactly is going on . . ."*

The control room fell silent for a moment, overcome by shock at the image, but the controllers soon snapped back into action. The flight director straightened his back, gritted his teeth, and pressed a button on his console to keep his communications limited to the loop in the room.

"Data retention procedures in place. Team, everyone turn to section one oh one dash two in your procedures manual. Security, please lock the doors." The director took a breath and steeled himself before pressing a button at his console activating a private line to the Kingfisher office on the mainland.

"Houston, this is flight." He took another long, slow breath. "Please tell Mrs. Nash we've lost the vehicle."

CHAPTER TWO

In the VIP gallery above the control floor, Jake Moran was already on the phone to his team back in Everett, Washington.

"Tam," he said through the commotion surrounding him. "Please say that wasn't anything on our end."

"Impossible," she told him. "We had ten-mile visibility, unlimited ceiling, and negligible wind shear. You can't get better conditions for a launch. That was positively nothing on our end."

Tamara Rinaldi was Jake's business partner and the director of operations at Cascadia Information Systems. She had two PhDs and zero reservations about telling Jake—or anyone else, for that matter—when he was full of shit. He took her counsel as gospel.

"I figured."

Through the glass of the control room, he viewed a scene of intense focus. Binders flipped open so checklists could be examined, each controller poring over every bit of data as they hunted for any obvious sign of what might have caused the failure. At the back of the room, the Kingfisher flight director—Jake's former colleague Andy Lang—turned and stared up into the gallery. When his eyes met Jake's, he shook his head dejectedly and gave a thumbs-down before returning to his console.

"It really wasn't us," Tam said again.

"Just the same," Jake said, "put a freeze on any data and systems we had working this, and have Stu make a complete pair of backups—"

"I'm already on it," a deep baritone said over the line. Stu Gallagher was the director of IT at Cascadia, an opaque title for a substantial job, given their diverse portfolio.

"Oh, so I'm on speaker?"

"We've been following in the Big Room," she said.

Jake's company had been providing meteorological asset support for today's launch. It was a minor deal but also highly visible. So much of Cascadia's work was classified, and the Kingfisher contract, while small, had been a high-profile marketing coup for their growing company.

"Who else is there with you?" Jake asked.

"Pretty much everyone," Tam said, followed by a chorus of "Hi, Jake!"

"Hey, guys," Jake said, turning to the wall and keeping his voice low in the somber room.

"Did you get to meet Helena Nash?" a voice asked.

"I am decidedly not cool enough to meet Helena Nash," Jake said.

They'd exchanged emails of greeting when Cascadia had come on to support the launch, and Helena Nash had invited him to be her guest in the VIP room at launch control; that had been the extent of their communications. As a self-made internet billionaire and head of Kingfisher, Helena Nash was truly an international celebrity. The younger staff at Cascadia were obsessed with her backstory, her poise, and her expensive, consistently on-trend clothes.

"If I get the chance to meet her," Jake said, "I'll let you all know."

A click sounded over the line, and Tam spoke again.

"You're off speaker now," she said. "What happened?"

"No idea."

"Liar. You probably have it all figured out already. What do you *think* happened?"

"Okay, I do have a thought. At that point in the boost phase, and the way it came apart . . ." Jake glanced back down to the focused concentration in the control room and lowered his voice. "I'd say it was a payload-integration issue. Somehow the satellite came loose from its mount up in the fairing. Vibration was amplified, and everything went to hell. It didn't look like that exactly on camera, but given what I saw, that makes the most sense to me." Jake turned back toward the rest of the VIP room. "Whatever it was, they're working it now. They'll have a pretty good idea before the end of the day, I bet."

"And you? What's your plan?"

"I doubt they'll need me for any kind of debrief. I'll head home a day early, catch up there for a day or two, then fly up to HQ after that?"

Jake's initial plan had been to establish Cascadia's base of operations back in his hometown of Jackson Hole, but Tam had pointed out that the cost of living and limited access might make it difficult to hire and keep employees. She'd suggested Everett, near her home in northwest Washington State, as a perfect alternative. Close to the culture, food, and city life of Seattle. And its proximity to mountain wilderness and Puget Sound made for easy getaways to outdoor recreation for their staff. Jake and Tam enforced flexible hours, too, encouraging their people to work from home when it was practical and security requirements allowed.

"And stay where?"

"I was thinking—"

"My guesthouse is open." Tam paused. "If you'd like."

Jake glanced around the gallery before responding, feeling ridiculous as he did it. "I think I'd like that very much." A young man in a light-blue polo shirt with the Kingfisher logo entered the room and looked around for a moment before spotting Jake and making a beeline in his direction.

"I think someone needs me here," Jake said. "I'll be in touch."

"Let me know when you're on your way?" Tam asked.

"I will." Jake ended the call and turned to face the young man.

"Mr. Moran?" the staffer said.

"Please, call me Jake."

"Mr. Moran, Mrs. Nash would like to have a word with you on the mainland."

Assuming all flights were grounded so soon after the failed launch, Jake asked, "Tonight? When is the boat headed back?"

"There's a helicopter up top for you now. She's waiting in Clear Lake."

Huh, Jake thought. *Apparently I'm cool enough to meet Helena Nash after all.*

After the air-conditioned chill in the dim VIP gallery, the humidity up on the platform hit Jake like a slap. The afternoon sky was blindingly bright, too, and Jake squinted as he searched through his laptop bag for a pair of sunglasses. Across the platform a midsize passenger helicopter waited with its rotors furled. A wind sock hung limp beyond it. Next to the helo, a stout Black man wearing a light-blue flight suit, aviator glasses, and a Kingfisher ball cap stood with his arms crossed. His expression remained wary as Jake approached.

"Sikorsky S-70," Jake said by way of greeting.

The man raised an eyebrow. "You know this chopper?"

Jake shaded his eyes with his hand as he peeked in through the canopy. "I saw these around when I started out at flight school," he said. "Thought I'd even get to fly one someday. But then 9/11 happened, and the Marine Corps decided it had other plans for me."

The man's face broke into a wide grin. "Shit, I thought I smelled a marine aboard," he said, pulling off his glasses as he extended his hand. "I'm Denny Wade. I was with the 169 out of Pendleton."

"Jake Moran," Jake said, shaking Wade's hand. "The 169. Vipers, huh? I supported some of your ops in Phantom Freedom."

Wade cocked his head. "You were in Fallujah?"

"In a manner of speaking," Jake said. "Intel. Eye in the sky."

Wade got the "classified" hint, left it at that, and gestured that other passengers were approaching.

"Marines ride up front," he said as he reached to open the helo's door. "Get yourself strapped in."

Jake pulled himself aboard and slid into the copilot's seat up front before latching his safety harness. He adjusted a headset over his ears as Wade helped the other passenger, an older, elegantly dressed man with a wild shock of white hair, into his seat.

"Dr. Taka," Wade greeted him. "It's good to have you aboard again. I wish it was under better circumstances."

"Thank you, Mr. Wade," Taka replied with a polite nod. He spoke with precise, accented English. "It is never good to lose a payload, but it happens from time to time."

Taka buckled himself in as Wade donned his headset and checked his comms.

A high-pitched whine sounded over their headsets as the chopper's twin turboshaft engines spooled up, and the cabin filled with a subtle vibration as the rotors began spinning overhead. Wade made a call to air traffic control to file their flight path.

"Houston Center, Kingfisher eight oh two departing restricted airspace GPS direct for Clear Lake City."

"Kingfisher eight oh two, Houston Center, you're clear for GPS direct; watch for southbound traffic out of Galveston Bay. Good day."

Wade glanced over his shoulder at their passenger and then gave Jake a sharp thumbs-up before pulling back on the cyclic to gently ease the chopper up and out over the Gulf. Wade was obviously a skilled pilot, and the flight was smooth as glass.

"So marines really can fly, looks like," Jake said.

Wade chuckled. "You know it. I got three thousand hours plus when I was in. So, you say flight school with Uncle Sam didn't happen, but did you ever get to fly?"

"I got my license after I was out," Jake said. "Fixed wing, though. Single-engine instrument rating. I've got a little Cirrus back home that I take around. Mostly for work."

"Sweet plane," Wade said, nodding as he scanned the airspace before them. "You get any time in rotorcraft?"

"Just a few hours in a Bell 206—"

"That bird nearly flies itself."

Jake laughed. "Not when I'm at the controls. Level flight was enough of a challenge."

"Life skills, my friend," Wade said.

They cruised high above the vast blue Gulf now. Far ahead, Jake saw a gathering of small boats.

Wade shook his head. "Man," he said, "I feel sorry for the guys who pulled perimeter duty today."

"What do you mean?"

"You don't know about the protests?"

Jake craned forward to better see the flotilla beneath them. "What's up?"

"It's a mess. Kingfisher has some plutonium-powered satellite coming up on the manifest in a few weeks . . . well, it'll probably slip after the shit that went down with the launch today, but there's a nuclear generator aboard and people are riled up. Environmentalists, mostly. They're worried if there's a failure like we just had now, an explosion or something, it's going to spread a green cloud of radioactivity all over Florida."

"Could it?"

"Hell no. I've heard all about how they encase that plutonium . . ." He stopped himself. "Let me walk that back. There's always a possibility. But the thing is made to survive, you know? I think the chances are slim. But I'm sure after whatever happened today, they're going to feel pretty fired up about their little party—"

A dark shadow flashed in front of them, causing them both to reflexively jerk backward. In the same instant the helicopter's canopy shattered with an earsplitting bang, showering Jake's lap with shards of plexiglass as the cabin filled with black, bitter smoke. Wade grimaced and doubled forward as Dr. Taka shouted from behind them.

"Mayday, Mayday," Wade managed to say through short breaths. "Kingfisher eight oh two is losing power twenty miles southeast of Galveston. Possible bird strike. Preparing to ditch." The leg of his flight suit was torn and dark with blood. "Gonna need some help here, Jake," he gasped, struggling to flip a switch on the overhead panel.

Jake whipped off his headset and twisted back toward their passenger. Taka met Jake's urgent stare.

"Get up here!" Jake told him, eyes watering from the acrid smoke filling the cabin.

Without hesitation, Dr. Taka unbuckled himself and scrambled forward, losing his footing in the lurching helicopter and crawling the rest of the way. He looked from side to side and nodded. "What do I do?"

"Help the pilot," Jake said, focusing on the shuddering copilot handle between his knees.

Taka immediately slipped off his belt and began to fashion a tourniquet around Wade's leg.

"Gotta autorotate," Wade said through shallow, quick breaths. Perspiration beaded on his forehead and upper lip.

Through the shattered canopy, the looming surface of the Gulf spun as the Sikorsky made a spiraling descent.

"Cyclic back half, Jake. Reduce collective. Full right rudder. All the way man, full right, do it!"

Jake mashed the rudder pedal all the way down with his foot as he pulled back on the control stick, and the helicopter stopped spinning through the sky. His old flight instructor had told him about autorotation—where an unpowered helicopter can make a safe landing with only the lift provided by its spinning rotors—but he'd never practiced the procedure. Now he was getting firsthand experience.

"Good, Jake. Good," Wade rasped. "Keep the stick still. Don't stir the pot."

Between the cockpit seats Taka knelt and worked to stanch the bleeding from Wade's wound. His hands and shirt cuffs were bright red, and the lower part of the canopy was smeared with a bloody boot print. Below them, the waves of the Gulf approached with frightening speed.

"Back on the collective, Jake," Wade said weakly. "Little more. We got five hundred feet. Four fifty. Okay, now, at fifty you're going to flare us out like that sweet little Cirrus you fly and set us right down on the water with a kiss." Wade gasped and winced, grimacing through his pain. "Here we go, man, here we go. Two hundred feet. On my call you're bringing that cyclic all the way back and giving it full collective. Get ready—"

"Brace yourself!" Jake shouted, both hands tight around the handle of the cyclic.

"You got it man, you got it."

"Get ready to crash!" Jake shouted again.

"One hundred feet. Okay, Jake. Now. Flare us out. Bring it on in."

Jake tugged on the vibrating cyclic. It resisted as the waves rushed closer.

"Do it now, man, do it!"

Jake pulled back on the stick with all his strength.

CHAPTER THREE

Creeping through the center of Old Tiraspol, René Ilonescu downshifted his rickety black Peugeot 205 and slowed to let some punks cross ahead of him on the Strada Sverdlov. His mangled right hand, missing the index and middle fingers and half the thumb, rested on the gearshift as the long-haired kids with skateboards and leather jackets sauntered toward the Hotel Russia. One kid grabbed his crotch and spit on the hood of the Peugeot, daring René with a glowering stare to say something about it. René sat unblinking and raised his damaged hand to the burn-scarred right side of his face, the flesh bright red with still-healing wounds. The kid blanched at the sight and turned away, moving quickly on.

Fucking weaklings.

Even on a rare sunny day like today, the old Moldovan city in the breakaway eastern republic of Transnistria had a way of looking gray and grimy, like it had never shrugged off the pallor of Soviet occupation from decades before. The exhaust haze from all the old cars and autobuses didn't help, and when René jammed the rattling hatchback's gearshift into first and eased off the clutch, a cloud of black exhaust belched from beneath the old vehicle. The catalytic converter had been chopped off and stolen years earlier, so a gray swirl followed René as he accelerated and turned south toward the Strada Odessa. René dodged potholes as he drove, and twice was forced to divert the car up onto the crumbling sidewalk to avoid low-hanging cables tapped into the overhead trolleybus lines to steal electricity. On his second diversion, René veered back quickly to the strada to avoid a body sprawled on the weedy concrete. Drunk or dead: either was equally likely here at 10:30 in the morning.

At the R27 the old Moldovan highway, the macadam became smoother and the going easier. René passed a tractor and floored the Peugeot, leaning forward as if he could physically urge the thing to move faster. He'd just barely made it to seventy kilometers an hour when he rounded a bend and was forced to slam on the brakes for a makeshift roadblock that had somehow sprung up in the two hours since he'd passed north that morning. René sighed. A dented Soviet-era UAZ-452 cargo van blocked most of the road, and two men, one old, one young, stood in the open lane. The young one was scrawny with a buzz cut and baggy jeans, while the old one had stubble and a huge belly that stretched his soiled shirt. A cigarette dangled from the older one's mouth. René knew both probably had pistols at their backs and were likely drunk, and that they had set up the roadblock to shake down travelers on their way to and from the republic's capital.

René slid his hand into his pocket as he slowed the vehicle and withdrew a four-inch Böker folding tactical knife, flipping it open with a flick of his thumb stump and hiding it blade-down between his knees. Even with a disfigured hand, René was skilled with a knife, far more lethal than he could be close in with a gun. The younger man on the road waved downward, and René cranked the Peugeot's window open as the car rolled to a stop.

"*Stoi!*" the younger one said in accented Russian. "Halt! Where do you think you're going today, huh?" He made a hesitant, staggering step forward, and René took the car out of gear and rested his hand on his leg close to the Böker. The kid didn't notice. "Just out for a drive I bet," he said, switching to Romanian. "Like they all say." He laughed like he'd made some kind of clever joke. René didn't laugh.

"I had business in Tiraspol," René said in Russian. "Slow going coming back. A lot of shit on the roads."

The older one scowled at this, and the younger one staggered closer to the car. "What are you trying to say, motherfucker?"

"I'm saying you need to get out of my way and let me through," René said. He reached down to the left with his good hand and pulled a pristine-looking Ericsson satphone from the door pocket, holding it aloft for both men to see. "Or I could make a call right now. I'm sure Vostok would send some of his guys to clean this shit off the road. They'd be happy about it, too, I bet. I think they're tired of just sitting around. A little action might be good for their morale."

The younger one furrowed his brow in confusion while the older guy visibly paled at René's words.

"Hey," the older one said, flicking his cigarette away and stepping forward to pull his younger comrade back by the shoulders. "Hey, we don't want any trouble from Vostok." He spoke in Russian, deliberately, like he was proving a point. "We're on his side, okay? Right? We're for the motherland, just trying to help. We're here looking for agitators—"

"Get the fuck out of here," René said, putting the car back into gear. "Vostok doesn't need help from clowns like you. If he did, you'd hear about it."

He let out the clutch and swerved around the UAZ, leaving the two men in a billow of exhaust as he folded his knife and returned it to his pocket. *Idiots.* If drunks like that were representative of the pro-Russian insurgents, it was no wonder the region was no closer to returning to Moscow's control. They were mostly addicts, hoodlums, and low-level scammers, every one of them piled onto a local pyramid of graft, with the Russian "advisors" sent by Moscow at the top of the heap.

Not Vostok, though. The soldier for hire was as clean as they came and dedicated at his core to the cause of the *Russkiy Mir*—the "Russian World," the expansion of which would counter the decadent weakness of the liberal West. Vostok was a true believer who inspired loyalty in his troops and fear in the locals.

René hated the man.

After a few more kilometers on the motorway, he entered the tired village of Sucleia. The highway was lined with low stone walls overgrown with weeds and brush, behind which stood ramshackle farmhouses with sagging roofs and clotheslines heavy with faded garments. Just past the village boundary he slowed and swerved to avoid a dead dog, then turned right toward the Dniester River. The road was unpaved as it paralleled the muddy waterway. René drove slowly for a kilometer and a half before pulling over and parking the Peugeot in a copse of dusty trees.

René grabbed a black backpack from the passenger footwell. He drew out a bottle of eye drops, tilted his head back, and applied some between the scarred, hard flesh of his ruined right eyelids. He returned the drops to the pack along with the satphone, zipped the top shut, and continued on foot toward the river. A dirt path followed the riverbank littered with plastic bags, soda bottles, and broken blocks of Styrofoam. Dead fish bobbed belly up at the water's edge. After a couple of hundred meters, René came to a concrete building erected over riprap at the bank. The glass from the old factory's windows was broken, and the building's lower level was tagged with colorful Cyrillic graffiti, and a rusty metal drainpipe—now painted to look like a massive, veiny phallus—jutted out from the foundation toward the water. At about twenty meters away, René unshouldered his pack, dropped it to his feet, and slipped his right hand into his pocket, ready to draw the Böker in an instant.

"Anton!" he called toward the building. "Anton! All good?" After a brief pause, a muffled reply came from inside the concrete husk.

"Tell me the word!" It was Anton's voice, but with a slight quaver. Something was off. René drew the knife from his pocket and flicked it open.

"Anton?" he called in reply.

"I said tell me the word! Say it!"

"Mountain!" René shouted. This was the code they'd agreed on to signal they were alone and safe. "Now you!" There was no reply, and

René stepped back behind a tree for cover. "Anton! What the fuck is going on?"

Anton's skinny figure appeared at one of the upstairs corner windows. "The Arab is here. Nabil."

René let his hand drop to his side. "Nabil? With the phosphorus?"

"There was a problem." Anton shook his head. "No phosphorus."

"Fuck," René swore, under his breath. He folded the knife and pocketed it. "Is it safe to come up?"

"It's fine," Anton said, and René raised his eyebrows. "He's clean," the kid added. "No weapons. I checked."

René grabbed the backpack, slung it over his left shoulder, and clambered up to a sagging loading dock on the north side of the structure, careful to step over the alarm trip wires he'd strung around the building. He crossed the room, treading through broken bottles and smashed, overturned furniture to a rusted iron stairway in the middle of the space. He climbed the stairs and knocked three times at the closed door at the top. Anton opened the door almost immediately and shook his head again.

"It's fucked," the kid said, looking gaunt and pale. A sheen of sweat sparkled on Anton's upper lip, and René wondered if the Dutch university dropout he'd taken in as his assistant had started shooting heroin again. *More shit to worry about . . .* He'd deal with it later. He moved past Anton and down a corridor lined with crates filled with AK-74M assault rifles and thousands of rounds of 5.45mm ammunition. An arsenal cached for a conquering army that was forever only days away.

René knew they'd never come.

The wall of plastic sheeting tented up for his lab rustled as he passed. In the far corner, beyond the lab, a short, pudgy man looked up and began visibly shaking when his eyes met René's.

"I can explain—" he started, but René held up his hand.

"The shipment didn't come through?" René asked.

"It . . . it arrived. But I couldn't take it."

"What do you mean you couldn't take it? Were there cops? There shouldn't have been cops, that was taken care of."

"I couldn't pay," Nabil said, and he looked down to his lap and started silently crying. René shook his head in confusion.

"How could you not pay? I gave you a hundred thousand, US."

Nabil opened his mouth like he was trying to speak, but no sound came from his mouth.

"What the fuck happened?" René asked. "You had the money, it should have been—"

"They wanted only Bitcoin," Nabil said, almost whispering.

"The deal was set up in cash. What was the problem?"

Nabil shook his head again. "They said they'd take only Bitcoin."

"You didn't," René growled, suddenly consumed by a white-hot rage. "You didn't!" He lunged forward, grabbing the Arab by the collar and slamming him into the wall. In the same instant the Böker was drawn, opened, and pressed to the folds of the fat man's neck. A trickle of blood ran over René's hand and down Nabil's sweaty, hairless chest. René smelled stale cigarettes and bile on the man's panicked breath.

"You traded the cash for fucking Bitcoin?"

"Don't kill me! Don't kill me!" Nabil openly wept now. "Please, René, don't kill me! I can fix this—"

"*Fix* this? You fat fucking idiot! We work with cash! I gave you fucking *cash* for this deal! But what, they wouldn't take the crypto? Why did it fall through?"

"The Bitcoin price dropped, almost twenty percent, we didn't have enough—"

"*Auughhh!*" René yelled, a primal, guttural roar, and he jabbed the knife into Nabil's soft belly. Not deep enough to kill the man, but enough to make him scream. He pulled the knife out, held the dripping crimson blade up to the Arab's face, then jabbed it into his gut again three times like punctuation as he shouted, "You *stupid! Fucking! Asshole!*"

Nabil vomited down his front, and René stepped back in disgust, letting the man slump to the floor.

"I'm sorry," Nabil said hoarsely. "I thought the price—"

René grabbed Nabil's hair and forced him to look upward. "You thought you'd make a little profit off me, right?" He yanked Nabil's hair again and leaned down so the two were eye to eye, only centimeters apart. "No one fucks me like this, you understand?" He slammed Nabil's head back into the concrete wall and stepped away. "No one fucks René Ilonescu. Ever. Anton!"

He turned to see the Dutch kid cowering in the shadows by the ammo crates, looking like he was going to be sick himself. "Pull yourself together, for fuck's sake. Finish him off and clean up the mess. Put him in the river—"

"Wait," Nabil gasped.

"When Vostok's guys find him downstream, they'll know what happened. A little reminder that we're still here—"

"I know someone," Nabil said, his glassy eyes staring far off into nothing.

René shook his head and stepped to the lab, pulling the Velcroed door flap open with a long *riiiiip*.

Nabil took a short wheezing breath. "He can get cesium—"

"Cesium?" René asked, cocking his head.

"Cesium. Yes. One thirty-seven, the radioactive isotope. And maybe plutonium—"

"How much?" René asked, letting the plastic flap drop. "How much plutonium?"

"Twenty grams at least. Maybe more. But twenty for sure."

"You're lying to save your ass."

"No," Nabil said weakly, shaking his head. "By God, I'm telling you the truth." He looked to René and shook his head again. "I swear."

René looked toward Anton, then to Nabil, and back to Anton again. "Clean him up," René said, and the kid's shoulders fell with visible relief. "Tape up his belly, and we'll have a word." He took a step into the lab before spinning back toward Nabil and pointing toward the west. “If you’re bullshitting me,” he said, “don’t forget, the river is right there.”

“I swear,” Nabil said as Anton crouched down next to him. “I’m telling you the truth.”

“You’d better be,” René said. He stepped into the lab, and the plastic flap dropped shut behind him.

CHAPTER FOUR

On the humid surface of the Gulf of Mexico, the protest, in the minds of its organizers, had been a massive success. There were only thirty of them in a handful of boats, but the media coverage they'd received from the two charter vessels following them had been extraordinary, and the visual provided by the distant exploding rocket over the group's banners and raised fists was *beyond* extraordinary. There'd been high fives and smiles as the cloud from the explosion dissipated, a true feeling that they'd accomplished something.

Like they'd practically been responsible.

As the cheers died down and the smoke cleared from far above them, they furled their banners and started up the motors on their jumbled collection of vessels: inflatable tenders, fishing boats, even an old sailboat had joined them. A speedboat chartered by the press fired up its rumbling motor and blasted away.

"Nice work, people!" a thirtysomething man announced over a megaphone from the flybridge of a nearly new fishing boat. He had brooding features and prematurely graying hair, but the smile on his face was genuine. "Let's head back and meet up in Galveston. I think Jenny has a suggestion for where we should celebrate, right, Jenny?"

A petite dreadlocked woman at his side was filming the scene with her phone. She paused to take the megaphone: "How do y'all feel about meeting back onshore at the Brick House?"

"The Brick House!" someone yelled, followed by shouts seconding the suggestion.

"The Brick House it is!" Jenny said. "And Duncan's buying!"

The group's leader pulled an exaggerated face of dismay before laughing along with the hoots and cheers from across the gathered boats. Duncan took the megaphone and raised it to his mouth, pausing for a moment to let the happy ruckus calm down.

"We'll see you all there. Everyone be careful on the way back—we don't want to do anything that's going to bring us any negative attention. Kingfisher gave us a gift today with that launch failure. Let's use it. Okay?"

"Right on, Duncan!" someone called, followed by whistles and claps. Duncan waved and flashed a wide grin before raising the megaphone once more.

"And one last thing," he started, "I wanted to tell all of you—"

A helicopter approached from the south, high in the air, and Duncan paused to let the engine noise pass. Another sound came, a sharp *boom!* followed by a whining groan, and all eyes turned to watch the damaged chopper trailing a thick plume of black smoke as it faltered downward in a ragged spiral. The aircraft leveled out, the *thump, thump, thump* sound of its rotors slowing like a dying pulse as it dropped from the sky. It struggled to stay aloft, hovering for an impossible moment before smacking the Gulf's surface a quarter mile away with a geyser-like splash.

"Holy shit!" someone yelled.

A deeply tanned kid called Tommy at the console of the fishing boat spun to face Duncan. "What do we do, man?"

Duncan froze for a moment, feeling the pressure of so many eyes on him. "We've . . . we've got to get over there," he finally said before raising the megaphone. He pointed to a nearby powerboat. "I want you with me over to that helicopter," he said, firmly now, composed once again. "Follow us. Everyone else, keep clear and stand by. Let's go!"

Tommy started the fishing boat's twin 150-horsepower outboards and took off toward the wreck, followed closely by the powerboat. As they approached, the helicopter listed to the side in the water, pontoons inflated at its sides and its tail boom half-submerged. Duncan keyed a handheld VHF radio.

"Hold up, let's approach slowly—there could be people in the water." The tanned helmsman coasted toward the bobbing machine, and Duncan glanced at Jenny before raising the megaphone back to his mouth. "Is anyone alive in there? Can anybody hear me?"

A tall, lean man appeared at the open side door and waved for the boat to slow down.

"We've got one seriously injured," the man shouted. "One other aboard, possibly in shock."

"Let's get the injured one," Duncan said. "Tommy, get us alongside."

The tanned kid expertly worked the throttles to gently bring the boat next to the listing chopper. Duncan threw a line, and the tall man snatched it from the air, pulling it tight.

"Is this the quickest in your group?" the man asked, and Duncan nodded. "Good. We'll send our wounded on here, and the other passenger can go on your other boat."

"Is the helicopter sinking?"

"It's not going anywhere. Get ready." He turned back to speak to some unseen people behind him. "Bring him up here. Bring him up easy. Wade, we're going to get you up on this boat. You just relax and let us do the work. We've got it."

A grimacing man appeared at the helicopter door, his face knotted in agony as he was lifted up by hands behind him. The tall man jumped aboard the boat before grabbing the injured man's coveralls and dragging him with Duncan's help over the gunwale into a heap on the deck. The left leg of the man's flight suit was ripped and bloody, with a black leather belt cinched tight up at the top. The wounded man squeezed his eyes shut, his breath coming in short ragged gasps.

"Christ, Jake, I'm . . . I think I'm blinking out . . . tell my wife—"

"Stop," the tall man—Jake—said. "You're going to be fine." He leaned over the rail and beckoned to a smaller, older man still aboard the helicopter. "Throw me that line. We'll see you ashore." Jake returned to the pilot sprawled out on the deck. "Just about home free, marine," he said. He turned to Duncan and Tommy and leveled a hard gaze. "Radio ahead and tell them we need an ambulance. Get us to the mainland. Fast as you can go."

Duncan hailed the marina on his VHF as Tommy checked the water around the boat and slowly motored away from the listing helicopter, making sure he was clear before bringing the throttles forward. The boat's bow leaped up, and it skimmed across the top of the water, launching from swell to swell as they powered back toward the coast. Jake crouched next to the bleeding pilot, gripping his shoulder and shouting encouragement as he checked the tourniquet on his leg. Wade grimaced each time the boat slammed into a wave, and the dreadlocked woman named Jenny knelt and held his hand. Duncan stood by Tommy and faced forward as they cruised around the easternmost end of Galveston Island and into the bay, slowing only when they rounded the breakwater at the Yacht Basin.

"There's the ambulance!" Duncan shouted, waving to the EMTs on the dock to get their attention. "The hospital's right over there," he added. "Your friend won't have to go far." The paramedics approached with a rolling litter and jumped down to the boat with a backboard.

"Deep puncture to the upper left thigh," Jake told them as they secured the pilot to the backboard. "Pretty substantial hemorrhage."

"We got him," one of the EMTs said, and they hoisted him up to the gurney and rushed him away. A pair of cops waited at the head of the dock.

"Man," Duncan said, shaking his head while Tommy, looking pale, sank down into the white chair at the helm. "That was something. I hope your friend there is going to be okay." He grabbed a water bottle from the console and took a long swig while Jake stared at him and nodded.

"Did you see anything out there?" he asked, and Duncan shook his head. He looked to Jenny, who stood with her arms crossed.

"You're protesters, right?"

"We were protesting the launch, yes," Duncan affirmed.

Jenny stepped forward. "You were part of it," she said, "weren't you?"

"I was observing," Jake said. "I wondered what you saw from down on the water."

Jenny opened her mouth to speak, but Duncan cut her off. "*Kingfisher Seven* was destroyed," he said. "Obviously we weren't expecting that."

"Obviously. But did you see anything unusual?"

"We weren't close enough to really see or hear anything."

"Except for that damn drone buzzing all the time," Jenny said.

"A drone?"

"Quadcopter," Duncan said. "Then we heard your chopper. They'd been going over all day, so we got pretty good at tuning them out. Wasn't really paying attention until we heard the bang."

"It was *loud*," Jenny said. "We thought you guys were dead."

"No," Jake said, his eyes following the ambulance's flashing lights as it pulled away from the dock. "Not dead. Not by a long shot."

CHAPTER FIVE

Vostok was quick to show interest when René called with news about Nabil's potential product. Even with the lagging delay of his voice over the satellite phone, his excitement was palpable.

"It's real?" he asked. "You've confirmed it?"

"I have no reason to doubt it," René replied. "The guy sent me a video. There was a Geiger counter in his hand—it clicked when it got close to the case with the material. I suppose he could have faked it, but it looked real to me."

"No, no," Vostok said. "This is good. Very good. Listen, we have some things we need to discuss. Things about the future. I think we can put this stuff to use. What do you think? Maybe a partnership again. You and me."

"Go on," René said. If this partnership was to be anything like their last one, he wanted nothing to do with it.

"Not on the telephone," Vostok said. "We need to speak in person. Can you get to Novi Sad? By Wednesday?"

Wednesday was two days from today; the city in northern Serbia was over a thousand kilometers away from Tiraspol.

"If I leave now, yes," René said.

"I don't want you on cameras," Vostok said. "No record of a border crossing. You'll need to smuggle yourself."

René closed his eyes and held in a sigh. This would be an uncomfortable trip; there was no way to avoid it. Fucking Vostok. The man was effectively his superior now, and René hated having him in a position of control.

"Yes," he said. "I can make it happen."

"Good. Get yourself to the Hotel Aleksandar. In the old city. Be there alone, and call this number when you arrive." Vostok gave a number with a Serbian country code, and René scribbled it down and read it back from his notepad. "Perfect. Correct. Use a burner phone and a fresh SIM card when you call. One of my guys will get you and bring you to me. I'm not kidding when I say you need to be alone, understand?"

"Why all the bullshit?" René asked. The order to hide himself seemed excessive; he'd known Vostok for more than a decade, going back to when they'd fought together in the Donbas. Before everything had gone to hell.

"Things are happening," Vostok said. "Big things. You can't take it personally. You're critical to all of it. I'll explain everything when you're here."

René had made cross-border runs like these many times. Anton had a nondescript Moldovan-tagged Škoda wagon, and they'd pulled out the springs and padding from beneath the back seat to move chemicals and finished product to and from the lab. The smuggler's space was just large enough for René to hide in for short periods of time. He was a slight, wiry man, only five feet, three inches, and by bending his knees and twisting to the side, he could fit himself into the space beneath the passenger seat with his lower back resting over the transmission hump.

He readied a bag with several changes of clothes along with some costume items to alter his appearance on the road. A gray beard and thick tinted glasses to cover the scars on his face, a mashed tweed hat, and a flesh-colored glove with five fingers to cover René's missing digits would be sufficient. A doctored Romanian passport with his long-dead father's name and image would come along, too, just in case they were pulled over and questioned at any point in the EU. With luck, they wouldn't need the identification. They never had before.

The next day, the two barely spoke for the first hours of their drive through the mostly sunny day; Anton, behind the wheel, played pop music at a low volume while René idly watched the passing farmland. A few kilometers from the border town of Sculeni, Anton turned left onto a dirt road and drove for a few hundred meters down an unpaved, brush-lined lane until they were beyond sight of the motorway. René quietly exited the Škoda while Anton twisted around and flipped up the wagon's back seat.

"Hopefully it will be fast this time," Anton said.

René shrugged before slipping inside, and the seat closed over him. The car began to move again, and René bumped his head as Anton executed a U-turn. It was loud on the gravel road, and then with a hard bounce, it was suddenly quiet and smooth as they returned to the motorway.

"It's all good in there?" Anton asked. After a year under René's tutelage, his Romanian was nearly fluent, if accented.

"I'm fine," René said, feeling the car slow.

"We're at the border . . . maybe eight cars ahead of us. Not so bad." The Škoda's engine stopped. "Everything's okay," he said. "Don't worry. They're shaking down some French tourists. Making them unload their caravan. It's gonna be a little while, those assholes have a lot of shit, looks like. Backpacks, chairs . . . you want some water?"

"I'm fine," René said.

The kid had good instincts. René was happy to have him around. But if he was really going to be trusted, and be part of Vostok's group, there was something he needed to know.

"Toni," he said, getting right to the point, "are you shooting junk again?" A pause, and no answer. "I'm serious. You need to be straight with me. You get into that shit again and it could come down on us—"

"I fucking hate being called Toni," Anton said, his voice distant in René's ears. "And you really want to bring this up right now?"

"If you're going to work with me, I need—"

"Moving again," Anton said abruptly, and the Škoda suddenly rumbled back to life. The car didn't go into gear, though. They sat still for five minutes, and five minutes more.

That skinny Dutch fucker, René thought. He had to admire the balls on the kid, shutting him up like that. Another twenty minutes passed, and finally the car began to creep forward. They paused again, and René heard Anton speaking to the border guard.

"No, nothing, going straight through. Seeing friends in Belgrade. Yeah. Yeah. Thank you." They moved on, accelerating on the smooth Romanian motorway. It was another ten minutes before Anton gave the all clear. René slipped out of the hiding place and made sure the rear seat was back in position. He grabbed his duffel from the footwell and wriggled forward between the seats into the front.

"Pretty funny, Toni," René said, unzipping the bag at his feet as Anton stared ahead. "You little shit."

"Is it any of your business?" Anton asked.

"If you're working for me, if we're setting up some deal with Vostok . . . yes, it is my business." René laid the fake beard inside out over his right leg and dabbed spirit gum from a tacky glass bottle over the mesh liner before raising it and pressing it to his face.

"It's not a problem," Anton said. "Just a couple times." He glanced over as René applied the disguise. "Does that shit hurt on your scar?"

"It's fine."

"I can't even imagine how big the explosion was," he said.

René didn't respond; he didn't want to talk about it.

"Could it happen to us? In our lab I mean."

"Could what happen to us?"

"An accidental detonation. An explosion. Like you had in Africa."

"It's not going to happen to us. It was a different sort of operation, okay? Much, much bigger. More people, more product. More chances to fuck up. Here it's just us, we're careful, we have the antistatic mats everywhere . . . Fuck's sake, I don't want to talk about this. What I want to talk about is if you're fucking dealing—"

"I'm *not.*"

"It's hard enough keeping the cops off our backs as it is." René leaned forward to don a dark-gray windbreaker. He pulled the tweed cap down over his head, put on the glasses, and slid his hand into the glove. "I don't want to clean up any new messes, understand? And if you're moving shit in the car, they have dogs at the border. They could have sniffed me out, even from traces—"

"I never had it in the car, okay?" Anton snapped. "I'm not stupid. It was a couple times, with a friend. He had some to share. I'm not buying, let alone dealing."

"Fine. I don't want to discuss this again."

"We won't."

The sun fell ahead of René and Anton as they pushed west through the farmland of Romania. The two spoke little as they rolled through the dark hours, the Mureş River flashing next to the motorway in the moonlight. Close to one in the morning, Anton stopped for gas at a twenty-four-hour rest stop.

"You want a turn?" he asked after they'd filled up the Škoda.

"Let's take a break," René said. "I don't want to show up at nighttime. I want us to be fresh."

Anton moved the wagon to the far western side of the rest area, near an idling lorry with Spanish tags. The two men reclined their seats and dozed for a few hours, then got back on the motorway just as dawn began to blush the sky to the east. They passed through the town of Timişoara, just coming to life for the day, and not long after they saw a sign indicating the Point Foeni border crossing was just ten kilometers ahead. Anton started looking for a place to pull over, but René shook his head, unbuckled his seat belt, and slithered to the rear and into the hiding space while the car kept moving.

In less than thirty minutes, they were in Serbia.

René returned to the front and checked in the mirror that his beard remained straight on his face. It was full daylight now, and the motorway was heavily trafficked with a nearly even mix of EU semis and morning commuters.

"We'll do a run through the city when we get there," René said. "More thorough than last time. I don't know what the fuck Vostok has up his ass, but whatever it is, he's going to be pissed if someone's following us. You'll drop me off and do another run while I walk to the hotel. Set up a few hundred meters away and watch. Look for the Maxi store—that's in the same building. When I catch my ride, I want you to tail me as long as you can, but don't worry too much if you can't hang on. You think they're onto you? Peel off and sit tight until I call, understood? Vostok's guys don't fuck around; you don't want to tangle with them."

They entered the outskirts of Novi Sad, rolling down narrow avenues in the residential part of the city and the wider streets of the industrial sector, all the time driving with purpose while René kept a watch behind them. After about forty-five minutes, the two entered a quiet area of warehouses and garages south of the canal. The streets were empty.

Certain all was clear, René gave the command: "Slow down, here, this corner. Don't stop, just slow!" He threw the wagon's door open and stepped out to the curb, catching his balance in a lurch before standing straight. "Go!" he shout-whispered, pushing the door shut.

Anton, like a pro, smoothly accelerated away. René was pleased. He straightened his jacket and began walking south toward the Danube River, keeping his head down so the bill of his cap would hide his face from any security cameras. *Everything is digital now,* he thought. Cameras everywhere. Some guys were bothered by the fact, always moaning about how the past was so different, so easy.

They were the ones most likely to be caught, René knew. Why fight the system? There were still plenty of flaws. It was like he'd told Anton a thousand times: find the cracks and slip between them.

Be invisible. Like now.

It took René twenty minutes to reach the old city, where the sidewalks were dense with young, well-dressed people. He was certain he wasn't being tailed, but just to be sure he ran an extra detection route through the streets lined with trendy hotels, restaurants, and bustling coffee shops. An environment where everyone angled to be seen, René knew, gave the best opportunity to disappear. No one paid him any attention. Half a block ahead on the Bulevar cara Lazara, René saw the telltale red awning of the Maxi supermarket on the first floor of the hotel. He was close. He drew the burner phone from his inside jacket pocket, powered it up, and typed from memory the number he'd been given. The call connected on the second ring.

"*Da*?" a voice said. Native Russian. Not Vostok's voice.

"*Ya zdes'*," René said. "I'm here."

"At the Aleksandar?" It was a man's voice but soft, almost feminine.

René slowed his pace and scanned the people around him, checking anyone speaking on a phone. No one seemed to match the voice in his ear.

"I'm close," he said.

"Go south. Toward the river. There's a sports complex behind the hotel. I'm standing in the parking lot on the east side. Look for a short guy. You'll recognize me. We met before."

René cut left and kept the phone up to his ear. He saw tennis courts and a park beyond, and a nearly filled row of parking spaces. He came close to the lot, walking slowly.

"I don't see you," René said.

"Parking lot to the east. Are you there?"

René moved forward, more cautiously. Something seemed off. He glanced at the sun to check his bearings. "I'm certain I'm in the right place. To the east." Then he glanced across the tennis courts and saw a short barrel-chested man with a phone to his ear. The man lifted his arm and waved.

"West!" he said. "So sorry. I meant the west side!"

René shook his head, disconnected the call, and started toward the far side of the complex. He heard a sudden movement behind him, and before he could react, a dark cloth bag was thrown over his head and his arms were held tight at his sides.

"Don't fight, asshole. Don't make things hard for yourself."

René struggled for a moment, then relaxed. There was no use resisting; they had him. He heard running footsteps.

"Check him," a voice said with calm urgency. The soft voice he'd been speaking to. René's wrists were held tightly behind his back as he was patted down. The burner phone and Böker knife were pulled from his pocket. "Get the phone. Smash it. Yes, on the ground. Fucking smash it. Use your boot—we don't want him tracked." A pause. "What are you looking at?" the voice called to some bystander. "Get the fuck out of here!"

René heard the clatter of his phone hitting the concrete, followed by a crunching sound. His wrists were bound tightly with zip ties, and he was spun to his side and roughly thrown into the back seat of a car.

CHAPTER SIX

The white passenger van moved steadily north on Interstate 45 toward Houston, hemmed in by traffic, not too fast, not too slow. The driver, clad in possibly the hundredth light-blue Kingfisher polo shirt Jake had seen today, seemed impatient.

"We'll get you there, Mr. Moran. I'm going as fast as I can."

"I'm not sure what the rush is, so feel free to get there whenever you want," Jake said with a yawn. Alone in the back, he didn't care. It was almost eight in the evening, and after the launch explosion, the helicopter crash, the boat ride back to Galveston Island, and the seemingly interminable questioning by local cops and a pair of too-serious rangers who were late to the scene, Jake was spent. The sky outside the car glowed orange in the clear evening dusk, and if he allowed himself, he could have easily dozed off to the hum of the van's engine.

Crashed in a helicopter, Jake thought, laughing to himself. And he'd lived to tell the tale. Not too bad, setting it down on the water like that. And Wade, Jesus, keeping his shit together enough to talk him through it. Calm, cool, and tough as hell. Jake wondered if Wade had dealt with something like that back in Iraq. What was it, three thousand hours the guy said he had flying in the marines? Plenty of time to run into some shit.

He'd go visit Wade in the hospital as soon as he could.

And what about those kids, the protesters, who'd pulled them all out of the Gulf? Not kids, really—they were likely only a few years younger than Jake. Earnest, but untested. Duncan seemed smart. Smart enough to get people to follow him. And the woman seemed to have the kind of passion that could inspire an army of protesters, not just some ragtag crew in a bunch of inflatable boats. They must have been thrilled by the Kingfisher failure, he thought. Good for their message.

"Mr. Moran?"

"Huh?" Jake snapped upright. "Sorry, I think I fell asleep."

"We're getting close. Right up here . . ."

They exited the freeway into a warren of strip malls, apartment complexes, car dealerships, and grocery stores that, after a few miles, gave way to long, flat buildings with the look of light industry. This was Clear Lake City, home to NASA's Johnson Space Center. In the acres surrounding the JSC campus, dozens of offices of supporting players and potential competitors had sprung up. Engineering firms, communications consultants, private spaceflight companies. They passed the low warehouse-type buildings with mostly empty parking lots until they came to a large fenced compound with a nearly full lot; the sign in front read: **KINGFISHER AEROSPACE—CLEAR LAKE CITY FACILITY**.

The driver badged through the security gate, parked, and led Jake into the main building. Even at this hour the place was humming with activity; people moved with quiet urgency in all directions, and above it all, in the building's spacious lobby, a flat screen replayed the explosion from earlier that day.

Jake signed in and was given a visitor's pass before a young woman emerged from a pair of double doors. She wore a dark business suit—seemingly the only person in the place clad so professionally—and had a tablet tucked under her left arm along with a sheaf of papers.

"Mr. Moran?" she asked, reaching forward to give Jake a crisp handshake. "I'm Janice Trout. Helena is almost ready for you. Please follow me." She guided Jake back through the doors from which she'd come and into a busy corridor lined with large framed prints of each of Kingfisher Aerospace's launches.

"Things seem to be hopping around here," Jake said.

"It's always busy like this on launch day," Janice said. "And with the anomaly, things are busier still."

Anomaly? More like *blew the fuck up*, he thought with a half smile.

Janice Trout didn't notice. "With our growth over the past two years," she went on, "more than half our team has never experienced the loss of a vehicle. Everyone drills for it, but those procedures get rusty when you don't need to use them. And when we were starting out, we got to use them quite a bit."

"I recall a few big blasts."

"We learned a lot from those failures. We were agile. We still are. The incumbent launch providers could never learn and adapt like we did."

"How long have you been working here?"

"Four years. Long enough to remember a time when making it to orbit wasn't guaranteed." Janice stopped at another pair of doors and held her badge up to a wall-mounted card reader. It beeped and clicked, and she pushed the right side open. Jake followed her through into a well-furnished waiting area. She held up a finger, indicating that Jake should wait, and poked her head through a door at the far end of the room.

"Excuse me, Helena?" she said softly. "Mr. Moran is here." Janice waved Jake into the room, staying behind as she closed the door.

Helena Nash's Texas office was appointed with modern furnishings and a broad desk with only a cell phone and slim open laptop on its surface. Helena typed intently on the keyboard.

"Just finishing this email," she said without looking up. "One second. There." She tapped the trackpad with a flourish, took off her glasses, and rose from behind the desk. "Mr. Moran," she said, smiling warmly as she reached for his hand. "It's wonderful to finally meet you face to face. I am so sorry about the trouble you experienced on your way back to the mainland."

Jake was surprised by how much smaller Helena Nash was in person. Her short, nearly white hair framed a youthful face with probing eyes, and Jake felt he was undergoing some sort of snap evaluation in her greeting.

"*Trouble* is one way to put it," Jake said. "I'm just happy everyone made it out of there alive. Especially your pilot."

"I heard from Dr. Taka that you rather saved the day." Helena spoke nearly unaccented English, but Jake knew that she'd been born in Sweden as Helena Sundqvist before marrying Gordon Nash, the eccentric British innovator. Fifteen years his junior, she'd helped his company produce the Nash 99, a personal computer that became as popular in Europe as IBM or Dell had been in North America. The Nashes hoped their creation would cross the Atlantic to become just as successful in the States, but when Gordon Nash died in a private plane crash, those aspirations died too. Helena came to the US instead and headed straight for Seattle, seemingly having a perfect knack for investing in just the right company at just the right time. Increasing her fortune by an order of magnitude, she began putting her money into side projects of personal interest: renewable energy, health care technology, solid-state batteries, and inexpensive access to low earth orbit through a tiny start-up called Kingfisher Aerospace in an Oakland warehouse.

It was all public knowledge. The backstory of her success.

Not many people had noticed Kingfisher back then. Jake had, mostly because it was his job to know and partially because he admired the small outfit's drive and innovation. He knew their successes, knew their failures, followed from afar as they tried and tried again to launch the single-engine *Kingfisher One* from a tiny atoll in the South Pacific. Three times they tried, and three times the rockets ended up tumbling into the sea. The fourth time, though, the little *Kingfisher One* went up and up and up to a not-quite-as-planned orbit around the earth, but into space nonetheless. A remarkable accomplishment for a nongovernmental entity, especially one made up of MIT and Caltech dropouts backed by a flashy Swedish billionaire.

Jake had been pulling for Kingfisher ever since and had admired Helena Nash's accomplishments from afar until she'd hired his company for this launch. Finally, here he was, shaking her hand.

"Dr. Taka was just as responsible for our safe ditch as I was," Jake said. "But we all made it out. And here I am."

"Here you are. Will you have a seat? I'd like to discuss something with you." Helena gestured toward a low modern couch under a bookshelf adorned with models of various Kingfisher rockets and payloads. Jake sat, and Helena slipped into a matching chair opposite him.

"We were very happy with Cascadia's support on today's launch," she said. "I wish we would have made it all the way up to orbit, but that is the way it goes sometimes in this business, you know."

"I'm sorry about the failure—"

"Don't be. It's a risk we take every time we fly. To be honest, I'm always prepared for them to not make it up. I work on the assumption that something bad is going to happen. That way I'm not surprised when things go wrong." She smiled. "Any guesses? On what caused our failure today, I mean?"

"I wasn't on a console, so obviously I wasn't seeing any of your data," Jake said. "But from what I could see, my first guess would be the payload coming loose from the second-stage adapter."

"A good guess," Helena said. "I thought the same at first, to be honest. But incorrect."

"You know the cause?"

"I do." There was almost a twinkle in Helena's eye, as if she relished doling out such privileged information.

"And . . . am I cleared to know?"

"Not yet, but I'll tell you anyway." She smiled again, then turned serious. "It wasn't any fault with our rocket, Mr. Moran. Not at all. The cause was external."

"External? You mean not involving the vehicle's hardware or software?"

"Precisely. The automated flight-termination system received an override command to destroy the vehicle."

Jake shook his head in disbelief. "Your rocket got a command to destroy itself from the range-safety officer?"

Helena Nash shrugged.

"Could it have been triggered on board?" Jake asked. "By some kind of error in the system?"

She shook her head. "I told you, the vehicle *received* a termination command."

"From an external source," Jake mused. "That signal travels on multiple frequencies . . ."

"Three. UHF."

"And the system won't start the termination-override sequence unless all three are in agreement."

"Correct."

"So, you have telemetry before the detonation showing a signal being received, yes?"

"You speak," she said, "like someone who has lived through this before."

"I have," Jake said. "I'm sure you know that I managed launches for the navy. And I suspect you also know I did that alongside Andy Lang, your flight director today."

"I am aware." Helena Nash leaned forward and tapped a finger on her chin. "Tell me," she said, "did you ever lose one? A rocket, I mean. When you were in charge of launching it?"

"On my watch? No."

"Did Andy?"

"Andy was very good at his job. He must have been, because you hired him, right?"

"But did he ever lose a military payload with a launch team under his command?"

"Mrs. Nash, I'm not—"

"Please call me Helena. We're not so formal here."

"I'm not trying to dodge your question, but most of the work Andy Lang and I did was classified. Some flights weren't, but most of them were, and I don't want to risk revealing operational details of something I might not be at liberty to discuss. I will say that Andy was one of the most qualified people I ever worked with. I support him without reservation." Jake held out his hands. "Is that good enough?"

"It will pass," she said. "Though I think your words say more about you than they do about Andy Lang."

This was a test; surely Helena Nash knew about the highly classified, multibillion-dollar National Reconnaissance Office satellite lost under Lang's command. There had been institutional pressure—"go fever"—they called it, and Andy felt he'd let himself get sucked into the frenzy to get airborne and missed some crucial detail that might have saved the expensive cargo. The investigation afterward found a design failure in the second stage, but Andy blamed himself, thinking that if he'd managed to recognize something in his preflight numbers, he might have called for a scrub and saved the mission. He took it hard, but he'd bounced back and sent many more payloads up to perfect orbits.

It was just the way this business was. Jake understood it, and he knew Helena Nash understood it too.

Helena clasped her hands. "Speaking of classified work, you have held on to your security clearances with the government, correct?"

"I maintain the appropriate level of access," Jake said. "For some of the work I do."

"A level of access appropriate for, say"—Helena Nash paused and tapped her finger to her chin—"alerting the US government when you've identified something in your work that might have national-security implications?"

Jake straightened in his seat. "I'm not sure I understand what you're getting at."

"Something like, say, a weapons depot in North Africa?"

Jake kept his expression neutral. "If we did identify such a thing," he said, "I would obviously alert the appropriate authorities. But regarding anything specific to Africa or anywhere else, I have nothing to say."

A year earlier, while working on a contract performing satellite-image analysis of archaeological sites across the Sahara Desert, Cascadia had discovered a sprawling, incongruous complex of structures in the remote north of the Republic of Mali. After some digital investigation pointing to possible Russian ties, Jake had back channeled the information to the Department of Defense. Two weeks later the site had been dealt with accordingly by a drone strike. The casualties were more than anyone was comfortable with: the result of a misjudgment in fractions of a centimeter and some minorly flawed intel. Hardly the worst shit show in Jake's past but not one that was easily forgotten. And apparently Helena Nash knew about it.

"Don't act like such a Boy Scout," she said. "I know you're not as saintly as you come across. Your public operations at Cascadia, weather, remote sensing, all of that, they all make great cover, don't you think?"

"Cover for . . . ?"

"Cover for information gathering for the US government when plausible deniability on their part is needed. Cover for operations run alongside perhaps some of your former colleagues in the CIA." Helena smiled, but her expression remained piercing. "This isn't an accusation, Mr. Moran. I quite respect the discretion you maintain. Which is why I've brought you here today."

"Cascadia has nothing to hide," Jake said.

"I think it's good to have enemies," Helena continued, as if reading Jake's mind. "It means you are *important*. But tell me, do you ever worry that some of your more, let's say 'hush-hush' contracts might come back to haunt you?"

"I agree that having enemies means something."

"Mr. Moran—" Helena started, and Jake stopped her.

"If I'm calling you Helena, call me Jake. Please."

She nodded. “Fine then. *Jake.* I know your company is very successful. You do exceptionally good work. Your reputation in information systems and the management of orbital assets is without peer.”

“You’re very kind to say so.”

“And because of your success and stature, along with the government work I should know nothing about, is it safe to say there’s no way I could convince you to consider joining us at Kingfisher?”

Jake paused for just a moment before answering. “I’m flattered by the suggestion, but I’m quite happy with my work and my team. Though we would be pleased to continue supporting your launches.”

“Well, this brings us to my question,” Helena said, leaning forward and folding her fingers over her knee. “We would very much like your support on future launches. Your team, by all accounts, worked flawlessly with Kingfisher and the engineering back room. They said you stepped in like old hands. No issues, no egos. And trust me, it’s not always that way with our support people. We appreciate that very much and would like to continue the relationship.”

“The feeling is mutual,” Jake said.

“But it does seem like such a waste of your ability,” she said, “having you support us in *meteorology*. All that knowledge of the process, top to bottom, and you’re giving us weather reports?”

“They’re a critical component,” Jake said. “And we’re happy to fill that role.”

“Of course they are. And I want them to continue. But I need something else. I want to take advantage of your skills. I’d like Cascadia to perform an audit, of sorts, of Kingfisher’s processes. You are an informed outsider. The most qualified outsider there is, possibly, and I’d like to hear your unfiltered impressions of our operation. What do we do well? Where could we do better? There are so few people qualified to provide an assessment like this, Jake. And fewer I would trust. Maybe only one person I could trust, and he's sitting in this room with me."

Jake said nothing.

"But with today's failure, I am in a peculiar situation," she went on. "There will be an investigation to determine the root cause—"

"You just told me it was the termination system."

"Of course, we figured that out right away. But there will be an independent group tasked with identifying how it happened and providing suggestions to prevent similar issues in the future. Space Force and NASA will be closely involved. Even though today's customer was a private operator, half of our manifest is made up of NASA and government payloads, so they'll want to ensure their flights won't experience a similar failure."

Jake again said nothing, waiting for Helena.

"You won't consider joining us, so I'm asking you to consider a private, quiet audit of our systems. But I am curious about something. Now that you know the cause, how do you think that termination signal got up to my rocket?"

"Well, with everything you've given me, the most logical explanation is that the range-safety officer accidentally sent the command. RSOs are good, but human. Even if they are Space Force."

"I agree with you," she said, but Helena's expression gave nothing away. "I can tell you right now, over the course of what is sure to be an irritating investigation, our partners at the Space Launch Delta 45 at Canaveral will exonerate us and conclude it was a fluke on their end, a gremlin in *their* system that sent the command. This will be good news for Kingfisher, as it won't be our responsibility, and Space Force, pressured by a backlog of upcoming flights, will modify systems and procedures to ensure it doesn't happen again. End of story. A delay, and an annoying one, but nothing more."

"But a simple resolution isn't what you're after."

She said nothing, so Jake dug a little deeper.

"You want a real answer. So you're proposing that—in a theoretical audit of Kingfisher—I should be looking for alternative ways a signal like that could have gotten up to the vehicle?"

Helena remained impassive for a moment, then nodded. "I would like to grant you complete freedom to explore every nook and cranny of our operation here," she said. "I want a warts-and-all report. If that exposes weaknesses in our telemetry and communications links, so be it. I want the unvarnished opinion of a true expert in the field. I want *your* opinion, Jake."

"Are you worried someone from outside the loop sent that command?" He thought for a moment. "It's encrypted, each link with its own key—"

Helena stopped him with a raised hand. "I am saying nothing of the sort," she said. "But if you and I can imagine it, Jake, then someone else can imagine it too. And if there is a weakness in the system, they will exploit it. You must understand there are others, competitors, who would like nothing more than to see me fail." She smiled a thin-lipped smile. "I want you to find anything. No matter how insignificant."

"I can't work solo on this," Jake told her. "I'm good at a lot of things, but I have people working with me who are even better."

"I don't want this to be widely known. Not because I have anything to hide, but because I want you to have absolute freedom to investigate all avenues while you develop your report."

"I'm only thinking of a couple of Cascadia people. Both have signed nondisclosures for you already. I trust them completely and value their skills. To do this right, I'd need their help."

Helena tilted her head. "Provisionally, let's say I'm fine with that."

"Do you want one of your people in here to write this up?" Jake asked. "I'm guessing you keep lawyers around for things like this. I do."

"I'd like to keep your task under wraps within the company," she said.

"Is that going to impact my ability to do my job?"

She shook her head. "People will understand that you're working with our systems in a contracting role. They won't know why, exactly, but they won't be surprised to see you nosing around."

"We'll need access to everything," Jake said. "Servers, backups, physical infrastructure. Personnel records. Everything."

"Consider it granted," Helena Nash said. "I will request that all data remain on site, though. Which means you'll be spending a lot of time on site as well."

"Understood."

"And you are a private pilot," she added. A statement, not a question.

"It's handy for the travel I do," Jake said. "And it sounds like I'll be doing a lot of it for this work."

"I would like you to fly commercial when traveling for us."

Jake cocked his head. "May I ask why?"

"My husband died in a single-engine plane crash, Jake. I know you are a brilliant man, and I'm sure you are a very skilled pilot, but . . . please allow me this one irrational request. Can you understand my concern?"

Jake nodded.

"Book your travel through Janice, wherever you need to go. And in many places, we have our own jets or helicopters—"

"Helicopters like the one I ditched in today?" Jake asked. For a moment he worried the dig might have been too much, but Helena shrugged it off.

"That," she said, "was entirely unexpected. We can control many things, but not the migratory flight of birds. At least we had security on the water to get to you quickly."

Jake didn't know if Helena truly believed a bird had brought down Wade's chopper or if this was part of his hazing. He decided it didn't matter. "Actually, the protesters got to us first. They were the ones who brought us to shore."

Helena straightened in her seat, her expression suddenly serious. "Do you recall who brought you in, exactly?"

“Academic-looking guy. A few years younger than me. With a short woman with dreadlocks—”

“Duncan? Was his name Duncan?”

“That’s it, yes. You know him?”

Helena Nash shook her head sadly. “I do know him,” she said with a sigh. “I know him very well. That was my son. Duncan Nash.”

CHAPTER SEVEN

René struggled to get himself upright in the back seat as he felt the car accelerate. His hot breath was stifling in the bag over his head, and the zip ties binding his wrists behind his back dug into thin flesh. He shook his head to try to get some fresh air and heard a laugh from the front seat.

"Try anything and you're a dead man." Again, the soft voice from the phone. "Don't be stupid."

"I'm not the stupid one here," René said. "Maybe you don't know who you're screwing with. Vostok won't be happy with this."

Now laughter erupted from the front. Two men.

"Oh, so you're some kind of big deal, huh?" A deep voice, from the driver's side. "You think Vostok gives a shit about you? What gives you that idea?"

René said nothing. In keeping silent, he could cling to a small thread of control.

"I said who the fuck do you think you are?"

René stayed quiet, breathed slowly, and took in the situation. Could Vostok have given him up for a bounty? There were plenty who wanted him dead, for sure, but would his old associate have done such a thing? He could hardly believe he'd been set up, after all they'd been through, but business was business.

Actually, the more he thought about it, the more plausible the idea became.

René tested the zip ties binding his wrists. Too strong to break, but in a quick move, he thought, given the proper opportunity, maybe he could slip his hands under his body to get them out in front of himself. Wait for the right time. Stay ready. René wondered if Anton had seen his abduction and managed to follow. He almost hoped he hadn't; the kid wouldn't last long against operators like these.

The costume beard on René's face was itchy and sagging, and he leaned his chin down to his right shoulder to scratch it. A gap opened at the bottom of the bag, and René saw his feet bathed in sunlight. They were headed east, then. Traveling fast, on a highway. He closed his eyes and tried to remember. National Highway 12, maybe. Or 102? The 102 went north out of Novi Sad. It had to be 12. If he was going to manage to escape, he needed to make a good guess of where he was.

After maybe thirty minutes, the car turned left and René felt the sun warming the bag at the back of his neck. Definitely northbound now. The car went through a series of stops and starts, city driving, and René made an educated guess about their location.

"Zabalj, huh?" he said. There was no response from the front. "This place is a shithole. I did a job here once—"

"Shut the fuck up!" the voice from the passenger seat said.

He'd flustered them. This was good. The car slowed, and René could imagine the silent, confused glances being exchanged between the two men up front as they tried to decide what to do. The vehicle came to a near halt before accelerating again.

"No more talking," the driver said curtly. René knew he'd gotten under the guy's skin, and he smiled to himself beneath the hood.

They drove on at highway speed for at least another hour. Then the car slowed and began making turns, lurching through potholes as gravel rumbled beneath the tires. René had no clue where they might be, and he stayed silent as he rocked about. After another half hour, the car came to an abrupt stop. A front door opened, and the car chimed about the keys left in the ignition.

René heard a voice from outside: Vostok.

"Idiot! What have you *done*?" The door next to René was thrown open, and he was quickly pulled out to his feet. The bag was yanked from his head, and there, in front of him, was Vostok: grayer at the temples but still hard and lean in the face and wide eyed in confusion. "Cut that off him. Now! Undo his wrists! Fuck, it wasn't supposed to be like this—" Vostok spun to face the two men standing next to the car. "Petr! What the *fuck* were you thinking?"

"You said—"

"I said bring him here! Not capture him! This is our *comrade*, not a prisoner!" Vostok stepped forward and slapped the man called Petr across the face, hard. Petr winced, and the taller man, the driver, looked to the ground as a flicker of a smile crossed his lips.

Someone cut the zip ties away behind René's back, and as soon as he was free, René ripped the beard from his face and pulled the glove from his sweaty, ruined hand. His skin was wrinkled, and the scars on the stumps of his fingers were angry red. He took in the scene around him as he rubbed his wrists. They'd come to a farmyard next to an old white barn with a mossy roof. A long solar array and a pair of Starlink-internet terminals stood beyond it. René saw no other buildings nearby, only rolling hills and overgrown hedgerows.

In addition to the chastened drivers who'd brought him there, three armed men in fatigues with balaclavas covering their faces flanked Vostok. One wore a floppy canvas hat and had a Chinese Type-95 automatic rifle slung from his shoulder.

Vostok shook his head. "Fucking morons," he said, spitting at the dirt. "How could you mess up like this? Was he armed?" Petr reluctantly pulled the Böker from one of his cargo pockets. "You took *that* off him? You idiot, give it back."

Petr hesitated a moment, then threw the folded knife at René's feet. "Eat shit," he said.

"Enough." Vostok reached down and snatched the knife from the ground before pressing it into René's hand. "Don't be a fucking kid, Petr." He slapped René on the back. "Come on. Let's go for a stroll."

The guard with the floppy hat began to follow, but Vostok waved him off. "Stay back, stay back," he said. "I don't need you. This guy's good. He's one of us."

Vostok made his way through a break in a slumping fence next to the barn and started along a faint trail through the overgrown grass. He'd been a mercenary nearly his entire adult life, much of it overlapping with René's, and his muscular body moved with the strength and grace of a dancer. The two were close in age. Maybe Vostok was older. Somewhere near forty, but wily and strong and not to be messed with.

"Fucking idiots," Vostok muttered. "How is the hand?"

"Better," René said. "It doesn't get in the way of my work."

"And your face? The scarring is tolerable?"

"I try not to think about it."

"Africa," Vostok said, shaking his head. "A disaster. I thought it was a sure thing for you." He spit in the grass and shook his head again. "Fucking Wagner."

René nodded. Fucking Wagner. Nearly eighteen months earlier, René had been an independent operator—an equal of Vostok's or more—dropping into conflict zones with a small highly trained team of chemists and IT experts that set up discreet labs to fabricate nearly undetectable explosives and digitally launder the money collected from their sale. A representative from the Wagner Group had reached out and set up a lucrative deal for René's team to produce explosives for Malian government forces fighting insurgents in the north of the country. Russia had hoped that through its influence, it might undermine the nation's postcolonial ties to France and the West and fill the vacuum left behind.

As soon as they'd arrived in Africa, René and his men set up a lab facility in a hastily erected complex of tents, shipping containers, and diesel generators around a prefabricated steel building outside the dusty northern village of Araouane. There, along with three Wagner-vetted locals recruited as assistants, they'd settled into the daily toil of bomb assembly and money laundering. His crew was focused, and the Malian hires were competent. They worked together with silent proficiency. Supplies and cash moved in; finished product moved out. Funds were exchanged and swapped for cryptocurrency by his tech guys with a slow but stable satellite connection to the internet.

For nearly thirteen weeks they worked with supreme efficiency, until one sweltering evening, after a long day loading tons of plastic explosive bricks into four open-bed trucks backed into the warehouse, René stepped out from the lab into the long shadows of the late day. He hitched his balaclava up over his nose and mouth to protect against the ever-present grit on the breeze and trudged through the uneven, loose sand to a pit latrine several hundred meters away on the northern edge of the compound. At the concrete block outhouse, he reached up to grab the edge of the sheet metal roof to support himself with his right hand while he fidgeted with the splintered door's reluctant latch.

Then in an instant there was something: everything, nothing, a shriek in the air, blinding light, and total darkness. The air was pulled from his lungs, and his ears thumped once, then twice more, and before René could make sense of any of it, he was on his back with the flaming wreckage of the outhouse on top of him. Cinder blocks pinned his legs, and a burning timber dropped onto his face, and he struggled to push it away as he wriggled through the stinking sand, damp with piss and shit and who knew what else, until he was clear.

René slowly sat up, and it took a moment for him to comprehend what had happened as he blinked the grit from his eyes and took in the scene before him.

His worst nightmare. An accidental detonation.

The buildings were gone, vanished like they'd never been there, and the desert was littered with crumpled sheet metal, tattered fabric, and charred, twisted corpses spread out across the blackened sand. An axle from one of the trucks stood upright next to a headless body, the wheel at its end still spinning in the silence. René's ears rang, and his body throbbed, and when he raised his arm, he saw with vibrant clarity the shredded remains of his thumb and index and middle fingers. René sat with his head slumped, cradling his wounded hand and trying not to touch the searing agony of his burned face. Some time passed—maybe five minutes, maybe thirty—until from the west he heard the slow thump of a Russian Mi-26 helicopter. He fell to his side in the rotor wash and closed his eyes. When he woke, he found himself in a rough Wagner field hospital, flies buzzing over the bandages on his face and his poorly sutured hand wrapped in yellow-stained gauze.

Eight weeks later, when he was well enough to travel again, he was sent to Transnistria. A consolation prize, of sorts, all arranged by Vostok. René was given money to set up a lab and train a new assistant, and coordinate with local separatists in advance preparation for the arrival of Russian troops—fresh from their easy victory in Ukraine—that would result in the overthrow of the Moldovan government.

A return to Soviet glory. The *Russkiy Mir*.

Months passed. Ukraine had become a quagmire; the invasion had never come. René knew it never would.

"I'm very sorry," Vostok said as he pushed the tall grass out of the way ahead of them. "For you, for your men. For all of this." He nodded back to the barn. "Especially for the behavior of those guys."

"It's fine," René said, even though it wasn't. None of it was.

"It's not. That was inexcusable."

"Okay, you're right," René said, finally letting his temper get the best of him. "What the fuck was that about, then? That's how you treat me? After everything I've done? After all the time I've waited? After this?" He raised his hand and wiggled his remaining fingers. "For fucking what?" René moved up so he was alongside Vostok. He glanced over his shoulder and saw the bodyguard far behind them, standing ready at the break in the fence.

"I know, I know," Vostok said, sighing. "Nothing is happening in Tiraspol. Ever."

"That's been obvious for months."

"Other things are developing—"

"What?" René said. "And you've been living it up with your private army while I'm rotting in the middle of fucking nowhere?"

"Listen," Vostok said. His voice was harder now. "You have a job. You do it well, but sometimes I think you forget you are part of a bigger action. I need you for it."

"*You* need me? You, or Russia? Aren't we working for the motherland? Or I answer to you now? Very handy now that all my guys have been taken out—"

Vostok glanced back toward the barn. "The motherland is fucked," he said softly. "The SMO proved it. Certainly you understand this."

René took a moment to gather his thoughts. Of course he understood it; Russia's military and political ineptitude in the "special military operation" in Ukraine had been obvious from the beginning. But to hear a patriot like Vostok say it out loud? That was jarring.

"We need to be realists," Vostok said. "That's why I wanted you here." He looked back toward the barn once more and waved, as if to let his men know everything was fine. "Those guys? They're nothing. Loyal, sure. But I can find them anywhere. Someone like you, though? With your skills? You're irreplaceable."

"That's something," René allowed.

"It's more than something," said Vostok. "It's *everything*."

Vostok grabbed René by the upper arm and turned him back to the barn. "Come with me. I need to show you something. Something you're going to be very interested in."

"The last time you said something like this, it didn't end well for me. Or my guys. Maybe I should sit tight and cast my lot with the Russians when they show up, yeah? They always seem to be just a day away."

"René, you and I both know it's never happening. Russia is rotting from the inside out. *Russkiy Mir* is a fantasy built on bribes and cronyism, and the whole structure is collapsing on itself. Everyone knew it was coming, but no one had the courage to say it. The SMO just hurried it along."

“Mother of Christ, Vostok. I never thought I’d hear you admitting such things.”

“Prigozhin saw it, but he made his move too soon, the idiot. You saw how the old grandpa took care of him.” Even here, away from everything, Vostok was reluctant to say the Russian president’s name out loud. “But Grandpa’s time is limited. Everyone knows it. When he’s out of the Kremlin, we’ll make our move. We need to be ready.”

René could hardly believe what he was hearing. It was treason.

“There’s a place for you, too, René. In the new Russia. The Russia that’s coming. I’m putting something together. We have muscle, sure, like Petr and the rest. But there will be vacancies that will need to be filled. Certain roles. I’ve brought together some experts, guys like you—”

“Explosives experts?” René asked.

“No, no. Different. Mostly computers. Cyber operators, people who can make things happen all over the world. Former GRU guys, mostly, but others too. Hackers, total specialists, these people. They’re good with code and moving crypto. They knew Ukraine was fucked from the start. A lot of them got out of Russia when the first round of conscription started. Went to Indonesia, Georgia . . . many came here to Serbia. We even have a couple operators in North America.”

René raised his eyebrows. “*Your* guys?”

“Well . . . their affiliations are a little more slippery. Grandpa funds them, but they keep us in the loop.”

“I see,” René said.

“But it’s more than just intelligence. I have rocket people too. Engineers and scientists from Energia and Roscosmos. Not as many as the cyber guys. And a woman also, a computer scientist. She might be smarter than all of them combined.” Vostok shook his head and laughed. “She could kick their fat asses in a fight too. From Rostov. A seriously tough bitch, I’m not kidding you.”

“These experts, they all answer to you?”

"Of course they do. I pay them. Or rather, I suppose I should say I disburse the payments. We have backers."

"Backers . . . like?"

"Big names. You know them, but better that you pretend you don't. So-called oligarchs, right? But here's the thing, René: They all know what's coming. And they all want to be ready to step in when the time is right to ensure a smooth transition to a new government. They're placing their bets, see? Getting ready. And when all this happens, there will be other opportunities as well. Business opportunities. For us."

"Such as?"

Vostok laughed, sharply, through his nose. "The smart ones, like us, they see what's coming. The others, well, they can't imagine Russia without Grandpa at the helm. And when he goes? They go too." Vostok formed his hand into the shape of a pistol and held it to his own temple, as if this one thing was too dangerous to put into words. René understood. "So there will be opportunities, see? Places for you. For your expertise. *Our* expertise together."

They were at the barn now. Vostok clapped René on the shoulder and shoved the tall barn door to the side on its rail. Inside, a pair of red Maersk shipping containers sat side by side, close, like they'd been welded together. A bundle of cables snaked from the far side of the barn to below the containers. On the container to the left, a steel fire door had been installed. Vostok pulled it open and beckoned René inside.

Inside the air-conditioned space was a long table with flat-screen computer monitors and cables arranged along its length. Three men wearing headphones sat tapping at keyboards, and at the head of the table a woman worked on a laptop. She looked up—first at her boss, then at René—and scowled as if bothered by their interruption. The man seated closest to the door noticed the woman's reaction and turned toward René. His eyes grew wide in shock, and he yanked off his headphones and dropped them to the table.

"René?" he said in astonishment. "It's really you?"

"Ilya!" René said, truly overwhelmed. "You're . . . you're alive?"

"I am, by fucking Christ, I am. I can't believe I'm seeing you here in front of me! I thought you were . . ." Ilya rose haltingly to his feet and made his way to René with a heavy limp. The two men he'd been working with glanced over before returning to their typing. "I thought you were gone. I thought I was the only one left." He grabbed René in a tight embrace. "We lost so many good ones that day, fuck! Dany, Vlody, I never thought those assholes would get us like that."

"What do you mean, 'get us'?" René looked to Ilya, then to Vostok. "It was an accidental detonation."

"Easy enough to think that," Vostok said. "Easy enough to let you believe it. But—"

"Brother, it was the Americans who fucked us," Ilya said. He shuffled back and slowly lowered himself into his chair. "Drone strike. Hellfire missiles."

René felt his stomach lurch as he absorbed Ilya's words.

"It's the truth," Vostok said gravely. "Wagner found parts from at least two separate pieces of ordnance. Right after they got you. When they found Ilya."

"I don't even remember what happened," Ilya said. "I'd gone out for a smoke. There was a place Dany found, a little wash. Three hundred meters, to be safe. That's how I survived. Even then, so far away, my leg still got fucked up. I got thrown against a cliff."

"And now?" René said, glancing back at Vostok. "You're here? With this guy?"

"I—"

"I hired him," Vostok said proudly. "Clearly, René, you had the best guys working for you. Ilya is the head of his team. Smart as hell. And loyal."

"Obviously," René said, turning to Ilya again.

"Work with us, René," Ilya said. "Vostok is a good boss. Like you, no joke. Work with us, and help take down those fuckers who got us in Mali."

“Listen to me, René,” Vostok interrupted, commanding his attention. “This is going to be difficult for you to hear, but it’s all the truth. You were infiltrated—”

“One of my guys? Bullshit.”

“No. I mean digitally infiltrated. You got hacked. We got data off of a couple of your hard drives after.”

“Fuck me,” René said, trying to process it. “Americans?” he asked, and Vostok nodded. “Government hackers?”

Vostok shook his head. “Contractors. Government affiliated. Elite.”

“The code was *tight*,” Ilya said. “So tight. They piggybacked on our crypto transactions. I’ve never seen anything like it. We went back and looked on the blockchain. All hidden in plain sight. They broke the code apart and stashed it in the metadata of each transaction; then it reassembled itself on one of our machines there in the desert. It activated itself silently and spread. Every fucking computer. Even the air-gapped hardware was infected.”

“Real pros,” Vostok said, as if that would make René feel better.

“Not so professional we couldn’t find it,” the woman at the table said without looking up. “Now it’s ours. And ours to improve upon.”

“Dasha is in charge of that,” Ilya said, looking at the software engineer reverently. She scowled, her attention still on her computer screen.

“And Ilya’s team,” Vostok said, “has been in charge of finding out where it came from.”

Dasha snorted at this, softly, and Ilya frowned before pulling a thick folder from a hanging file at his feet. He dropped it on the table in front of him and threw it open.

“Look, René, here, they used command and control servers all over the world, hacked machines, totally shady, like a GRU operation almost—” Ilya cut himself off, looking up at Vostok questioningly.

“He’s fine,” Vostok said. “Go on. Show him who did it.”

Ilya flipped several sheets forward and unfolded a color satellite photo. “They bounced the data packets around to cover their tracks, VPNs, things like that. It was smart. Dasha reverse engineered the virus and had it send out a modified payload. Just a little message to ping us each time it made a hop on the network." He tapped his finger on the map. "And this was the last hop. The packet went right up to the firewall of a place in Washington State in the US. Commercial building. Big satellite installation."

"What's their story?" René asked.

"Government contractors—launch support. They call themselves Cascadia. Lots of ex-military. We believe one of the principals is ex-CIA. That's . . . yes. That's him." Ilya had flipped to a printout of a photo that appeared to be from a government ID, a lean, green-eyed man with close-cropped hair.

"Jacob Moran," René said, reading the name below the photo. "The motherfucker." He looked up at Vostok. "Can your North American operators take care of him?"

"Not yet," Vostok said. "We're going to keep an eye on him. He's leading us to maybe . . . what they call 'bigger fish' in America. And once that happens, maybe you'd like to take care of this Moran asshole yourself?"

"Explain," René said.

"Come with me," Vostok said with a wave of the hand. "Ilya, excuse us." Vostok guided René to another steel door opposite the one they'd entered. It accessed the second container, which held another long table. Vostok motioned for René to take a seat, then shut the door behind them and crossed his arms.

"First, I have a question for you," said Vostok.

"Go on."

"Those materials you have the opportunity to purchase," he said. "What would be the best way to disperse them over a wide area in a rapid way?"

There was a long silence. "Are you asking me about a dirty bomb?" René asked, and Vostok raised his hand and wagged his index finger.

"I never said that. Never, never." He tapped his finger to his lips. "Please don't speak those words out loud again, understand? Besides, this operation needs something more sophisticated." He nodded. "But for the sake of argument, for maximum dispersal of the material, how might you do it?"

"A plastic of some sort, Semtex, C-4 explosive maybe, at the core, the material tightly bundled around it." René put his hands out in front of him, demonstrating a sphere in the air.

"Wouldn't that be easily identified by authorities afterward?"

"Absolutely. Commercial explosives like that are all chemically tagged to make it trivial to figure out where they were manufactured. If you're talking about a target in the third world, don't worry about it. They don't have the resources or time to investigate. But a Western target, or a job in a Western country? Very different. I'd make my own stuff to avoid tracing."

"You could fabricate an untraceable device?"

"Given the proper supplies and enough time, a few months maybe, of course I could."

"Months are too long," Vostok said. "Weeks are too long, really. But I have a question for you. Could you possibly quickly build a dispersal device using rocket fuel?"

René paused and pondered the absurdity of it. Then he laughed. "Like kerosene and liquid oxygen? It would be complex, and massive, at least car size or bigger for an energetic detonation, and you'd need to manage cryogenic temperatures for the oxygen." René cocked his head and thought for a moment. "But hypergols, maybe . . ."

"What are hypergols?"

"Hypergolic fuels. Hypergols. Liquid at room temperature, relatively easy to store, and they react explosively on contact. Violently. Hydrazine and dinitrogen tetroxide are the most common. Russia's *Proton* and *Soyuz* vehicles use them. Not *quite* as energetic as kerosene or methane with liquid oxygen, but dead simple because they don't need an ignition source."

"Do any of the US space companies use these hypergols?" A touch of excitement entered Vostok's voice.

"Of course they do. Everyone in that industry uses them. Mostly in upper stages or satellite-propulsion systems. For reliability, you can't beat them. They just come together and . . . *boom*." René clapped his hands for emphasis. "Foolproof."

"Now another question for you," Vostok said. "If there was an explosion at a rocket facility with these chemicals, it probably wouldn't be questioned, correct?"

"Well . . . ," René said. "In the right location, with the proper circumstances, it would look like an accident. But it wouldn't explain the presence of radioactivity everywhere."

"Are you saying the explosion would be strong enough to spread your materials around in the air?"

"What the hell are you scheming here?"

A broad smile covered Vostok's face, and he grabbed René and shook him by the shoulders. "The operation is coming together, old friend," he said, beaming.

"You mean an 'operation' to take out this asshole who wasted my guys?"

"Yes, René. Take him out, and so much more. If you decide to join me, you'll learn about it all." Vostok paused. "But one last question," he said, raising an eyebrow.

"What's that?"

"If we buy the materials, can you get them into the US? Are you good enough to make that happen?"

CHAPTER EIGHT

The tidy house, built in the 1930s on Galveston Island, hadn't been used as a residence in more than a decade. The place had white siding and yellow shutters and flowers growing in planters out front, and an electric bicycle leaned against the side of the covered front porch. A sign reading **GREATER GULF DEFENSE FUND** hung from the eaves.

Inside, the space was bright and airy, with hardwood floors and practical office furniture. There was a reception area, some comfortable-enough chairs, and a brochure rack with different materials about how to get involved or donate. The kitchen remained functional, with dated fixtures and a perpetually running coffee maker. Behind the kitchen, the former dining room had been converted into a conference space with a long table and numerous chairs. A wall-size map of the Gulf of Mexico hung on the far wall.

Duncan Nash sat at the head of the table.

Despite the sunny day, Duncan had the room's blinds closed, instead illuminating the space with twin banks of adjustable LED lights on either side of the room. On the table was a short tripod with a professional video camera mounted to the top of it, connected by a cable to a MacBook Pro off to the side. Duncan fiddled with a lapel mic at his collar, and a soft knock tapped on the door.

"Quick," Duncan said. "Come in, what is it?"

The door opened, and Jenny leaned inside.

"There's someone here for you," she whispered.

"CNN is calling any second," Duncan said. "I should be done in ten minutes if they want to wait . . . or tell them to come back this afternoon."

"He looks important."

"Babe, are we not important?"

Jenny frowned. "You know how much I hate it when you call me that."

"Come on," Duncan said before shooing her out. "Fifteen minutes, tops. Tell him to wait."

The door shut, and Duncan made one last check of his camera. The map as a background—Jenny's idea—was a brilliant touch. He could have gone up to a TV studio in Houston to do a remote, but doing an interview over Zoom, he'd discovered, looked better for their cause. Scrappier. Not as polished. That mattered to people, especially people who might want to donate. He checked that his tie was loosened just so, pulled his unbuttoned collar open, and pushed his rolled-up sleeves a little higher on his arms.

A chime sounded in his earpiece to alert him of an incoming Zoom call, and he tapped the trackpad on his laptop to answer.

"This is Ben Ford at CNN studios, Atlanta," said a voice in Duncan's ear. "I'm your producer today. How are you? Do you hear me okay?"

"I hear you fine, Ben. How are you doing?"

"Good, great. Even better now that I hear how good your audio is. Terrific. We've got an excellent picture from you too. This is a two-minute segment, so you'll want to keep to the point. Ashley Knight will be anchoring the spot." The producer paused, and Duncan scribbled the anchor's name on his notepad. "We're wrapping up a segment—then we're out to commercial. Please hold for me. Jet Propulsion Pasadena, still with me? Great. Please hold." There was a long period of quiet before Ben Ford came back on the line. "Okay folks, we're coming out of commercial. You're live in twenty."

In a window on his laptop, Duncan saw the anchor, Ashley Knight, soundlessly talking. Below her, the words "Peaceful Nukes in Space:

Time to Reconsider?" were printed over an endlessly crawling breaking-news chyron.

"You're live in three, two, one," the producer said. Duncan heard the show's audio feed come on in his earpiece, and on his laptop he saw himself on the right side of a three-way split screen.

"—time to think again about nuclear-powered satellites orbiting the earth, or is the risk too great? Joining us now to discuss is Dr. Sandra Rodriguez from the NASA Jet Propulsion Laboratory in Pasadena, California, and Duncan Nash, director of the Greater Gulf Defense Fund in Galveston, Texas. Thanks so much to both of you for joining us today. Dr. Rodriguez, let me ask you, how exactly do these space generators work, and should we be worried about them?"

"Radioisotope thermoelectric generators work by turning naturally occurring thermal energy from certain elements into electricity. Think of it as something like a solar panel that generates power from heat instead of light." Dr. Rodriguez spoke with an assertive, well-practiced tone. "There are no moving parts, so the generators are stable and safe. In fact, in nearly fifty years of use in space applications, there's never been a failure."

Duncan sat quietly and smiled. He could have cut in here, could have told her she was lying, but he knew remaining impassive would bolster his cause.

"But why do we need it now? What does this technology provide that, say, solar panels couldn't?"

"That's a great question, and let me tell you, we love using solar where we can, but sometimes in space it's not the best solution, maybe if you're far from the sun or you need high wattage. Places like Saturn, where our very successful *Cassini* mission was powered by an RTG, or the surface of Mars, where our *Curiosity* and *Ingenuity* rovers are still going strong with generators of this type."

Duncan noticed how cautiously Dr. Rodriguez avoided saying anything like "nuclear" or "radioactive." For her, Duncan knew, saying the word "plutonium" would be like dropping an f-bomb on live TV.

"And for this upcoming mission? Why can't you use solar there?"

"We're launching a satellite called high-energy electric-propulsion demonstrator, or HiPEP-D, to test lighter and more efficient propulsion systems for our next-generation missions to the outer solar system. The power requirements for HiPEP are quite great, though. So large that we'd need a tennis court–size solar array for it, and that's simply not practical. So we use an RTG, which gives us all the power we need. And, like I've pointed out, has proved to be completely safe."

"Duncan Nash, I see you shaking your head there. Do you disagree?"

"Ashley, thanks so much for having me on, and I have to say I disagree completely. The radioactive generators Dr. Rodriguez is talking about are powered by plutonium 238, which is refined from deadly waste left over from nuclear power plants. Just a couple grains of this plutonium dust, if inhaled, would cause a rapid and unpleasant death. Milligrams of plutonium are all it takes, and HiPEP is launching with nearly seventy pounds of it—"

"It's encased in durable graphite blocks," Dr. Rodriguez cut in. "They look like little marshmallows, inch-square cubes. They're indestructible—"

Duncan continued to smile and shook his head. "Your own engineers have admitted they have no idea what it would take to destroy those toxic plutonium blocks. You've had JPL scientists resign over the fact they felt their concerns about this were being ignored."

"You're talking about something from ten years ago, a disgruntled—"

"Think about this, Ashley: Seventy pounds of radioactive plutonium, with a half-life of eighty-seven years. Imagine an explosion, a catastrophic failure like we just had with the *Kingfisher Seven*. Imagine it over South Florida, atomizing that material and raining it down on Naples and Miami. Now imagine every living thing in the Everglades dying from radiation poisoning in the days and weeks that followed, the area contaminated for a couple generations—"

"You're talking about a scenario that's virtually impossible," Dr. Rodriguez said.

"Virtually," Duncan said, raising an eyebrow, "or entirely? You're admitting there's a chance."

"I'm not—"

"That's certainly a chilling picture you're painting for us," Ashley Knight cut in. "But, Mr. Nash, there's something else we need to talk about here, your mother—"

Duncan nodded. He was ready for this.

"—Helena Nash, is the head of Kingfisher Aerospace, the company launching HiPEP-D next month. How does her involvement affect the situation for you?" The screen cut to a replay of Monday's launch and explosion.

Duncan stared into the camera. "I'd be raising red flags even if this launch was being managed by NASA or SpaceX or anyone else. Kingfisher Aerospace and the rocket industry have been part of my life since I was a teenager, and I think that exposure has given me a better understanding of the risks than a regular observer."

"Kingfisher has an incredible safety record," Dr. Rodriguez said as the explosion footage played from a different angle. "They've proved themselves to be—"

"To be *human*," Duncan said as the split screen returned. "They showed that when their launch failed two days ago. Human beings sometimes make mistakes. Period. Three more minutes in flight and the debris from that explosion could have hit Florida. Now imagine it had been radioactive." Duncan paused to let his words sink in. Dr. Rodriguez's lips parted as she tried to formulate a comeback, but Ashley Knight jumped in before she had the chance.

"Obviously a very important discussion here, but we've run out of time, and I'd like to thank my guests again for joining us. We'll be following this one closely through the summer." The split screen ended, and Ashley Knight cracked a smile. "I'd love to be a fly on the wall at the Nash family's Thanksgiving dinner this year. Coming up, farmers in the heartland—"

The anchor's voice cut out, replaced by the producer's.

"Thanks, folks, this is CNN Atlanta terminating." The video call ended, and an instant later the door to the room opened and Jenny leaned inside.

"Great, huh?" Duncan said, flashing a double thumbs-up.

"Great, yes, super. Um, Duncan, this guy *really* wants to talk to you."

CHAPTER NINE

Back in his home office in Jackson, Wyoming, Jake closed the CNN tab on his browser after the interview ended. Duncan Nash was smooth, Jake thought with a shake of his head, wondering if he'd had some media coaching at any point, or if the guy was just naturally slippery. He seemed nothing at all like the guy who'd plucked him out of the Gulf of Mexico two days earlier.

He was good, Jake thought. *But not so good I couldn't see right through him.*

He rose from his desk and walked to the tall windows in his office, crossing his arms and leaning against the sill as he took in the view. His house, nestled in a stand of towering pines, was built high up on a hillside on the east side of town with an unimpeded view north across the valley to the vast Teton Mountain Range beyond. His parents had bought the property along with a small cabin in the early '80s, and Jake had made it his home after leaving the marines, building a house for himself and keeping the cabin as an occasional rental.

It was sentimental too. His late parents had loved that little cabin, and it held the fondest memories from his childhood.

Jake was 99 percent of the way to saying yes to Helena Nash. His instinct told him it was the right thing to do, but he wanted Tamara's and Stu's opinions first. And while Helena Nash had requested him not to do any private-plane piloting for Kingfisher, she'd stated no restriction on what he did with his personal time, so Jake decided he'd make the trip to Seattle in his own aircraft after all.

At first light, he would fly from his home base to the Pacific Northwest and spend a few days at the office, bunking down in Tam's guesthouse. If his colleagues agreed to proceed with Kingfisher, he'd fly commercial to Houston, find a place to stay, and get to work. Jake didn't want his enthusiasm for the job to lead him into doing anything stupid. Stu and Tam were trusted partners, and they'd become good friends. If there were any gotchas, Jake knew, they'd help find them.

Jake went upstairs to his bedroom and packed two bags. One small one he'd take up to Seattle, and a larger rolling bag for his stay in Texas. Enough work clothes for a couple of weeks at least and running clothes for a few days. Hopefully he'd find a place with a washing machine. In the middle of his clothes, he had a Wüsthof eight-inch chef's knife in a clamshell travel case. Jake liked to cook, and few things bugged him more than being stuck with lousy cutlery in a long-term rental. Nestled beneath the knife was a locking plastic gun case holding a SIG P226 pistol and loaded clips. Cascadia had been backing away from the shadier work, mostly, since the debacle in Mali—there were fewer reasons these days for "cover," as Helena Nash had put it—but Jake would never be dumb or relaxed enough to travel unarmed.

Jake lugged the big bag downstairs, leaving it inside his door before running back to his bedroom to retrieve his flight duffel. Back in his office he checked through his tech go bag: sixteen-inch laptop; a spare smartphone; a flip phone with a prepaid, unused SIM; travel chargers; cables; more cables; a wireless router with custom firmware installed by Stu; a notebook; five roller-ball pens; aspirin; Altoids; sunscreen; spare toothbrush; and toothpaste. All cables wrapped with Velcro ties, everything with a proper place. The order of it all made him happy. Jake zipped up the stout canvas messenger bag containing everything, slung the strap over his shoulder, double-checked that his desktop computer was off, and locked the door to his study.

Later, in bed, Jake kept his eyes shut, waiting to hear the owl who lived nearby, but instead he heard a vehicle on the road, fast, then slow. Then something peculiar: a motor growing closer and the coarse rumble of gravel under tires. He opened his eyes and blinked against the darkness, straining at the window to see through the deepening night. A dark shape ghosted up his drive, stopping just shy of the cabin. It took Jake a moment to process it. The headlights were out, and the vehicle crept to a stop. He stepped back from the window frame and felt the bed for his clothes. He pulled his phone from his pants pocket and went into the bathroom so anyone looking from outside wouldn't see the light of the screen.

There, Jake quickly pulled on pants and a shirt. In bare feet, he stepped softly down the two flights of stairs to his workshop space. It smelled of grass clippings and gasoline and was pitch dark inside. Jake walked with his hands held out in front of him as he shuffled forward. His fingers hit something smooth: the hood of his riding lawn mower. He reached to his right and felt his workbench. Jake slid his hands over the top and against the wall behind, and found a hammer hanging from a pegboard.

Better than nothing, Jake thought, testing the hammer's weight in his hand.

He slowly opened the door and took cautious steps through the grass toward the cabin. There was a low twisted cedar tree close to the front corner of the building, and he made for it and crouched behind. Jake breathed as quietly as he could and listened. Twenty feet to his left, the car's cooling engine made a pinging sound that seemed louder than a gunshot. Jake kept still. He heard footsteps as a man's shadow emerged around the far corner of the cabin. Jake tightened his grip on the hammer, lowered into a crouch, and prepared to—

A sudden rush came through the night, followed by an explosive impact to his chest. The intruder had rammed Jake with a shoulder to the sternum, and Jake flew backward into a heap, seeing stars as his head struck the ground and he gasped for breath. The hammer was gone from his hand. The man was on top of him in an instant, rearing back with his right fist, but Jake slipped aside so the following blow only clipped his ear. Somewhere through the fog of surprise, Jake's long-ago training kicked in; his muscle memory took over to fight back. He drew up his knees under the weight of the form straddling him and threw a wild headbutt. It wasn't perfect, but it connected. The guy got a handful of Jake's shirt and raised his right arm; once again Jake avoided the punch, this time dodging the blow entirely. He clawed at the guy's eyes with his left hand while scrabbling for the hammer with his right.

"Who are you?" Jake grunted. "What the hell do you want?"

His hand found the man's throat, and he closed his fingers as tightly as he could. The man wheezed as he tried to rear away. In the grass to his right, Jake's hand brushed over something firm. Not the hammer, but a fist-size rock. He picked up the cobble and swung, but the guy sensed the movement and blocked the move with his forearm and made a sound almost like . . . laughter? In his confusion over the sound, Jake relaxed his defenses. The assailant sensed it and landed a solid, heavy punch to the left side of Jake's face.

Jake groaned, seeing stars again. He raised his left arm defensively as he swung wildly for the guy with his right, but the attacker lurched to the side, his weight suddenly gone from Jake's body.

The dark form struggled to his feet and ran away, followed by the sound of a revving engine and spraying gravel. Jake rose to a seated position, his temple throbbing, and the world spun around him. Then he leaned over to be sick.

CHAPTER TEN

Even at three in the morning, the breeze coming off the bay by the Montenegrin city of Kotor was warm and heavy with humidity from the Adriatic Sea. René and Anton had hidden in some dense brush high on a hillside overlooking a car park on the northern outskirts of the city. Below them, illuminated by a single yellow lamp at the edge of the lot, Nabil leaned against the back of a boxy Dacia van, chain-smoking as he glanced nervously about. René had a Soviet-era bolt-action Mosin-Nagant Model 91 rifle resting across his lap, and he raised the old gun's scope to watch the fat man drop a cigarette butt to the ground and grind it out with his heel. Nabil immediately lit another from a pack in his breast pocket and peered up anxiously into the night.

"He's going to need more smokes if he keeps going like that," Anton said softly. "How long has it been? They're late."

"These things are always late," René said, scanning the area through the scope before returning to Nabil, who gazed plaintively in their direction as he took a pull from the cigarette. "Stop looking at us," he whispered to himself.

Through the scope René saw Nabil abruptly straighten and turn to peer up the road. René swung the rifle northward to see approaching headlights. His body tensed, but the car passed the lot without slowing.

"Fuck's sake," Anton said. "When will they come?"

"Keep your phone off," René said, barely speaking above a whisper. He returned the rifle to his lap and took a long breath. "I don't want any light on us. No tracking. We'll let your guy know after the transfer. When we're on the road. Tell me again what happens in Malta?"

"Everything is coming together—"

"Anton, it needs to *be* together."

"No, no, listen. Everything's lined up. Almost—"

"Toni."

"Stop! Stop, okay? Listen to me."

"Fine, go on." He raised the scope again to observe the area while the kid spoke.

"Your guy there was solid, like you said. He's got us a plane lined up—he's still working on cover for the stuff when we fly it over. That's the thing we're waiting on. We can't just move those lead cases around in the open, right? We need to hide them in something good. It's mostly figured out, but he'll wrap it up while we're on our way there on the boat. And once we *are* there, no one's going to check us when we move everything to the airport from the harbor. He's paid off the right people."

"What boat?"

"Maltese-flagged catamaran. Tour boat, but the guy makes most of his money running cigarettes from there to here. Lots of space to hide things. He'd be returning home empty, so this is just gravy for him."

"Does he have any clue what we're moving?"

"I've let them all think it's gold bars—"

René closed his eyes, took another deep breath, and shook his head. Gold would only draw their attention.

"I know it's flashy," Anton said quickly, anticipating René's concern. "But it's the only thing that makes sense for us to be moving that would be so heavy. The lead cases for the stuff, there was no way around it. People seriously worry about radioactivity. I had to come up with something."

René didn't like it, but Anton was right. It wasn't the way he normally would have conducted such a thing, but the deal felt like it was coming together. Vostok had given them nearly a blank check to purchase the material and get it moved to the United States. And in the greatest irony of all, at least to René, the transaction was being conducted in Bitcoin after Vostok encouraged them to use cryptocurrency for the purchase.

"What, you think we could do this deal with a sack full of rubles?" Vostok had said. "Even a truckload of notes wouldn't do it. The currency is worthless. At least the value of Bitcoin might go up. See if the seller will take it."

The seller reacted enthusiastically to the suggestion. Crypto would simplify things. For the physical exchange, they'd chosen the centrally located Montenegrin city of Kotor, in a parking lot that had once been used for a now-closed school for the blind. The lead casks made to contain the radioactive samples weighed about ten kilos each, the seller informed them, and with eighty of the containers, they'd be moving nearly a ton of material. To manage the load, they borrowed a Dacia van from one of Vostok's old contacts outside Podgorica, the capital. They also acquired a Geiger counter from the University of Novi Sad so Nabil could quickly test the product on site. Even with the material sheathed in a lead canister, enough alpha particles from radioactive decay would pass through to make the counter click. Nabil swore the stuff would be real.

"By God, René," he'd said, "I'm staking my own life on this. I won't let you down."

Now, in the dark, René lifted the rifle again. Nabil still leaned against the van. The fat man sighed, checked his watch, and took a long drag from his cigarette. It felt strange, René thought, to hold a gun with half his right hand missing. He braced the rifle as usual with his left palm under the barrel and the stock against his right shoulder, but now his damaged hand pressed awkwardly at the trigger guard, his ring finger awkwardly against it. Suddenly his body tensed. A new sound came from the north. Nabil flicked his cigarette away into the night, and René swung the rifle northward to see a pair of vehicles coming: a battered Toyota Hilux pickup truck with a tarp over the bed, followed by a sedan. The truck slowed and entered the parking lot, followed closely by the car behind. René lowered the rifle to take in the whole scene. The truck made a sharp turn as if it were driving away before backing up to the rear of the van. Nabil stood straight, his head held high, as a bearded man exited the idling truck. The two shook hands stiffly. René raised the gun again and tried to get a good look at the man waiting inside the car. It was too dark to see, and his right hand kept slipping on the trigger guard. He turned back toward the two men, and his hand slipped again. The bearded man shook his head, irritated, pointing to the truck. High on the hillside, the sound of rising voices was barely audible.

"No, Nabil, no," René whispered. "Come on, just say okay and be done with it."

"What's going on?" Anton asked softly.

"I don't know, some problem. He's fucking this up." René pulled the rifle's bolt handle back slowly, ready to chamber a round, and repositioned his hand—sweating now—as he peered through the scope at Nabil's face. René's Arabic was limited, but he could see the man's pudgy mouth repeating one word over and over as he vigorously shook his head.

"La, la, la." No, no, no.

René pressed closer to the eye cup. His hand slipped, and he felt his ring finger catch in the trigger guard. Nabil was shouting now, his hand lifted in the air. The scope's crosshairs were centered on his mouth.

René held his breath.

Then a loud crack sounded through the night, and the top of Nabil's head disappeared in a spray of red mist.

CHAPTER ELEVEN

Duncan followed Jenny out into the reception area. A stern-looking man in a dark tailored suit was seated there. He had close-cropped hair and an attaché case at his side and looked tired of waiting.

"Good afternoon," Duncan said, holding his hands wide. "I'm very sorry that took as long as it did. How can I help you?"

The man rose to his feet. "You are Duncan Nash, yes?" he said, speaking with an Eastern European accent. "You are the head of this organization, this is correct?"

"I am, yes," Duncan said, offering his hand. "And you are?"

"I am Mr. Strelka." They shook hands, firmly. Duncan nodded and smiled, but Strelka's lips remained pressed tight.

"How can I help you?" Duncan asked. "I already talked to the police about what happened Monday, I'm not sure what more I can add—"

"I am not here about that," Strelka said. "You are opposed to the upcoming Kingfisher launch, yes? This is the purpose of the organization?"

"It's really more about keeping plutonium out of the atmosphere—"

"I wish to talk about stopping rocket," Strelka said in a deep, nearly robotic monotone. "With you. Is there a place," he said, glancing at Jenny, "where we may talk in private?"

Jenny crossed her arms tightly across her body and frowned.

"Jennifer Bean here is our outreach coordinator. I value her input on—"

"I wish to speak alone with you," Strelka said. "A private issue about rocket."

"Sure, sure. No problem. Come on back." Duncan led the man through the kitchen into the conference room, throwing open the blinds as they entered. He turned to close the door and saw Jenny in the kitchen, her arms still crossed and her face twisting into an expression of angry indignation. Duncan held a finger up in a "hold on" gesture and shut the door.

"So," he said, smiling, "what do we need to discuss? You want to stop this launch? We'll take all the help we can get." Duncan was usually good at getting people to loosen up, but the man remained impassive. "Who are you with? You're not really like most of the people we get showing up here."

"I represent Russian interests in Miami," Strelka said. "I am . . . a lawyer." He placed his attaché on the table and flipped it open to take out several color-printed maps of South Florida.

"Ah," Duncan said, suppressing his excitement. This was an angle he'd never considered.

"You must know," Strelka said, "that many Russian nationals have homes and property in Miami."

"I've heard, yes."

"Very many Russians," Strelka said. "Important people. Powerful people."

"There *is* a lot of wealth there," Duncan said.

"The people I represent are not interested in having to leave their homes for a rocket that explodes plutonium on them."

"I don't think anyone is," Duncan said. "There are nearly seven million people who could be—"

"My concern is with only Russian nationals. Please understand. This is why I am here. I believe you can stop this rocket."

"With enough resources, personnel, financial . . . yes, I believe we can stop it."

"What is your plan for stopping this rocket?" Strelka asked, spreading the maps out on the table.

"Well," Duncan began, "it's not like we can go disable the thing. So we need to focus on shifting public opinion." He was slipping into pitch mode now, pulling from a script he'd recited hundreds of times to potential donors. "Rocket launches are nothing like the spectacle they were in the sixties and seventies. Or even the eighties, at the beginning of the shuttle program. Back then, launches were a national event, a shared experience. Now it's commonplace. People regard launches about the same way they look at a plane taking off. Boring. Sure, there are fans who tune in to the webcasts, but we're talking about a tiny fraction of the population. Most people, though? Rocket launches never even cross their minds."

"I am not seeing the point here," Strelka said impatiently.

"The point is, when you take the time to educate people, their opinion changes drastically. We ran some targeted ads with some facts about the upcoming launch and payload in the South Florida media markets—print, TV, and online—and asked some polling questions. Are launches safe? Only thirty-one percent of the people in the target area responded yes. How is your life impacted? The averaged response was one point one. Strongly negative. Do you see what I'm getting at here?"

Strelka said nothing.

"What I'm saying is, if we had the resources to really cover South Florida with ads about this, public opinion would turn so strongly against Kingfisher, they'd be forced to cancel the flight. I'm talking a big buy here, a big, sustained campaign. With enough messaging, we're certain public opinion can be shifted in such a way that citizens would contact their elected representatives to bring a halt to the launch. Probably the public relations nightmare would be enough to put the launch on hold, but with enough momentum and political will, it could be stopped—"

"You have a personal connection," Strelka interrupted. "I wish to ask about this."

"You mean my mother?"

"Yes, your mother. I wish to share information with her that could make her reconsider proceeding with this launch."

"Information?"

"Documents," Strelka said. He pulled a USB stick from his briefcase and held it in front of Duncan's face.

"What sorts of documents?"

The Russian smiled. "There have been no terrestrial failures of nuclear generators in the US space program. In Soviet times, there were several."

"I know of the *Lunokhod* mission failure that spread polonium over the Soviet Union in 1969. And Russia's *Mars 96* reentering over Chile. But there was never confirmation—"

"Here is confirmation," Strelka said, placing the thumb drive gently on the table. "Here are top secret reports after *Lunokhod* reentry. From USSR. Reports on dispersal of polonium, cases of radiation sickness, mass fatalities. Images and video also. Data until 1990. Not only from there, also there is documentation from three failed launches at Baikonur—"

"Are you serious?" Duncan said, his eyes growing wide. He reached for the thumb drive, but Strelka pulled it out of his reach.

"Not for you," he said.

"But this could change public opinion completely! And prove a threat of harm in the courts. If this shows the true danger of these generators—"

"I agree it could work this way," Strelka said. "But Helena Nash must see it first. Can you arrange it?"

"I haven't spoken with my mother in more than a year. It could be difficult."

Strelka spun his attaché toward Duncan and slid some papers aside to reveal multiple bound stacks of one-hundred-dollar bills.

"This is fifty thousand US," he said. "My backers wish to give it now to the Greater Gulf Defense Fund. A donation."

"That's very generous," Duncan said, his eyes still on the USB. Strelka slid the drive closer across the table.

"You take this USB," he said. "If you get it to Helena Nash, we will give you five hundred thousand. If she cancels launch, you get two million more." He paused and shook his head slowly. "But is not for you to see, these files."

"But if we *showed* people," Duncan said, "if they could just see how terrible—"

"*Not for you to see*," Strelka repeated gravely. "Only for your mother. If I find you have seen, it is very bad for you."

"I . . . I understand," Duncan said.

"Get this to Helena Nash," Strelka said. He drew a business card from inside his jacket and placed it on the table. "Call this number to tell me when she has seen. Then we discuss how you can use for your cause."

CHAPTER TWELVE

"What the fuck?" Anton gasped. "You killed him?"

"That wasn't me," René said, though for an instant he thought it might have been. It was impossible for him to have taken a shot, though; the 91's breech remained wide open. "Stay down. Keep quiet." Gunfire began to pop-pop through the night. Below them, the bearded man lurched and fell dead to the ground, too, slumping over Nabil's splayed-out legs.

"What is going on?" Anton asked, close to panic.

"I said be quiet." René swung the rifle to the south just in time to see muzzle flashes from a drainage ditch a couple of hundred meters away. "Stay flat on the ground."

René shoved the old rifle's bolt forward to chamber a round and forced himself to breathe slowly. The passenger car began to accelerate away, and a renewed volley of gunfire from the south shattered the car's rear window, causing it to veer up a berm by the entrance of the lot. René watched a short, stocky man in fatigues emerge from the drainage area, a balaclava covering his face and an automatic rifle in hand. His gait tickled something in the back of René's mind.

Petr?

A taller man followed, his face masked and weapon raised to cover his comrade.

The guy from Novi Sad: the driver.

René looked over the scope to view the entire scene. None of it made sense. Would Vostok have sent the two men to undermine him? Were they working on their own?

"Who are these guys?" Anton whispered.

"I said shut up."

The short one, the one who looked like Petr, ran toward the stopped car, hesitated, then pulled the door open. He drew a pistol from a holster low on his leg and fired two rounds into the car to finish off the man inside. Back at the truck, the tall one lifted the tarp and peeked underneath. Then he knelt next to the bearded man on the ground and patted his hands over the dead man's pockets.

René took a breath, sighted on the man's head, and pulled the trigger. He missed high; a bullet hole appeared in the side of the truck. The tall man lowered into a crouch and froze. René calmly chambered a second round, adjusted his aim, and pulled the trigger. The man's head snapped back, and he dropped dead over the pair of bodies sprawled on the ground before him.

"What's happening?" Anton said again, hyperventilating now.

René chambered another round and turned his weapon toward the short man, who hurried to take cover behind the truck. The man had a broad chest and swung his arms wide as he ran. René was certain it was Petr.

Fuck this guy. René had no reservations about eliminating the two men. He had a mission, and he intended to complete it.

The short man—Petr—raised his pistol over the hood of the truck and fired wildly into the hillside to draw René's fire. The shots thudded harmlessly into the earth ten meters to the right of René and Anton's position. René stayed calm, his breathing steady. More shots came from behind the truck, and headlights appeared out on the highway from the south. Local police forces? Reinforcements? The car passed, its driver oblivious to the gun battle next to him.

"Come on," René whispered. "Show yourself." He sighted just above the truck's hood, waiting for Petr to peek over to take a shot.

"Come on, motherfucker." The wind had stopped; only the sound of the Toyota's idling motor hummed softly in the night.

"He's getting in the truck!" Anton cried.

René looked to the left to see the dome light illuminating the cab. He tightened his ring finger to pull the rifle's trigger but had overcorrected his aim; a bullet hole appeared harmlessly in the door. The truck, slowed by its heavy cargo, began to creep forward, and René chambered another round and fired. The passenger window exploded, but the truck kept moving. He took one more shot and missed wide.

"Fuck!" he shouted, jumping to his feet. "Come on!" he said. "Let's go! Come on, come on, come on!" Anton seemed frozen. René grabbed the collar of the kid's sweatshirt and dragged him along, staggering and tripping down the hillside. He lost his grip on the rifle but didn't turn back to retrieve it. The two got to the pavement just as the truck turned out onto the highway.

"Get in the van!" René shouted. "Quickly, get in!" He pulled open the driver's side door and scrambled into the seat and pressed the ignition, the seconds feeling like hours as the diesel engine turned over. Finally the motor rattled to life, and René threw the transmission into drive as Anton pulled his door shut. The kid was really panicked now, his breaths coming in a racked wheeze as he clutched the armrests of his seat.

"Why did they do that? What just happened?"

"It's Petr, one of Vostok's guys," René said as he turned out on the highway and stomped on the accelerator. "Maybe they're on their own. Or maybe Vostok tried to fuck us." None of it made sense. "Get yourself together," he said. "I need you to be calm."

Anton mumbled something in Dutch and took a halting breath. "What . . . what do we do now?"

"We catch Petr and take the material."

Ahead of them, maybe half a kilometer away, they saw the Toyota's taillights as the loaded truck labored up a hill.

"Put down your window," René said. "Put on your seat belt. Listen to me. I said put down the fucking window! Things are going to get crazy in a moment. I have to depend on you. Are you listening to me?" The kid said nothing, staring ahead into the night. "Anton!"

"Yes," he finally said, seeming to collect himself. "Yes! Tell me what to do." He toggled the control, and the window lowered. The taillights ahead drew closer.

"Get your seat belt on. Strap in. That's it, good. I'm making a move at the top of the hill. You stay put while I work on this guy. When you see a chance, get in the truck. Give me thirty seconds. If I'm not there, you get the truck to the boat and get the stuff to the States, okay? I'll get there on my own."

"I won't leave without you," Anton said.

"Shut up. You will. Thirty seconds. Any longer than that and you get out of here, understand?" They were on the hill now, catching up with the laboring truck, maybe sixty meters ahead. "Tell me you understand."

"I understand."

"Watch what's going on. Hang on tight now. You'll know when to move."

With no cargo and a high-torque diesel motor, the van flew up the rise, easily closing in on the overloaded truck. Ahead, the pickup lurched as if the driver was downshifting. The crest of the hill was less than thirty meters away, and René kept the pedal floored and moved into the oncoming lane. They sped past the truck, and René threw the wheel to the right, blocking Petr's path and causing his own top-heavy Dacia to swerve and roll onto its side with a screeching slam. A half second later the fugitive truck collided with the van's undercarriage, ramming them forward on their side. René checked Anton, hanging wide eyed and sideways in his seat. The kid was fine, if shocked. René cut the motor, unbuckled himself, and scrambled upward, pulling himself toward the sky and out the passenger-side window. He lay flat on the side of the van, steadied his breathing, and pulled his knife from his pocket. A single headlight beam cut through the night in the settling dust, and the scent of diesel fuel and motor oil hung on the air. The pickup continued to idle behind them. This was good, René thought. He'd wanted a collision that left the loaded vehicle drivable.

A sound came from behind: the Toyota's door creaking open. René almost smiled. Petr was impulsive. And he'd been humiliated over René by Vostok following the clusterfuck at Novi Sad. Of course he'd want revenge.

René held his breath and silently peered over the side. Petr walked cautiously, almost tiptoeing alongside the roof of the van, his pistol held out before him. He paused at the van's cab, taking a wide-footed stance and bracing his weapon with his left hand.

René flicked his knife open, rolled from the topside of the van, and landed on Petr from above. His right foot connected with the gun, pushing it away, as René clung to Petr's back, his left arm over his shoulder. He raised the blade for a killing blow but was thrown backward by a hard right elbow to the gut.

Petr spun to face him. René lunged forward and was barely clipped by a wild punch to the left side of his head. He ducked to miss a follow-up left, and feinted to draw another punch from Petr's right. René used the miss to slash Petr's forearm with the Böker.

"*Ah!*" he cried, clutching his arm. Behind him, the air brightened over the crest of the hill from approaching headlights.

"*Politsiya!*" René shouted in Russian. "Police!"

Under the balaclava, Petr's eyes widened as he turned slightly.

René's blade slashed across the side of his face, splitting his balaclava and cheek open in a wide gash.

A high-pitched scream filled the night just as the headlights crested the hill and slowed. Petr pressed his hands to his face, howling, and René drew back to finish him off but froze. The car had stopped. René turned and ran. Behind the van, Anton was at the wheel of the loaded pickup truck. He'd backed away from the wreck and had the passenger door open.

“Lights off,” René said, climbing in and slamming the door closed. “Down the hill. Get us away from here, hurry.”

Anton reversed into a three-point turn and accelerated into the dark.

“Did you kill him?” he asked.

“No,” René said. “I fucked him up, though. He’ll probably wish he was dead.” He paused to catch his breath, feeling his heart slow, letting the rush of the fight leave his body. “Was it thirty seconds? I told you to get out of there.”

“Not quite. But I said I wasn’t leaving.”

“You did fine,” René said. “Now get us to the harbor.”

CHAPTER THIRTEEN

Outside in the predawn, Jake's twentysomething former tenant, Katie Warner, waited for him by the garage. She'd come to Jackson to ski for a winter after college a few years back and had, like so many others, fallen in love with the valley and ended up staying. She'd moved out of Jake's rental cabin and in with a boyfriend the previous summer, but Jake still threw her a few bucks in exchange for watching the house while he was away. Often she'd shuttle Jake to the airport in Idaho where he kept his plane; this morning, her green Subaru wagon waited in the driveway with the hatch open.

"Thanks again for taking me over," Jake said as he loaded up the bags and shut the door.

"Aw, I'd drive you to Seattle if you asked me." They pulled out of the drive and headed down the hill. Katie's eyes fluttered to his bruised cheek, but she had the decency not to comment. "How long does it take you to fly there?"

"About five hours. I could do it faster, but I'll make a pit stop and weather check in Boise."

Katie nodded. "When can I go flying with you again?"

"We can go up when I'm back. How about that?"

"Okay. I'm holding you to it." They passed through town and made their way westward on the highway to Wilson and Teton Pass. "So this rocket thing, is that the one with Helena Nash?"

"It is," Jake said. "She's pretty nice. Intense, but—"

"You met her?"

"Well, yes. I'm doing work for her."

"You met Helena Nash. Holy shit, Jake."

"How do you know about her?"

"How does someone *not* know about her?" Katie asked, truly excited. "She gave that amazing talk at South by Southwest, and have you not seen the video of her dancing last year at Coachella? It's adorable. She's like the coolest cool mom."

Jake laughed. "I was surprised by how much smaller she was in person."

"She's like a little elf or something. That is so amazing you get to hang with her."

"I don't think we're going to be doing much hanging out. She's a busy person, and I will be too."

"Okay but—" Katie paused. They were headed down the steep mountain pass now, and she focused for a moment on her driving. "If you get to be in the same room with her again," she continued, "definitely get a picture with her, okay? And send it to me."

"I'll see what I can do," Jake said. "But I need you to do me a favor for now. Two, actually."

"Anything. What's up?"

"I'd like you to not mention to anyone that I'm working with her. I'm going to be involved in some sensitive stuff, and my involvement could . . ." Jake struggled to find the best way to phrase it. "It could ruffle some feathers. Like some of the other things I do. Keep it under your hat for now, and you can tell them about it after I'm done. News gets around, especially with social media and all that. Okay?"

"Of course. Mum's the word." Katie nodded with finality, and Jake knew she meant it.

"Thank you."

"What's the other favor?"

"Don't sleep at the cabin while I'm away this time, okay? Just check in on the place every few days. In and out." Jake threw her a stern look.

"You were a spy, weren't you?" Katie said nonchalantly. "When you were in the army."

"Whoa, Katie. Marines. *Marines.* I was in the United States Marine Corps."

"But you wore a uniform and carried a gun and all that, right?"

"I did, sometimes."

"So it's like the same thing."

"Not at all," Jake said.

Katie screwed up her face. "Did you have a title? Like Sergeant Moran or something."

"Rank. I held the rank of major."

"Major Moran! I love it. Can I call you that?"

"I think I like Jake better."

"Whatever, Major Moran. And you were a spy. Am I right?"

Jake said nothing for a moment as he pondered the best response.

"I'm right," Katie said, grinning. "I know it. You aren't saying anything, because you're not allowed to. Right?"

They crossed into Idaho now, and Katie slowed the car as they entered the little town of Victor, a bedroom community to Jackson.

"So by 'spy,'" Jake said, "what do you mean exactly? What's your definition?"

Katie leaned her head from side to side. "Like, you sneak around and check people out without them knowing. You get important secrets and send them back to your boss or whatever. But you were a good spy, because you were a soldier and you were helping the country. That's kind of how I imagine your spy life."

"If that is your definition," Jake said, "then yes, I was pretty much a spy."

"Okay," Katie said, nodding and grinning. "Okay. I am actually driving a real spy. In my car."

"Retired spy."

"Whatever, it's fantastic."

"Probably also not the kind of thing you want to be telling your friends," Jake said.

"Hey, I am the most trustworthy person you will ever know. Do you think I would . . . wait, do you say 'blow your cover'? I wouldn't ever blow your cover. That's how you say it, right?"

"There's no cover to be blown. The work I did was called SIGINT. It was like—"

"Whoa, now you are talking to me in *code*? This is unreal."

Jake laughed. "It's not code. SIGINT means signals intelligence. We got intel—intelligence, I mean—from various electronic sources, satellites and things like that, so it could be interpreted for our guys in the field. So it was kind of high-tech spying." Jake deliberately left out some of the recon work he'd done early on, and his liaisons with the CIA. It was okay to answer Katie's questions, he thought, but there were some things she didn't need to know.

"Still, that's amazing."

"And later on, I worked with the navy on launching some of their satellites for gathering all of that intel. I loved that work. I really loved my time in that world."

"So why did you quit? Or retire? Whatever you do when you stop being part of the army. Or marines, I mean."

"I left," Jake said. "I had fulfilled my obligation—there were new people coming up. They didn't need an old guy like me in there taking up space that they wanted." It was mostly the truth.

"You're hardly old."

"In that world, yeah, I was pretty old. I worked with a lot of contractors, too, and I saw that there were still some opportunities in the private sector where I could try a lot of new and different things but still be able to serve. So . . . here I am."

"Here you are," Katie said. "That's pretty awesome." They were slowing down for the town of Driggs, Idaho, now. The buildings had straight facades and were occupied by restaurants, real estate agencies, and tourist shops.

Katie drove them back to a parking lot next to a fence topped with razor wire, with rows of airplane hangars just beyond. Jake got his things from the back of the car, and Katie leaned against the side of it.

"Hey," Jake said, "there's a bag inside the front door back at the house. I'll need you to FedEx it to me once I get settled in and have an address in Texas."

"No problem." Katie gave him a mini salute. "Fly safe, Major Moran."

Aside from some moderate turbulence as he came over the Cascade Mountains, Jake had an easy day of flying. It cleared his head, being in the air; seeing everything from above gave him a sort of lasting clarity. After nearly five hours in the skies, his mind felt sharp and ready.

Jake contacted Seattle air traffic control and was slotted into the approach pattern for Paine Field, the large private airport in Everett, Washington, on the north side of Seattle's metropolitan area. He touched down smoothly in a moderate crosswind, exiting the runway as soon as he had slowed enough. He taxied to the parking area, tied down, grabbed his bags, and headed to the office to pay for fuel and a month's parking. Outside the front door, Tam waited for him. His colleague leaned against an Audi wagon, wearing aviator glasses and pulling a wind-whipped strand of dark hair from her face.

"I saw that landing," she said, cocking an eyebrow.

"Was it okay?"

She shrugged, and her face turned serious. She looked like she was going to say something, but she stopped herself and came to Jake instead, grabbing him in a close embrace.

"I was so worried," she whispered. "That helicopter crash—"

"It was fine," Jake said. "I'm fine."

Tam pushed herself back and touched her hand to Jake's cheek. "You can't blame me for worrying. What the hell happened?"

Jake shrugged. "Birds, they think. Freak accident."

"And last night? Was that a freak accident too?"

Before Jake could answer, she said, "Does anyone at the office know about your intruder?"

Jake shook his head.

"Does Stu?"

"Only you."

"Why don't we hold off on the office, then?" Tam said. "Let's just go talk."

Tamara lived on Whidbey Island in the Puget Sound. It was less than an hour from the airport, but taking the ferry to the island from the sprawl of the mainland was like traveling to another world. Her house sat up on a wooded bluff looking north, and on this cool day the view across the water to Camano Island was clear. The main residence was a restored farmhouse with rustic furnishings and decor from her travels around the world. Gems and fossils collected on her journeys were displayed in glass-front cases, and an antique Fresnel lens from a lighthouse in Normandy stood in the corner. Mounted on the wall in an antique frame was a spare mirror from a spaceborne imaging platform she'd designed.

Tamara's first doctorate, earned at age twenty-five, was in planetary geology, with a second, two years later, in optics. Tam's parents were academics, her mother Iranian, her father from Italy, and she'd inherited their considerable intellect and easy charm. She'd always believed she'd spend her life in academia, or maybe at NASA designing probes to search for life on other planets. Her abilities, though, led to her quick recruitment by the petroleum industry. Tamara became an innovator in using satellites to discover oil deposits, and when she found the generation of satellites were lacking in capability, she designed from scratch a new system that met her needs. The oil industry burned her out, though: the pressure was tiresome, the personalities grating, the endless sexism offensive. Eight years was enough. Royalties from her imaging patents allowed her to buy herself a beautiful place in the Pacific Northwest, and she never needed to work again. A life of consulting gigs, gardening, and philanthropy would have suited her just fine.

But it was hard to leave that world completely. She attended a few conferences a year, here and there, just to stay current, and kept crossing paths with a tall ex-marine named Jake Moran. Their exchanges were cordial, friendly even, and the level of their conversations showed that Jake had a deep understanding of the work she'd done. Their consulting jobs often overlapped, and they found themselves emailing each other for advice on technical issues or referring clients if the other was a better fit. At one of their meetings a few years back, Jake had asked if she'd join him for lunch so he could pick her brain on a satellite-imaging problem he was dealing with.

"I have a confession to make," he'd said once they were seated at the restaurant, spreading some papers out over the table. "I want to ask you about something more than just image resolution." Tam froze, thinking for a moment he was going to ask her out on a date. He picked up on the reaction and laughed. "Oh, no. No, no, no," he said, waving his hand. "Not . . . no." He laughed again. "I'd like to ask if you'd ever think about working with us at Cascadia?"

Now it was her turn to laugh nervously, unsure whether she was relieved or possibly disappointed. "I'm flattered," she said. "But I'm quite content working as a consultant right now. I just couldn't see myself being someone's employee again."

"I'm not talking about working *for* us," he said. "Would you consider being a partner?"

Tam was taken aback. She said she'd consider it.

It wasn't only his intellect that made her take the offer seriously. It was his passion, his certainty, his clear desire to do the right thing. And those eyes, those green eyes, crinkling at the corners when he smiled, the way they always met her own eyes with interest and respect—it was something she'd only fleetingly experienced before in her professional life.

After chewing on the pros and cons, she'd finally said yes.

Now she entered the living room to find Jake staring in wordless thought out over the Sound. In her left hand was a pair of tumblers with ice, in her right was a mostly full bottle of Wyoming Whiskey small-batch bourbon. Jake had given it to her as a birthday gift the year before. He glanced toward her and laughed.

"So I'm out of town a few weeks and everyone starts drinking on the clock?"

"I'm considering this on-the-job therapy." Tam pulled over another chair across from him and filled each of the tumblers halfway. She passed one to Jake and held hers aloft.

"To safe landings," she said.

"Safe landings." They tapped glasses and both took a long sip.

"I think we're going to need to put in your contract that you can't fly anymore."

"That makes you the second person who wants to ground me."

"Who else? Helena Nash?"

Jake nodded.

"From a completely practical point of view," Tamara said, "from a risk-reducing posture, it's something we should at least talk about."

Jake took a long swallow of his bourbon and laughed.

"I'm not kidding. When it comes to things like this, you *are* the company. If something happens, that's gone. We depend on you."

"You're the company, too, Tam."

"It's not my picture on the orbital-assets web page, last I checked. People want to hire *you*. Helena Nash wants you in there, not me."

"She wants you too. She knows about you. And Stu."

"It's *your* reputation that got us that gig. But more than that. We need you, Jake. All of us. I worry, okay?"

Jake shrugged.

"I'm being serious," Tamara said. "But you don't really need to stop flying. Maybe just keep yourself out of helicopters with big targets painted on them."

"It's the strangest thing," Jake said. "You'd think something like that, a helicopter crash, you'd see at least something about it in the news. But nothing. I read about an 'incident over the Gulf of Mexico' the day after, but there were no details. And I kind of expected investigators would keep wanting to talk to me about it. Like the FAA or NTSB. I haven't heard from anyone after the local cops."

"Kingfisher," Tamara said quietly. Then, shifting in her chair, she continued, "Was it frightening?"

"It's funny, I was so focused on what was going on, I didn't think about anything other than trying to get us down. The pilot, that guy Wade I told you about, he was unflappable. Even with a chunk of plexiglass through his leg, he talked me through all of it. He saved us more than anything I did."

"You were lucky."

"We *were* lucky. All of us."

Tamara lifted the bottle from the floor next to her chair, uncorked it, and topped off both their drinks. "And then you were unlucky. Who was it, Jake? Last night?"

"I'm . . . I'm just not sure. Like if those guys from Mali—"

"Wagner?"

"Yeah," Jake said. "Except, even if they figured out my role in it, I can't see the remnants of that group getting their shit together enough to hassle a guy in the States."

"So maybe it wasn't Wagner?"

"There are plenty of people we've pissed off. I need a better security system. I'll get one. I'm fine."

"You're fine. And I'm through being emotional for the moment." She wrinkled her nose with a little smile. "What about this job offer?"

"It's a big deal for us. You'll see what I mean when we get down there—"

"*When* we get down there? I thought the purpose of this chat was to sort through the offer. You sound like you've already decided. And I'm not saying that's a bad thing. But lay it all out for me so I can back you up. Or tell you you're an idiot."

"Maybe I have decided," Jake said. He swirled the ice cubes in his glass and took another long swallow. "Maybe I have. Maybe you're trying to get me drunk."

Tamara smiled again, wanly this time, and shrugged. "Seriously . . . why take the job?" she asked. "I assume the money is good."

"The money will be very good."

"Is that all?"

"No, it's much more than that. Ever since she asked me, I've been thinking: Could someone penetrate a launch system like that? I can't let go of it. I think of every launch I ever managed, every little fault that might have been in the system. I never even considered it then. Did I assume it was secure? I've been lying awake at night thinking about this. Were there ways it could have been taken over? Was I clueless? And part of it's like . . ."

"Like what?"

"Some of the hacking Stu's team has been doing. A little black hat—"

"Maybe a *lot* black hat," Tam said. "I hold my nose and keep my head turned. And you two keep doing what you do."

"No shit," Jake said, taking another long sip. "Sometimes I wish I didn't have to know about it, or do anything with it. But the results. You can't argue with the results. And we can't just do nothing with the results, Tam."

"Never to be discussed."

"I wish it was that easy. This remote access kit Stu's guys developed, it's scary how capable it is. And the way they slipped it into that Wagner operation in Mali—"

"I couldn't believe it myself," Tam said.

"I *didn't* believe it at first. That was part of the reason I approved it: I didn't think there was any way it would work. But it did work. And if we could do it, why couldn't someone else?" Jake raised his glass like he was going to take a sip of his bourbon and shook his head. "Flip it around, Tam. Why couldn't someone else build a hacking kit like that too? I mean, Jesus, what if someone got into a rocket-launch system and took control of the vehicle. The eastbound overflight regulations have them threading a pretty tight needle through Florida and the Caribbean. So, what if? What if they blew something up on purpose?"

"Come on, I've been to a few launches myself. I don't know the details like you do, but I know it's a tight system. And what, fifty years of rocket launches, and nothing like this has ever happened."

"Fifty years of *government* launches. All overseen by militaries with operational-security measures drilled into them. But these new guys, private space, they push back against that oversight. They're so green . . . What if that creates an opening for someone? Do you see what I'm saying here?"

"Maybe you're getting a little conspiracy theory on me here."

"Maybe you're feeding me too much bourbon."

"I guess I can see it. But it seems a little far fetched."

"It's our job to see it," Jake said. "If we want the job."

CHAPTER FOURTEEN

Jenny tried to start an email, but her lingering fury over being shut out of Duncan's meeting with the Russian the day before made it pointless. She got up, sat down, and got up again before stomping back into the kitchen. What did he think she was, his secretary? She was a partner, *his* partner, and she was beyond angry at being excluded from something important. The Russian had said nothing as he sat in her office, staring at her the whole time. She'd wanted to burst into the conference room and give them a piece of her goddamn mind, but she didn't. She'd held herself back and instead clomped back into the lobby, and Duncan had known better than to stick around afterward.

From behind the desk, she grabbed her bag and bike helmet and stormed out of the house and down the front steps, letting the door slam behind her.

On her e-bike, down Broadway, she tried to make herself calm down. Who did Duncan think he was, anyway? Calling her *babe*? Seriously? Jenny unclenched her teeth. She turned down her street, but instead of stopping at her house, she went all the way down to Seawall Boulevard and turned left to head along the beach. Out in the Gulf an endless line of freighters was queued up, straight from the Panama Canal and headed for the depots of Galveston Bay. Beyond the freighters the sky had taken on a dark cast, like storms building beyond the horizon.

Jenny rode along, passing bars, hotels, and restaurants to her left and the seawall to her right, passing the Pleasure Pier and its roller coaster and trinket shops, heading eastward until the development died off near the end of the island. The road halted right at the channel, and Jenny dismounted. A couple of old-timers were fishing, spin casting with long rods out into the water, and one of them waved hello.

"Nice to see you out, Miss Jennifer. How's your mama been?"

"She's great, Mr. Nelson. How are you?"

"Doing all right. All right. You tell your mama I said hello, will you?"

"Sure thing."

The freighters here were closely spaced coming into the channel between Galveston and Goat Islands, like beads on a giant garish necklace. Ships coming in, ships going out. Jenny walked along the sand, thinking of being here with her grandmother, her Grandma Hazel, who told stories about hurricanes, and pirates, and the old Spanish fort that had stood in this very spot. So much had changed, she knew. What a place to grow up . . . Her whole family had left, now; her brother gone to the East Coast, her mother up in Dallas, her father lost. And Grandma Hazel dead for years.

Who would keep those memories alive? Jenny felt it was her job, her duty, to stay behind. Four generations on the island. She had to stay. This was her home. And protecting it—from plutonium, or pollution, or rising sea levels, or anything else—had become her reason for being.

Jenny closed her eyes and focused on the sound of the waves rolling in. Pirates had been here, right here, nearly three hundred years ago. The dread pirate Jean Lafitte wrecked ships, buried treasure. When she was a little girl she'd hunt with her cousins, digging in the sand, nickels and pennies standing in for gold doubloons. Someday, if she had a little girl of her own, she could pass on those stories. Her own children could dig in this very sand.

Jenny opened her eyes and took a deep breath. It was all worth it, protecting this place. And someday, kids would be a happy addition to her life.

But kids, though . . . with Duncan? She couldn't see it.

She started walking back up to where she'd left her bike. Mr. Nelson and his friend both waved as she pedaled away. They knew the old tales. They'd boarded up their homes to ride out the great named hurricanes. Rita, Ike, the deluge of Harvey. After the waters had subsided, they'd stayed. Just like Jenny would.

The ride back seemed quicker than the trip out had. The street was lined with tidy houses, and hers was single story and white with green trim and a screened-in front porch. It had been her Grandma Hazel's childhood home. The office on Broadway was where Jenny had lived as a child. She owned both places now and kept an eye on a third house that her mother owned and rented out. Her father had lived there for a little more than a year following her parents' divorce when she was nine. Then Hurricane Ike came, and he was gone. Maybe he drowned in the storm surge. Maybe he just ran away. Jenny didn't dwell on it. There was the house, though, and a little insurance money, enough to get her comfortably through college at the University of Texas with a degree in botany.

Duncan's car, a Tesla sedan, was parked in front of the house when she made it home. It stood out there at the curb among the old Chevys and Fords. Given how concerned her partner was with his image, Jenny wondered how driving a $100,000 car worked with the man-of-the-people message he was trying to convey. She tried not to pay attention, but it was getting harder to overlook his contradictions.

Jenny wheeled her bike past the Tesla, leaned it against the side of the house, and bounded up the porch steps. She saw Duncan seated on the couch inside, a laptop open on his knees. He placed it to his side on the couch and jumped to his feet as Jenny entered.

"Babe!" he said, smiling broadly. "Where did you go? I was trying to call—"

"Sorry," she said. "I haven't looked at my phone."

"I have some pretty big news. That guy—"

"That guy had news for us?"

"Huge news for us."

"For *us*? Or for you, Duncan?"

"For us!"

"If it was for us, why wasn't I allowed to be in there?"

"Come on, babe, you know I—"

"Please, *please* stop calling me that."

"The guy, he was, I don't know, old fashioned. Russian. Conservative about that stuff."

"Are you conservative? Are you old fashioned? You couldn't have said something to him? You couldn't have told him that I am your partner in this thing?" Jenny's voice was rising, and Duncan waved his hands toward the floor to try to get her to quiet down.

"Come on, the neighbors are going to hear—"

"I don't care if they hear! Duncan, I started the Defense Fund! That was my thing! When you came on, we were supposed to be equals! Partners! How did you think that made me feel when you went with that guy—"

"Hey, hey," Duncan said, stepping close and putting his arms around Jenny.

"Don't 'hey, hey' me!" Jenny shouted, twisting out of his embrace. "If we're partners—"

"We *are* partners."

"If we're partners, you need to treat me like one. But I sure as hell don't feel like a partner right now."

"Okay," Duncan said. "I'm sorry. I want to tell you about what he had to say."

"Fine. Great. Please tell me. What did he have to tell you that was so amazing?"

Duncan grinned. He reached in his pocket and pulled out a black USB thumb drive, raising it up between their faces.

"This," he said, hardly able to contain his glee. "This, Jenny!"

"What is it?"

"It's the last piece of the puzzle. It's proof, proof that the failure of an RTG can be fatal to people on the ground."

"Proof how, exactly?"

"There are documents on here. Pictures and videos. Radiation measurements, casualty figures. Evidence of how things can go wrong. If we show this to the world, Jenny, there's no way Kingfisher can launch that rocket."

"That's . . . that's amazing?" Jenny whispered. Despite herself, she was getting caught up in Duncan's enthusiasm.

"Right? This is it, babe! This really is the last piece of the puzzle."

"Can I see it?"

Duncan shook his head. "Nope. We're not allowed."

"What do you mean 'we're not allowed'?"

"I mean I have to show it to my mother first—"

"Oh, Jesus, Duncan, what the hell—"

"We got fifty thousand dollars from him just for talking."

"Fifty thousand?"

"In cash!"

"You aren't sketched out by this?"

"And if I can get the documents to my mother, we get another five hundred thousand—"

"This doesn't seem weird to you? At all?"

"What have we got to lose?"

"They're trying to get access to your famous mother is all! You're going to open that up, and it's going to be a love letter from some rich Russian guy. They're *using* you, can't you see that?"

"If they want to give us that kind of money, they can use me all they want. The same thing goes for my mom."

"This isn't right, Duncan. I don't feel right taking that money. I don't think you've thought this through."

"But if it's proof, babe, we can't pass this up!" Jenny crossed her arms, and the two of them stared at each other for a long, silent moment. "And besides," Duncan finally went on, "it's half a million bucks just for talking to my mom. And a two-million-dollar bonus if we stop the whole thing."

"Duncan!" Jenny shouted, practically shaking. "That guy is shady. He's going to own you!"

"Babe," he said, grabbing her shoulders. "It's so much money."

"I don't want to hear it," Jenny said, turning away from him. "And I think you should stay on the mainland again tonight."

CHAPTER FIFTEEN

Jake had planned to cook for Tamara, but they'd put a big dent in that bourbon, so they ordered pizza instead and talked until the sun went down. It was a comfortable friendship. One of the best Jake had ever known. There could have been more to it, maybe, but she was too important to him, and he didn't want to complicate things.

But sometimes—like tonight, his brain lubricated by spirits—Jake wondered, What if? He laughed it off. What if? *Right.* In looks and intellect, Tam was far out of his league. He'd never even have a chance.

He laughed at himself for even thinking it.

It was amazing enough that Tam had come to work with him. Sometimes he had a hard time believing she'd accepted his offer of a partnership.

I'll take it, Jake thought. *I'll take it.*

"You seem more sober than you should be," he told her as she opened the guesthouse door for him. The light inside was harsh, and Jake shielded his eyes with his right forearm.

"One of us has to be," Tam said. "Sit, okay? I'm going to get you some water."

Jake collapsed on the bed while she rustled through the freezer. He turned his head and blinked; on the nightstand was a SIG P226 like his own. He laughed.

"What's so funny?" Tam asked as she returned. She handed him a glass.

"That gun," Jake said. "It's the same as mine—"

"I know. That's the one you told me to get. I'm not leaving you alone up here, Jake. What if he tries again?"

"We should take turns keeping watch, then. We'll stay up here and watch the house. I can go first if you want."

"You need to rest," she said. "I'll keep an eye on everything. Then you can have a turn."

"Are you sure?"

"I'm sure. I'll let you know when it's time for you to wake up."

"Fine then," Jake said, suddenly feeling very tired. He lay back and looked at Tam, backlit by the light over the sink. "We . . . we should turn out the light."

"I'll get the lights," Tam said. "You try to get some sleep."

Tam put her hand over Jake's and left it there for a long moment. Then she rose and snapped off a wall switch, and the space felt impossibly dark.

The next morning Jake blinked his eyes open to harsh sunlight coming straight in the guesthouse window. He was fully clothed, and his head pounded. At some point in the night a duvet had been laid over him. He turned his head to see Tam seated in a rocking chair, scrolling through her phone with a half smile on her face. On the table next to her was a mug of coffee, a mostly-empty glass of water, and her pistol.

"Morning, Jacob," she said, not looking up.

"You . . . you were supposed to wake me," he said, pulling himself upright against the headboard. "I was supposed to have a turn."

"You needed the rest. I was fine."

"You stayed up all night?"

"It wasn't difficult," she said. "Not with you snoring the way you were."

"I don't—"

"You do," she said. "Not so much. I'm just teasing you. How's the head?" Tam went to the studio's kitchenette and took a mug and water glass from one of the cabinets and filled each.

"I think I'm feeling the whiskey more than getting punched. And I don't understand how you look so fresh."

"Hydration," she said, holding up the glass. "And coffee." She placed the mug and glass on the nightstand and took a seat at the foot of the bed.

"No one came by?"

"It was completely quiet."

"You must be exhausted."

"I dozed, here and there. I felt like we were safe. I would have heard someone approaching, and the outside door is solid and dead bolted. I'd call this, oh, what would you call it? A military term."

"A defensible position."

"Something like that. Exactly." Tam patted Jake's foot and got to her feet. "Let's get cleaned up and head in. I want to see what Stu has to say about everything."

"You feel okay going over to your place solo?"

Tam picked up the pistol and pulled the slide to check the chamber. "I do," she said, letting the slide snap back. "But if I need any help, I'll let you know."

Two hours later, Jake and Tam found the Cascadia parking lot was half-filled with cars when they arrived. The building was single story and made of architectural concrete, metal, and glass—modern and functional yet comfortable and airy inside.

Tam held her badge to the card reader at the door, and it unlatched with a resounding clack. Inside, a guard to the left nodded and smiled. The sun shone through the windows on a circular reception desk made of pale wood. The receptionist, Jessie Kane, jumped up from her seat at Jake's and Tam's entrance.

"Welcome back, Jake!" she said, grabbing him in a hug. "Mail is on your desk."

Past the reception area, they entered the space everyone referred to as the Big Room. It was naturally lit by high windows and served as a comfortable area for meetings or quiet work. A handful of people sat chatting at the scattered tables and couches, and a few called out greetings as Jake appeared at the doorway.

"I'll be in my office if you need me," Tam said. Jake made his way across the room, taking time to say hi and catch up with anyone who needed or wanted to chat, and hoping no one would ask about the fading bruise on his cheek.

Jake crossed to the IT wing, where Cascadia sequestered its server farm along with the staff responsible for keeping it all running. While so many businesses had shifted their computing infrastructure to the cloud, the sensitivity and specialization of Cascadia's contracts demanded a sizeable in-house hardware installation. Down the right of the hall were climate-controlled server rooms with rack after rack of hardware connected by neatly bundled runs of networking and power cables, with a third room at the end of the hall serving as a termination point for the pair of redundant fiber-optic connections to the internet backbone. Emergency generators and backup satellite dishes were housed in a fenced enclosure outside.

Down the left side of the hall were the offices of Stu and his staff. Stu's was the first open door. The room's blinds were pulled shut, and an old-fashioned Tiffany lamp with an incandescent bulb gave the space a mellow golden glow. A U-shaped desk filled the office, its surface covered by four large flat-panel displays, two open notebook computers, and some neatly arranged textbooks and technical documents. On the wall to the right of the doorway were shelves filled with a mix of books, bound journals, and models of sailboats. On the wall to the left was a waist-high workbench with a draftsman's stool beneath it. The bench was covered by parts of disassembled computers and devices, with a pegboard wall behind from which soldering irons, screwdrivers, and various meters and gauges neatly hung. For all the projects he was running simultaneously, it was amazingly orderly. At the center of it all was Stu Gallagher, a prematurely graying, barrel-chested man with biceps straining at the sleeves of his polo shirt. He was reading some sort of technical manual, leaned back with his feet propped up, and he peered up over his glasses from the book in his lap to take in Jake at the doorway.

"Looks like it hurt," Stu said, slapping his book shut and sitting up straight. "You get into a fight?"

"Yeah," Jake said, closing the door behind him. "It was a weird one."

CHAPTER SIXTEEN

The Dassault Falcon 7X, a newer, three-engine private jet with a nearly six-thousand-mile range, droned over the Atlantic. Almost five hours into an eleven-hour flight, René rested his head against the oversize cabin window next to his seat. He wanted to sleep, needed to sleep, but he was far too keyed up. He glanced across the aisle at Anton. The kid was under a blanket in his fully reclined seat, pale and shaking and covered with a sheen of sweat.

After the shoot-out in Kotor, they'd quickly transferred the materials to the catamaran and had an easy passage to Malta. The captain had asked no questions, as advertised. As soon as they got underway, René had called Vostok for an explanation.

"It couldn't have been Petr," Vostok had said emphatically. "Absolutely not. Impossible. There's no way. He's in Novi Sad right now. I just spoke with him. But don't worry about the mess you left in Montenegro. Our guys will clean it up. And listen, one of our contacts in the States tracked down our target. The one responsible for Mali."

"Did he take care of him?"

"We need him, René. We will eliminate him, but for now, we need him. Our guy roughed him up and got out of there—he was only meant to install eyes for us, but the target was already home," Vostok said. "Like I said, I don't have direct control over these operators in North America. If I did, I'd figure out another way, and Moran would be a dead man."

Aside from the Falcon's first row of seats, which René and Anton occupied, the plane's remaining fixtures had been removed to make room for music cases and trunks, all of them battered and spray paint stenciled with the words "Property of the Raptors." Their Maltese contact had found it all; the equipment had belonged to some long-disbanded musical group and been abandoned in a warehouse for more than a year. The cases and gear made perfect vehicles for smuggling, and an even better cover story. The cesium casks, their cases wrapped in black cloth, were tucked into the backs of amplifiers, keyboards, and drum cases. The plutonium was wedged into the open underside of a sound mixing board and secured with black gaffer tape. And the two men accompanying it all? Simply roadies, traveling in advance to set up for a private party at some millionaire's private Bahamian enclave.

"So they see this when we land," Anton had explained. "Maybe they bring in some dogs to check for drugs. Not explosives. Certainly not radioactivity. It's perfect. I'm telling you. We're setting up for some wedding is all. A corporate retreat for rich Americans. Some private party. We don't even need to know. We're just there to set things up."

"And when we move all this stuff to a boat?" René asked. He felt confident about the cover story, but he wanted to see it from every angle. "What then?"

"It's no different. Some rich person has a private island. That's where we're going. Why would we need to know anything? We're just roadies, right? We have so many opportunities to act like we know nothing. And if things get hot? Someone starts nosing around, looking too closely? We slip away and live. But I don't see it coming to that. This cover is ideal."

The more René thought it over, the more he knew the kid was right. He couldn't have come up with a better story himself. The only potential point of failure, he thought, was if the crates or cases had been used to move drugs in the past. What if a dog signaled on that, warranting closer inspection by the authorities? Anton assured him they'd be okay.

"The cops went over those crates with a microscope already when the gear entered Malta, you can believe it. Any hint of dope or anything else and they would have kept it as evidence. We're good, René. I mean it."

Now, after a departure that seemed almost too easy, they were on their way, chasing the sun over the sea toward North America. René felt like he should be relaxed, but something nagged at him—a tension, a pressure, a worry he couldn't identify. He crossed his arms over his chest and looked ahead into the open flight deck. A pair of thirtysomething Germans in aviator glasses and white short-sleeved button-down shirts with epaulettes at the shoulders piloted the plane. Did they have any clue what they were carrying? It didn't matter. René hoped he wouldn't need to kill them. It would only make things messy. Why seek complication?

René heard a sound to his right and turned to see Anton shaking as he fumbled at the button to raise the back of his seat. When he was finally upright again, Anton looked at René, a grimace on his pasty face.

"Are we landing?" he asked.

"Not even close," René said. "You don't look so good."

"I'm fine, really."

"Toni, you're going through withdrawal—"

"I said I'm fine!"

Anton jumped to his feet and stepped forward into the galley area at the front of the plane. He rummaged through a cabinet and took out two bottles of water, shakily handing one back to René. He faced the cockpit again and exchanged a few words in German with the flight crew. The pilots laughed, and Anton returned to his seat.

"What's so funny?" René asked.

"The pilot says five more hours until he's with two girls on the beach," Anton said. "I asked if he knew some girls; he said he could find us some easy on Cat Island. I told him no thanks, we'd be into plenty of girls at our gig. He asked if he could come. They had a laugh at it. Stupid, really. But he believes our story completely."

René spent the rest of the flight in a fitful half sleep with the window shade next to him pulled down. After a while he sensed a change in the Dassault's engines, a lowering in tone, and a slight pitch forward that let him know they were beginning their descent into the Bahamas. René turned to nod at Anton; the kid still looked twitchy and pale, like he hadn't slept at all.

"Is everything okay?" René asked.

"What do you mean? Of course everything is okay. Why would it not be?"

René looked to the cockpit. "Ask those guys," he said. "Check that everything is going as it should."

"Don't be so jumpy. Everything is—"

"I said *ask* them."

Anton called up to the cockpit in German, and the pilots replied cordially. They chatted back and forth, René understanding none of it, until Anton nodded and gave them a half wave in thanks.

"We're fine. Landing twenty minutes early. I asked if customs would be a hassle, and they said it's always been easy in the Bahamas. You can relax now."

"I am relaxed."

Anton managed a laugh. "Right," he said. "You really look it."

The two men said nothing else as the plane descended straight into Cat Island. René watched the deeply hued water flash beneath him, so clear in places he could see the sandy bottom below as they passed over. Minutes later they landed. The plane taxied off the runway and over to a set of tie-downs where another jet and a small prop plane were parked. The copilot pulled off his headset and twisted back, calling out something in German.

"He says welcome to the Bahamas," Anton said.

"Welcome to the Bahamas!" the copilot said again, this time in English. "Enjoy your stay at the Hawk's Nest Resort. Right on the beach!" He flashed a leering grin toward Anton. "Plenty of girls for all of us."

The pilots opened the door and lowered the steps, then got to work tying down the plane.

"They won't help us unload," Anton said. "Not in the contract."

René followed Anton down the plane's steps and into the hot Caribbean air. The pilots finished up and waved, the copilot saying something in German before calling in English: "We see you later! Thank you very much!" He pointed to a low building a couple of hundred meters away. "Send customs over there for us, okay? We go find a drink. And some girls! Maybe you join us after, yeah?"

"*Danke!*" Anton called back with a wave. "Thank you!"

"The deal is done?" René said.

"All paid in advance. Now we unload."

"No help from those guys? Really?"

"I told you, not in the contract."

"Fuck's sake. Fine. Let's get at it."

René and Anton spent the next half hour dragging the crated instruments out into a line on the tarmac. Anton made a couple of calls and pointed toward the end of the runway after pocketing his phone.

"Truck is coming in ten minutes. Twenty max. They'll take us to the boat. The boat is owned by a Russian guy in Miami. He knows Vostok's people, apparently. He's being paid by them."

René heard a rumbling at the far end of the runway and shielded his eyes to see an open-top Jeep with a Bahamian Customs and Immigration seal on the side. Anton looked unfazed, waving not too eagerly or reluctantly. The Jeep stopped and a uniformed man stepped down from the passenger side. He had dark skin and curly gray hair. A younger man exited the driver's side of the vehicle, went to the back, and helped an old German shepherd out of a crate.

"Passports?" the older man asked. "Where you fellows come in from?" His questions were directed more toward Anton than René. Anton turned to René and acted dumb. He knew to keep quiet.

"He asks us where we came from," René said to Anton in French, pretending to explain. Anton nodded in understanding, and René looked to the uniformed man. "We came from the Côte d'Azur," René said in English. "By way of Malta."

"I see," the man said as he looked over their passports. The young man and the dog had come to his side. "And your friend? Doesn't speak English?"

"Just French," René said.

"Bon-joor," the older man said in an exaggerated way, and Anton smiled and tipped his head. "What brings you to Cat Island?"

"Our boss has a gig. His band. We're here early to set up."

"Where is the gig?"

"Private party," René said. "Some little island." He nodded to Anton and switched to French. "What's the name of the island? Any idea?"

"Maybe Pleasure Island? Try that."

"Pleasure Island?" René said in English. "Something like that? We don't know, we just go where he sends us."

"Pleasure Cay," the older man said with a nod. He repeated it, drawing out the syllables. "Plea-sure Cay. That's the name. Fancy-fancy. You're rolling with the big boys, huh?" He walked along the line of cases and crates. "There's nothing in here that would get you in trouble, is there? Nothing inside you wouldn't want a fellow like me to see?"

"No," René said. "We keep out of trouble. Take a look if you need to. None of those cases is locked."

The man laughed, a dry cackle in the breeze. He leveled a long stare at René. "You're good," he said. "You're good." The hairs on the back of René's neck prickled. The man laughed again. "I know how men look when they're hiding something. When they're up to no good." He pointed from René to Anton with a stern face. René's pulse picked up, but the man's face broke into a genial smile. "You guys? Not you. No way." He laughed. "What you fellows need is a cold beer, followed by a long rest. Let's have old Roy here give a little sniff-sniff, and we'll be on our way." The young man guided the limping dog down the line of cases while the older man stamped their passports. The dog hobbled along, its tongue lolling out, never pausing as it went down the line.

“Okay,” the older man said as he returned their documents along with a pair of clipboards. “No sweat, all good. You fellows fill out these papers while I go find your pilots. In the bar already, huh? If I’m not back to get these and your entry fee, just give them to my partner, Arthur, here. Good afternoon, then. Enjoy your stay in the Bahamas.”

“And a good afternoon to you,” René said. He willed his pulse to slow and exchanged a look with Anton as the Jeep trundled off in a cloud of exhaust.

“Easy,” Anton said, wiping the sweat from his face with his wrist. “Just like I told you.”

CHAPTER SEVENTEEN

"So the guy just hit you in the head?" Stu asked. He'd leaned back in his chair again, feet up and his fingers laced across his broad chest.

"He wasn't there to kill me. He got in a couple of good shots and took off. I don't think he expected me to be in Jackson." Jake sat on the draftsman's stool and leaned forward with his hands clasped and elbows on his knees.

"Looks like he delivered you a message all right. But who was the sender?"

"Who have we pissed off?"

Stu laughed. "We've pissed off plenty. Was the guy foreign?"

"Hard to say."

"And you let this guy knock you around? I thought they trained you guys to be tough in the Marine Corps." Stu was a navy vet and took any chance he could to good-naturedly stoke the interservice rivalry in the office.

"Cut it out. I'm being serious. We need to figure this shit out."

"Okay. Sorry. Any description? You probably didn't get a very good look at him, correct?"

Jake shook his head. "Not at all. The guy wasn't ripped or anything. Maybe about my build—"

"Definitely not ripped."

Jake sighed and rolled his eyes. "You never let up, do you?" he said, and Stu smiled and shrugged. "I have zero description."

"Probably didn't see the car either."

"Negative visual on the vehicle. A sedan, from the sound." Jake sighed. "I'm leaning toward Wagner."

Stu crossed his arms and sat up straight. "Reasonable thought, but doubtful. There's nothing left of Wagner. Not enough to mount an op stateside, and no way the current Russian regime would back them working over here. And another thing: those Wagner guys were never very subtle. If someone took the trouble to track you down, he probably would have finished you off. I'm not trying to trash-talk your skills here, pal, but if we're really talking Wagner PMC, you'd be dead."

Jake had to admit the logic was sound.

"Okay then," he said. "Who?"

"How's your OPSEC been? Anyone following you?"

"Nothing's set me off recently."

"Have you been paying attention? *Really* paying attention?"

"I do my best, Stu. I sniffed out that guy at my place, didn't I? No one showed up at Tam's."

"What about Kingfisher? I want to go back to that."

"What about it?"

"Set the scene for me there. Anything out of the ordinary?"

"The platform was secure. There was private security around the perimeter. Andy Lang was out there . . . he was pretty distraught about the failure—"

"Lang? What the hell was he doing there?"

"He was flight director."

"Are you shitting me?"

"I'm not. Kingfisher hired him two years ago."

"I never trusted that guy."

"Stu, drop it with Andy." Jake rose from the stool and stretched his arms over his head. His body remained stiff from the tussle. "He's solid."

Stu twisted his chair, grabbed a yellow legal pad and pen from his desk, and began taking notes. "You say so," he said. "Fine, then. So then your chopper went down. Funny, that, huh?"

"It's a good thought, but there's nothing there."

"Nothing there but birds, allegedly . . . And what size bird, exactly, can take down a Sikorsky S-70?"

"Pelicans? The kids on the water did mention hearing a drone. I'm letting it breathe for a minute. Are we doing this thing? For Kingfisher?"

"Probably. We'll have deep access, correct?"

"That's what Helena Nash told me."

"HR access?"

"I can't see why not."

"I think on top of their systems, we need to run background on their people."

"Select individuals, or the whole shebang? There have to be several thousand people at Kingfisher."

"We can manage. I want to look at their whole staff. Quietly."

"We can't take data off site," Jake said, and Stu shook his head.

"Quietly," he repeated with exaggerated softness. "The quiet way I do things, Jake. They won't ever know. And another thing: I want schematics of their network. Documentation, service records, trouble tickets. Hardware invoices. Until I can get there, you need to get your ass into every server closet you can and take as many pictures as possible for me."

Jake smiled. "You're talking like you want us to take this gig."

Stu shrugged and grinned. "How could we not?" he said. "It's right in our wheelhouse. Am I wrong?"

"I thought the same thing. Helena Nash seemed to think the same thing too. Like she knew more about us than you'd find on the website."

"You have a reputation, Jake."

"We do have a reputation. All of us. Let's hope it doesn't get us killed."

There was a tap at the door, and the two men turned to see Jessie Kane leaning into the doorway.

"Jake, I'm sorry to bother you," she said. "There's a call waiting for you. And before you say anything, I tried to put them through to voicemail—"

"Can I call them back? I'll call them back this afternoon, I promise. I'm trying to catch up with everyone. I want to catch up with you too. Maybe an all hands in the Big Room after."

"I think you really want to take this call."

"Maybe it's the guy who beat you up," Stu quipped. Jake grabbed a paper towel roll from the workbench and flung it at Stu.

"These navy guys," Jake said, shaking his head. "Who is it?"

"It's Janice Trout," Jessie said. "She says Mrs. Nash is holding for you."

Jake and Stu turned to each other.

"Do we take it?" Stu asked.

Jake nodded firmly. "I think we do."

Jake shut the door to his office and quickly took a seat behind his empty desk. The throbbing in his temples was momentarily forgotten as he lifted the phone's receiver. He cleared his throat and tapped in on the flashing line.

"This is Jake Moran," he said.

"Mr. Moran, I have Helena Nash for you. Please hold the line while I connect you." There was a click, and a moment later Jake was being warmly greeted like an old friend.

"Jake! It's Helena. How have you been? Please tell me everything is going well?"

"I'm okay," Jake said. "How are you?" He tilted his head for a moment, puzzled by the familiarity, and puzzled more by being tracked down. "How did you know I'd be here?"

"I didn't, actually. I don't have your cell number, so I had Janice call your office to get it, or see if I could get on your schedule. But there you were! I'm very happy you were able to pick up. I'm going to get right to the point here. Have you given any further thought to my offer?"

"I have," Jake said, strangely savoring how he let the moment linger. There was a pause and the slightest sound from Helena Nash, a tiny clearing of the throat.

"And?"

"And I am strongly considering. I'm here at my office today to consult with my associates. The ones I told you about."

"I'm assuming they've responded favorably?"

"They have. I'm not ready to say yes, but we're leaning in that direction—"

"Well, we've had something come up that's brought new urgency to this. The investigation of our failure is going to be briefer than I suspected."

"You've heard from Space Force?"

"Not formally, but via back channels . . . I'm not supposed to tell you this. I'm *really* not supposed to be talking about this. I'll share it with you, but first tell me truthfully, are you really considering saying yes?"

"I am." Jake's curiosity had grown to the point that he might've said yes simply to hear the reason why. Space Launch Delta 45 was a tight ship; getting anything out of them was virtually unheard of.

"They determined a fault mode. An exceedingly rare edge case where one system out of agreement could have caused a condition that would have caused all three to autonomously send the termination command."

"So you have your answer."

"*They* have an answer, and *we* have caught a break. Instead of a monthslong investigation on our end, we're going to be cleared for flight with only a two-week delay. I thought we would have the whole summer for this project, Jake, but now we have less than a month. Given this, I *really* need to know: Are you interested?"

Helena had said Space Force would claim responsibility when Jake met with her after the crash. He had half believed her and half thought she was full of shit, posturing to convince him of her power and influence and to make Kingfisher seem ever more appealing to him and to Cascadia. The fact that she'd pulled it off left him speechless.

"Of course it's not official," she said, "and this is entirely off the record, but when their report is issued, that will be indicated as the most likely cause."

"Well, I guess this is pretty good news for you. Are you sure you still need me?"

"Now we need your services more than ever. And urgently." The eagerness in Helena Nash's voice made Jake pause. He had taken a pen from his desk drawer and idly twirled it in his fingers as he solidified his thoughts. Finally he spoke.

"May I offer a frank opinion here?"

"I welcome your opinion. And I encourage you to always speak freely with me. You're not going to upset me by telling me something disagreeable, Jake. There are few things I hate more than sycophants, and trust me, a person in my position attracts them like moths to a flame. So please, tell me anything."

"I think you should go ahead and delay the next launch."

"Would you like to tell me why?"

"I think you could use the time to ensure your systems are in order. Not just my audit, but have Andy Lang check things top to bottom as well. It will be good public relations, too, looking like you're not giving in to some kind of launch fever."

"Trust me, I've thought about all of these things. I don't think extra time is going to reveal anything beyond what you can do in a month. JPL is in no rush to get HiPEP-D flying, but we have other customers down the line in the manifest who would feel pinched by the schedule slipping to the right."

"So it *is* a case of launch fever, then."

"No," she said firmly. "The issue is the plutonium, plain and simple. The longer we wait, the more chance those protests could gain some traction. If they get in the ear of someone important, someone up the road at NASA or worse, in Washington, we could find ourselves in a regulatory mess. Do you understand what I'm saying?"

"I do, but do you really think a little time is going to hurt?"

"Are you saying you can't do the job in the window we have?"

Jake stopped flipping his pen. "Helena, I need to speak frankly again. Is this something personal? Something with your son that's driving this decision?"

There was a long, long pause, and Jake wondered if he'd gone too far. Finally, he heard a sigh on the other end of the line.

"Of course it is personal, Jake. It's personal for Duncan. Do you think he really cares about radioactivity in the atmosphere? For him it's just another way to get at me. To try to break my heart. Personally? Yes, I will confide that it bothers me. It upsets me quite a lot. Professionally? It's simply another obstacle to be confronted. If that's what I need to reduce him to in my mind, I will do so. Am I clear?"

"You are."

"Any other questions?" She laughed bitterly. "Be as frank as you want."

"There's a chance of a failure on the next launch."

"There's always a chance of that. I know it better than anyone."

"If there is a failure, even if no radioactivity is released, are you ready for the public relations nightmare that will follow?"

"We are prepared. Absolutely prepared. Our marketing and communications department has messaging at the ready. In the event of a failure, we will have atmospheric scientists on call to confirm there has been no release of radioactive material. We have two deep-sea submersibles ready to retrieve any debris from the seafloor as soon as possible. We want to show the public that the thermal generator survived any failure intact. So yes, we have a plan in place. Is there anything you would add?"

"I'd like to see that plan in writing, but yes, it sounds as though you have your bases covered."

"When you accept my offer, I'll send it to you. Only then. When can I have an answer?"

Jake's cell buzzed in his pocket, and he checked it to find a message from Tam.

Are we in? it said.

"Jake," Helena said, "are you still there?"

"Sorry," Jake said. "One sec."

He typed out a reply to Tam: Stu's in if you're in.

Helena gave a little irritated cough.

The phone buzzed with another text from Tam: I'm in if you're in.

"Jake?" Helena asked.

"I can tell you right now," he told her. "We're in."

CHAPTER EIGHTEEN

Helena tapped the phone to end the call. From the thirtieth floor of the Four Seasons Houston, the late-day sun gleamed gold on the windows of the downtown's skyscrapers. It was a place just right for the city's transient elite, kids out of school and flush with family wealth, or young men from the Arabian Gulf region who needed a home base when they came to the States to learn the ins and outs of the American petroleum industry. Helena Nash had made it her Houston base, too, and she stood by the broad living room windows in a comfortable, baggy sweater and a pair of old jeans, looking out over the city as she dialed her most trusted assistant.

"Janice," she said, a smile on her face. "Jake Moran has accepted our offer."

"That's great news!" Janice said. "I'll reschedule my time off to assist—"

"No," Helena said. "Absolutely not. You're absolutely taking a couple weeks off, do you hear me? You are indispensable to me, yes, but I'm not so hopeless that I can't manage Mr. Moran and everything else while you have a vacation. Even if we need more than one person to fill your shoes, which we probably will, it would make me so happy to know you got to have a little time off to recharge yourself."

"I don't know," Janice replied with a sigh. "We have so much going on. Why don't we wait until after the next launch, and I'll think about it then?"

"That's what you said before the last one. And the one before that, if I remember correctly. Work is work, and it will go on. You can miss a launch. There will be a place for you on the next one."

"But this one is different."

"What makes it so different?"

"You know what. The payload. Your son." Practically all the Kingfisher executive staff and board avoided mentioning Duncan. Helena was glad that Janice never felt like she needed to hold back. "What if his protest works? I swear, it keeps me awake nights."

"That's not healthy."

"But it does. He bought more ads. I saw the media report—"

"I've seen it too. I know. But it means nothing. Trust me. Duncan is not going to stand in the way of the next launch. I can guarantee it."

"How can you be so sure?"

Helena wanted to say "Jake Moran," but didn't. While she hadn't quite envisioned how Moran could be used to quash Duncan's efforts, she had a feeling he would be instrumental in the problem's resolution.

"When does Mr. Moran start for us?" Janice asked, and Helena laughed.

"Did you read my mind? I was just thinking about him."

"See? I *am* indispensable. Who will read your mind if I go on vacation?"

"Jake Moran apparently will arrive at our Clear Lake office the day after tomorrow. I'm not sure how he's planning to begin, but it should be interesting to watch."

"I want to ask you about something," Janice said. "The helicopter crash. Have you heard anything further from the FBI?"

"You know as much about it as I do. You see all the same things."

"Do you really think it was a bird?"

"It happens," Helena said. "As improbable as it sounds, it happens."

"What if it could have been something else, though?" Janice asked. "What if it was someone intentionally trying to bring the helicopter down?"

"What are you trying to say?"

"I have an idea that might help us," Janice said, almost coyly, "and make the protester problem go away. But I wanted to run it by you first."

"I'm listening."

"What if we made it look like it was your son? Sabotage. An attack or something. We float the idea in the media that his people brought down the helicopter. With a rocket launcher, or a strong gun maybe? Do you follow me?"

"Janice, that's ridiculous! A rocket launcher? Duncan wouldn't do something like that. Where would he even get something like a rocket launcher?"

"It doesn't matter if he would do it, or if he could get his hands on a weapon that could do the job. It's the *idea* that he could. The idea that people might think he had a strong motive to do so."

Helena didn't speak for a very long time. "I can't believe you're actually suggesting this."

"Imagine the publicity . . . fantastic publicity."

Helena Nash said nothing. She dropped down onto her sofa and stared out at the lights of the city.

"And," Janice went on, "it will be a tremendous distraction for Duncan. Defending his reputation will divert his attention from his protests, and the discord and doubt will cause him to lose followers. And probably donors as well."

"Janice," Helena said with a frown, "this is brilliant, but horrid. When did you become so Machiavellian?"

"I believe in the company," Janice said firmly. "I believe in our mission. If we do this, I truly think the problem will be solved. Duncan can clear his name afterward, maybe, but it might take months, even years, long after the HiPEP-D mission is launched and over. The only lasting damage might be to your son's reputation, but are you that concerned? Look at what he's doing to you. Don't let him. If we push back, we can stop him, and the lesson he'll learn will be enough to keep him from ever interfering again."

Was she really hearing this from Janice? Janice, her protégé, first hired as a simple scheduler? She showed such drive and verve and cunning . . . everything Helena had once imagined her own son would be by her side. And it broke her heart.

"Oh, I couldn't, Janice. I can't do this to him."

"*You* can't," Janice said. "But does that mean I can't?"

"I don't want to hear about this," Helena said. "I don't want to know."

"You don't need to know a thing," Janice said.

She took a long, deep breath. "I don't want to hear a word about it ever again."

"We could use Jake Moran—"

"I told you, not a word! I need to go. Check in with me tomorrow."

Helena ended the call, placed her phone on the sofa cushion next to her, and leaned back and closed her eyes. Then she turned her head to stare out at the city, the blinking radio towers, the blur of traffic on the freeways, the comings and goings of commercial planes. What a miserable place, Houston, she thought, hating the fact that political patronage a half century earlier had placed Johnson Space Center in the swamp that was Clear Lake City. If only there were some other place she could stage her launches. If only the usually placid Gulf weren't so perfect, far enough south in latitude and filled with cheap oil rigs ready to be converted for her use.

If only.

Helena craved a glass of wine. Something to calm her thoughts. That's the problem with brilliance, she thought, it never turns off. The duty of genius. She padded to the too-big kitchen and got a glass for herself. So many of her wealthy peers had live-in help, but that had always seemed ridiculous to her. She never wanted to let go of her origins. She never wanted to let her head get too big.

Duncan, she thought as she returned to her comfortable seat. *My little boy, Duncan.* Did I miss something? I was there, Duncan, I was there. I helped with homework—I came to your sports. When your father was gone, I was there twice as much.

A soft buzzing snapped Helena out of her self-pity. The phone to her side vibrated with an incoming call; the screen showed "Unknown Caller." Not so unusual. Very few people had her personal cell, and those who did were often the sorts of people who preferred to keep their own contact details obscure. She tapped to answer.

"Hello?" she said, leaning back again and closing her eyes.

"Hello, Mother." The voice was flat, without affect, but unmistakable.

"Duncan?" Helena snapped upright. "Duncan, is it you?"

"It's me."

"How . . . how are you? How are things? I'm happy you—"

"Mother," he said. "I need to see you."

CHAPTER NINETEEN

After a direct flight from Seattle to Houston's George Bush Intercontinental Airport, Jake picked up a rental Chevy Bolt and headed south, down Interstate 45 and over the causeway to Galveston Island. He slowed as the car's navigation system guided him south down Thirty-Seventh Street, and he glanced down at his phone to double-check the rental home's location.

"Your destination is on the right," the nav software's voice cooed, and Jake slipped the Bolt into an overgrown parking space next to a tidy two-story house with blue siding and white shutters and trim. A broad covered porch spanned the front of the house with dormer windows above. Jake turned off the electric car and brought up the check-in instructions on his phone. He scanned through the message to find the lockbox code and scrolled down until he got to a personal greeting at the bottom.

> Hello Mr. Moran! I hope you enjoy your extended stay. Having someone there for nearly a month is new for me, but I think you'll find my home suitable for your needs. I'm in Dallas, but please don't hesitate to call or text if you have any issues. I have people there in Galveston who can help you if you have any urgent issues or concerns. Take care—Sherry

The lockbox opened on the first try. Inside the house, the windows were open and a pleasant, fresh breeze swayed the curtains in the bright and airy room. Throw rugs covered the wood floors, and the walls were painted in light blue and white. The home's decor had a nearly over-the-top nautical theme—seashells on the end tables, a seascape print above a plush couch—but the space didn't feel cluttered by it. Jake moved to the kitchen and happily found it was stocked with good pans and—even better—adequate knives. Still, he was glad he'd packed his own chef's knife.

A small bedroom with kid decor was at the back of the house by the staircase. *Stu's room,* Jake thought with a laugh. At the top of the stairs, he found a bathroom with a claw-foot tub, with two equal-size bedrooms off to either side of it. The bedroom to the left, at the front of the house, had a queen bed and a large desk. Jake chose this one for himself. When he slid the curtains open, he was happy to see the steely-colored water of the Gulf of Mexico to the south. He took a deep breath of the salt air, closed his eyes, and smiled.

It all felt right.

Jake grabbed his bags from his car and began to unpack. His big bag from Wyoming probably wouldn't arrive for another day. Katie had only gotten things to FedEx yesterday morning; there was a chance it could show up tonight, but Jake wasn't holding his breath. He ducked into the bathroom and checked the bruise on the side of his face. It had faded, a little, but still seemed obvious.

It took some searching to find the house's cable modem tucked into a utility closet back by the downstairs bathroom. Jake disconnected the basic consumer wireless router and replaced it with the one he'd packed. Stu had programmed it with custom firmware to support a strongly encrypted virtual private network connection back to the office in Everett. Aside from giving him secure access to his company's electronic resources, it also blocked any internet-connected devices in a rental home like this from eavesdropping on him. Jake grabbed his laptop from his bag and checked the National Weather Service home page to test his connection. It worked well. The forecast for the coming week said highs in the upper seventies with a chance of showers and thunderstorms each afternoon.

The evening was quiet. Jake ran to the store for some basic staples, made a simple dinner, and went to bed early.

The next morning, after an easy forty-minute drive to Clear Lake City, getting a permanent badge for the Kingfisher facility was straightforward. Human resources expected him, they had most of his paperwork signed already, and it didn't take long for them to snap a new picture and present him with a key card.

"All access, huh?" the man said, raising an eyebrow. "Don't lose it. And if you do, tell us immediately so we can deactivate it. Are you using your own computer? You'll need to see IT to get that set up. They're right down the hall."

Jake made his way down to the IT office. Working for Kingfisher was a coveted job, and even its IT support staff were reputed to be among the best in the world.

"What have you got?" the young man behind the desk asked warily. "If you're contracting, we're going to need to install some software on your laptop."

"That's not going to fly," Jake said. Maybe they were among the best in the world, but they weren't going to touch his laptop. "If you have guest access, just give me those credentials, and I'll take a Kingfisher laptop for anything I need to do internally."

"Yeah, ah, I'm sorry, but we don't just hand stuff like that out here. I'll need to put our monitoring software on your laptop."

"Why don't you call Janice Trout, and she can explain it to you," Jake said.

"Janice Trout?" the man said with more than a little incredulity. "I don't think we need to elevate it to that level quite yet, Mr.—"

"Moran. Mr. Jake Moran. Please call Janice Trout and let her know my request."

The man looked up Janice Trout's extension on a web directory, picked up the handset of his desk phone, and clicked her name to call. He fidgeted in his seat and sat up nervously when the call connected.

"Ah, hello, Ms. Trout, I'm so sorry to bother you, but this is Sandip Ray down in IT and . . . yes, that's his name, Moran . . . oh. Oh, I see. Yes . . . yes. I will. I understand. I'll tell him. Okay, you too. Thank you. Goodbye."

Sandip hung up his handset and stared at it for a moment.

"She says you get whatever you want," he said. "And she'd like to see you after we wrap up. I'm very sorry, Mr. Moran. I honestly thought this was just a normal contractor onboarding."

"It's really okay," Jake said, holding out his hand. Sandip took it and they shook. "Please call me Jake. Can I ask you a couple questions?"

"Of course, anything."

"How long have you been here?"

"Almost a year. A year in June. I got recruited straight out of Rice University."

"You work in IT support? What did you study?"

"Yeah, I mean, everyone in IT starts out on desktop support. My undergrad is in electrical engineering, and my master's is in artificial intelligence. I could have made so much money going anywhere else, but working for Kingfisher? You can't pass something like that up. We all start out doing desktop support. Which can be a little . . ." Sandip stopped himself, and Jake smiled.

"Go ahead, say anything. I've handled some rough support gigs myself."

"I mean, it can suck, right? There are a lot of smart people here, but man, some people just don't get technology. Mrs. Nash is a wiz, though. We never get calls for her. She takes care of her own IT stuff. Both for security reasons, like, so no one can mess with her computers, and because she's smarter than all of us." Sandip laughed. "But how many bosses do you know who can set up a printer on their own or replace a hard drive? You can't help but respect that."

"She is a very talented person," Jake said.

"So anyway, we all start by doing support. Which is kind of brilliant, because we learn Kingfisher inside out. Systems, staff, everything. And if you do a good job?" He shrugged and smiled. "The cream rises to the top, as they say."

"I wish you good luck all the way to the top," Jake said.

"Thanks. Hey, on that laptop, do you want Windows or Linux? We have our own in-house Linux distribution for our engineers and programmers."

"Linux would be great," Jake said. While not as intuitive as Windows or the macOS, it was more secure and capable for IT work.

"It's going to take me a little bit to get the machine set up for you. You want to go see Ms. Trout while I work on that? I should have it done before you get back."

"Sounds perfect."

After the conversation, Jake made his way back to the lobby and down the hall toward Helena Nash's office. The door across the corridor from her office was open, and Janice Trout called out from inside as Jake passed.

"Jake!" she said, jumping to her feet to shake his hand. Again she was dressed professionally, almost severely, in a charcoal gray suit. Her smile was warm, though, and she seemed genuinely happy to see him. "Won't you sit down? Helena is in back-to-back meetings this morning, but I hope I can get you on your way. I know you've seen HR, and we've got an office set up for you down the hall. How can I help get you started?"

"I'd like to see an org chart," Jake said. "And I'm going to need access to your human resources software."

Janice didn't flinch at the request. "Consider it done," she said, making notes with a stylus on a tablet computer on her desk.

"Organizational chart will be in your email within the hour, and I'll have HR contact you. IT will be setting you up with a mobile phone as well."

"Just another thing to carry around, I guess."

"And everything is okay after your troubles with our aircraft the other day?"

"Thankfully, the doctor and I were fine," Jake said. "I'm hoping the pilot's recovering well. I want to check in on him."

Janice nodded thoughtfully. "I know they said it was a bird collision, but that's not what it sounded like when the FBI was back here this morning—"

"The FBI was here?" Jake asked. "About the crash?" Janice nodded. "Do they think it was something other than a bird?"

Now Janice shrugged. "Hard to say what they might be thinking. It all seems very suspicious, though, especially when they started asking about the protesters down on the water. You didn't see anything strange from up above, did you?"

"I—" Jake started before stopping himself. "I'm sure I'll have a chance to tell the investigators in person. You can tell them where to find me."

"Of course. Anything else I can do? Any other questions?"

"In fact," Jake said, "I do have a couple. Can you get me a list of everyone working launch control last Monday?"

CHAPTER TWENTY

It had been at least two years since Duncan Nash had been to Kingfisher's headquarters in Clear Lake City. The interior of the building was exactly as he'd remembered, and the foyer bustled with activity below high skylights and a quarter-scale model of the *Kingfisher Seven* suspended from the high ceiling. Duncan made his way toward the reception desk. Behind it, on a massive flat-panel display, a montage of Kingfisher launches and satellite deployments played on a never-ending loop. After each launch, the footage cut away to Kingfisher employees crowded in this very lobby, cheering and clapping.

Propaganda. The employees were there not by choice but because they would be given negative scores in their performance reviews for showing "inadequate enthusiasm" during launch operations. Everyone on the outside believed it was a progressive, amazing company, but Duncan knew it was more like Soviet Russia, with backstabbing, intrigue, and the always-possible threat of being reassigned to some gulag backwater like the hardware test facility in the bug-infested swamps of Louisiana.

A young man in a blue Kingfisher polo looked up from his computer behind the reception desk as Duncan approached. He gave a fake smile. "Good morning!" he chirped. "Welcome to Kingfisher. How may I assist you?"

"I'm here to see—" Duncan was cut off by the sudden arrival of a slender woman in a dark suit. She had blond hair pulled back into a bun, and a clipboard and tablet computer in the crook of her arm. Maybe thirty, Duncan thought, maybe even older, but in great shape. He took in her figure without being obvious. The woman gave him a thin smile.

"Mr. Nash," the woman said coolly, extending her hand. "I'm Janice Trout, Helena's assistant." She gave his hand a brief professional shake and nodded to the man at the reception desk. "I'll take it from here, Randy. Thanks." She turned toward the doors leading to the administrative hall. "Come with me, please. I'm sure you know the way."

"I do," he said, eyeing her from behind.

"Helena is wrapping up a meeting," Janice Trout said over her shoulder. "You can wait with me until she's ready for you."

They entered an office across the corridor from his mother's suite, and Janice gestured to a chair before going around to sit behind her desk.

Duncan sat, placing his computer bag next to him on the floor.

"It's been a while," Janice said.

"Excuse me?"

"We've met before," she said flatly.

They had?

"It's good to see you again," Duncan said, doing his best to project warm sincerity. "I meet so many—"

"*And* some time since you've met with Helena."

"Our goals," Duncan said, speaking carefully, "have diverged in the past few years."

Janice Trout said nothing. She simply laced her fingers atop her desk and stared at him. Duncan shifted in his chair. Maybe he hadn't read this woman right at all.

"What exactly *are* your goals, Mr. Nash?" she asked, and Duncan laughed.

"I have a feeling you know."

"I'd like to hear it from you directly."

"I want to stop radioactive plutonium from contaminating the environment."

"That's quite admirable. What have you done to achieve it?"

"Excuse me?"

"You say you don't want plutonium in the environment. That seems noble. I want to know what you've done to try to stop it from happening."

"Obviously we've held protests."

"Obviously."

"And we've sought legal recourse, trying to block any launches of radioactive material."

"I am aware of your legal maneuvering."

"Then why are you asking me these questions? If you want to interrogate me, maybe I'll just wait out in the hall instead."

"Do you feel like you've exhausted every avenue to try to stop this?"

"Of course I have. This has been my life for almost two years now. I'm sure you know about—"

"Mr. Nash," Janice said. "In all this time, have you considered simply asking your mother to stop the launch?"

There was something in her voice, something about the shift in her use from "Helena" to "your mother" that made Duncan pause.

"If you think you have some insight into my mother's behavior that I don't, you're—"

"Don't you think talking to her directly before trying any of your stunts could have saved a lot of effort? Or saved your donors a lot of money?"

"She has her mission. I have mine."

"She loves you, Duncan. More than the world. More than this company, for sure. She would have listened."

"Are you not hearing a thing I'm saying?" He lifted the computer bag from the floor and placed it in his lap. "I *know* how she would have responded."

"I think, Mr. Nash," Janice said, leaning slightly forward over her desk, "that this has nothing to do with plutonium."

"It has everything to do—"

"I think," she continued, "this is something personal between you and Helena. Some unresolved issue. If you would not take the simplest, most direct path to solving the problem, how could I, or the FBI, think otherwise?"

"The FBI? What are you talking about?"

"This is personal for you. It has nothing to do with radioactivity. Why else would you have had someone shoot down one of your mother's helicopters?"

"Are you kidding me?" Duncan shook his head in disbelief. "You don't really think—"

"You're a capable, well-connected man. With significant resources, and motivation to use them."

"Personal or not," Duncan said, "there is no way I would do something so insane." He rose to his feet. "And jeopardize my organization? You're crazy, and brainwashed, just like everyone else here. You're all part of a cult." He stabbed his finger in the direction of his mother's office. "And your leader is right across the hall."

"You would know, wouldn't you?" Janice said coolly. "I've seen your followers on the news, on social media, everywhere. They think you're a god. If anyone's a cult leader—"

"They believe in the cause."

"It's you."

They stared at each other. Duncan kept his breathing under control, his rage in check. He forced himself to smile and stepped to the door. Any lust he might have felt for this woman had completely vanished.

"You've got it all wrong," Duncan said. "You have no idea."

"Think what you want," Janice said. "The FBI will come to its own conclusions as well." She glanced down and tapped at her tablet screen. "I believe Helena is ready to see you now."

CHAPTER TWENTY-ONE

The first position on Jake's list, telemetry, had been staffed on the CommSat launch by a woman named Tricia Cruz. Her office, along with the other flight controllers', was on the second floor of the engineering wing. The central atrium was large and open, not unlike Jake's own building back in Washington State, under a glass skylight with launch-support rooms on the first level and offices above. Tricia's door was open, and she was reading something on a large desktop computer monitor as she absentmindedly worked at a bowl of yogurt with fruit. She was casually dressed in jeans and a pullover, and she wore reading glasses with her hair pulled back in a bun.

"Knock, knock," Jake said as he leaned in the doorway. Tricia jumped in her seat, put her breakfast next to her keyboard, and turned in her chair to face the doorway.

"Hi," she said, looking a little surprised. "Are you . . . there's supposed to be someone coming in today to talk about the launch?"

"I'm him," Jake said, waving the Kingfisher badge hanging from a lanyard around his neck. "Do you have a few minutes? I have some questions I'd like to ask. Only if it's convenient."

"Sure," she said. "You want to talk in here? Or there's a nice space down at the end of the hall we could use too."

"Let's go there."

The two strolled down along the balcony overlooking the space below until they came to an open area at the corner of the building.

Wide windows overlooked a grassy expanse, and inside there were angular chairs and a low sofa along with a pair of wooden tables. A dartboard hung on the wall next to a pair of classic cycling posters. Jake winced at all the decorative touches intended to impart a Silicon Valley start-up feel. They were trying too hard.

Trish took a seat in the corner, and Jake unshouldered his bag, pulled out a pen and notebook, and took a seat facing her.

"Janice Trout sent an email to all the flight controllers on the CommSat mission. We're supposed to answer anything you ask."

"Within reason," Jake said. "I'm here because I'm doing a systems review. Trying to see what works and what doesn't, or what can be improved. I've spent a lot of time at telemetry on launches, so I understand its importance. How did you end up there? And I guess more broadly, how did you end up here at Kingfisher?"

"Well, at MIT I was working on encrypted frequency-hopping communication links," she said. "I started interning at the Draper Lab my junior year. I was planning to work there through graduate school. Kingfisher knew about me pretty early, though, I guess. They invited me down to observe a launch my senior year, and I was hooked. I got my master's and came straight here. I could have worked at Draper—they really wanted me to stay—but . . ." Tricia waved toward the complex with her hand, as if that said it all. "Kingfisher, right? How could I pass this up?"

"Helena Nash seems to inspire serious devotion in her employees."

"Helena is amazing. Look at what she's done. Look at what we've accomplished with her leadership. We've successfully launched more payloads in the last eighteen months than all the US launch providers combined. That doesn't happen by accident. Helena hires only the best. We are devoted. We are a tight team, and we have to be."

"CommSat was your first launch, you said?"

"My first as a console lead. I've done backroom support here in Clear Lake for five other launches, both telemetry and INCO."

INCO, short for the instrumentation and communications officer, was another role Jake knew well.

"Tell me about the launch Monday. How did it go? Were you nervous out there for your first time?"

"I wasn't nervous at all," Tricia said. "The funny thing was, it felt more like a sim. We'd been doing training simulations for CommSat here on the mainland for nearly five months, and we did three sims out on the platform in the week prior to launch. So it wasn't foreign or weird. It was very familiar. In fact, the weirdest thing was *how* familiar. Exactly like a sim. Kingfisher really trains it into you before they turn you loose on the real deal."

"That's one thing they have in common with the government," Jake said.

"You went through simulations too?" Tricia asked.

"Probably a hundred to every single real launch I worked on," Jake said. "But tell me about launch day. Anything off nominal? Anything that stood out?"

"Nothing significant, except I did have a blip during the terminal count—"

"A blip?" Jake uncapped his pen and flipped open the notebook.

"A comms dropout," Tricia said. "Sometimes over the wireless-communication link between the two platforms, you'll get a quick glitch in the signal that ends up in weird or frozen data. Telemetry is usually the only station that sees it, because I'm looking at the signal as it's coming in. They're not common, but also not unheard of."

"What's your procedure on that?" Jake asked, not looking up as he scribbled notes.

"The rule book says a data drop longer than ten seconds means an automatic twenty-minute hold in the countdown to reestablish a solid link. If we can't get a good link in that time, it's a mandatory clock recycle to T-minus ninety minutes. But because that often means refueling or missing a launch window, it's usually a twenty-four-hour scrub. So we try to avoid it if we can."

"Is that automatic, or up to you?"

"Totally at my discretion. And the truth is, when we're within T-minus two minutes, we're so close to the vehicle's onboard computer taking over, I'll usually let it go. I wouldn't do that if we were getting weird data on other terminals or if something seemed off nominal with the vehicle or payloads. But all the calls had been 'go' that day, no one was working any issues, so I was ready to let it keep going. As it was, it was hardly more than a second or two before I had good data again."

Jake took a moment to finish a note and looked up to face Tricia. "You're probably pretty familiar with that data link, yes?"

"I designed it."

"Can you get me all of the documentation on that?"

"You're sure you're authorized to see it?" Tricia asked. She waited a beat and laughed. "No, I know you're authorized. I'll send you a link to that system on our intranet. If you aren't allowed to see it, you won't be able to open it. But I suspect you won't have a problem."

"I like that you're by the book," Jake said. "If I were still running launches, I'd ask you to be on my team in a heartbeat."

"Thank you. That means a lot."

"Anything else that seemed weird?"

Tricia tilted her head to the side and pursed her lips. "Like I said, it felt so much like a sim. Now that I think about it, we even had a blip in our prelaunch simulation. Right around the same time in the count. But it was shorter, not even half a second."

Jake made a note of it. "Anything else? Anything on your console, or anyone else's?"

Tricia shrugged. "Before the vehicle came apart, guidance called out some motion in the vehicle. But that happens every flight. Winds aloft, usually."

"Who worked the guidance console that day?"

"Elliot Hsu. He was a year ahead of me at MIT."

"Do you know where I can find him?" Tricia grinned and pointed back toward the second story balcony.

"Right that way," she said. "He's my next-door neighbor."

Elliot Hsu's office looked to Jake like a room in a college dorm. Strewn papers, open journals, and multiple coffee mugs covered most of the surfaces. A hammock hung diagonally across the room over a mountain bike propped against the wall. In the far corner, a wiry young man in cycling shorts and a pro-racing jersey was hunched over a laptop, typing at amazing speed. He wore a massive pair of over-ear headphones, his body silently bouncing to whatever music he was listening to.

"Elliot," Tricia said, rapping hard on his open door. "Elliot!" He didn't move, so Tricia grabbed a pair of running socks—clean, Jake hoped—from a chair next to the doorway and threw them at Elliot's head, scoring a direct hit. The young man jumped in surprise and pulled his headphones down to his neck as he swiveled in his chair to face the doorway.

"Jesus Christ, Trish, just message me on Slack if you need to talk." He looked genuinely startled, but he smiled. "Who is this?"

"This is Jake Moran."

"The guy from the email?"

"The guy from the email. Jake, meet Elliot."

"How's it going?" Jake asked. Elliot rose to shake Jake's hand and pointed to a pair of chairs covered in stacks of technical printouts.

"You guys can sit there," Elliot said. "Just put that shit on the floor or wherever."

"I'm smart enough to not set foot in here," Tricia said. "He wants to talk to you. And, Jake, if you have any more questions, you know where to find me."

"Thanks for your help."

She left for her own office, and Elliot got to his feet. "Sorry, man, it's a mess in here. You want to grab some coffee? We can talk down in the cafeteria if that works for you."

"Coffee sounds great."

Elliot kicked off his cycling shoes and slid his stocking feet into a pair of Birkenstock sandals before grabbing a travel mug from the shelf above his desk. "We need to look at data?" he asked, reaching for his laptop. "I'm assuming we're talking about the failure, right?"

"You can leave the computer," Jake said. "I'm just meeting people. Getting to know the lay of the land." Jake followed Elliot downstairs and back out into the reception area before heading down the hall that led to Helena Nash's office.

"So is this an investigation of the CommSat failure, or are you getting things ready for HiPEP-D?"

"Little bit of both," Jake said. As they passed the entrance to Janice Trout's office, the door flew open, and Jake was stunned to see Duncan Nash emerge. Duncan held a computer bag tightly and didn't seem to notice Jake as he strode purposefully across the corridor. Elliot kept walking. He pointed to one of the large launch photos lining the hallway.

"That was GOES-West," he said. "Weather satellite. My first launch on the platform. It was, like, the best launch ever too."

"You never forget your first time in the trench," Jake said.

"I know, man. It's almost as good as sex." Elliot paused. "Who the hell am I kidding? Launching a rocket is better than sex!" He laughed and shook his head. "I'm such a fucking nerd."

They entered the cafeteria, which seemed more like a food court in a high-end shopping center. Skylights illuminated a large common area with tables, couches, and beanbag chairs surrounded by dining options like a sushi bar, a taco stand made to look like a food truck, a wood-fired pizzeria, and a coffee shop, which Elliot made a beeline for. "What do you want?" he asked. "I'm buying. Lattes here are really good." He laughed again. "Not like I need any more caffeine. I already had two espressos before I rode in today." A man in line in front of them glanced back over his shoulder.

"Elliot, you're a twenty-four-volt guy in a twelve-volt world," he said dryly.

"I know, right? But I get twice as much shit done!"

They got their coffees and took a seat on a pair of chairs next to a tall potted plant. A shaft of midmorning sun hit the gleaming white floor next to them. Elliot sat back, took a sip of his latte, and crossed his legs.

"So what's up? Process review? JT didn't say much in her email."

"What *did* she say, exactly?"

"Just that you knew your shit—not those words exactly, she's a little more corporate, obviously. She said you had a lot of experience in the industry, and you'd be asking us some stuff, and we should all do our best to help you out with any questions you have."

"Seems about right," Jake said.

"You work some launches?"

"A few. I was in the military. Observing birds, weather, some stuff I can't talk about."

"Right on," Elliot said. "One of my professors did that shit in the navy."

"What was his name? I might have known him."

"Her. Dr. Wendy Brunner. You know her?"

"I know of her. She was there before me. Anyway, tell me about the CommSat launch. Anything weird for you or off nominal?"

Elliot took another sip from his travel mug, licked some foam off his upper lip, and shook his head. "It was a smooth countdown. Too smooth for my liking, to be honest."

"What do you mean by that?"

"What I mean is, I honestly prefer to be working a couple issues on launch day. Nothing so major it's going to cause a scrub, but some little fluke to keep us on our toes. Questionable instrument readings, or intermittent comms, you know what I mean? Stuff we can work around without impacting the mission. When it goes too smooth, I feel like people get lazy. And if we get lazy, that's when we run the risk of missing the big stuff. For a few hours after we lost CommSat, that's exactly what I thought happened. Smooth sailing, too smooth, and it bit us in our asses."

"But then what?"

"Word got around about a possible cause." Elliot frowned, looking like he was holding something back.

"I've heard it," Jake assured him. "Flight-termination system was activated."

"Okay, good. I hate spilling secrets. It was so weird, man. FTS triggering was like, the *least* likely thing in my mind. But after I heard, and the more I thought about it, I was like, well maybe someone back at Delta 45 in Florida got an itchy trigger finger. And then I was freaking out: Was it because of my call on the net?"

"What was your call? Tell me about that."

"We had a bobble," Elliot said. He held his forearm out in front of him parallel to the floor. "Stable flight, nothing moves." His arm stayed steady. "But wind shear, even really minor wind shear, makes the vehicle move like this." He tipped his arm up and down like a teeter-totter. "We started seeing a bobble."

"And you called it out verbally."

"We always call it out, no matter how minor. The oscillations I was seeing were completely in normal bounds, nothing serious at all. But we call it out because sometimes the payload team sees those same movements, and they might be freaking out it's something going on up there. If my console lets them know we're seeing it, too, and we aren't calling for an abort or anything, it calms them down. Better still, it shuts them up." Elliot laughed.

"Principal investigators and satellite operators can be pretty uptight," Jake said. "I've worked with a few."

"That's an understatement. Though I have to say Dr. Taka, the guy who designed CommSat, was totally chill. So easy to work with. That made me feel even worse about the possibility of it being my fault, because he's such a nice guy."

A nice guy and a good one to have around if your pilot's injured, Jake thought. "So you're saying you were worried that your call might have encouraged someone back at Canaveral to push the big red button?"

"Yeah man, for a couple hours I was freaking out. But then I was like, Hsu, what's your problem, dude? They have all the same data we do—they operate in the same parameters. They wouldn't have sent the destruct command unless it was making a beeline for Miami or something. But even then they'd probably give us a few seconds to see if the thing would straighten out. So I knew it wasn't my fault. And it sounds like it was a computer problem over there instead of someone pushing the button. Though we're not supposed to know that."

"Do you remember who told you?" Jake asked, and Elliot shook his head.

"We heard it was FTS from an internal report. It was really general. It was sent to the controllers from Andy Lang, but anyone could have written it for him. Then Lang told us a little more in a meeting yesterday. After that, I kind of heard bits and pieces all over."

"You've never experienced anything like that before, even in a simulation?"

"Man, I hope they start putting it in the sims, because we were all floored when we found out. I would have liked to have had some training to prepare myself, you know? Our last sim certainly didn't prep me for it."

"What do you mean?"

"It was nominal all the way uphill to orbit. It was crazy—the supervisors never give us sims that easy. It was just like launch day, right down to the bobble around T-plus one oh two seconds. I made exactly the same call as I did during the live flight. Total déjà vu. Except for the explosion, of course."

"Anything else? Anything weird after?"

"Nah, once we got our shit together, it was totally by the book. Lang got our heads back in it."

"How's Andy to work for?"

"No complaints. He runs a tight ship. Hey, wait, he's ex-military, too, right? Did you ever know him back then?"

Jake nodded. "I knew him then. I know him pretty well now. He's a good guy."

"Hell of a guy," Elliot said. "Anything else for me?"

"I think that should do it. Thanks for your time."

CHAPTER TWENTY-TWO

The door to Helena Nash's office closed with a resounding click, and Duncan, for the first time in nearly two years, faced his mother. The two watched each other warily—she behind an immaculate desk, he at the door with his computer bag—as if testing to see who would make the first move. The look on his mother's face was sorrowful, almost pathetic; her eyes shone with something like emotion, and Duncan wondered if he could see the slightest tremble in her chin. Duncan remained still, clutching his laptop bag to his front, and when he blinked, the soft expression on his mother's face was gone. Her eyebrows narrowed, and she frowned. It was the same look she'd given him as a child if he had a bad grade or had gotten into some sort of trouble.

"Duncan," she said.

"Hello, Mother."

"You look . . . agitated. Is something wrong?"

There were a thousand things he could have said, but he stuck with the one that was troubling him the most.

"That woman. Your assistant. She's terrible."

"Duncan. *That woman* is the best employee I've ever had. She is shrewd, brilliant, and observant. She could run this company herself someday if she wanted to." Her expression hardened. "Like you could have, if you'd had the desire. But you had other plans."

"Saving people from radiation poisoning is not 'other plans.' It's the most worthwhile thing I've ever done."

“Oh, is it, now?”

“It is! I can make a difference here. People believe in me. They depend on me.”

“Depend on you for what? Throwing away your fortune on a caprice? Saving them from a risk that isn’t even there?”

“It is there.” Duncan held his bag out in front of him and shook it. “It is real. I have proof of it right here.”

“Proof of what? What are you talking about?”

“Here, Mother. Here. Let me show you.” Duncan flipped open the top flap of his bag and pulled out the USB drive, holding it up between his fingers like a precious gem. “Right here is proof of the danger of radiothermal generators.”

“Proof how? Documents? Photos?”

“Documents, photos, hard data . . . it’s all here. Acquired from well-placed sources. Let me show you.” Duncan stepped toward his mother’s desk and held the thumb drive out to her. “Look at it. Open it up. I have all the time in the world.” Helena took the drive and turned it over in her fingers. She made no move to open her laptop and look. Instead she lifted the handset from her slim desktop phone and pressed an extension.

“Janice, will you have someone in IT bring me a new laptop? One from engineering. I need a fresh install of Linux, not Windows. Something that hasn’t been used on the network yet. I’ll need to be able to view Word documents and PDFs. Thank you.”

“That hardly seems necessary,” he complained.

“I will look at your little files but not on a computer connected to the Kingfisher network.” She gestured to the couch across the room. “Will you sit? I imagine this could take a little while.” Duncan took a tentative step toward the couch and slowly took a seat. Mother and son stared at each other quietly for a long, awkward moment.

“You’re . . . looking healthy,” Helena said tentatively.

“Mother, seriously,” Duncan said dryly. “I’m not here for—”

The door buzzed and opened, and Janice Trout poked her head in the room.

"IT is here with a computer," she said in a near whisper. "They had one ready right when you called."

"Have them bring it in."

Janice pulled the door open, and a twentysomething man in a blue Kingfisher shirt entered the room pushing a gray equipment cart ahead of him. On top of the cart was a folded HP laptop, and on the shelf below were cables, an external mouse, and various other peripherals.

"Good morning, Sandip," Helena said.

Duncan knew she memorized all her employees' names. It was a parlor trick, and she used it to make her underlings feel valued. It disgusted Duncan so much he could hardly watch the exchange.

"Where should I set this up for you?"

"I only need the laptop for a few minutes. I have some data I need to look at isolated from the network. When I'm done you can wipe the hard drive, reinstall the operating system, and put it back into circulation."

"Sure thing," Sandip said, placing the laptop on the desk. "It's got our default first-use password, so you'll need to change it when you boot up. Just give us a call when you're done." He smiled and left the room with the cart. Helena had already opened the laptop's screen and was typing away on its keyboard. The USB sat on the desk.

"Let me disable networking so it's truly air gapped; then we can take a look," she said softly as she typed. She must have noticed the anticipation on Duncan's face, because she rolled her eyes and shook her head. "You can come over and have a look, too, you know."

Duncan dropped his bag to the floor and slowly stepped around to his mother's side of the desk. He kept his distance, a step behind, looking over her right shoulder as she inserted the drive into one of the laptop's USB ports. She browsed to the drive's contents, revealing a handful of Word documents and JPG images. She clicked on the first image listed, and an image-viewer app opened showing a photo of a rocket with Cyrillic writing on a launchpad. She clicked the next one, which showed a similar scene. Three more static shots, and finally the rocket was lifting off in a billow of orange fire.

"This is *Mars 96*," Helena said. "It failed."

"I know."

"Everyone knows." She scrolled through more pictures before closing the image viewer and opening one of the documents at random. It was in English—a summary of a mission. She closed it and opened another, and another. She opened a PDF file and closed it. She opened a video and played a twenty-second clip of a Russian *Proton* rocket lifting off into the sky.

"Well?" Duncan said.

"Well, indeed. Where is the proof?"

"It's right there."

"Duncan," Helena said with a sigh, "there is nothing new here. I've seen all of these documents before. Look." Helena opened her personal laptop and opened Wikipedia in a browser window. She typed "Mars 96" into the search bar and clicked through to the entry for the failed Russian mission. "Here's the same photo. And down here . . . your document is just a cut and paste from this text. This is supposed to be earth shattering? You downloaded a worthless load of files from the internet to prove what?"

"Wait," Duncan said, squeezing in next to his mother and pivoting the laptop toward himself. His mouth had gone dry, and his hands shook as he clicked open the files on the drive one by one. "Just wait. Wait, they told me it's here."

"Duncan. Why are you doing this? Was this simply an excuse to come in to talk with me?" Helena's voice cracked as she spoke. "Did you think you needed to do this to have an excuse to talk with me? You know—"

"I needed to show you this, Mother. This was why I came!"

"You *know* you can come talk to me anytime. You are my son, and no matter what sort of differences we have, I love you. I will always love you, Duncan. Always."

"But it was this!" Duncan said, fumbling to open the last files. "There was supposed to be proof!"

Helena reached over and slapped the HP's screen shut. "Did you not hear a word I just said to you?"

Mother and son stared at each other.

"It was supposed to be proof," Duncan repeated.

"Take it then," Helena snapped, yanking the USB from the closed laptop. She slammed it down to the surface of her desk with a crack. "Take it and leave. If that is the only reason you came to see me, take it and go. Go!"

"But, Mother—"

"*I said go!*" Helena roared.

Duncan snatched the USB drive from the desk and grabbed his bag. He didn't look back as he left the office.

CHAPTER TWENTY-THREE

By the end of the day, Jake had interviewed nearly half the launch controllers from the CommSat failure. None had anything new to report, and each said something about how much it had felt like a simulation. There was nothing too strange about that, Jake knew; it was the whole point of training, to make everyone feel like they'd been there before.

There was someone else Jake wanted to talk with, off campus, and he departed a little early to make the meeting. He'd parked in a normal spot that morning, not an EV-charging space, and he hadn't plugged the car in for the day. The battery indicator showed 38 percent as he headed southward to Galveston Island. Traffic on I-45 wasn't light, but it was steady, and it only took Jake a little over half an hour to make it to the island. He headed east down the center of the island on Broadway, but instead of turning right toward his rental, he continued straight for a couple of more miles and turned left toward the University of Texas hospital. The EV parking was close to the front, but both spaces were occupied, one by an idling black SUV. Jake shook his head and parked in a normal spot. Once inside the main building, he was greeted by a young volunteer at the front desk.

"I'm here to visit a patient," Jake asked. "Denny Wade."

The teen typed something into her computer and nodded. "He's accepting visitors. Room 2021 in the PCU." The girl pointed to her left. "Primary care unit is that way. I'll need you to sign in and wear this badge, please."

Jake signed his name on a digital screen and affixed an adhesive visitor badge over his breast pocket. The PCU was easy to find—down the hall and up an elevator—and Jake found Wade's room open with the sound of a TV coming from it.

"Visitor," Jake called, knocking at the door.

"Visitor?" a booming voice replied. The television volume went down. "Now just who would come to visit me?"

Jake stepped into the room, and Wade, propped up in his bed, broke into a broad grin.

"God*damn*," he said, reaching out with his hand. "Jake Moran." Jake reached out to shake, but when their hands clasped, Wade pulled Jake toward him and grabbed him in a backslapping embrace. "Goddamn," he repeated. "Thank you, man."

"No, thank you," Jake said, pulling a chair to the side of the hospital bed. "It would have been game over if you hadn't talked me through that autorotation. How are you feeling?"

Wade shrugged. "It's nothing. I might get discharged tomorrow. Seems like a little nerve damage when I got hit, so I'll need some physical therapy so I can get to wiggling my toes again. Jesus Christ, did I say thank you? Thank you."

"Look, we can thank each other all day. I'm glad I could help. I guess I'd have been happier if we didn't have to deal with that at all. But we came out of it, right?"

"Hell yeah. How you been?"

"I've been okay. Doing some work for Kingfisher for the next couple weeks."

"I heard. Hey, I got a question. Anybody talk to you about what happened on the helo?"

"Crickets after the local cops day of, though I hear the FBI has been on it at Kingfisher HQ. What about you?"

"Same deal. Couple guys had a word with me right when I was out of surgery. Feds, looked like. I hardly remember. But after that, nothing. That seem weird to you?"

Jake nodded. "Really weird. I don't get it. I'm going to ask some questions while I'm down here this week. If the feds won't do anything, shouldn't someone?"

"Good luck with that, man. Unless you can talk to Helena Nash herself, I don't know if you'll get anywhere."

"As a matter of fact," Jake said, "I *can* talk to her."

Wade raised his eyebrows.

"You got Helena's ear?" Wade asked. "You must be some kind of big deal, marine." Jake shrugged. "She actually came out here to see me. Day after. Real sweet, seemed like she felt pretty bad about everything. Told me not to tell anyone she'd come, like she wanted to keep it quiet."

"You're telling me about it, though."

"Well, you're different. You were in the shit too. I think she just wanted to keep it on the down-low, not have people make a big deal about it."

"Anyone else come to see you?"

Wade shook his head. "Other than my wife, no. But Taka called to check in on me yesterday. *Doctor* Taka, I should say. You know his company made the hardware in CommSat? Anyway, I thanked him too. But otherwise, it's been weirdly quiet, you know?"

Jake nodded. "I keep hearing about birds being what knocked us down, but . . ."

Wade raised a finger. "About that . . ."

The pilot reached beneath the adjustable-height table next to his bed, grabbed a slender, dull-metal tube about the size and shape of a Magic Marker, and handed it to Jake. "Tell me, you ever seen anything like that before?"

Jake turned the metal over in his hands. It was flattened into an airfoil shape, the ends were jagged, and it seemed impossibly light for how rigid it was. *3D printed,* Jake thought. The outer surface was grooved, and the center was filled with ultrafine metal webbing in a honeycomb pattern.

"Featherweight," he said, flipping it in his hand. "Where'd it come from?"

"They pulled it out of my leg here in surgery," Wade said. "I can tell you what it's not: It's not part of a Sikorsky helicopter. And it's not part of a pelican, either, which is what we supposedly ran into."

"Something from the back maybe?" Jake mused. "Dr. Taka had it, and it ended up in you when we hit the Gulf?"

"You buy that explanation?" Wade asked, taking the object back.

"Not really, but can you think of anything better? Did you show this to Helena?"

A knock sounded at the door, and the look on Wade's face brightened. "Another visitor?" he boomed. "This is my lucky day! Who's there?"

A stocky man in a white T-shirt and track pants stepped into the room. A visitor sticker was askew in the center of his chest. He stepped purposefully into the room with his right hand behind his back, stopping abruptly when he saw Jake.

"Do I know you?" Wade asked.

"I . . . must have wrong room," the man said with a thick Slavic accent. He paused for a moment, then quickly raised his arm.

"Gun!" Wade shouted.

As the man leveled a pistol at Wade, Jake, still seated, kicked the rolling table at him as hard as he could. It clipped the side of the man's leg, throwing off his aim, giving Jake just enough time to stand and hurl the chair at the intruder. The back of the chair made solid contact with the side of the man's head, but the intruder managed to half deflect the chair and shove it back in Jake's direction, knocking him against the wall.

Instead of attacking, the man turned and ran. When Jake looked to Wade, he saw why: Wade was aiming his own pistol at the empty doorway.

"He went right," Wade said. "Be careful."

Jake vaulted the chair and entered the corridor, then ran after the big man, who was hurrying toward an elevator bank. Jake ducked into a nurses' bay when the intruder called an elevator. Lights began flashing in the hall, and a recorded voice over the PA system repeated, "Code silver, PCU. Code silver, PCU. Remain in place. Code silver . . ."

Fire doors at the end of the corridor began swinging shut between him and the gunman. Jake dashed for the doors and pushed through shoulder first, but the intruder had disappeared.

Jake ran to the adjacent stairway and bounded down two steps at a time to a landing. He started down the final flight but halted as a man's voice from the main corridor shouted, "Stop! Sir, I need you to stop!" Jake returned to the landing and kicked at a half-open window, shaking away the screen from his foot. He eased himself through and shimmied down a standpipe before dropping the final few feet to the ground and crouching in a landscaped flower bed.

A moment later, to Jake's left, the big man ran at a sprint out the building's sliding front doors. No one followed. Jake watched him get into the driver's seat of the Escalade idling in the EV spot. The SUV had Texas plates and what looked like a rental-car barcode in the driver's side rear window. The vehicle took off while Jake dashed for his rental Chevy, cursing himself for not plugging the car in earlier in the day as he turned it on. The console showed only 19 percent charge.

He put the car in drive and swerved around a vehicle exiting the lot in front of him, completing the sketchy pass in enough time to swing westward onto Broadway. Jake hoped the SUV was headed toward I-45; he moved the car as far to the left as he could in his lane and craned his neck to try to see ahead in the column of moderate traffic. He pushed forward, cutting someone off abruptly enough to get a honk from the car behind him. Jake slipped the Bolt into a gap two cars behind the SUV. In a moment they'd merge onto the interstate; he'd have a chance to get closer then.

Jake sat tight and pondered his next move. What happened if the guy stopped? What happened if he made Jake as a tail? The battery indicator had dropped to 14 percent. In any event, he wouldn't be able to follow for long. He pulled his phone from his pocket and unlocked it with his fingerprint.

"Call Stu Gallagher," he said, putting the phone on speaker and placing it on the center console. Stu picked up on the second ring.

"Jake!" he boomed. "You're calling me on cell. This means either you need lady advice, or—"

"Shut it. I need your help right now. Cadillac Escalade, rental car. Texas plates, I'll give you the number in a second."

"You in trouble?"

"Hang on and be quiet. Get ready for those numbers."

The road curved to the right and seamlessly became Interstate 45, and Jake pressed the accelerator to the floor to slingshot himself around the two leading cars and the Escalade.

"LJK3821!" Jake said as he sped past the SUV. He tried to steal a quick glance at the driver but only saw the same short dark hair and sunglasses. He kept speeding until he was three cars ahead of the Escalade before slipping over into the right lane and slowing to the pace of the other traffic around him.

"Jake, talk to me," Stu said. "You there?"

"I'm here."

"Give me five minutes. You all right?"

"I'm good," Jake said. "Find out whatever you can. I'll talk to you later."

He ended the call and picked up the phone again, opening the camera app and tapping the icon to switch to the front-facing camera. He eased off the accelerator, forcing the cars behind to slow to his pace. The Escalade got into the left lane, and Jake smiled. He got over, too, continuing his slow speed so the Escalade ended up right on his bumper. Jake kept his eyes on the road and raised his phone. He held his finger on the camera button to make it take pictures in burst mode, moving it around slightly as he did so in hopes that at least one of the pictures of the guy behind him would be clear. He assumed if the driver even noticed what Jake was doing, he'd simply think he was some dumb tourist taking pictures of the road.

After about fifteen seconds the SUV crept closer and flashed its brights, the driver irritated by Jake's slow speed. He put the phone down and waved apologetically.

"So sorry, asshole," he muttered.

About two hundred yards ahead he saw an approaching exit. He put on his right turn signal. The driver to his right slowed to create a gap, but Jake waited until the exit was on them and quickly swerved all the way over across both lanes and onto the ramp, keeping his head turned to the right to hide his face. When he looked back to the interstate, he saw the SUV far ahead of him. The driver had made no attempt to brake and follow.

At the top of the ramp, Jake pulled to a stop on the shoulder and grabbed his phone. He searched for the number to the hospital and had his call put through to Wade's room. Wade's "Hello" was clipped and tense.

"It's Jake. What's going on there?"

"Jesus, man, I've been worried about you. Some people came and asked if I saw anything. Feds, again. I played dumb. What happened to that guy?"

"He moved out in a real hurry. I got a good look at his vehicle and tried to get some pictures of his face. A friend's looking into it. We'll see where it gets us. How's your discharge coming?"

"No word from the doctor yet about when I can leave," Wade said.

"I think you should take matters into your own hands and bug out pronto. That guy wasn't there to bring you flowers. If he comes by again—"

"I hear you. I'm packing my bags right now."

"I guess I'm not so surprised you had a piece there under the covers with you," Jake said. "Wade, tell me truthfully: You don't have anything going on in your life, do you? Any reason someone like that would come after you? I don't get the feeling you do, but I need to ask."

"I get it, man. I got nothing going on. My life is clean. No serious debts, nothing shady on the side."

"I figured. You have any place you can go off the grid for a little while?"

"My brother-in-law has a condo not too far away. I can use it whenever I want. It could be a nice place to stage my recovery."

"I agree. Get your family out of your house, and get to your brother-in-law's place. And, hey, that honeycomb thing you showed me—"

"I've got a mechanic buddy I'm going to show it to. He's like Rain Man when it comes to shit like that."

"Sounds good. Lie low, and let me know if anything weird happens. Got it?"

"I got it. Listen, you keep me posted too. And keep yourself out of trouble! Don't go chasing anybody around with no reason. Kingfisher has security, real body men for that Nash lady. Use 'em if you have to. Don't do anything stupid."

"I appreciate the concern. Get yourself safe, and let's stay in touch."

After they exchanged numbers, Jake ended the call and opened the camera roll on his phone. None of the pictures of the man in the Escalade was great, but a few were clear enough, and Jake attached them to an email for Stu with: "Get these to Josephine and Miles in Tam's image-processing team. If anybody can clean these up, it's them. Check them against any facial recognition databases you can get access to. 60% match is worth keeping. Flag anything with an Eastern European/Russian-sounding name. And call me back about the rental car ASAP, for fuck's sake."

Jake took a deep breath. Maybe Wade was right; maybe he shouldn't have gotten involved. Too late now, though. He had a thread, and he intended to follow it. Jake pulled onto the ramp once more, crossed the overpass, and headed back south on the interstate toward Galveston Island.

CHAPTER TWENTY-FOUR

Duncan still shook with anger as he took a seat in his car out in the Kingfisher lot. The fucking Russian had played him. He dug through his laptop bag for Strelka's card. Proof or not, they'd made a deal, and Duncan had held up his end of it. Now he wanted payment. He drew his phone from his pocket and dialed.

"You have news?"

"I showed her the USB."

"And does your mother stop the launch of plutonium?"

"No. She won't stop the launch. She said the documents were worthless. She had seen them all before."

"Too bad."

"Yes," Duncan said. "I was very hopeful." He paused. "So now . . . do you pay me?"

"Yes. Now I pay you. Let us meet right away. Do you know where is the intersection of Red Bluff and Underwood?"

"Of course," Duncan said. "You're actually very close. That's only a couple miles from where I am right now."

"How lucky that we happen to be in a similar area."

"Yes, it is. And do you have the money?"

"I have means with me to pay you."

Duncan started the Tesla and headed for the exit of the Kingfisher lot. "What are you driving? So I can find you."

"Don't worry. Go to Red Bluff and Underwood, and I will be waiting for you there. You won't miss me."

Sure enough, after several minutes of driving, Duncan saw a black Cadillac Escalade SUV stopped on the shoulder of Underwood Road next to a fenced-off, overgrown vacant lot. Strelka stood behind the SUV. He wore dark glasses, a tight white T-shirt, and Adidas track pants with black sneakers. A fresh gash ran from his left temple to his upper cheek. It looked like he hadn't even bothered to stanch the blood.

Duncan pulled up behind the Escalade and got out of his car. "It was strange," he said. "She said she'd seen everything on the USB before."

Strelka nodded and opened the rear hatch of the Escalade. He pulled out a very large tan duffel bag. Large enough to hold a lot of money, Duncan thought, but it appeared to be curiously empty.

"You were not supposed to look," Strelka said.

"Wait, what?"

"You were not supposed to look at contents of USB."

"Hey, I only saw when my mother was looking—it's not like I could help it."

"I told you," Strelka said. "It is very bad if you look." He unzipped the duffel, drew out a pistol, and aimed it at the center of Duncan's chest.

"Whoa, whoa, what the hell!" he said, putting his hands in the air. "I did exactly what you told me! What is going on—"

"Get in the bag," Strelka said. He threw the duffel into the back of the Escalade, where Duncan saw a roll of duct tape and zip ties.

Strelka gestured to the bag with the pistol. "In."

"I'm not getting in that bag," Duncan said.

He felt his pulse pounding in his neck and temples, and the coppery taste of fear filled his mouth. He took deep, slow breaths and forced himself to stay calm. If there was one thing in this world he was good at, he knew it was projecting confidence and composure.

"You're crazy," he said, and he turned back toward his car. Out of the corner of his eye he saw the Russian swing the pistol at his head. Duncan ducked, but not in time, and the last thing he felt, before his knees crumpled and the world went black, was the lightning-bolt crack of steel against the back of his skull.

CHAPTER TWENTY-FIVE

Back on the island, Jake found a grocery store on Seawall Boulevard to grab supplies for dinner and a six-pack of beer. He left the Bolt to charge in the grocer's EV parking spot and walked back to his rental. There was nothing more he could do about the guy in the Escalade; it wasn't like he could have maintained a tail in his barely charged EV. He'd gathered information, and that would have to be good enough.

At the house, Jake found his big bag waiting for him on the front porch. This was good news. Inside the home, though, he was surprised to discover that none of the lights, appliances, or outlets were working. Jake looked outside at one of the neighboring houses and saw kitchen lights on and a TV glowing in the living room, so he knew power wasn't out in the neighborhood. It was almost 7:00 p.m., and there was still enough daylight coming through the windows that he could see pretty well inside the house, so he opened his bag, took his SIG from the gun case, and searched the house with his pistol at his side. When he was satisfied no one was hidden or waiting for him, he made a second pass, still armed, this time looking for a circuit breaker panel. Toward the back of the house, there was a locked owner's closet. *Probably in there.* He stowed the pistol, took out his phone, and opened the rental app to send a message to his host.

> Hi Sherry, the place is great, but it seems like the electricity has gone out. Can you let me know where the breaker panel is so I can try to fix it? Thanks, Jake

Jake put his groceries into the fridge—being quick about it to keep things cold, given the lack of power—and hauled the big suitcase upstairs. He unpacked and changed into running clothes. His phone buzzed on top of the dresser as he was pulling on his shirt, and he checked to find a reply from Sherry.

> Oh shoot, I'm so sorry. They've been doing utility work on our street and sometimes it pops the main breaker. The panel is in a locked storage closet, so I'll need to send someone over there to open it up and reset it. I apologize for the inconvenience!

This, Jake thought, was a relief. A known condition. After the episode at the hospital, he was on edge. He put the gun back in its case and hid it in his empty suitcase in the closet. He headed downstairs, laced up his shoes at the door, and slipped out into the humid air, locking the place behind him. He walked a few strides while his watch synced up with GPS and headed south at an easy pace. He smelled the sea air, so unlike the air of the Puget Sound—thicker, with a greater density in his nose and lungs. It wasn't unpleasant, only different, and it wasn't long before he found an easy rhythm. He made it to Seawall Boulevard and crossed to the broad sidewalk, heading east with his back to the sun. Down on the beach to his right a few people ambled in the damp sand: retirees, a mother and two children with sand pails, a teenage couple holding hands.

At three and a half miles out, Jake turned around and started back. The sun was low in the sky, and it enveloped everything on the island—the beach, the hotels, the roller coasters, and the pier—in a warm glowing light. He picked up his pace as he passed the pier, breathing hard with his mouth open as he ducked and weaved through the shuffling pedestrians, until he reached the road back to his rental. He eased his pace to a cooldown jog, trotting along until he reached the little blue house. He was looking forward to taking a shower and cooking a nice meal for himself, but that vision was shot when he got inside and tried to flick the switch to the living room light. Still nothing. So instead of a shower or food, he grabbed a beer from the still-cool fridge, popped it open, and went back out to take a seat on the front porch. He put his feet up on the railing, tipped his chair back, and took in the evening. Music from an open window across the street. Laughs and shouts from a pack of elementary school–age local kids riding past on their bicycles. An elderly African American woman walking up the street with a strong gait, a grocery bag in each hand. She noticed Jake on the porch and nodded, and he nodded in return. A strange noise hummed like a far-off insect, and an electric bicycle buzzed up the street and wobbled to a stop right in front of the house. The woman riding it dismounted, took off her helmet, and hung it from the bike's handlebars before climbing the steps to the little house, muttering "Shit!" as she fiddled with the lockbox to the side of the door.

"It's unlocked, you know," Jake said.

The woman jumped.

"Don't scare me like that!" she breathed. "Jesus. I don't like being scared like that. Are you the guest?"

"I am."

"I'm sorry about the power. Let me reset the breaker. It should only take a second." She finally got the door open and disappeared inside. Less than a minute later, the porch was awash in sudden illumination from the living room. "Sorry about that," she said, standing just outside. Her features were silhouetted by the light from the door. "Look, my mom would kill me, but I don't think you want to wait for me to come over if this happens again, so I'm just going to leave the lock open for you, okay? Breaker box is to the left—it's the main breaker at the top. You're not going to steal anything, are you?"

"Not really the way I operate," Jake said.

"You don't look like—" The woman leaned forward, peering at Jake. When she was out of the glare of the light, her eyes widened. "I know you," she said. "I know you from—"

"The boat," Jake said. His feet remained up on the railing, and he nodded. "I was on that helicopter. You came and rescued us. I didn't get a chance to thank you." He raised his beer bottle. "Thank you. You saved the pilot's life. Maybe my life too. I'm Jake Moran, by the way."

"I'm Jenny Bean."

"Would you like a beer?"

"Wait a second. You work for the rocket company." She put her hands on her hips. "You're part of launching that thing."

"I don't work for them. I'm a consultant."

"Same difference."

"I'm double-checking their safety procedures," Jake said.

"Well, if you want to keep things safe," Jenny said, her voice starting to rise, "you can stop them from launching that damn thing!" She shook her head. "I have half a mind to kick you out of this house right now."

Jake leaned upright and got to his feet. "Wait," he said. "Don't leave."

"What do you mean don't leave?" They were face to face at the doorway now, and she looked up at Jake, her eyes burning with intensity.

"I mean don't go yet. Let me get something." Jake went to the kitchen and finished off his beer with a long pull. He placed the bottle in the sink and grabbed two new bottles from the fridge. Back on the porch he found Jenny standing in the same place with her arms crossed. Jake offered one of the bottles, but she didn't take it.

"What, you think you're going to get me drunk and change my mind?" she said.

"Not at all," Jake said. "I wanted to give you the opportunity to change mine." Jenny's brows narrowed, and her stance relaxed. "I just want to listen," he said.

Jenny tentatively accepted the beer. "Thank you," she said softly.

"I hope you like ales," Jake said. "I've never had this one before tonight."

"This one's okay," Jenny said, staring at the label. "They brew some other good ones here on the island too."

Jake took a seat on the farthest chair from the door and gestured toward the chair next to him. "Please," he said. "Sit."

Jenny hesitated. "You're just going to tell me I'm wrong."

"Try me."

She came over, slowly, and sat down next to Jake. She leaned forward, almost closed in on herself as if she were chilled, though the night remained comfortably warm.

"This rocket," she began. "This payload. It could be really dangerous." She stopped, as if conditioned for pushback, and waited for Jake to say something. He raised his eyebrows and took a sip of his beer. The lack of confrontation seemed to throw Jenny off script, and she almost stammered as she continued. "There are people, down here, everywhere, in Florida especially . . ." She looked at Jake, and he nodded for her to continue. "It could be so bad. The plutonium, the radiation in there, it's alpha decay—those particles are deadly if they're inhaled or ingested in any way."

"Yes," Jake said.

"Yes?"

"Yes, it would kill you pretty quickly." He took a sip of his beer, and Jenny took a long one of hers. "Go on."

"If it blew up in flight, over South Florida, those particles could be dispersed in a way that could make a lot of people sick. Thousands, even tens of thousands if it blew up in the right location. Do you understand what I'm saying?"

"I do," he said.

"But there's the old oil rig they're launching from. Right out there only thirty miles away. I guess it's personal for me. I grew up here. If the rocket blew up out on that rig, before it even got to take off, and the wind was blowing inshore, it's not impossible to think . . . I've seen computer models, legitimate ones, where particles could make it here. *Here.* People could die. This place could be contaminated. Ruined." She laughed softly. "There are some people who would say it's ruined already. Refineries, hurricanes. All the spring break tourists."

She laughed again, a little more warmly now. "But I love this place. It's my home. For better or worse. If I knew about the risk, if I *believed* there was a risk . . . how could I live with myself if I knew and I didn't do something about it?" She sipped her beer and shook her head. "Do you even understand what I'm trying to say?"

"I do," Jake said.

"Okay, now it's your turn to tell me I'm stupid. Overreacting because it's all fine. This is where you tell me why I'm wrong and there's nothing to worry about and on and on."

"You're not," Jake said. He put his feet up on the rail again and tipped his chair back.

"Pardon me?"

"You're not wrong. There absolutely is risk involved. A lot of it."

Jenny Bean said nothing.

"Launching rockets is a risky business. It's become less risky, but there's always a chance something is going to fail, some fault in the system, or human error. People mess up. Big time. And most of the time, you know, the risk is financial. Satellites are expensive, rockets are expensive, facilities, tracking, support personnel . . . every time something goes up, there are hundreds of millions of dollars at stake. Physical worry? Not much. In nearly sixty years of orbital launches, no person has ever been hurt by orbital debris falling to Earth. It's a big planet we're on, and rockets are relatively small. But something like this? Yeah. There's more risk. Maybe something could go wrong. In Russia, the old Soviet Union, things did go wrong a few times." Jake took a swallow of beer and let his chair go upright. "You're totally right to be worried. And you're totally right to be pointing out the risks."

Jenny laughed, an incredulous bark of a laugh, and shook her head. "I don't understand how you could be working with Kingfisher and talking this way, to be honest."

"I'd be a fool to not consider it. Anyone in this business would be."

"If you know all that," Jenny said, "if you feel that way, how in the world could you let it go on?"

“Well,” Jake said, “If I found out the risk is too great, I’d stop it.”

“You could do that?”

“Sure I could.”

Jenny looked to her side, eyes unfocused as she pondered something. Twice she looked like she was going to talk before stopping herself. Finally she spoke.

“If I could show you proof,” she nearly whispered, “of how bad it could be, would you really stop it from happening?”

“I know a lot about this stuff. But if you showed me something new, data I can consider, I’m always ready to have my mind changed.” Jake was curious, even though he had a feeling this was a ploy to buy time. Jenny seemed sincere, though, genuine, and he wanted to learn what information she had.

“Duncan,” she said. “Duncan got some documents. If I could get them and show you . . .”

“What kind of documents?”

“I can’t tell you yet. I don’t think I’m supposed to even know about them. But let me try. Let me try to get them for you.”

“Where did Duncan get these documents?”

“From a guy. A rude asshole, actually. But Duncan . . .” She suddenly started, and her head snapped upright like she had woken from a daydream. “Duncan. Jesus, Duncan.”

Jenny got to her feet and placed her not-quite-empty bottle on the railing. “I need to go,” she said abruptly. “I’m sorry. Thank you for the beer. Thank you for listening.” She quickly turned and bounded down the steps before mounting her e-bike and riding off into the night with a soft whir.

Huh, Jake thought.

He tipped his chair back again, looked out into the night, and finished his beer.

CHAPTER TWENTY-SIX

The old fishing boat—a worn-down diesel trawler with an equally worn-down, gin-blossomed captain named Oleg—took two days to make it through the Bahamas and across the Gulf Stream to Florida. The waves and engine noise lulled René into a deep, dreamless sleep through the crossing, but sometime in the darkness he woke abruptly. René blinked his eyes open and looked around the cabin. Something had changed—the pitch of the engine, the motion over the waves—and René sat up in his bunk. In the darkness, the luminescent hands on his watch read ten till five in the morning. Anton slept deeply in the bunk across the cabin, his knees folded up toward his chest. René padded up the companionway to the helm, where Oleg sat like a statue, a smoldering cigar clenched in his teeth and bathed in bluish light from the screen of his GPS and radar displays. He indicated René should look forward and off to the left with a jut of his chin.

"Miami," Oleg said. René spun around to see the lights of the city reflected over the black water.

"We're going there?" René asked.

"*Da*," Oleg said. "Well, a little north."

"North? I thought you were taking us to Miami?"

"Look, it's all Miami," Oleg said with a wave of the hand. "But we're going a little farther north. Easier to unload what you've got. No customs, that was the deal. I know it's not drugs. I won't carry drugs. No way. I know you've got gold aboard. I'll get you there."

“Get us where?” René asked, keeping his tone flat. They were essentially hostages now. What could he do about it? He could eliminate the man and take over the boat, but where the hell would he go?

“Near Fort Lauderdale,” Oleg said. “It’s much easier. We were out for a fishing trip, see? Like I said, no customs.”

René kept quiet, staying above on the deck and watching as they drew closer to land. The sky above lightened with the faint blush of dawn, and after another thirty minutes, when they were close enough to the shore that René could hear the hum of morning traffic, Anton dragged himself up the companionway.

“Ah, good morning!” Oleg said. “Can I get you something—”

“Nothing,” Anton said. There was a quaver in his voice, and he looked ghostly pale in the dim morning light. He stepped to the stern, unzipped his pants, and pissed over the rail.

“You want some water?” Oleg asked. “Eggs?”

Anton glowered at the old man as he took a position behind René. Oleg gave up on talking and turned his gaze back to the water. Nothing more was spoken as they headed north, parallel to the shoreline. A police helicopter buzzed overhead, speeding to the south. René flinched at the sight of it, but it passed over them without pausing. After another half hour they approached a buoy marking an inlet, and Oleg slowed the engines and spun the boat’s wheel to enter.

“Welcome to America,” he said.

René did not reply, and neither did Anton. The boat passed under a high bridge, busy with morning commuters, and into a canal lined by massive houses with boats and Jet Skis docked out front. The canal twisted and turned inland, and the farther they got from the Atlantic, the smaller and shabbier the houses and boats became. After twenty minutes and many more turns—Oleg never hesitated, he knew exactly where he was going—many of the houses were not houses at all, but trailers and mobile homes. Frequently the docks were empty, but the few boats that were tied up were sun bleached and worn. One more turn, and Oleg pulled back on the throttles completely, guiding the boat between some gull-stained pilings next to a rusty seawall. A green mobile home with a sagging porch awning and closed storm shutters sat ten meters from the canal.

So, this was the States, he thought. The United States of America. It felt anticlimactic. He looked over his shoulder at Anton, and the two men exchanged a nod as Oleg stiffly made his way forward to secure the boat.

"Now what?" Anton asked.

"Now we wait," Oleg said. He pitched the stub of his cigar in the water and coiled the end of the faded line in his hands before dropping it to the deck. "Your guys are driving here. It could be some time."

They spent the day hiding from the sun beneath the trawler's sagging Bimini sunshade. Oleg, seated at the helm with his ever-present cigar, seemed unbothered by the heat. Anton looked sicklier by the hour, his skin pale and sweaty and his forearms red from continual scratching.

"Hang on, Toni," René said softly. "We'll be out of here soon, and you can look for what you need, okay?"

The kid merely nodded, staring blankly into the distance.

A few minutes before ten o'clock that evening, a black Escalade came to a stop next to the mobile home.

Oleg pointed. "Your guys," he said.

The front doors of the SUV opened, and two men emerged, both in tracksuits. Their movement toward the boat was nearly reptilian, and they stopped at the edge of the seawall. One, wearing aviator glasses, had broad shoulders and a fresh scab on the side of his head, and the other, short and stout, had an angry red, poorly sutured scar running down his cheek from his temple to his chin.

Petr.

"Looks like you cut yourself," René said, rising to his feet. "Maybe too close a shave."

"Fuck you," Petr said. He crossed his arms and spit into the water.

"Too bad you couldn't get the stuff back in Kotor, huh?" René asked, clenching his fists to check his rage. "Were you trying to win points with Vostok by eliminating the middleman?" He stepped up on the rail so he was face to face with Petr. "Vostok and I have a history, you know. I suggest you watch your back."

Petr sneered, the pus oozing from his wound glistening in the mobile home's porch light. "If it wasn't for Vostok looking out for you," he said, "you'd have been a dead man the minute we arrived."

Oleg, still at the helm, looked rattled by the posturing. Anton's pasty face dripped sweat, and his eyes darted back and forth between the men. Behind Petr, the taller man in the tracksuit started to laugh.

"What is this, the fucking circus?" he asked the pair. "This is like watching two dwarves get ready to fight. Will the dancing bear come out next?"

"Who the fuck are you?" René asked. The guy stank of FSB, or GRU.

"I'm your boss now," he said. "I don't give a fuck about how long you and Vostok have been sucking each other's dicks. When you're over *here*, you listen to *me*, understand? Just like this little fuck listens to me."

Petr scowled at this but said nothing.

"And your name?"

"You will call me Strelka." He nodded to the companionway. "The product?"

"It's down below," René said. "Hidden. I'll show you."

"Not you," Strelka said, pointing to Oleg. "Him."

"Sure, fine," Oleg said. René saw the old man's hand shaking as he started toward the cabin. "Let's go. I didn't see any of this. I was never involved."

"Go," Strelka said. "Take Petr there." He nodded to Anton. "And you too."

"He stays topside," René said. Petr stepped aboard, bumping René as he passed.

"The kid will help carry the material," Strelka said.

Oleg stepped through the companionway, supporting himself on the hatch slides as he made his way down with Anton right behind him. Petr followed.

The old man gestured toward the bunks. “It’s all down under these—” Petr silently drew a pistol from the back of his waistband, placed it against the back of Oleg’s head, and pulled the trigger. The sound was oddly soft, like the cracking of a dry twig. Blood sprayed over the bulkhead, and the old man collapsed to the deck.

Anton appeared stunned, unable to understand what had happened in front of him.

“What the fuck?” he managed.

“Calm down,” René said, softly but urgently, dropping down into the cabin. “Anton, lis—”

Petr turned and calmly shot Anton in the neck, and the Dutch kid crumpled in a twisted heap.

René stared at Petr. “You didn’t need to kill him,” he said through clenched teeth. “You could have told me you were going to—”

“He was an addict,” Petr said with a shrug. “You think we didn’t know? A junkie like him would only cause problems.”

“He has connections, family . . . you don’t think killing him is going to cause problems?” René asked. He couldn’t bring himself to look down at Toni’s body, instead glancing out the portlights to see if anyone had noticed the commotion. It was silent along the canal. Strelka, still on the seawall, crossed his arms and grinned.

“He won’t be missed,” Strelka called from above. “Don’t lie to yourself.”

René covered Anton with the same blanket he had slept under the night before.

“But look,” Strelka said, stepping aboard to lean in the companionway, “you two midgets need to make peace so we can all work together. We need your help now, René. Delivery is only part of the deal. Even if I’m the boss in America, you’re lucky to have a powerful friend in Vostok. He says you can help us.” The man grinned again and spit in the cockpit. “He says there’s a man here you need to take out. An American agent. He fucked you up in Africa, yes?”

“Something like that,” René said.

“I’m here to help you with that. Uncle Strelka has come to do what the Romanian gutter trash cannot handle on his own.”

CHAPTER TWENTY-SEVEN

The twenty-seven-foot Boston Whaler, with Kingfisher logos on either side of its hull, skimmed over the surface of the Gulf of Mexico. Up by the helm, Jake Moran shielded his eyes from the morning sun as he stared out toward the hazy blue horizon. To his side, Stu Gallagher, who had arrived the night before after driving his van all the way from Washington State, stood with his arms crossed. Andy Lang was seated on a bench behind, his skin taking on a greenish cast as the Whaler rolled over the Gulf swells.

Jake had interviewed all the controllers from the CommSat launch in the first three days. Everyone had said practically the same thing: the flight seemed too easy, and it felt like a sim. *Too much like a sim,* a couple of the controllers had said; for some of them it had felt oddly unreal. The sentiment was almost always followed by praise for Kingfisher's simulation supervisors for creating training routines that seemed so real they were indistinguishable from an actual launch.

It was impressive. Jake wanted to see how they did it and would visit the simulation crew when he found the time.

A gray, angular form on the horizon seemed to rise from the water as they approached. The object loomed taller and taller still, and Jake had to crane his neck to take it in as the boat drew near. They moved toward one of the platform's four stout pillars from the north, and as they came close Jake saw the words **WARNING—PRIVATE PROPERTY—AUTHORIZED ACCESS ONLY** stenciled at multiple heights and angles. The pilot slowed and approached a steel dock to the side of the pillar, where they were met by a guard in a blue Kingfisher jumpsuit who helped tie off the boat. Jake, Andy, and Stewart stepped up to the dock. Its surface felt so stable it was hard for Jake to believe the giant ex–oil rig was not firmly anchored to the seafloor. The dock was bisected by a painted steel grate acting as a security barrier, behind which were flights of stairs leading many stories up toward the deck of the structure. The guard punched a code into a keypad to open an access gate and beckoned for the three visitors to pass through. The gate latched solidly behind them once they were on the other side.

"Andy," the guard said, giving a half salute.

"Hey, Jerry," Andy said. "Got two new ones today. Stu and Jake, this is Jerry Burke, the mayor of Platform One. You'll both need to show him your badges and sign in."

Jake held out the badge dangling from his neck for Jerry to scan, and Stu did the same. Next to the security station was a bin for their personal electronic devices.

"Need your phones, folks," Jerry said as he handed out hard hats. "Secured facility."

Stu frowned as he handed over a phone from his pocket, and Andy shrugged.

"I don't even bother bringing stuff like that out here anymore," he said. "Cell frequencies and Wi-Fi are jammed out here on the platform anyway, so it's not like there's any point."

Jake drew his Kingfisher-supplied phone from his pocket, leaving his personal phone in place. "I don't think I've even turned this thing on yet," he said as he handed it over to the guard.

After they were signed in, Andy led them to the bottom of the steps. The treads and railings were a freshly painted white and blue. Everything was perfectly clean and well maintained.

"We'll go up to the top and work our way back down," Andy said. "But this is where the barges tie off to when they bring the stages out here for integration. There's a pair of cranes two hundred feet above us that lifts the stages and payload up to the integration shack. Come on, I'll show you." He started up the stairs at a good clip, but Jake paused to let Stu catch up.

"I didn't see StairMaster anywhere in the job description," Stu grumbled.

"You need more cardio, big guy," Jake said.

Andy glanced back at them. "I'll get the shack open. See you up top!" He bounded upward two steps at a time.

"What do you think so far?" Jake asked.

"I think Lang is a weasel."

"I don't mean about Andy. I mean about Kingfisher."

"Impressive, mostly. Hardware installations seem pretty tight. Listen, I'm going to try to hang a few steps back on this tour and get some supplemental documentation."

"What are you talking about?"

"I'm talking about this," Stu said, and he pulled a small digital camera from his pocket. Jake smiled and quickly showed Stu his own cell phone.

"Funny," Jake said, "I was kind of thinking the same thing. You probably have a better idea of what to get pictures of, though."

"You keep that knucklehead occupied, and I'll get the pictures."

"You need to lay off," Jake said. "He's okay. And I need you to engage with him. Just because I used to do this doesn't mean I know everything, especially about how these guys do stuff. Ask lots of questions. Play dumb if you need to. Shouldn't be hard, right?"

"Fuck you, Jacob."

At the landing at the last flight of stairs before the top, they passed a pair of doors with a sign over them reading: **BLAST SHELTER—THESE DOORS TO REMAIN UNLOCKED AT ALL TIMES**.

"Very nice of them to include that out here," Stu said. "I wonder how often they need to use it?"

"If you're running for the blast shelter," Jake told him, "it's probably too late."

They reached the top of the staircase and exited a door out onto a sunlit surface. Immediately before them was a sign that said:

KINGFISHER LAUNCH PLATFORM ONE

HARD HAT AREA. STAY INSIDE YELLOW PERIMETER LINES.

DO NOT ENTER RED PAINTED ZONES.

Below that, the words **NEXT LAUNCH** were followed by a digital display with **T-13D 4H 22M 13S** counting down. Below that, it said **STATIC FIRE 05/22 7:25 TENTATIVE DATE**. Jake looked at his watch. Three days away. At the bottom of the display, it said **PLATFORM WORK STATUS GREEN**.

"Green means all areas of the platform are open for work," Andy's voice called as he approached from behind them. "It goes to yellow when we're within twenty hours of a static fire or launch. That means only tech specialists can be up here in restricted zones. It's pretty much whenever the vehicle is upright on the pad. Anytime within four hours of launch or hot fire is status red, and no one is allowed out here on the platform. That means the tanks up here are charged and the vehicle is ready to be fueled."

"How does the fueling happen?" Jake asked.

"Two tankers come out when we're in status yellow before static fire—"

"I don't want to sound stupid," Stu asked, flashing Jake a wry look, "but tell me again what static fire means?" He pulled a small bound notebook and pen from his pocket and prepared to take notes.

"Not stupid at all," Andy said. "Static fire is a test firing of the rocket's engines. It's our most important test before launch. Anywhere from four days to a couple weeks before the real thing we go through the entire countdown sequence, complete with fueling the vehicle and igniting the engines. We let them go at full thrust for four seconds before shutting down to make sure the team and the vehicle are all working correctly."

"If those engines are going full blast," Stu asked, "how does it not take off?"

"Hold-down bolts," Jake said. "It's literally screwed to the platform with very strong hardware. In a real launch, when the rocket's computer verifies that everything is running smoothly, it sends a command for the bolts to be cut with an explosive charge, and the rocket can lift off."

"It all happens in milliseconds," Andy affirmed with a nod. "If the computer senses anything wrong like failed ignition, bad combustion, maybe too much vibration, it's smart enough to shut the whole thing down before the bolts blow."

"Got it," Stu said, scribbling away in his notebook. "It would be a hell of a mess if those bolts failed during a test, wouldn't it?"

"It would," Jake said. "But they're reliable."

"Anyway," Andy continued, "the tankers come down here, one with liquid methane, and the other with liquid oxygen. They get pumped up into those tanks over there." Andy pointed to two large round tanks, almost like water towers, on the far side of the platform. "They prechill those tanks for a day before we fill them from the boats. We have enough fuel to handle three recycles or long holds in the count, maybe four if it's a smaller payload—"

"I'm sorry again," Stu interrupted. "Recycle?"

"You want to answer, Jake?" Andy asked. "I'm curious to see how much you know about the way we do it here."

"Sure," Jake said. "So, if the countdown is stopped and started over for any reason, that's a recycle. Just a pause where they stop the clock and pick it up again, that's a hold. It can be a technical issue, or maybe some boat or private plane goes into restricted water or airspace and they have to stop the count. If it's a long hold, something that means the countdown has to be restarted at a later time, the fuel can be off-loaded back into the tanks. But you lose some of it to evaporation."

"Any more than four times and we need more fuel," Andy added.

"Four times," Stu murmured, scribbling.

"Come this way," Andy said, walking to their left. "Here's the integration shack."

Ahead of them was a steel building, more like a small warehouse than a shack. On the exterior wall below the Kingfisher logo were the words **HORIZONTAL INTEGRATION FACILITY**. Two tall cranes stood behind the building, and a pair of long steel objects with crisscross girders, looking almost like radio towers laid on their sides, stretched between the building and the edge of the platform.

"That's a strongback," Andy said, pointing to one of the towerlike structures. "It serves as a support backbone for the rocket before liftoff. The stages get hoisted up by crane from their barges and placed on a strongback. They get rolled in and checked out in horizontal position here in the shack before we push them outside and stand them up for static-fire tests and launch out on the pad. The strongback pulls away a minute before ignition. If anything goes wrong and we halt the terminal count, the strongback returns upright and clamps on to the rocket to support everything. We can work on three vehicles at a time if we have a high launch cadence going. One on deck and two in the shack."

Inside, the three of them were dwarfed by a *Kingfisher Seven* resting on its side. A blue-painted strongback supported the rocket from below, and circular hydraulic clamps, like some giant insect's pincers, closed around it at regular intervals. Back where they stood, by the base of the vehicle, the eight-foot-wide mouths of the rocket's seven engine bells were covered by red protective hoods with the words **REMOVE BEFORE FLIGHT** stenciled on them.

A fat black cable emerged from an open access panel at the base of the rocket. Andy walked briskly toward the engines, waving for Stu and Jake to follow.

"You guys need to see this," he said eagerly. "SimSups—"

"*Sim soups*?" Stu asked, raising an eyebrow.

"Simulation supervisors. We call them SimSups for short. See that cable plugged in to the first stage? There's one up at the interstage too. They're hooked up—" Andy stopped himself for Stu's obvious benefit. "Sorry. The interstage is basically a ring connecting the first and second stages of the rocket. Anyway, these cables are hooked up because our SimSups are setting up our first integrated simulations with the flight controllers. Up until now the controllers have been working with computer systems back on land that mimic the vehicle's systems in flight. All fake. And that's how everyone else in the industry simulates a launch. But do you have any idea how we do it, Jake?"

Jake shook his head as his ex-colleague's face cracked into a devious grin. "You do something different?"

"Not just different," Andy said. "More like *groundbreaking*. When we get this close to launch, we start doing training simulations with the *actual flight hardware*, not just simulation software. Are you following me?"

"Go on," Jake said. He was following, but he couldn't believe it.

"We bring the controllers to Platform Two," Andy said, "which is only a few miles south of here. Then we load a flight profile into the vehicle itself. Every single detail: altitude, acceleration, thrust, trajectory, all that stuff is read by the rocket's computer and sent back over the comm link, which has no idea it's not real! To the computer, data is data. It tests everything in the system: communication links, launch systems, the flight hardware itself." Andy gave Jake a friendly punch on the shoulder. "What do you think about that?"

Jake shook his head. This was all news to him, and he had to admit, it was brilliant. "So that's why everyone I've interviewed has told me the simulations seem so real."

"Right!" Andy said, still excited. "Because they practically *are*! The rocket is responding to what it thinks is actual flight telemetry. And the control team is too. Sometimes, when we work an early sim to get everyone warmed up, we'll replay an actual flight profile from a previous mission all the way up to orbit. We even play video from an old launch on the displays. Or if we've had a previous failure, we'll run that through the system and see if the control room crew can catch what went wrong."

"That's amazing," Jake murmured. "Virtual launches. I can't believe no one else has thought of doing it this way."

"I don't understand what's so amazing about it," Stu said.

"The more realistic you can make your practice missions," Jake told him, "the greater your chances at success when the real thing happens. Kingfisher is making it as real as it possibly can without firing up the engines."

"Amazing, right?" Andy said.

"How does a simulation end?" Jake asked. "How does the system know it's over?"

"If communications go blank across channels simultaneously, the rocket is smart enough to assume there's been a failure, so it sends commands for all systems to enter safe mode. Which is basically the default before a launch anyway. Once we confirm everything's been reset, we can start a new simulation. It usually doesn't take us more than fifteen minutes to set one up. I'm telling you, the only difference between a sim and a real launch for us is loading fuel and lighting the candle. Well, we don't arm the flight-termination system either. It wouldn't be so good to have a rocket blow up here on the platform. That said, we get guys from Delta 45 sitting in on training runs too. Space Force loves it. We offer the most realistic training experience there is."

Stu scribbled furiously as Andy spoke, and Jake shook his head.

"In everything I've read and heard about Kingfisher," Jake said, "I don't think I've ever heard anything about this."

"Trade secret," Andy said, shaking his head. "Not *ever* discussed publicly. It gives us an incredible corporate advantage. Sure, it will get out someday and will probably become the norm in the industry. But we want to keep that from happening for as long as we can. And for as incredible as this system is, Jake, you know what amazes me the most?" He winked. "*You* didn't think of it first."

CHAPTER TWENTY-EIGHT

The three men—two Russians and a man with no country—had driven through the night and into the next day, stopping only for fast food and gas. The one called Strelka had taken René's phone before they'd left Oleg's old trawler back near Miami.

"Anything can be traced," Strelka had explained, giving René a smartphone, an older LG with a large screen. "This device is safe. We're going to Houston. Make a shopping list for the things you need; find places in Houston for us to purchase them. Use that phone to search. We'll get your things as soon as we arrive so you can get straight to work."

René said nothing as he took the phone, resentful at being given orders by a GRU grunt. He sat in the back seat as they rolled over the flat landscape, searching online for various shops that might have the equipment they needed. They entered the afternoon rush hour, and Petr cursed at the traffic. It was the first time René had heard the man speak in nearly fifteen hours.

"Where do we go?" Strelka asked from the front passenger seat. "Give me an address so I can navigate us there."

The first place on René's list was a ranch-and-irrigation supply store. He read the location, and Strelka plugged it into his own phone; moments later a female voice began giving directions in Russian. It took nearly half an hour to get across town to the store. After they parked, the two men up front made like they were going to get out of the Escalade.

"Just me," René said. "You both stay here."

"We're coming with you," Strelka said.

"You're both too obvious," René said. "Two bloody-faced, tracksuit Russians in an American farming store? Stay in the car. What, you don't trust me? Ask Vostok if you're worried."

The two men up front looked at each other, then pulled their doors shut.

"You go, then," Strelka said. "Anything funny, and you'll end up like your friend back on the boat."

"Fuck you," René said. Strelka turned and gave a hard stare, but René didn't flinch. "You have money for me to buy these supplies?"

Petr worked through a bag in the front and handed René a thick stack of newly minted hundred-dollar bills bound with a rubber band. René shook his head and laughed.

"You're giving me this shit?" he said incredulously. "Don't you have smaller bills? Older bills? Something a little less obvious?" The two men looked at each other again, saying nothing, and René laughed again. "Whatever, fine. I'll work with this." He unbanded the notes and handed half the stack back. "Crumple them up. Make them look used. Come on, do it." The three men worked in silence for a few minutes wadding and unwadding the bills before René stacked them back together and slipped them in his pocket.

"You should get a less-obvious car," René added as he stepped out to the pavement.

"The car is fine," Strelka called back. "But we are getting another."

"Good!" René shouted. "Because this one has GRU written all over it!"

He slammed the door and crossed the lot. It was true, the black Cadillac stood out harshly against the handful of old pickup trucks in the lot. Inside, René grabbed a shopping cart and worked quickly. He found a shelf with the most important item, low-voltage DC ball valves made of aluminum alloy. He grabbed twenty and threw them into the cart, followed by another five as spares. Then he cruised the aisles, grabbing any tools and fittings he thought he might find useful. On an endcap he found multicolored rolls of tape and added them to the pile. In an aisle by the back, near bulk fertilizers and pesticides, he found protective gear, and he grabbed nitrile gloves, thick chemical-resistant rubber gloves, a pair of full-face respirator masks with organic vapor filters, and a six-pack of Tyvek full-body safety suits. Last he found citrus-based degreaser; four gallon-size bottles went into the cart. The checkout up front was staffed by an indifferent-looking kid; she hardly glanced at René as she rang up his items.

"I'll need two of the ninety-gallon fuel-transfer tanks out front," René said. "The aluminum ones for a truck."

"Uhhh-huh," the girl replied, her eyes glued to her terminal. "You need help loading those up?"

"I can get it."

They had to put one of the back seats down to make room for the diamond-plate tanks in the Escalade, but everything fit just fine. They then drove to two different industrial-supply stores to get the next items on René's list: aluminum pipe fittings in a variety of sizes and two long spools of Teflon-lined hose sheathed in braided aluminum.

"Why so many stops?" Petr asked. "We don't have much time to do our work."

"He can't work without the proper supplies—" Strelka began.

"Everything needs to be aluminum alloy," René explained. "Any other metal could react with the chemicals and explode. Plastics could melt and make a dangerous spill. Don't worry, the rest of the stuff will be easy to find."

Next, they detoured to a used-car lot at a corner in the middle of nowhere. The building was gray and dilapidated and looked like it had been a gas station in the past. Strelka looked back over his shoulder at René.

"I'm getting us another vehicle," he said. "Petr will take you from here. Don't fucking kill each other. I'll see you tonight. I have some work to take care of."

René stayed in the back of the SUV while Petr drove them to an electronics-supply store. Again René went in alone, quickly searching the aisles. He wanted to spend as little time as possible here. The place had too many security cameras, too few customers, and a too-eager staff. He grabbed twelve-volt golf cart batteries, resistors, spools of wire, a soldering iron kit with spare tips, and a dozen personal walkie-talkie radios. He made a second pass through the shop and found stretchy black tape and heat-shrink tubing. Two heavyset boys at the counter angled to ring up the sale. René didn't like the attention, but there was nothing he could do.

"This looks like a big project!" the boy at the register said.

René smiled and nodded, paying and leaving as quickly as he could. In the same strip mall, there was a fitness store; René ducked in and purchased three large tubs of creatine-AKG bodybuilding supplement powder. The muscle-bound man at the register said nothing during the transaction.

Now it was almost seven in the evening, and they went next to a brewing-supply store. René told Petr to join him inside. "I might need help," he said. "They won't notice you here."

Inside at the counter, René asked for ten mini kegs. "Anything you have. It's fine if they're dented, they just need to be very clean inside."

"They're steam cleaned and dried," the man at the counter said. He was older and balding, with a mustache and a ponytail. "You need taps too?"

"Ten taps," René said. "Flat taps. Aluminum, not chrome."

"I think they're aluminum—"

"Check for me," René said. "I need to be sure."

"Says right here on the box. Aluminum alloy."

"Good. I also need ten five-gallon CO_2 pressure tanks."

"Ten of them?"

René nodded. "It's a big party. And give me two extra taps."

The ponytailed man rang up the sale. "Pull your vehicle around back. We'll load you up there."

CHAPTER TWENTY-NINE

After the integration shack, Andy Lang hustled them through the rest of their tour. The platform-operations manager, a jovial Englishman introduced as Robert, appeared at their sides to let them know that a line of thunderstorms was maybe ninety minutes to the east and they probably wanted to plan their return travel to miss the weather. At the launchpad, Stu seemed particularly interested in the sound-suppression water system.

"We dump thousands of gallons of water down the flame aperture at liftoff to minimize the effect of sonic shock waves bouncing back from the platform structure or the surface of the Gulf," Andy said. "Those sound waves could damage sensitive systems on a satellite, so all that water at the time of launch helps muffle things. It also protects the lower part of the platform's structure from the heat of the engines, so there's less for us to repair here between turnarounds. Usually all we need to get ready for a new launch is a freshwater rinse and some new paint."

"You use seawater for the dump?" Jake asked, shielding his eyes with his hand as he looked over the assortment of tanks and insulated pipes around the far edge of the platform.

"We've got all we need all around us," Andy replied. "Pumping it up from below is a lot more economical than bringing a freshwater tanker out here every time. Rinsing things down only takes a few thousand gallons versus sixty K and a shitload of diesel."

On the far edge of the platform was a large tank for the rocket's methane fuel, along with its refrigeration equipment.

"By supercooling the propellants," Andy explained as Stu took more notes, "we can increase the fuel density by about seven percent. The extra fuel gives us greater payload capacity to orbit and better margins for landing the rockets downrange on our landing platform."

"Does it land on another oil rig?" Stu asked.

"We considered that, but our landing software is accurate enough now that we can land on a barge. Practically a postage stamp. It's nice to have some flexibility where we can place it, too, based on fuel requirements for the mission. It gets towed out there by a tug, waits on station, and after landing, most of the time we can bring it right back here to refurbish. Once in a while we send stages back to the mainland for heavier repairs, but that's only about every ten launches. We like to do a deep inspection of the engines then anyway."

"And that reusability," Stu said, not looking up from his notepad, "is the main reason Kingfisher has become so dominant in the industry, right?"

"It's made us nearly forty percent less expensive than our legacy competitors," Andy said, grinning proudly. "We're even cheaper than SpaceX these days. So the economy we provide, plus our reliability, makes us pretty much a no-brainer for someone looking for a launch service to low earth orbit."

"And the rocket that blew up a week ago?" Stu asked. "How does that affect reliability?" He stopped writing and crossed his arms.

"Rockets fail," Andy said. "Every once in a while, they fail spectacularly. Right, Jake?"

"Anyone who tells you otherwise is full of it," Jake agreed.

Robert appeared at their sides again, tapping the face of his watch with his index finger. "There's a ferry leaving for Platform Two in fifteen minutes," he said. "If you don't make that one, you're going to be stuck on the worker boat at four thirty."

"We'll be on it," Andy assured him. "I'm going to show them the data room; then we'll be down at the dock." He waved them forward again. "Sorry about the rush, but you heard the man," he said with a shrug. "You guys can get back out here if you need to, but the server closet isn't anything too special."

He pulled a key chain from his pocket and worked at a lock on the door to a shedlike steel building at the far corner of the platform. To the side of the shed was an industrial air-conditioning unit and a backup generator with a red, eighty-gallon diesel tank next to it. Above it was a steel tower with two large dishes, one pointed to the southwest, and the other back north toward the mainland. Beyond the dishes, the sky had grown dark, and the surface of the Gulf was ruffled with whitecaps.

"We have point-to-point data links from here to a station at Freeport, west of Galveston, and another to the launch-control platform. Encrypted, frequency hopping in the seven-hundred-megahertz spectrum. Still capable of high bandwidth, but at much longer distances than something like your home Wi-Fi. Because the other platform is only a few miles away, that link tends to be super solid. Thirty miles back to shore can be a little more dicey. That's a backup for relaying telemetry, not control for the vehicle." He finally got the door open and let out a little whoop. "I'll show you this—then we'll be out of here." They were met by a blast of cold air as they stepped inside. "We keep this room at fifty-five degrees for the electronics," he explained.

In the center of the small space, Jake saw a tidy server rack with computers and networking equipment mounted in it, all cables neatly bundled and labeled. A shout from Robert came from outside the open room.

"Andy Lang, your ride is leaving in six minutes!"

"Guys, I'm sorry, but we need to get down to the dock," Andy said. He stepped out, shouting "Coming! Don't let that boat leave without us!" Jake exited the room after them and turned back to see Stu block the door from closing with his foot.

"Go with Lang," Stu whispered as he pulled the camera from his pocket. "Make a distraction. Don't let the boat leave without me."

That evening, after a boat ride to Platform Two and a trip in a helicopter back to the mainland, Jake headed to the bare office they'd given him in Clear Lake and finally began to set up his workspace to begin processing some of the information he'd collected over the past few days. He booted up the laptop they'd given him back on his first day and watched it sit for a long time doing seemingly nothing. Jake wondered if the machine was even on, but he heard the gentle whirring of the machine's fan as it powered up, and when he looked closely at the side, he saw an amber hard drive light flickering with activity. He waited about half a minute for a log-in screen, then entered the temporary username and password he'd been given before the machine seemed to freeze once more.

After thirty seconds of waiting for something to happen, Jake turned his attention to his phone and scrolled through his contacts to Denny Wade's number. He tapped to call, and Wade picked up on the second ring.

"Hey, Jake," Wade said, "you got an ID on my visitor yet?"

"Still waiting. My guy is pulling some strings to check with the feds. How are things on your end?"

"Quiet. Mostly. I've been getting a few calls from numbers I don't know. Not picking up, though. I don't want to give anyone an opportunity to triangulate my position."

"Good man. Maybe think about getting a burner phone if you can?"

"Already done. I've told my wife and brother-in-law to be on the lookout, too, but so far it seems like no one's digging too deep. My daughter's at college, and same deal for her."

"Good," Jake said, impressed by Wade's sense of operational security. "You act like you have some experience."

"I might have a little."

"Anything that might come back to bite you in the ass?"

"Like I told you, man, I'm clean."

"Plus, you can't talk about it."

"I can't. I suspect you got things you can't talk about either."

"Your suspicion would be correct. Listen, when this shit clears up, I'll buy you a beer and we can see if we've got any overlap in the shit we're not supposed to talk about."

"I'd consider that. You're on for the beer, at least."

"Keep me posted if anything changes."

"Right on. You do the same. We'll be in touch."

By the time Jake ended the call, the laptop showed a window requiring that he change his password. Jake did so, sending the laptop into another long churn. If the thing was this slow all the time, Jake thought, he wouldn't get to look at many files at all. Shouldn't a company with Kingfisher's resources be able to supply people with faster laptops?

While he waited, Jake opened his personal laptop and searched Google for his fellow chopper passenger, Masahiro Taka. Toward the top of the results was a link to a company called Incremental Systems Incorporated, with offices in Tokyo, Los Angeles, and Houston. A biographical link for Taka was below. Jake clicked through to learn that the company had worked on several different communication-satellite platforms that he was familiar with, though none he'd worked with directly. The lost CommSat mission was a new footnote in their corporate history.

On the "Staff" page was a bio for Dr. Masahiro Taka, director of operations and chief engineer. Born in Osaka and educated in Tokyo and at Caltech, Taka specialized in high-bandwidth communication systems to moving targets on the ground, like planes and ships. Jake scrolled down and found a contact link and entered the number in his phone. An autoattendant system picked up, and when Jake made his way to an operator, he was immediately transferred when he asked for Dr. Taka. After a moment, a woman's voice came on the line.

"I'm sorry, we have no comment at this time," she said.

"I'm not looking for a comment, I'm trying to get in touch with Dr. Taka," Jake replied. "I think I got transferred to the wrong extension."

"You can't speak to him," the woman said.

"May I ask why not?"

The woman on the other end of the call sighed and possibly sniffled. "Because Dr. Taka was killed in a car accident two hours ago. I'm very sorry if this is the first you heard. And I'm sorry that I'm not able to tell you anything else. We'll be releasing a statement shortly. Hello?"

Jake said nothing.

"I'm sorry, are you there?"

In front of him, the laptop screen continued to flicker.

CHAPTER THIRTY

In the dark room where he'd been kept, Duncan lost track of any sense of time. How long had he been here? Days? A week? His captors were cruel, experts in sadism, keeping music playing, bringing his meals at odd times, giving him a smack on the face when he least expected it. And a slap to the back of the head where he'd been hit by the pistol—that was the worst. At first he'd kept himself from crying out; he didn't want to give them any sort of satisfaction or let them believe they'd broken his spirit. After days of the abuse, though, days of no sleep, days of pissing and shitting in a bucket, Duncan would wail at the blow, weep, slump in the chair against his restraints, and beg for mercy.

"She has not seen it," the one named Strelka would say, grabbing Duncan by the hair to force him to look up. "Why has she not seen it?"

"I don't know. I don't know!" he'd sob. "Please, why are you doing this to me?"

"Help me understand why your mother has not seen the USB we gave you. Why are you lying to us?"

"I swear to God, I showed her—I did!"

Sometimes Strelka would rise up to his full height, twist his body, and strike Duncan across the face with the back of his hand. There was nothing he could do to brace himself or get out of the way; sometimes the crunching of the broken bones in his face made him vomit. Strelka would shake his head with disgust.

"Why has Helena Nash not seen it?"

"I told you I don't know!"

"For your health, mama's boy," Strelka would say with a sneer, "you had better pray she looks soon."

Duncan's head sagged, the music was turned up louder, and time became meaningless once more. They hadn't checked on him for days, it seemed. Sometimes he saw his mother. And sometimes, through the fog and noise . . . was that his father? Could he even remember the man's face? It had been so long.

Suddenly there was silence.

It took Duncan some time to realize the music had ceased. The lights came on in the room. He lifted his head and blinked his eyes open to see one of his captors, the short one with the scar down his face, standing before him. The man held a water bottle in front of him. The other one, Strelka, stood to the side of Duncan's chair, grasping a knife in his hand.

"Don't kill me," Duncan rasped through his broken teeth and chapped, bloodied lips. "Please don't kill me."

"Kill you?" the short one said, snickering. "We are not here to kill you."

Duncan felt a strong hand on his wrist, and the zip tie that bound his right arm to the chair was severed. An instant later his left hand was freed as well.

"Please don't kill me," he repeated.

"We can't kill you. We need you." Strelka crouched to cut away the zip ties binding Duncan's ankles. "You are useful to us."

"Useful? What?" Duncan's head lolled about, and he closed his eyes.

The shorter man grabbed him by the hair and put the water bottle to his lips.

"Drink, mama's boy. Drink!"

Duncan tried to swallow, but water ran from the corners of his mouth down his filthy shirt. "I need a doctor," he said. "I need to see a doctor."

"We take good care of you," Strelka said. The two men had a good laugh at that.

"A little rest, and you'll feel much better, mama's boy."

"But why? Why are you doing this to me?"

Strelka took Duncan by the chin and tilted his head upward. The Russian's eyes were black, and his teeth flashed as he grinned.

"Oh, don't you know?" he said. "You were right. We should have believed you all along."

"What are you talking about?"

"Your mother," the Russian said, spreading his arms expansively, almost jovially. "We have confirmation. She has seen the documents!"

CHAPTER THIRTY-ONE

"What's to say the guy didn't have an accident?" Stu asked over his beer later that night. He and Jake were seated upstairs at a Galveston bar just across the main road from the beach. "I checked the cops' communications, witness statements, the driver of the other vehicle," he went on. "This was a normal car crash, Jake. He ran a red light while he was texting and got T-boned. The phone was there, active messages, the whole thing. No cloak and dagger. Dr. Taka was an idiot."

Jake knew if anyone was going to find a whiff of something fishy in a situation, it was Stu, but he couldn't let go of the feeling that there was more to the story. He opened his mouth to speak, but Stu waved his hand and cut him off.

"I know what you're about to say. But I looked into your guy Wade—"

"You did?"

"I did. No reason to doubt he's a great human being. I do have reason to doubt that his past is as lily white as you're thinking, though. He was in Iraq, yes. Afghanistan too. You know what he did after his stint in the marines was up?"

"He became a corporate pilot, I'm pretty sure."

"Correct. He was corporate, all right. But not back here in the States. He stayed over there. There's no record of who he worked with, but listen to this: in the marines, he got 3,277 hours of flight time, mostly in Sikorsky CH-53E Super Stallion helicopters. That's all public record. But on his next stateside job application—"

"Stewart," Jake said, "how do you even get this stuff?"

"It's a lot easier than you think. Anyway, on his next job application, he lists the marines as his last gig, but suddenly in his flight log, he's got more than five thousand hours in the cockpit. He lists the Super Stallion again along with some other heavy-lift birds, but also he's got experience in a Russian Mi-17 chopper. You know who used to fly Mi-17s in the Middle East?" He didn't wait for Jake to answer. "The CIA, that's who. They had a deal to lease Russian hardware. Easy deniability. I don't think he'd get hours like that unless he was flying for Uncle Sam."

"I'll be damned," Jake said.

"So sure, Wade's visitor could have been there because of some work he was doing for the Company. Possible, yes?"

"Possible, sure," Jake said. "But I'm not closing my mind off to anything."

"And you shouldn't! Because your Russian in the Escalade, if it's him, has some interesting connections."

"Russian? Did you get a match?"

"Possible match. We kept getting hits on a guy named Gavril Strelnikov. Major in the intelligence services."

"FSB?"

"Not FSB. GRU. Military intel. In fact, he managed to piss off some FSB big shot during a Fancy Bear turf war a few years back when they had their fingers in our election. But—and I say this assuming we've identified the right guy, and I think we have—this Strelnikov guy is tight with a gentleman named Sergey Romanov. That name ring a bell with you?"

"Holy shit," Jake said.

Of course it rang a bell; Romanov was an executive at Energia, the Russian rocket and missile manufacturer. Jake had even met him once at a dinner following a European Space Agency technical summit in Germany. "So what's their connection?"

"Nothing solid. Just moving in the same orbit. See what I did there? But if you look at Strelnikov's patterns of travel over the past few years, you can begin to make some guesses."

"Guesses like . . . ?"

"Well, if you knew someone who had connections with Russia's biggest missile factory, and you saw he was making multiple trips to Pyongyang to meet up with guys close to the Kim regime, what might that lead you to believe?"

"Jesus Christ, Stu."

"Jesus Christ, indeed."

"Where else has he been?"

"Tehran, Lagos, Dubai, among other places. Oh, and some trips to North Africa in the past year. Mali, specifically. Isn't *that* the damnedest thing?"

Jake leaned back in his chair and laced his fingers behind his head. Stu drained his beer and glanced toward the bar.

"Tam gets in tomorrow, correct?"

"That's what she told me."

"That reminds me: I'm supposed to tell you she's getting a car, so you don't need to pick her up at the airport." Stu grinned.

Jake nodded, ignoring him. "So, tomorrow. What's our plan?"

"I say we hunker down in that office they gave you and start combing through our data. We got a ton of photos, but there might be some supplemental stuff I'll need."

"You see anything in the pictures you took of the server closets?"

"Nothing stands out to me, but I'm going to have a couple of my guys look too. Don't worry, they don't know what they're looking at. I blurred all the equipment stickers. I just want some fresh eyes on it. Anything turns up, I'll let you know ASAP. Meanwhile, maybe you can track down as many schematics as possible for me tomorrow. I think it's most productive for you to do the asking while I hang out in the shadows."

"Agreed," Jake said. "I'll dig up what I can."

They ordered another round, and Jake excused himself to run outside to make a call.

Sergey Romanov was a name Jake hadn't thought of in a long time. With the ascendance of private launch operators like Kingfisher and SpaceX, Russia's launch industry—dogged by corruption at all levels—had been damaged more than other state-sanctioned providers. Romanov had faded into irrelevance in the industry along with the Energia corporation. The guy was a snake oil salesman, a nothing, had never garnered favor with Putin or even the lower tiers of his regime. The last Jake had heard, he was doing time in the Donbas, selling stolen junk parts to paramilitary groups for pennies on the ruble.

Jake pulled out his personal phone, scrolled through his contacts, and placed a call to Denny Wade. Wade picked up on the second ring.

"Jake Moran," he said, deep and soft, like he didn't want to be overheard by someone nearby. "You got something for me?"

"Depends," Jake said tersely. "If you know anything about operational security, and I suspect you do, you'll know the right way to ask for it."

Without another word, Jake terminated the connection. Three minutes later, he received a text containing a DC phone number and the words:

SIGNAL APP. TOMORROW PM. USE A CLEAN DEVICE.

CHAPTER THIRTY-TWO

Jake and Stewart spent the next day working with a silent efficiency the two had honed over years of shared operations. A whiteboard was delivered to the office, and while Stu began to sketch the layout of Kingfisher's network, Jake got a new laptop from Sandip, who apologized profusely for the trouble, then visited staffers to fill in any remaining gaps in their understanding. Late in the afternoon, after a bout of rapid typing, Stewart froze, staring at his screen with a puzzled look on his face.

"You see something?" Jake asked.

"Not . . . no," Stu said. He shook his head, pushed up his glasses, and blinked like he was waking from a dream. "Ghosts. Weird data. I got halfway through the Mali reports, and it crapped out. It's nothing."

"You've been looking at a screen too long, old man," Jake said. "Let's wrap it up for the day. Tam's getting in—we can make dinner and plan our next steps."

"You go," Stu said. "I need to finish writing this monitoring script. I won't be far behind."

"That's what you always say."

The drive back to Galveston Island was uneventful. Jake checked behind him repeatedly, getting no sense that he was being tailed. He took an exit halfway to the island to be sure, pausing at a gas station to check for any unusual traffic that followed. Nothing.

The neighborhood was quiet when he parked in front of his rental. No traffic on the street, a pleasant warmth in the air. Humid, but not unbearably so, with puffy cumulus clouds high in a perfectly blue sky. Inside the house, Jake ran upstairs, pulled his go bag from the closet, and took out a never-used Android burner phone. The device's stock operating system had been overwritten by a hacked version developed in house by Stu's team with an encrypted file system and secure messaging apps. Jake booted up the phone, opened the Signal app, and composed a message to the DC number Wade had sent him the day before.

"Does anyone else have this contact?" he wrote.

Almost immediately the phone buzzed with a reply. "No one." A moment later, the app chimed with an incoming voice call.

"Yes?" Jake said.

"Jake Moran." It was Wade. "What was I wearing the day we met?"

"Flight suit. Ball cap. Aviator glasses. What mission did I support?"

"Phantom Freedom."

There was no preset code by which the two men could establish their bona fides; this limited questioning would have to do.

"You were an operator," Jake said. "You've been holding out on me."

"Not entirely true," Wade said. "I was a contractor."

"For the Company."

Wade said nothing; Jake took this as a yes.

"Anybody mad at you?" Jake asked. "Someone who might hold a grudge?"

"Like I told you, no. I wasn't holding out on you about that either. I kept my nose clean. I was just a deliveryman, you know?"

"Black sites?"

Wade paused. "Maybe. I tried not to see anything. And when I did see things, I tried not to think too much about it. Or ask any questions."

"You ever run into any Russians over there?" Jake asked.

"Wait up, wait up. It's my turn to ask some questions. You did some work for the Company too. Am I right?"

"Early on," Jake said. "I spent some time on the ground. There were some operators. Not too long for me. I had some contacts in the Company later. Sometimes they wanted backup on what they thought they knew. Probably for ops guys like you running on the ground."

"We probably worked more closely than we knew."

"It's possible," Jake said. He peered out the upstairs window at a car that seemed to be going unusually slowly down the street; when it came close, he saw an elderly man at the wheel. False alarm. "Anything weird going on for you? You worried for your safety?"

"I am at a secure location," Wade said. "My wife is in another. I did tell her what's going on—"

"You trust her?"

"Completely."

"How's your daughter?"

"I have someone keeping an eye on her at school."

"You feel okay with that?"

"I do. What about you? Anything off?"

"Plenty. I got some news today. Looks like our intruder is ex–Russian intelligence. GRU, not FSB. You cross paths with any of those guys when you were consulting?"

There was a long pause.

"I worked with a few of them, mostly because we were leasing their choppers. They all said they were mechanics, but obviously some of those dudes were higher up. I kept my mouth shut. Zero fraternization. Shit was tense. Tell me more about this guy. You got a name?"

"Strelnikov. Gavril Strelnikov. That ring a bell?"

"Nope," Wade said. "You say he's ex-intelligence, but what's his deal now?"

"Ex-GRU. Here's the thing: if this is our guy, he's been tight with a former bigwig with access to Russian missile technology. Energia. Remember those fuckers?"

Wade said nothing for a moment, then let out a low whistle. "Corporate espionage, you think?"

"Seems a little heavy handed to me for just lifting trade secrets," Jake said.

"You have a point."

"One more thing. Maybe a coincidence, maybe not. The guy in the chopper who helped you out with your leg—"

"Dr. Taka."

"Right. Dead. Car crash, yesterday."

There was a long silence.

"You're not shitting me," Wade finally said. "But I sure wish you were."

"One of my guys looked into it and is convinced it was an accident. I'm not so certain. GRU operatives are pretty good at making people disappear in natural-looking ways."

Wade was silent for another moment. "Jesus Christ. I owe that guy my life."

"If keeping out of sight seemed important before—"

"I get you, man, I get you."

"So here's the question," Jake said. "Let's say it wasn't an accident with Dr. Taka. Let's say they wanted to get rid of you too. What do the two of you have in common?"

"Nothing. Zero. I was just giving him a lift. First time I met him was that morning in the ready room at the helipad in Clear Lake City, on the flight out. He was getting a briefing before we left the mainland—"

"What kind of briefing?"

"Personal safety," Wade said. "Even though he had nothing to do with HiPEP-D, he was starting to get some heat from protesters."

"Who did the briefing?"

"Who else? Mrs. Nash herself."

"Seriously? What did she say? I need you to remember everything, Wade. Who else was there?"

"It was about security. Her, Taka, me, and another support guy."

"Tell me about the other person. You know the name?"

"Nah, just like Taka, it was the first time I met the dude."

"How did you know he was support?"

"He was wearing the blue polo. Visiting scientists always wear ties. Taka had a coat and tie, remember? The A-Team at Kingfisher, scientists, engineers, all that? They wear whatever they want. Now, support staff? Guys like me? Welcome to the baby blue polo. Or flight suit, depending on the day. This guy was support all the way."

"What did he look like?"

"I don't know, thirtysomething white guy. Maybe forty. Dark hair. Not scrawny like a nerd. Little edgy. Maybe custodial. Maybe shop crew. Easy enough to find his name, just check the passenger manifest that day. Everybody signs in."

"I'll do that," Jake said. "Did Helena say anything to the guy?"

"Maybe hello, but that was it. She was focused on Taka. She wanted to give him a bodyguard to follow him around because of the way the protests were heating up. I thought it seemed a little excessive, you know? Like, scientists versus environmentalists and you need to put a body man on the guy? Taka laughed it off. Guess he should have taken the offer a little more seriously."

Jake paced the room in thought. "Anything else? She say anything to you?"

"Just that they were expecting a bunch of boats, and I should be happy I was in the air that day and not down on the water."

"Shit, Wade, there has to be something else. Something we're missing here."

"I told you everything I remember."

"All right. Listen, if anything else pops into your brain—"

"I've got your Signal."

"Take care of yourself, Wade."

"You do the same, man."

Jake leaned against the desk for a moment, lost in thought with his arms crossed and the phone in his right hand. He shook his head, powered down the phone, and popped out the battery and SIM card before putting it back into his gear bag.

He pulled his running clothes from the dresser, quickly changed, and grabbed a long drink of water in the kitchen before he bounded out the front door and down the porch steps, hitting the street at a run. He sprinted hard, as hard as he could, trying to clear his head. He went out just a little more than a mile and slowed his pace before turning around and hitting a full-on sprint pace on the way back. The sky to the west had darkened with an approaching squall line, and the air smelled heavy with rain. Far-off thunder rumbled in the air, and when he reached Thirty-Seventh Street, he slowed to a cooldown jog back to his rental.

With the rental in sight, Jake eased into a walk and pressed the stop button on his GPS watch. A flicker of lightning sparked over the rooftops along the street. He checked the stats of his workout as he made his way up the porch steps, stopped by a sniffling sound as he reached for the door. Jake spun to his right to see Jennifer Bean seated on one of the deck chairs, her legs drawn up and arms wrapped around her knees.

"Are you trying to get me back for startling you the other night?" Jake asked. "If so, it almost worked."

Jenny shook her head, and Jake saw that her eyes were red and cheeks wet with tears.

"Hey," Jake said. He came over, crouched in front of her, and touched his hand to her elbow. "What's wrong?" She shook her head again. "Do you want to tell me what's wrong?"

"It's Duncan," she said, straightening up and wiping her eyes with the back of her wrist. She sniffed again. "Something's happened to him."

Jake immediately thought of the "something" that had happened to Taka but kept his expression neutral.

"What makes you say that?"

"He's . . . he hasn't answered my calls for a long time. After I saw you, I tried to get in touch with him. I wanted to show you . . . the stuff he got, the . . . those documents . . ." She began crying again, and she covered her face with her hands. "I was mad at him, before," she sobbed.

"But he's not answering, and I think something bad has happened. It's not like him . . . his car was left in Clear Lake."

A chill went through Jake's body, magnified by his damp running clothes. He stood up and touched Jennifer's shoulder. "Hang on," he said. "I'll be right back." He went inside, ran upstairs, and threw on a sweatshirt. Back downstairs he grabbed a box of tissues from the bathroom and got two glasses of water from the kitchen before returning to the front porch. The sky was darker now, and the trees on the street shook in a gust of wind.

"Hey," Jake said, holding out the tissue box. Jenny took one, then another and another after that, and wiped her eyes and nose before clutching the wadded tissues in her hand. "Maybe have some water," he said, offering a glass.

"I'm okay."

"It's here if you need it," Jake said, setting it on the porch next to her. "Can you tell me everything? I want to help, but I need to know everything." Jenny nodded rapidly and wiped her eyes again. "How long has he been gone?"

"Four days. I was mad. I told him I didn't want him staying here—"

"Staying here on Galveston Island you mean?" Jake asked, and Jenny nodded. "You two are a couple?"

Jenny shrugged. "It's complicated."

"It always is." Jake thought briefly of Tamara. "Why were you mad at him?"

"The guy who came. He had something he wanted to show Duncan, the documents. Just him, not me. He was creepy, like, a foreign lawyer—"

"Foreign?" Jake asked.

"He had an accent."

"Russian accent?"

"Maybe. I'm not sure."

Jake unzipped the pocket of his running shorts and took out his phone. He unlocked it and quickly scrolled through his photos, stopping at the pictures he'd taken of the guy from Wade's room at the hospital.

"I know it's hard to see," Jake said, zooming in on one and angling the phone's screen toward Jenny, "but does this look like the guy?"

Her eyes widened. "That's him! He just sat there and looked at me. That's his car too. It was parked right out front."

"You're sure?"

"One hundred percent. He just sat there and stared."

"So he came to see Duncan. Where was this?"

"Our office, it's right down on Broadway. Duncan couldn't meet with him right away—he was doing a remote for cable news." Jake nodded. He'd seen it. "After, he went in and talked with him. They left me out of it, and I was steaming. I was so mad I left." A plunking sound began out on the street behind Jake—raindrops hitting parked cars. "Later Duncan came over to my house. He was all excited. He said they had proof that radiothermal generators were super dangerous. The Russian had given him files. And a bunch of money too."

"What kind of proof? Did you see?"

Jenny shook her head. "He had it on a USB stick. Said he wasn't allowed to look until he showed it to his mom—"

"Shit," Jake said. He stood up straight and paced down to the end of the porch and back. He leaned his left shoulder against the corner post and watched across the street. The rain picked up for a moment, heavy with a gust of wind before easing off. The sky flashed, and the sound of thunder came sooner.

"What?" Jenny asked.

"It's a Trojan horse," he told her. "A virus on that USB. They were using Duncan to get it into Kingfisher to hack their network."

"I *knew* that guy was using him for something! He gave him so much money, like fifty thousand dollars, and he was going to give him a ton more if he could prove he showed the stuff to his mom. Even after he left Galveston, I was texting with him, trying to get him not to go. Then he just stopped texting back. I knew something was wrong with it; I asked him if he didn't think something was fishy, too, but Duncan, sometimes I feel like . . ." Jenny's chin began to tremble. "Sometimes I feel like he's not motivated by the right stuff. He's got a big heart, he really does, but he's always had money. That's his life, money, he's always been famous, had this famous mom . . . I didn't have anything, you know? When I was little, we didn't have squat. He's got everything, and all I've got is . . . Galveston."

"Galveston's a lot," Jake assured her.

"You think so?"

"If you love it, isn't that enough?"

Jenny was quiet. She pulled her feet up onto the chair, wrapped her arms around her legs, and rested her chin on her knee. "I do love it," she sighed. "I thought I loved Duncan too. But I always knew . . ." Her voice trailed off, and Jake didn't press. The rain fell hard and steady in the street, and it ran in a muddy rush next to the sidewalk out front. "I always knew it would never work out," she said softly. "It was easier to keep going, though."

"I understand," Jake said.

"Do you?"

"Yep," he said, hoping she'd let it go.

"I know there's not a future for us," Jenny said. "But I still care about him. And now . . . I'm so worried. I'm *terrified.* Do you know . . . the foreign guy?"

"I know enough to tell you he isn't a lawyer," Jake said. "He's a Russian ex–intelligence agent. A real bad guy. This isn't easy to say, and it won't be easy for you to hear, but Duncan could be in serious trouble."

Jenny bit her lip, working hard to keep her composure. She started to cry, the sound faint in the passing storm.

"I should have never let him in! I knew he was a fraud the moment I saw him. I knew it!" She looked down so her forehead rested on her knees, and her body shook with sobbing.

Jake crouched down again and rubbed her shoulder. "Hey," he said. "Jenny. Listen to me. Listen, okay? Look at me." She lifted her head, blinked, and then sniffed. "I need you to listen. If you want me to help, I need you to listen. You said something about Duncan's car. What happened with that?"

"They found it over in Clear Lake City. A couple miles from his mom's complex. Parked, unlocked. His phone was in there; he's never ever without his phone. He had business cards in there, too—that's how the police knew to call me before they towed it."

"Do the police know he hasn't come back? Have you filed a missing person report or anything?"

Jenny shook her head. "No," she said. "I've spent all this time trying to make myself believe nothing was wrong. I wanted to believe he wasn't calling back because I was mad at him. But when they called about the car this morning . . . that car is his baby. He never leaves it unlocked either. I knew something had to be wrong."

"Okay. You're going to be okay. Listen, those Russian guys don't mess around. If he found Duncan, he can probably find you. I don't want you staying at your house, okay?"

"I could stay at the office," Jenny said. "There's a bedroom and kitchen there—"

"No, that's just as bad. It's the first place he'll look. Who owns this place?"

"It's my dad's, but my mom's name is on the deed. My dad's been dead for a long time."

"Same last name as you?"

"Her maiden name is on the deed. They'd been apart for a while when she got the house back. So, no."

"Okay," Jake said. "I've got two other people down here, too, people who can help keep you safe. I trust them, and you should too."

"Is it really that serious?"

"It really is. We can go to your place so you can pick up some things if you need them, but we're going to have to get out of here for a while."

Jenny stood up and turned like she was walking to the porch steps; then she put her hands on her head and spun back toward Jake. "Is he going to kill Duncan?"

"He's the kind of person who could," Jake said. He wanted to be honest with her. "But if I have anything to say about it, he won't."

The rain was easing, but Jenny broke down completely and staggered forward into Jake's arms.

"I shouldn't have let him in," she wailed, burying her face into Jake's shoulder.

"Hey," said Jake. "Shh. It's not your fault. It's not. He would have gotten to Duncan anyway. At least you saw the man. That's helpful. We're going to do our best to help Duncan, okay?"

Jenny looked up at him but said nothing. A car sprayed water from a puddle as it passed through the ending storm. Finally, she pulled away.

"One question," Jake said. "Why did you come to me? Why here and not the police or anyone else?"

Jenny sniffed again and blinked, and the way she looked up into Jake's eyes was piercing. "Because you're the only one who listened."

CHAPTER THIRTY-THREE

The heavy rain ran in sheets over the windshield of Tam's rental Volkswagen despite having the wipers on at the highest speed. The windows were fogging, too, and she put the defrost on at full blast to try to improve her view. The taillights of the cars ahead looked like red smears through the rain. As she headed south from Houston's Bush Intercontinental Airport, the storm had come on fast, rising up over the flat Texas landscape like a wall of blue cloud. Tam peered forward as she tapped the brakes, then glanced down at the Google Maps navigation on her phone.

In half a mile, keep left on Interstate 45 . . .

She came off the interstate onto the surface streets of Galveston Island, and the rain pounded the roof of the car. It seemed almost biblical, the way it fell in torrents. What must it be like in a hurricane? she wondered. It would be an amazing thing to see. Not this time of year, no way, but maybe someday.

In a quarter mile, turn right on Thirty-Seventh Street . . .

The rain eased, and Tam flicked her windshield wipers to low speed as she made the turn.

Your destination is on the right . . .

Tam slowed and leaned to her right to try to see the rental house's number. On the porch she saw—*is that Jake?*—a man and woman embracing. Not a fleeting embrace either; a deep, caring, rocking-from-side-to-side sort of clinch. The man tenderly held his hand to the back of the woman's head and whispered something in her ear.

Tam pulled into the closest parking space, jumped out of the car, and walked through the rain and up the steps of the house.

"Hey!" she said. "I didn't know you'd have company."

The two separated quickly. Jake peered into the rainy gloom.

"Who are you?" the woman asked, startled.

"Tam," Jake said. "This is Jennifer Bean."

"Hi, Jennifer Bean."

Tam schooled her face into something near neutrality.

Jake's expression went from confusion, to aggravation, to something like exasperation, making Tam wonder if she'd misread the situation.

"Jenny," Jake told Tam, "is not only the owner of our rental, she's also the founder of the Greater Gulf Defense Fund."

"From . . . the protest?"

"Yes. The protest," Jake said. He stepped forward and gently took Tam by the arm, bringing her closer. "Jenny, this is Tamara Rinaldi, my business partner."

"Pleased to meet you," Jenny said, offering her hand and looking as confused as Jake had.

"I told you about Jenny's partner, Duncan."

"Helena Nash's son."

"Correct. Jenny's just told me that he's been kidnapped."

"Kidnapped?" Tam repeated, as she started to understand the seriousness of the situation.

"Yes, kidnapped," Jenny said, covering her face with her hands as she let out a heaving sob.

"Kidnapped," Tam said. "Do you know who—"

"I do know who," Jake told her. "GRU. Bad news."

"Oh, shit," Tam said. She looked to the crying woman, then to Jake. She opened her mouth, wanting to apologize, but not knowing how to express it. Jake seemed to understand. He raised his hand and shook his head as if to let her know nothing needed to be said. Tam stepped close to Jenny and wrapped her arm around the petite woman's shoulders.

"Jake said you own this place?"

"My mom owns it," she said, dropping her hands. "I help the renters when she's out of town."

"If we're really dealing with GRU—" Tam started.

"It's not safe for us to stay here," Jake said. "Jenny, now that I'm thinking about it, I don't think it's safe for us to go back and get your stuff either. Not yet."

Jenny nodded like she understood.

"Where do we go, then?" Tam asked. "Those guys . . . we don't want to use a credit card or check in anywhere with an ID."

"I know a place," Jenny said. "I know someone who can help us out."

The motor lodge, on the far west end of the island, was a relic from the early '60s. Its faded sign, crooked under the still-dark sky, advertised color TV and cable. After a long, roundabout route in Tam's rental to make sure they weren't being followed, and a stop at a gas station for a toothbrush for Jenny, they pulled into the motel's lot. Jake instructed Tam to park far away, out of the light.

"You sure this is good?" Jake said.

"I've known the owner since I was a baby," Jenny said. "He was my grandma's next-door neighbor when they were kids. I trust him."

"Okay," Jake said. "Tam, would you send Stu the address on Signal?"

They followed Jenny into the office. The fixtures were tired but clean, and a flickering blue light from a television illuminated the back room.

"Mr. Nelson!" Jenny called. "Mr. Nelson, are you here?"

A moment later an elderly man in a T-shirt and jeans held up by suspenders shuffled out behind the desk.

"Miss Jennifer," he said, giving Tam and Jake a long, appraising stare. "Isn't this a surprise. What can I help you with?"

"We need a room," Jenny said.

"Two rooms," Jake said. "One for them, one for me."

The old man gave Jake another long look. "I'm sure you wouldn't mind," he said slowly, "if I had a word in private with Miss Jennifer, here?"

"You certainly may—" Tam started, but Jenny stepped forward and leaned against the desk.

"They're good people, Mr. Nelson," Jenny said. "I appreciate you looking out for me. I really do. I know we're like family but—"

"Mr. Nelson," Jake cut in, "we're helping Jennifer with her organization. Her partner is in trouble."

"Duncan," Jenny added. "You've met him."

"The boyfriend," Mr. Nelson said, nodding slowly. "With the flashy car."

"He didn't do anything wrong. And he's my ex-boyfriend now."

"Well, isn't that a relief."

"There are people who don't agree with Jenny and Duncan's work," Tam said. "Ruthless people. We think they've harmed Duncan. We're trying to keep them from hurting Jenny too. We're worried they might come to her house."

"So you need a place to stay," Mr. Nelson said. He was silent for a moment as he seemed to chew on the situation. "A place where nobody knows." He reached under the counter and raised a pair of keys, holding them at arm's length as he peered at them over his glasses. "Here we got room two, and here we got room three. All made up and ready to go."

Jenny ran around and gave Mr. Nelson a long hug. Jake drew out his wallet and placed five hundred-dollar bills on the counter.

"For your trouble," Jake said.

Mr. Nelson scoffed and slid the money back toward Jake. "If Miss Jennifer says you're good people," he said, "that's enough for me. She can get me back later."

"For the housekeeper, then," Jake said, pushing the money toward him once more. "A tip."

The old man tilted his head and gave Jake a long look. Then his wrinkled face turned up in a wry smile. He took the bills, folded them, and slipped them in his pocket.

CHAPTER THIRTY-FOUR

Jake woke the next morning to a loud rapping on the room's front door. He grabbed his SIG from the nightstand and ran to the side of the door.

"Who's there?" Jake called.

"Jesus Christ, Jake, it's me," Stewart boomed. "Open up the door."

Jake checked the safety and held the gun at his side as he unchained the door and ushered Stewart inside.

"What the hell, Jake—"

"Shh," Jake said with a finger to his lips. He placed the gun on the dresser and locked the door before checking out the window. Aside from Stewart's unmarked, windowless Sprinter van parked off the highway, nothing seemed amiss. He glanced down at his watch. Quarter after six in the morning.

"What's going on?" Stu asked.

"Keep your voice down."

"You are twitchy as fuck, Jacob. What the hell is going on?" Stu lifted the SIG from the dresser, checked the chamber, then set it down again. "You looked like you were ready to take my head off in your skivvies."

"Not the time to joke around," Jake said. He began to make coffee in the room's single-serve machine and checked again out the front window.

"Did you stay at Kingfisher all night?" Jake asked.

Stu took a seat on the bed and crossed his stout arms across his chest. "Better than the kids' room over at the rental. Seriously, though, Tam told me to stay in Clear Lake. Where is she?"

Jake took a sip of his coffee and started a cup for Stu. "She's asleep next door. Hey," he asked, "when you loaded up your rig to come down here, did you bring computer toys or ballistic toys?"

"A mix of both."

"Good. I think we're going to need them."

"Will you tell me what the hell is going on?"

Jake handed over the coffee and told the story from the beginning. When he got to the part about Duncan and the USB, Stu let out a low whistle.

"If that guy you showed me is really GRU, they have some nasty tools in their digital kit. Have you connected to Kingfisher's network with any of your gear?" Stu narrowed his eyes at Jake.

"Personal laptop. And then the machine I had with you yesterday. But the first one they gave me was a shitbox, so slow it was practically useless."

"Consider them all infected. Highly contagious. We'll FedEx them back to the shop and have Grant do a little reverse engineering in the isolation room while I take a look on site. And you need to tell Helena to shut down the network. All of it, and immediately."

"Good," Jake said, already tapping out a message to Janice Trout. "Very good idea. Helena and Duncan barely talk. His choice, not hers. I wouldn't be surprised if she has no idea he's missing."

"Do we let her know?"

"Yes. But not by text."

On this, Jake was adamant. This was her son.

Stewart nodded his agreement. "Now for your new friend . . . you think it's smart to leave her here? And for that matter, you think it's smart for *us* to be here? Tam said you checked in with no ID, but if we're dealing with Team Russia—"

"If those guys know about us and want to get to us, we're probably going to need to get inside a secured perimeter."

"Like Kingfisher," Stu said, and Jake nodded.

"I don't know about Jenny, though," Jake said. "I thought about sending her away, but it's probably safer for her if we keep her with us. And maybe she can help us find Helena's kid somehow."

As if on cue, a knock came at the door. Stu opened it, and Jenny entered, wrapped in a blanket. She looked up at Stu and turned to Jake.

"This is one of your guys?" she asked.

"One of the best," Jake said.

Stu smiled and offered his hand.

"Captain Stewart Gallagher, US Navy, retired."

Jenny's hand was dwarfed by Stu's as they shook.

"It's nice to meet you," Jenny said. "I'm usually pretty reluctant about navy guys, but if Jake here can vouch for you, I guess I'm okay with it."

Stu made a face, and Jake stifled a laugh.

"Damn," Stu said.

Jake shrugged. "She calls 'em like she sees 'em."

"Anyway," Stu said, "what's next?"

"What's next is we go see Helena Nash."

Jenny and Tam rode in the back of Stu's van on the drive to Clear Lake City, while Jake sat up front and Stu drove. From the outside, the vehicle looked like something that might be driven by a plumber or electrician: gray in finish and slightly dirty, with a ladder and long pair of thick PVC tubes filled with smaller copper pipes and steel conduit on top. The cargo space in back was lined on the driver's side with racks of plastic bins filled with assorted hardware, and the passenger side had a long workbench with a shelf above and bins below.

Only a close inspection would reveal that some of the bins had false bottoms and were filled with digital hardware like circuit boards, relays, and handheld radios. The other bins, even more benign looking, contained several pistols and ammo, along with scopes and night vision goggles. Even the ladder and pipes on the roof were deceptive: the ladder, if it wasn't being used to scale a wall or fence, could be used with the pipes in one of the PVC tubes to erect an antenna for long-distance shortwave communication or surveillance. In the other PVC tube behind a dummy plug of galvanized conduit ends, a heavy canvas case contained a McMillan TAC-50 sniper rifle with a bipod, sound suppressor, and scope.

Stewart had trained as a sniper as a naval cadet.

Jake spent the drive trying to fill Stu in on any details he'd forgotten. Stu listened quietly, making none of his usual jokes or jabs, taking in every detail as he sought out patterns or connections that Jake might have missed.

"So there it is," Jake said. "Initial thoughts?"

"Obviously we need to find out who else was on that outbound chopper from Clear Lake with your guy Wade and Taka."

"Do you still think Taka was killed in a car accident?"

Stu said nothing for a moment. "I think it bears further investigation," he finally said.

"Where did they find the kid's car?"

Jake turned to the back of the van. "Jenny, do you know where exactly they found Duncan's Tesla?"

"The police said on Red Bluff Road and Underwood."

"Find it on your phone," Stu said. "I want to do a drive-by."

Jake searched for the location on Google Maps, realizing nearly too late they were almost to it. "Slow down, slow down," he said. "It's right here. Take this right." At first the road was lined with low steel-and-concrete buildings like every place else around the NASA complex, but after a mile or so, it became less developed. Some buildings and homes could be seen far off to the south, and to the north, separated from the road by a swampy irrigation ditch, was a field of tall grass.

"Good place to pick someone up," Stu said. "If you didn't want to be noticed."

"Should we stop and take a look?"

"He's not here," Jenny said flatly.

"How do you know?" Jake asked.

"I just know it."

"She's right," Stu said, continuing to drive. "Whoever it was, they took him away. Maybe he resisted. Maybe the car was a message to his mom. But he's not here. If our friends in the GRU wanted him to be found, they'd have left him. If they wanted anyone to know anything, they'd send a message. I am surprised they left the Tesla sitting there, though. They probably didn't move it because they couldn't figure out how to drive the thing. How do we get to Kingfisher from here?"

Jake looked at his phone, cocking his head to orient himself. "Take this next left. We'll swing around and go in from the back. I've never gone this way." They drove into denser buildings and over a set of canals. Off to their left were more canals, scrubby trees and brush, and some cinder block buildings with corrugated steel roofs. In between the buildings were tall tanks with warning signs too far away for Jake to read.

"What are the tanks?" Stu asked.

"This is all Kingfisher property. I bet they fill up their fueling barges here to take out to the launch platform. There's probably rail access here too." Sure enough, only a moment later the van went over a railroad crossing. "It's probably a lot cheaper for them to handle the cryogenic stuff in bulk on their own instead of using a contractor. Ditto for the hypergolics."

"Seems like those guys have all the angles covered," Stu said.

"They sure do. That's how they beat everyone on price. Take another left here. You'll go another couple miles—then another left and we're there."

At the Kingfisher gate, the guard recognized Jake and waved them through.

"What's our plan?" Stu asked.

"First, we get Jenny settled into our office. Tam can keep an eye on her and check if we have any new info back in Everett. I want you to meet Helena Nash as soon as possible."

Outside the entry, Jake told Jenny to make up a name to sign in with. "If they've hacked into the network," he said, "I don't want them to see you're here. If they ask for ID, say you forgot it. I'll vouch for you." Jenny nodded. Inside at the front desk, Jake was stopped from scanning his all-access badge.

"I'm sorry for the low-tech form," the young man said, handing over a trio of clipboards. "A network glitch has taken down a lot of our systems."

Stu and Jake exchanged a glance.

"Just what kind of 'glitch' are we talking about, here?" Stu asked.

"IT isn't saying much. But I'm very sorry for the inconvenience." He pawed through a drawer for pens. "Fortunately," he said without looking up, "the internal card readers are all battery powered, so you can still open doors."

Jake peered over the desk at the small pile of guest paperwork accumulating on the surface. "Helena Nash is waiting for us."

"Oh, she's behind closed doors at the moment—"

"Call Janice Trout. Tell her Jake Moran is here. It's urgent."

"Of course. Just a moment." The young man punched a number on his phone and turned away, speaking softly so Jake couldn't hear. He hung up the phone and nodded. "Ms. Trout is very sorry, but Helena is going to be tied up all day getting ready for the static-fire test. She says you should check back tomorrow morning, but that could be busy too."

Jake said nothing for a moment, confused.

Stu shrugged. "This is your show, Jake," he said. He swung his pass on its lanyard. "At least she shut it all down like you asked."

Jake led them all to the office. "There's food right down the hall," he said.

"I need coffee before I do anything else," Tam said. "I'll be back in a moment."

Jake followed her out into the corridor, letting the door close behind. "Hey," he said softly, grabbing Tam by the elbow. "Did you bring that pistol of yours?"

"I wasn't quite sure how to check it in my luggage," she said sheepishly.

"The black duffel in my office. There's a yellow gun case at the bottom. My SIG is in there if you need it."

Tam nodded and left, and Jake returned to the office and gestured for Jenny to take a seat at his desk. "Make yourself comfortable," he said. "Stu and I have something to take care of, but when we get back, we can figure out a good time to introduce you to Helena. Sit tight for now." He turned to Stu. "Let's go check out the helipad."

He left the room at a brisk pace, and Stu, with a surprisingly nimble gait for such a bulky person, kept up at his side.

They exited the building and walked under an awning toward a small glass-and-concrete structure. Parked beyond was a Sikorsky S-70 helicopter with a Kingfisher logo on the tail boom like the one Jake had flown in with Wade. Inside the structure, a digital display on the wall was unpowered and dark; a piece of paper had been taped to it with the printed message: No Flight Updates Due to Network Outage. Please see Ashley for More Information. Through a window, a young woman in a Kingfisher polo and ball cap rose to see who had entered.

"Hey, fellas," she drawled. Her badge said **ASHLEY—FLIGHT OPERATIONS**. "Midmorning flight is shut down. If you need to get out for static-fire ops, soonest we'll be flying is noon, looks like."

"No, it's okay," Jake said. "We aren't flying today. But what's going on?"

The woman thumbed back in the direction of the main building. "Network crashed. Sounds like everybody's been hit. It's a big scramble to get things working so they can keep the static-fire test on schedule, but people like us working out on the fringes . . . out of sight, out of mind, as they say."

"Are your passenger manifests accessible?" Jake asked. "Or is that messed up by the network too?"

"We have a paper record. They need a real signature on file."

"Can I see the entry for the tenth?" Jake asked. He held up his badge, unsure if it would make any difference. "You can call Janice Trout if you need confirmation."

"You're fine," Ashley said. She went to a shelf and grabbed a three-ring binder, placed it on the pass-through, and started to page through. "It's funny," she said, "in all the time I've worked here, I've never had someone ask to see the manifest before, and now I get two people in a week."

"Who else was here?"

"Some guy. Worker pass. Not a contractor like you." She quickly flipped a couple of pages, then flipped back. "Did you say the tenth?"

"Yes. It was a Monday."

"Weird. The page isn't in here."

"May I see?"

Ashley spun the binder so it faced Jake. Denny Wade was listed as the pilot on most of the flights, but other names showed up too. The pages were all in order for the days before and the days following; only the tenth was missing.

"I'd show you the manifest on the computer," she said, "but I can only do that when we get the network back."

"That's okay," Jake said. "The other person who looked at this . . . you remember what he looked like?"

"Big guy. Talked kind of funny. Mechanic, I think. Anything else?"

An idea occurred to Jake, and he quickly drew his phone from his pocket. He swiped through his pictures of Strelka.

"Did he look anything like this?"

Ashley tilted her head to the side and squinted. "Yeah, you know . . . I think that's the guy. Not a hundred percent sure, but it could be."

Jake and Stu exchanged a look of alarm.

"Anything else?" Ashley asked.

"No, we're good. Thanks for your help."

Jake and Stu left the flight-operations building, walking faster now than they had before.

"What do you make of that?" Stu asked.

"Something here is very fucked up."

"So where do we go now?"

"Straight to the top."

Back in the main building, the two headed directly to the front desk. Jake sped past and badged through the door leading to the executive hall. At the door to Helena's suite, he waved his badge. Nothing. He crossed the hall to Janice Trout's office and tried the same with no luck, so he pounded on the door with the flat of his palm.

"Janice? Janice! Open up." He spoke so loudly that a couple of people walking down the hall stopped to stare. "Janice! Open your door!"

"Jake," Stu said softly. "Behind you."

The door to the suite had opened, and Janice Trout poked her head out into the hall.

"Jake. We did as you asked, but Helena can't see you right now."

Jake barreled toward her and through the door, pushing her firmly but gently to the side. "Wait, no, Mr. Moran, you can't! Stop, please don't make me call security . . . you can't see Helena now!" Janice grabbed at Jake's arm to stop him, but he strode across the waiting area to the doors of Helena Nash's office.

"Stop!" Janice said, nearly at a shout. "You can't . . . you can't go in there!"

Jake pushed through the door and was met by the last thing he expected to see: Helena Nash, alone and seated at her desk, with her forehead resting on her crossed arms. Her shoulders trembled, but she didn't look up. An open laptop was next to her on the otherwise bare desk.

"Mr. Moran," Janice begged. "Please, please don't—"

"Helena," Jake said. "I need to talk with you. I think your son is in trouble."

Slowly, Helena lifted her head to face Jake. Her eyes were red, her complexion blotchy from crying. "You think so?" Her voice was faint, almost weak. "I think so too."

With that, she spun the laptop around so Jake could see the screen. Filling it was a paused video image of Duncan slumped in a chair with his lips bloodied and his right eye swollen shut. The clothes he wore were filthy, and in his hands he held up a copy of the *Miami Herald*. Jake peered forward and saw the paper was dated two days prior.

"Go ahead, Jake," Helena whispered, and a tear slipped down from the corner of her eye. "Go ahead and hit play, and see how much trouble my son is in."

Jake reached forward slowly and tapped the laptop's trackpad.

"Mother," Duncan said, his enunciation hampered by his ruined face, "if you proceed with the launch of the *Kingfisher Seven*, I will be released. But if you alter the countdown in any way"—he paused to take a breath—"I will be killed and returned to you in pieces."

CHAPTER THIRTY-FIVE

Quietly, crowded around Helena's desk, Jake and Stu watched the video of Duncan over and over again. Helena had gone to the couch, composed now, her arms crossed and her lips pressed together in a tight frown. Janice Trout sat at her side.

"Play it again," Stu said. "Don't look at him. Look at the room. Look for shadows." Jake tapped the trackpad, and the room filled with Duncan Nash's broken voice once more. The handheld image was mostly still but wobbled from time to time.

"For the past two years I have supported effort to halt the forthcoming launch of the HiPEP-D technology demonstrator by your launch company, Kingfisher Aerospace. I now know this effort has been mistake, and I renounce such effort. Mother, I wish for you to proceed with this launch. I have learned the hard way that this technology is important for humanity, and I will not stand in way of launch—"

"Freeze it," Stu said. "Shadow, there." He pointed to the lower right side of the screen. "We'll get a still and boost the contrast. There's at least two in there with him."

"Two?" Jake said.

"One holding the camera at the back of the room and one making that shadow. Probably holding his script. Hit play again."

"I was wrong in my judgment, and I renounce all efforts of the Greater Gulf Defense Fund. Mother, if you proceed with the launch of the *Kingfisher Seven*, I will be released. But if you alter the countdown in any way, I will be killed and returned to you in pieces. If all countdown and launch effort proceeds without delay or hesitation, I will be released unharmed. If effort is seen to be delayed in any way or authorities are contacted, you understand what will happen to me. Please, Mother, I wish to see you again. Do not allow this thing to happen to me. You will receive a message confirming the goodwill of my captors in the next several days, following the static-fire test. Please be ready for it."

The video blurred as the camera turned away, and then it went black.

"So, two in there," Stu said.

"And a Russian-written script, I'd say," Jake added, "given the grammar."

"Hmm. Most guys would subconsciously correct the mistakes," Stu said, thinking. "Either he got a stern command to read it exactly as written, or he's smart as hell and sending us a message."

"He *is* smart," Helena said, not looking up. "He's brilliant."

Jake and Stu crossed the room and stood before the couch.

"Helena," Jake said, and her eyes met his in a hard stare. "Your son is in terrible trouble." She nodded. "If his captors are who I think they are, it's especially bad. I am certain they killed Dr. Taka, and they tried to kill one of your pilots, Denny Wade. I'm guessing they wanted to eliminate Wade and Taka for something they saw, possibly the identity of a passenger who flew with them on the outbound from Clear Lake on the morning of the failed launch. We believe that person gained physical access to the compound, and probably to the launch platforms as well."

"What?" Helena said, sitting up straight in her seat. "I don't understand how that could even be possible."

"These men are associated with the Russian intelligence services," Stu said. "They have a vast set of tools to work with. Their de facto leader in the States is a man called Gavril Strelnikov. He was a GRU major, and he's bad news. I'll get a photo distributed to your security staff so they can keep an eye out for him if he tries to return."

Jake pulled out his phone again and showed the man's photo to Helena. "I know you briefed the passengers for that morning flight, that you had concerns about the protests. Do you recall seeing this man at any time? He goes by Strelka."

Helena shrugged and shook her head. "I see so many people. It's possible? I can't be certain."

"He's ruthless," Jake said. "We need to assume he's part of a team. They've tried to eliminate the people who were aboard my chopper one by one. At some point, when you or your son are no longer useful to them, they will eliminate you too. Both of you."

"Oh, Duncan," Helena sighed, her expression softening a little. "Duncan, Duncan, Duncan."

"But there is hope," Jake continued, and Helena looked up again. "I'm sure he's alive now. As your son, he has value to them. By having him, they believe they have leverage over you. If they lose him, they lose that leverage."

"I agree with your assessment," Helena said. "What would you suggest we do?"

"The launch is scheduled for what, ten days from now?"

"T-minus eleven days and roughly two hours." Janice said. "Provided tomorrow's static fire proceeds without interruption."

"Eleven days is a lot of time," Jake said. "With some help from the feds in Miami, we can cover a lot of—"

"Absolutely not," Helena said, sitting upright. "The federal authorities will not be alerted."

Jake crossed his arms. "May I ask why not?"

"Your Strelka will know it the moment we contact the FBI, don't you think? They will have some way of knowing."

Jake nodded. "It's probably true," he said. "Stu, what do you think? Helena, apologies, this is my associate Stewart Gallagher."

"Ma'am," Stu said, "your network has been infiltrated. You should assume all of your systems have been compromised and your operations are under constant surveillance."

"I can hardly believe it. Explain how."

"The USB drive your son showed you, it contained bogus information, correct?"

"It did, but I only opened those files on an air-gapped Linux machine. The hard drive was wiped before it was returned to service."

"Is there any way we can find that machine?" Stu asked, and Janice began typing a message on her phone's screen.

"I'm sure the reinstallation was logged by our IT department. But like I said, they would have wiped it before putting it back into circulation."

Jake shook his head. "The people we're dealing with, the men we believe have taken your son, are former agents of the Russian intelligence services. If that suspicion is true—"

"They have access to very sophisticated malware," Stu broke in. "State-sponsored development. Viruses with encrypted payloads that can infect a hard drive's master boot record, or overwrite a motherboard's BIOS or advanced boot firmware. Wiping the operating system and starting over isn't enough to clean a machine infected like that. Even if you're not connected to a network, some of these payloads are capable of using a computer's speakers and microphones to communicate with other infected machines using ultrasonic frequencies."

"I've read of such things," Helena said. "But we have exceptional procedures here. Strong antivirus—"

"A motivated and well-funded adversary can get around the best antivirus," Stu told her.

Janice sat up straight, staring at her phone with a puzzled expression. "Sandip says that computer went to Jake Moran after it got wiped."

Jake and Stu shared a look.

Jake sighed. "That explains why the computer was so slow when I used it for the first time. The virus was going through its installation routine, probably from the machine's BIOS."

"It's everywhere," Stu said. "You need to assume everything here is infected, and probably many of your staff's personal devices as well."

“How do you suggest we mitigate this intrusion, then?” Helena asked. “And in a way that doesn’t disrupt our countdown going forward? My IT staff did as I asked and shut us down immediately, but they’re baffled.”

Stu nodded thoughtfully and pulled a tablet from his bag. “I’ve had a good look at your network schematics,” he said, opening a file on the tablet. “The architecture is top notch. Well designed. I suspect the virus is trying to communicate over standard IP ports. I’d guess it’s imitating regular web browsing or domain name requests in an effort to be stealthy. Your security software is smart enough to realize the ports are being spoofed with nonstandard packets, so it was already blocking the traffic, and the virus is jumping to a different port to get around the block. I can’t know for sure without investigating a little.”

“It doesn’t seem so stealthy,” Helena said, “if you can figure it out just like that.”

“Well,” Stu said, “I have two things helping me out. A strong sense of paranoia and a pretty good idea some Russian guys slipped an infected thumb drive in here. It’s no surprise your IT staff isn’t thinking malware, because they run a very tight ship. And I’m sure none of their antivirus software has triggered any sort of alert, so they still believe they’re fine. They’re probably thinking it’s faulty hardware throwing out bad data packets, and they’re trying to track it down by process of elimination.”

“So what do we do?” Janice asked.

“We stop blocking the ports. Let the packets go through.”

“Why on earth would we do that?” Helena asked incredulously. “Are you saying we just open the door and give everything away?”

“Not at all,” Stu said. “Just because we’re opening the door doesn’t mean we can’t control the speed at which things are happening. We can throttle the connection to slow down how much is getting out. Not fighting it will make them believe everything is fine in here as well as reduce their level of suspicion. We’ll act like we don’t know anything. Even better, by playing dumb we can analyze the traffic here on our end and try to see what's going on. Find the IP address of their command-and-control server and try a little reverse engineering to determine the mode of infection, how the payload is hidden, all that."

"Let's say I am okay with this," Helena said. "How do we make it happen without it being common knowledge among my staff?"

"If you have one trusted staff member in your IT department, I can give him or her some direction . . ."

Helena sat, tight lipped, and slowly shook her head *no*.

"Or," Stu added carefully, "I *could* go in and do it myself. Depending on the brand of network hardware you're using, it shouldn't take me too long to figure it out."

"But if you can delegate one trusted person to this job," Jake said, "it would be best. I need Stewart's expertise elsewhere today."

"If it's for anything other than keeping our countdown on schedule," Helena said, "forget it."

"Keeping the countdown going is exactly what it is," Jake said. "Stu?"

Stu scrolled to a new diagram on the tablet. "The network connection to your launch-control platform is locked down like a fortress," he said. "And from what I understand by looking at these schematics, your launch-operations network is completely segregated from anything here onshore, am I correct?"

"You are absolutely correct," Helena said. "For security and autonomy, we keep traffic going one way to follow vehicle telemetry. Voice and data communications are on a different physical network completely."

"Yes," Stu said. "That's what I've seen. But there are many opportunities for bad security, for things to bleed from one network over to the other—"

"Staff on the platforms get extra training in data security before they are allowed out there," Janice said, almost looking insulted. "Our people are trained *very* well."

Stu smiled for a moment. "Yes. True. I saw that in your documentation. But again, these are human beings we're talking about, and even the smartest human beings do stupid things sometimes. I'd like to go out and stay at launch control for a couple days with some monitoring equipment. Just to see if there's anything going on. It's also important to see if any virus has somehow made the leap out there. I'll watch in real time as your static-fire test is conducted. The timing is ideal."

"If we do see anything abnormal," Jake said, "it's low risk, because it's only the static-fire test. We can quietly correct it before we get too close to launch day in the count. And hopefully, we'll have found Duncan by then."

"Wait, by 'we' do you mean you're going out there as well, Jake?" Helena's expression was displeased.

"I am," he said. "I need to get Stewart oriented, and I want to see for myself how your static-fire operations are conducted."

"I think our issues here onshore are a bit more pressing at the moment," she countered.

"We have someone onboarding right now who will take over here—" Jake's phone vibrated in his pocket. He pulled it out and unlocked it to see a Signal message from Tam.

I'm back from coffee. Where are you guys?

"In fact," Jake said, raising his phone in the air, "I'm going to get her now. We'll send her right over. Stu?"

The two returned to the corridor and took off for Jake's office.

"How secure are you on that virus assessment?" Jake asked. "Do you really think it's working that way, or did you just put it out there to give Helena something to grab on to for now?"

"A guess," Stu started, "but an educated one. I have about eighty percent confidence that's how it's working. It's just how it feels to me. And it's exactly how we did it on the Mali job, so I guess it's fresh in my head. I'm going to take a quick look before we head out to the platform."

"Sounds good to me," Jake said.

They found Tam waiting for them in the office. Stu immediately took a seat at the desk and started working on his laptop, and Jake dug through his bag for his gun case.

"So what's the word?" Tam asked.

"You need to get over to see Helena Nash," Jake said. "Shit's blowing up. Don't let Jenny out of your sight. And here, you should have this." He pulled his SIG and a full magazine from the case and handed it over.

She checked that the chamber was clear and slipped the gun and ammunition into her bag.

"What about you?" she asked. "What will you carry?"

"I suspect Stu has me all taken care of." Stu, deeply focused on his laptop, didn't notice being mentioned. "Go out to the front desk and tell them you need to see Janice Trout. Tell them you're with me if you need to."

Next Jake dug through his gear bag and pulled out the spare smartphone. He powered it up, opened the Signal app, and made an encrypted call to Wade. The call connected on the second ring.

"Jake, I was just about to message you," Wade said. "I've got some news."

"Me too, what's up?"

"That honeycomb piece. My guy took a look. Said he saw something like it in Afghanistan. Not a positive ID, but he thought it looked like a strut from a Russian military quadcopter. They call it a Blizzard drone. *Buran* in Russian. Not a weapons platform, but they started using it that way in Ukraine. It's got only a fifty-kilogram payload and limited flight time—they originally used it for shit like dropping supplies or setting up short-term communication relays. But it works pretty well as a guided weapon, too, turns out."

"Communication relays . . . ?" Jake shook his head and turned to the wall, and suddenly everything clicked. "Holy shit. The Russians used it to bring down CommSat. It was small enough to get close and spoof the termination signal, and everyone assumed it was some media drone covering the protest. Then we got in its way."

"It didn't even need to be armed," Wade said. "My guy said Buran carries a five-hundred-gram explosive charge in its default configuration to self-destruct if control is lost. Which would have been just enough to fuck up our shit."

"Your guy," Jake said. "How much does he know? Does he have the strut now?"

"He assumed it was a souvenir I kept from the 'Stan, and I said nothing to change his mind. The piece is in my hand right now."

"Okay," Jake said. "Good. Listen, I'm going off the grid for a couple days. I'm going to give you the contact info for one of my associates. If anything comes up, I want you to get in touch with her ASAP."

"She's solid?"

"More than solid. I trust her with my life."

"Jake, wherever you're going, take care of yourself, okay? We still need to get that beer."

"You take care too. Keep lying low. When we get this figured out, drinks are on me."

Jake terminated the call. He composed a message to Wade with Tam's contact information, pressed send, and powered off the phone.

Across the room, Stu suddenly jumped to his feet. He walked in a tight circle behind the desk, shaking his head as he ran his fingers through his hair.

"What's going on?" Jake said. "You learn anything about that virus?"

"I . . . sure did," Stu said.

"What's up? Are you okay?"

"I think I just disabled it completely on the Kingfisher network. Everything should be fine now. We can tell them to bring everything back online."

"What? How the hell did you manage *that*?"

"So, remember how I said it felt like the Mali job? Well . . . I put a kill switch in our code for that payload."

Tam, across the room, had been following closely. "A kill switch?"

"Yeah. Just in case it got loose on our network or something. I coded in a stupid password, Gallagher123. If the virus receives that text on a specific port, it runs a routine where it disables itself."

"So you sent it Gallagher123?" Jake asked. "And it worked?"

"Yes, it worked perfectly."

"That seems impossible," Tam said.

"You'd think," Stu said. "But not if it's our own code." He shook his head again in disbelief. "And it was. *Our* code. The same fucking code. Someone got it from Mali and used it against us."

CHAPTER THIRTY-SIX

Strelka slammed the bulky encrypted satphone on the hotel-room table.

"We have trouble," he told Petr. "Trouble that could have been avoided—"

"What are you talking about?" Petr asked.

René looked up from where he was soldering the circuit board of a walkie-talkie and watched the exchange from across the room.

"If you'd just done your fucking job," Strelka spit. "Vostok has infiltrated the facility. They know about the drone. They can trace it to us. Do you understand? This was supposed to be a ghost operation. Invisible!"

"But it's impossible—"

"They've identified it *by name*. They know it was a Buran! You might as well have written our fucking names on it."

René watched as Petr clenched and unclenched his fists. "Who the fuck are you, talking to me this way? What have *you* done beyond taking out the Japanese scientist who knew nothing? The two men who *do* know something are still out there! Anything would have worked better than this shit plan you put together. And you've fucked up every chance to eliminate the witnesses." Spit flew from Petr's mouth as he grew more indignant, and his shouting grew louder. "You had the chance to eliminate JacOb Moran and the pilot *together* at the same time in the hospital, and you fucked that up too!"

"Listen to me, Petr, I don't care that you washed Vostok's balls for him over in Europe, I'm in charge over here, got it? But here, if you think I'm so shitty at my job, Vostok is giving you the opportunity to show me up. He has a task for you."

"What's that?"

"You're being sent to eliminate the pilot. You get off on shit like this, right? We don't need to worry about Jacob—he'll be on the launch platform in an hour. He'll be useless there, stuck, once the operation begins. But the pilot's near Houston. Vostok's hackers were able to associate an IP address with the pilot's communications. From that they'll soon be able to determine a physical location. You will leave here now and head north toward the city, and as soon as I have a correct address—"

"I should be here, with the operation."

"Vostok says otherwise, asshole. And I agree. You should be able to eliminate him and be back here early tomorrow. There's a piece of the Buran with him—you need to get that as well. We can't leave a trace of this operation. *Nothing.* Do whatever you need to do to get what's left of the Buran, kill the pilot, and get back here immediately so we can distribute the devices. This isn't me talking—it's Vostok's order. Do you understand?"

Petr glowered over the table and slowly rose from his seat. "I understand," he said. He grabbed a small bag from the counter in the kitchenette, checked inside it, and left the room without saying another word.

René watched the door for a moment, then faced Strelka. "You want to explain that to me?"

"It's nothing. He'll take care of it and be back."

"Right," René said. "Sure."

A cough came from behind the closed door to the adjoining suite, and Strelka turned in the noise's direction and scowled. The racket had been nearly constant when they'd first set up in the hotel, but René had tuned it out when he'd gotten to work on his detonators. "And that?" René asked. "Do you care to tell me about who's in there?"

"I have no idea."

"Bullshit. Tell me what's going on here, everything, or I walk."

"Go ahead," Strelka said. "The moment you touch that door, you're a dead man." Strelka lifted his shirt to show the pistol tucked in his waistband, and the two men stared at each other. The coughing sound came again, a weak rattle.

"You need me," René finally said. "If I leave, you're fucked."

"I'll kill you if you try to go," Strelka said. "And I'll wash my hands of this and return home."

"You think Grandpa will be happy with that? You know you can't walk away now. They'll kill you the second you step off the plane."

Strelka shook his head and pointed at the table. "Just make your fucking bombs, okay?"

"The devices are complete," René said. "They only need fuel now so they can detonate."

"Whatever. You know what I mean. Finish your job. Get revenge for your guys slaughtered in the desert. Do it so we can all leave." He paced around the room and spun to face René once again. "Who are you with, huh? Vostok thinks you have training."

"No one."

"Come on. Are you with the Mossad? You look Israeli. You talk Russian like an Israeli too. Just tell me. Those guys are badass."

Was Strelka trying to soften him up? It wasn't going to work. "Tell me who's in the other room," René said.

The muscles in Strelka's jaw tensed. "It's an insurance policy," he said. "Someone important."

"A hostage?"

"Someone important, okay? You don't need to know who exactly. Having him gives us cover when we need to leave. We'll hang on to him until we're certain we're safe, then eliminate him."

"If he's important," René said, "maybe he has value. We could set up an exchange—"

"Not part of Vostok's operation," Strelka said. "We do our job, make the hostage disappear, then you go." He grabbed a manila envelope from the kitchenette and drew a stack of passports and some documents from inside. "Belgian identities for you and Petr. Business class passage from Dallas to Reykjavík tomorrow at noon, then on to London and finally Moscow. Vostok takes care of his people. So, work with me. Do your job." Strelka tossed the envelope back on the counter. "The chemicals you need to finish. When do we get them?"

"Tonight. I think it'll be safer in the dark. And it shortens our exposure. It's bad stuff. Toxic and explosive."

"Understood," Strelka said. "Tonight. Maybe Petr will be back to help by then." The satphone chirped, and Strelka glanced at the display. "It's the boss again," he said. "Wait." He connected the call and brought the phone to his ear. "Vostok. You have it? Give it to me." He grabbed a pen from the suite's desk and scribbled on the back of the envelope. "It's fine that we don't have the exact unit. Petr can set up and watch the place until the pilot shows his face. We have time, we're making good progress on the devices—" Strelka looked to René for confirmation, and René nodded. "He indicates they're going well. Good. Thank you. What's that?" He paused, frowning as he listened. "Understood. It shouldn't be a problem." Strelka terminated the call and looked at René.

"Change in plan. Kingfisher's network is back online much sooner than we expected. If we're going to use our credentials to get past their security, we need to get your chemicals now."

CHAPTER THIRTY-SEVEN

They took a different helicopter out to the platform than they had on Jake's previous flights—a sixteen-seat Bell 525—filled with technicians and engineers supporting tomorrow's static-fire test. Wade was right; there *was* a distinction in dress: the techs all had blue polos and name tags, while the engineers wore ties and swagger. Jake recognized a couple of the controllers from his earlier interviews, and they all exchanged polite hellos before boarding and donning their headphones. Even with noise cancelling, there wouldn't be much conversation over the heavy racket of the chopper. Stu dozed off as soon as they were in the air, and Jake was left to his thoughts.

He was conflicted about spending so much time out on the Gulf while there were also jobs onshore he could be doing. Stu had been adamant, though. More than adamant; he'd practically demanded they go, and sooner rather than later. Jake had suggested they go the morning of the scheduled static fire, but Stu had crossed his arms and shaken his head. Cryptically he'd said, "It will all be clear when we get there."

What did that *mean, anyway?*

The wave tops on the blue water of the Gulf of Mexico flashed like jewels as they passed over, and Jake thought about the last time he'd made this flight, the morning of the CommSat launch. Just another launch. How many had he seen up close in his life? Fifty? A hundred? The failures stood out, the close calls, but so many of them blurred in his memory. Not CommSat, though. And HiPEP-D certainly wouldn't either.

The chopper rose up over the launch platform's helipad and spun to turn into the wind as it touched down. Jake gave Stu a quick elbow in the side to wake him up.

"Did I miss anything?" Stu asked as he pulled off his headphones.

"It was completely unremarkable," Jake said.

"Just the way I like it."

They grabbed their bags and followed the other passengers past a series of communications dishes and tall antennae through a doorway into the structure. The group descended two flights of metal stairs and entered a well-lit corridor with Kingfisher logos on the wall at regular intervals. A few techs disappeared through a set of doors. Jake and Stu stayed with the others until Jake held up his hand.

"VIP gallery," he said, reaching for a door. "This is what you wanted, right?" The door was unlocked, and he opened it to reveal a dimly lit room with desks, rows of chairs, and a high counter with printers and an ancient fax machine. The angled glass wall opposite the door looked down over the launch-control room, which was busy with the calm but focused energy of the controllers and support staff preparing for tomorrow's test.

"Fax machine?" Stu said, dropping his bags into a pile on the floor. "I thought this was a modern outfit."

"It's for the press," Jake said, unshouldering his own bag. "Some of those agencies still file reports by fax, I guess. But tell me about the virus. You're *certain* it was ours?"

"As soon as I decompiled the thing, it was obvious. I'm a little troubled by the fact that it's out in the wild."

"We'll figure it out after this is over," Jake said. "Let's get going on the task at hand."

Stu dropped to his knees next to his duffels. He unzipped them and rifled through, taking out a black canvas tool case followed by an industrially hardened laptop and some cables. He shuffled on his knees to the table with the fax machine and unscrewed a utility plate on the wall underneath it.

“Getting right at it, I see,” Jake said.

“There are two networks here. Administrative, with a connection to the Kingfisher office and limited access to the internet. For staff communication, email, file transfer, shit like that. The other is technical operations. Totally segregated from the internet and Kingfisher. That’s for rocket telemetry. Command and control. That’s the one we need to get on.” He placed the plate and its screws on the carpet next to him and eased a cable from the junction box in the wall.

“You yank out some random cable under the fax machine and hope it works?”

“If you did any kind of research, Jacob, you’d know this room is set up to support a public affairs officer. PAOs get a technical-operations console so they can monitor critical systems as they do their reporting. This”—he held up the cable—“was for that console. Kingfisher ended up giving the PAO a spot down in the control room itself, so they never needed to use it.”

From his tool bag Stu pulled out an ethernet jack and snapped it onto the end of the cable. He stuffed everything back into the wall and plugged his laptop into the new jack. Jake saw text flash by on the laptop screen as it powered up. Stu logged on and began typing commands at amazing speed. He nodded and grinned.

“We’re in.”

“That easy?”

“In your report, maybe you could mention they should stop using the same password on all of their networking gear out here.”

“Noted,” Jake said. “Now what?”

“Now we set up phase two,” Stu said. He strolled to the window overlooking launch control and put his hands on his hips. “Oh, fuck me,” he said with an exasperated sigh. Jake came over to his side.

“What’s up?”

“That’s up,” Stu said, pointing to the control console closest to them. “Andy Lang is working this?”

"He works all the important ones, I think," Jake said. "Come on, now, Stu: This beef is ridiculous. He's navy too. He's fine. And besides, we need to work with him."

"Yeah, yeah. What we need is to get to Platform One ASAP. According to their protocols, we wouldn't be able to get over there tomorrow so close to the static fire. It'll be shut off to personnel."

"Why exactly do we need to get there?"

"I took those pictures of the platform's equipment closet."

"And?"

"Something's out of place. A piece of hardware that shouldn't be there. It's been bugging me since I saw it. One of my guys picked up on it too. Could be nothing, but there's only one way to know for sure. I need to get into that room."

"You're going to need to get over your issues with Lang, then. I think he's the only one with enough pull to send us over this close to the test."

"Fine," Stu said. "Let's get down there and have a word with him. You do the talking."

"Um. You don't just barge into launch control," Jake said.

He went back to the window. Andy Lang wore a lightweight communication headset and had a pen clenched in his teeth as he flipped through a three-ring binder. How many times had Jake been there himself, searching the rule book for some obscure procedure or fault mode? He waited until Andy had found whatever he was looking for, sat up straight, took the pen from his mouth, and twirled it in his fingers. Fifty years ago, Jake thought, Andy Lang would have been a chain-smoker. He let Andy have a moment with his thoughts, then rapped a knuckle sharply on the glass. Several heads in the room turned, surly at the interruption. Andy Lang turned, too, and his eyes widened in surprise at the sight of Jake and Stewart. He waved, and Jake waved in return before gesturing for Andy to come up to the observation lounge. Andy glanced back at the room. He tapped his watch and held up all five fingers on his right hand.

"Five minutes," he mouthed before turning back to his work.

"Be friendly," Jake said, slapping Stu on his muscular shoulder. "Big smiles. Get over yourself and sharpen up your pitch, because this guy has the power to say no, okay?"

Stu gritted his teeth into a false grin and nodded.

Twenty minutes later the two men, along with a skipper in Kingfisher blues, were aboard a rigid inflatable boat, pounding over the waves in the three-mile gap between launch control and the main platform. Stu had brought one of his duffels, and he knelt down on the deck and began digging through the bag. He pulled out a laptop and cables and small black boxes, and sorted things into different piles.

"This no-electronics-gear-on-the-platform rule is really cramping my style," he said. "But I can work with it." He glanced up to check that the pilot wasn't paying attention and wordlessly handed Jake a pair of black network cables. He returned everything to the duffel except for a pair of black boxes, each about the size of a deck of cards, and a roll of stretchy black electrical tape.

"Secure those on your person," he said, pointing at the cables. "Sneaky-like." He unbuttoned his pants and began to slip the boxes down his underwear.

Jake laughed. "Jesus Christ, Stewart, they're not going to pat you down. They trust you. Just bring a regular phone or something to leave in the bin, and you're fine."

Stu sheepishly withdrew the boxes from his briefs and moved them to his pockets.

Five minutes later they were docked at the launch platform. Stu explained to the boat's skipper that they'd only be a few minutes, ten at the most. Would he be able to stay while they did their work? The skipper was fine with it. They signed in and left their phones, just as they had done on their previous visit, and donned the hard hats given to them by the security officer at the gate. Stu stayed on Jake's heels as they dashed up the steel steps, two at a time, and burst out into the bright space of the platform. The scene was one of controlled urgency, workers moving with purpose from place to place. No one paid them any attention. Jake started for the equipment closet but stopped to ensure that Stu was behind him. His friend had stopped, too, shielding his eyes as he craned his neck to take in the rocket standing upright in the center of the platform.

"That is one big motherfucker," Stu said.

Jake paused to take it in too. After so long in the business, he'd almost forgotten how awe inspiring it could be: that a machine—pencil thin and impossibly tall, built by human beings with all their flaws and shortcomings—could rise on a tower of flame and go beyond the atmosphere? He chided himself for taking it for granted.

"It's really something, huh?"

The launchpad itself was surrounded by a high steel fence. Inside it, a group of engineers was clustered at the base of the rocket, dwarfed by the engine bells as they looked over some technical document on a tablet computer. Off to the side of the platform, a digital display counted down the hours and minutes until the test.

STATIC FIRE TEST IN T-18 HOURS 7 MINUTES 22 SECONDS, it said.

"Let's go," Jake said, slapping Stu on the back to break him out of his trance. "We can get a closer look after all this is over."

The two crossed the platform, taking care to stay within the yellow-lined paths designated for foot traffic, and Jake pulled out a ring of keys given to him by Andy Lang. Getting permission from Andy to visit the platform had been hard enough; getting the keys to the equipment closet had been almost impossible. But when Jake hinted there could be a piece of unauthorized equipment on the launch platform, the keys were in his hands a moment later.

Now, outside the door to the closet, Jake searched through the keys dangling from the large split ring for the proper one. An air-conditioned chill washed over them as the door finally unlocked and swung open. Stu took charge and stepped inside.

"Anything look funny to you here?" he asked, pulling the boxes and electrical tape from his pockets. He handed one of the boxes to Jake. "Hang on to that. Give me those cables."

"It looks like a pretty tidy installation," Jake said, handing over the contents of his pockets.

"Makes it even harder to see when something's out of place," Stu said. He dropped to his knees and tapped a small black cube on a shelf in front of him. "Tell me what this is," he said.

"Looks like a power supply," Jake said. It sat squarely on the shelf, its excess cable neatly coiled and zip-tied.

"Correct." Stu pointed to another similar box. "How about this?"

"Another power supply?"

"Yep." Now Stu pointed to a box down on the lowest shelf. "And this one?"

"So, they've got good power and cable management. Stu, what the hell are you trying to—"

"Come down here," Stu said. "Look closer."

Jake crouched down and reached for the box.

"Don't touch!" Stu barked. "Just look. It probably has an accelerometer to detect if it gets moved. Look close and tell me what you see."

Jake leaned closer. The box was black plastic, about four inches long by two inches wide and an inch and a half tall. A red LED glowed on one end where a thick power cable emerged. Jake visually traced the cable—its slack also neatly bundled with a zip tie—to the back, where it was plugged in to an outlet. From the other side of the box, another thick cable disappeared upward behind the shelving. Jake rose to his feet, found where the cable emerged behind the next shelf up, and followed it higher. On his tiptoes, above the highest shelf, he saw the cable split into two. One half went to a small silver coaxial connector, and the other looped back down. Jake followed the downward loop, along with a neat bundle of network cables, to where it was plugged in to a networking switch.

"What the hell . . ."

"Why would you plug a power supply straight into the network, huh?" Stu plugged the two network cables they'd brought into a pair of ports on one end of his little black box and rose to stand next to Jake. "You do it because it's not a power supply at all in there. There's a minicomputer system inside that box. And that other half of the cable? Coaxial. Going to a little patch antenna stuck up on the roof, I bet. Probably somewhere in the sixteen-hundred-megahertz frequency band."

"Holy shit," Jake said. "That's Iridium."

"Uh-huh," Stu said. "Short-burst-mode satellite communications. Whoever put it in here has remote access to the launch-operations network."

"This is potentially very, very bad."

"That's one way of putting it." Stu snapped one of his network cables into an unused port on the switch and nodded. "Which one is the bad guys' cable? Show me where it goes into the switch." Jake pointed to it, and in one swift motion Stu unplugged it and snapped it into his black box, replacing the open port in the switch with his own network cable. Now Stu's device was in line with the cable coming from the rogue device.

"Network tap?" Jake asked.

"You got it," Stu said. "My own creation. Raspberry Pi minicomputer with two extra network ports and power over ethernet. We 3D printed the cases in the shop. That one you've got is a spare. I didn't want to take any chances." A tiny green LED on the side of the tap flashed for a few moments before it glowed steadily. A grin spread across Stu's face.

"Bingo," he said. "That solid light means we're connected and talking over an encrypted data tunnel to the laptop I set up back at launch control. Now anything that comes in over this"—he pointed to the device on the bottom shelf—"gets copied to us too."

"You are a mad fucking scientist, Stewart."

"Maybe so," his friend said, grabbing the spare tap from Jake's hand. He turned the little box over and over, cocking his head as he appraised his work. "But you wouldn't have it any other way."

CHAPTER THIRTY-EIGHT

In the hotel room, Strelka checked his watch.

"Almost eleven hundred hours," he said. "Petr should be with the pilot by now." He pulled a blue Kingfisher shirt and a security badge from a duffel and handed them to René. "Take these."

"This man looks nothing like me," René said, looking over the ID.

"It doesn't matter. They never check closely. If things work as expected, we won't even see another person while we get your ingredients."

René put on the blue shirt and tucked the pack of Tyvek safety suits under his arm along with the gloves, respirators, and a pack of black electrical tape. The rest of the hardware and supplies were out in the car. He waited as Strelka leaned close to the door to the neighboring suite.

"Everything good in there, mama's boy?" he called in English. "You feeling okay?" A low moan came in reply. "Don't worry, we'll have you out of there very soon, yes?" He nodded to René. "Come on."

Down in the parking lot, René threw the supplies in the front seat of the gently used white Nissan Armada that Strelka had procured, and circled to the back of the SUV.

"We won't need the transfer tanks," he said. "I figured out a better way. We'll fill the kegs directly; it will be safer and faster. Help me pull these things out of here."

"Not here," Strelka said. "We'll do it someplace where no one will notice."

They drove a mile to a more deserted stretch of road, and the two men muscled the tanks out of the back of the Armada and pushed them into the ditch. Beyond was a high chain-link fence topped with razor wire; a **No Trespassing** sign was posted every hundred feet or so. They drove along the fence for another half mile to a gate with an empty security shack. A printed paper taped on the shack's window said: "Due to network issues, we are unable to process visitors at this entry point. Please proceed to main entrance at Port Road."

"What do we do?" René asked.

Strelka, saying nothing, waved his badge and jumped out of the SUV. He went to the gate and held the card up next to a white reader by the latch. A buzz sounded, and Strelka pushed the gate open and returned to the driver's seat.

"That's what we do," he said, slowly driving the vehicle in through the perimeter. He left to pull the gate shut behind them and got back in the car. "Where will they have your chemicals?"

René looked over his shoulder at the fence, amazed that they'd just entered the facility so easily. "We can't just drive around looking for it," he said. "Someone will see, cameras or—"

"The cameras are on the network, and we currently control the network. Fuel transfer happens three days before they test or launch—otherwise no one is out here. I observed their procedures closely for weeks to learn their routine. And even if we do run into someone, we have ID. But you said this should be a quick job, yes? Tell me where to go."

René pointed to some low buildings next to some tanks erected on girders. "Try over there. The tall tanks are probably for cryogenics. Hypergols should be nearby. And, yes, it should be fast. Only a minute or so per tank."

They pulled up next to one of the windowless buildings. A sign on the side said **DANGER—HYPERGOLIC FUEL TRANSFER FACILITY—AUTHORIZED PERSONNEL ONLY**.

"This is it," René said.

Strelka cut the engine, and the two got out. The air was dense with humidity, and the sounds of insects and frogs filled the air. A canal lined with cattails and thick with algae ran behind the building. Strelka tested the building's door. Locked. Attached to the building on the north side was a roofed steel cage with four massive tanks inside. Its gate was locked as well.

"Can you pick locks?" René asked.

"No time. This must be done now."

Close to the canal the ground was soft and mucky. The area between the building and canal was a concrete deck beneath a steel awning, and a fence extended out to the edge of the water. Razor wire was coiled loosely at the edge of the fence to keep people from going around onto the concrete. Inside the fenced area, a pair of alloy swing arms with valves at the top were secured upright. These, René figured, must be used to load propellant into the barge when it was tied up at the building.

Strelka reached out with the cutters and snipped away the razor wire so it dropped into the water. René easily swung around the fence and onto the deck.

"Perfect," René said. He swung back over. "Work on making a hole in the bottom of the fence so we can pass the tanks under after they're filled. Give me the keys so I can bring the car right here."

Strelka hesitated for a moment, then got up and went around the building. Seconds later the Armada backed up to the edge of the canal.

"You don't trust me?" René asked.

"Just get to work," Strelka said. "I'll watch for any guards."

"You said there wouldn't be anyone."

"We're fine. Get working!"

One by one, René grabbed the kegs and swung them around the fence onto the concrete deck, arranging them in two rows of five. He took several trips to shuttle all his supplies and hardware onto the deck. When he was finished, he stripped naked next to the Armada. Strelka looked up from where he knelt to cut the fence.

"Will it be too hot in the suit?"

"Too hot, yes, and if any spills on me, I'm going straight into the canal," René said. "Don't follow me in if that happens. I'll deal with it." He pulled on one of the Tyvek suits and zipped it up, and put on another over that. Then he slipped his hands into a pair of nitrile gloves, pulling the ends over the wrists of the safety suit. "Come here," René said. "Get that black tape. Seal up the wrists." He held out his arms, and Strelka wound tape around them. René pulled on the thick chemical-resistant gloves, and Strelka sealed them as well. He pulled up the hoods of the suits and put the respirator over his face. "Tape around the mask too," René said.

"This tape isn't sticking," Strelka said.

"Use duct tape, then. There's a roll in the front seat."

After his suit was secure, René shuffled forward and swung himself around onto the deck, taking extra care not to catch his gear on any jagged edges of the fence. Sweat ran down the small of his back, and the face mask fogged from his breathing as he stood and looked over his gear. He reached for a roll of tape but stopped at the sound of a distant hum.

"What's that?" he called to Strelka, speaking loudly to be heard over his mask.

"It's nothing," Strelka said, peering back toward the entrance gate. "No vehicles here. Some faraway machine. Just focus on your—" The sound grew suddenly louder, and Strelka spun in place to face the canal. "Get down!" he breathed, dropping into the tall grass. "Hide!" From behind the brush lining the bank, a small inflatable boat piloted by a middle-aged man in a plain white shirt appeared. There was no time for René to move; he stood still, frozen. The boat came closer, and René felt his blood rushing in his ears. The man in the boat turned his head toward the transfer depot. He seemed completely unconcerned at the sight of René and raised his hand in a casual wave. René raised his gloved hand in return, and the man continued on without looking back.

When the sound of the outboard faded to almost nothing, Strelka rose from the grass, slipping his pistol under his shirt as he got to his feet.

"What the fuck was that?" René said, as the pounding of his pulse eased.

"I didn't—" Strelka shook his head. "I shouldn't have let him go like that. If he comes back, I'll take care of him." He nodded to the gear. "Just do your business so we can get out of here."

René returned to work, marking five of the kegs with red tape and the other five with blue. He marked the swing arms connected to the building in the same way: one red, one blue. From his assortment of aluminum fittings, he found a threaded end that fit onto the swing arm. He screwed that piece onto a reducing ring clamped to a length of shiny braided hose; the hose was fitted to a modified keg tap. He marked the assembly with red tape before putting together an identical one that he marked with blue.

"We keep everything separate," he said to himself out loud, pointing to each of the pieces of tape as he made a mental tally. "Two fill lines, one red, one blue. Ten tanks, five red, five blue. Okay." He took a deep breath and nodded. "Okay."

He walked forward with one of the red-taped kegs and pulled one of the swing arms—also marked in red—down so it was parallel with the deck. He connected the tap to the ball valve at the top of the keg, then stood up straight and held the keg by its handle at his left side. With his right hand he very, very slowly turned a lever on the swing arm. Gradually he felt the keg growing heavier. It didn't need to be completely filled, only a third or so for his purposes, and when the keg had gained an appropriate heft, he pulled the lever shut. René disconnected the keg, stood it on the deck, and grabbed one of the tubs of bodybuilding powder. He unscrewed the lid and liberally dusted the top of the keg with powder.

"What's that?" Strelka asked.

"Alpha-ketoglutaric acid," René answered. "It's a sham for building muscles, but not bad for neutralizing hypergolic fuels." He let a moment pass, then poured some of the citrus degreaser over the keg. “Citric acid will take care of anything the AKG misses,” René said. He repeated the process with the rest of the red-flagged kegs before placing them at the side of the deck closest to Strelka and the Armada. René disconnected the red filler hose and neutralized it thoroughly with AKG and degreaser before setting it to the side as well. Then he connected the blue hose and put the first keg into position.

Strelka observed the process from outside the cage.

“Strelka, let me offer you a couple options,” René said, looking up for a moment. “Either put on a suit and the other respirator and come in here with me, or get about a hundred meters away over there by the canal while I finish this.”

“Why should I do either?”

“Because if these chemicals contact each other, they’re going to explode. If they do, you might be killed standing where you are. But if you’re not killed”—René grinned behind his mask and flexed his scarred fist—“you’ll be messed up enough to wish you had been.”

Strelka walked a hundred paces down the canal to wait.

CHAPTER THIRTY-NINE

Jenny sat in the comfortable space outside Helena Nash's office and waited. Five minutes had passed since Tam had gone in; Jenny tried to distract herself by looking at her phone, looking for the news, looking for anything. She checked her messaging app for a text from Duncan, but nothing was there. Another five minutes passed, and Jenny got to her feet and began to pace. What if Mrs. Nash didn't want to see her? What if she thought somehow Jenny was to blame? She pushed those thoughts away. Jenny wanted Duncan to be safe. No matter what happened between them in the future, she just wanted Duncan to come home.

The door to Helena's office cracked open, and Tam leaned out.

"I'm sorry that took so long," Tam said, swinging the door wide. "Come on in."

Jenny entered a modern-looking office to find two other women inside: Helena, standing next to her desk, smiling warmly with her arms outstretched, and a blond, professionally dressed woman about the same age as Jenny. The professional one was seated, smiling thinly and visibly tense, but she got to her feet as Jenny entered the room.

"You are Jennifer?" Helena said. "Duncan's friend Jennifer?" Petite like Jenny, the older woman stepped across the room and drew Jenny into a close hug.

"I'm so sorry," Helena said softly into Jenny's ear. "I'm so very sorry."

Jenny swallowed back the feeling of oncoming tears, and she drew away to look Helena in the eye. "I'm sorry too," she said. "I'm sorry for you, Mrs. Nash. I'm sorry for your son. This must be so . . . it must be very hard for you."

"Please. I want you to call me Helena."

"And I've been . . . I've caused you nothing but trouble." Jenny couldn't help it now; tears began spilling down her cheeks, and she sniffed and used the back of her sleeve to wipe them away. The woman across the room looked like she was about to start crying herself, and she turned away from the scene.

"You believe in what you do," Helena said. "I respect that."

Jenny didn't know what to say. Duncan's mother, under the most impossible burden, was comforting *her*?

"You need to meet Janice, my assistant. Oh, come on, Janice, buck up, we've all been sad enough. Come meet Jenny."

Janice stepped closer and offered her hand. "Hello," she said. "I've followed your work very closely."

The absurdity of it, the ridiculousness of the pleasantries being exchanged, seemed to hit everyone at the same time, and they all broke out laughing.

"Maybe if we'd met sooner," Helena said, "so much of this could have been avoided." Her eyes misted, for an instant, and she composed herself again. "Tamara has caught me up. I know you've told her and Mr. Moran everything that happened, but maybe we could all have a seat and you could go over it one more time for my benefit? Only if it won't be too difficult for you."

"Oh, no," Jenny said. "Not at all."

They all took seats, and Jenny retold everything she recalled from the day the Russian showed up at the Defense Fund. Janice took notes on her tablet without looking up.

"And when he came over with that damn thumb drive and all that money, I thought, I don't know, there was a love letter for you in there from some rich Russian or something."

Helena smiled. "If only."

"I tried to tell him. I knew it wasn't right—I knew he shouldn't take that money. Even if that guy hadn't been such a creep, even if it had been the nicest person in the world offering money like that . . . I don't know. It wasn't right."

Helena closed her eyes and shook her head.

"Duncan," she said with a sigh, "has often in his life been drawn to the path of least resistance, shall we say." She opened her eyes and smiled wanly. "You are a good person, Jenny. I can feel it. I'm happy Duncan found his way to you. You two were together, but Tamara tells me that might not be the case anymore."

"We were," Jenny said. "I knew it couldn't last, though."

"I understand."

"But I still care about him. When they found his car, I don't know, I wasn't sure what to do. I knew Jake had something to do with your company, so I went to him."

"I'm glad you did," Helena said.

"Helena," Jenny said hesitantly, "may I see the video? Of Duncan?"

"It's so awful," Helena said. "But of course you may. Tamara, why don't you show her? I've seen it enough."

Tam went to Helena's desk, and Jenny followed. An open laptop sat askew on the otherwise empty surface. Tam brushed her fingers over the trackpad to wake the machine up, then tapped to play the video. Jenny clapped her hand over her mouth in shock and stood motionless as she watched. When it was finished, it took her a moment to speak.

"Play it again, please," she said, and Tam restarted the video. Jenny closed her eyes and listened to the way he spoke, the cadence, the way the words were thick through his broken teeth.

"He's reading something," she said when it finished, not opening her eyes. "That's how he reads from a script."

"That's exactly what we thought," Tam said.

Jenny opened her eyes. "Can you play it again?" Tam tapped the trackpad, and this time Jenny leaned in closer. Duncan sat stiffly in the chair, nothing like his normal relaxed bearing. His eyes were bruised and bloodshot.

And a newspaper from Miami. Miami? That Russian-sounding guy had been from Miami. That's what he'd said. But the way Duncan held it, his hands . . .

His hands.

Jenny leaned forward and squinted at the screen.

"Do you see something?" Tam asked softly.

"His hands. Look at his hands. Play it again. Watch his hands! Go back . . . back more . . . there. Start it there. Wait, look. See his fingers? Now hit play." Helena and Janice came over to join them, and they all leaned in close. On the left side of the paper, Duncan's four fingers were close together, while on the right the top three were close, while his pinky was slightly spread downward. Duncan's raspy voice began to speak.

"Turn off the volume," Jenny said. "Mute it." Helena reached forward and tapped a key, and Duncan's voice went away. The video played on, and she again watched Duncan's fingers spread apart before returning to their original position. They stayed that way before briefly opening again, but this time they went so the index and middle closed together on the left, and the index, middle, and ring fingers closed on the right. His fingers parted again, so slowly, staying apart for a long moment, before returning to their original position with the right pinky away from the other fingers. The motion was subtle and barely noticeable.

"Is it something like Morse code?" Janice whispered.

"They're numbers," Tam said, looking at her own hands as she reproduced the motions. "He's telling us numbers. Seven seven five seven. Maybe it's—"

"A combination?" Jenny said. "To some lock? Where they have him, maybe?"

Helena stood and crossed her arms. "You're missing something," she said. "When he opens all his fingers and pauses. It's another number. A zero. Seven seven five *zero* seven."

Janice gasped. "Oh my God," she said. "That's our—"

"Our zip code," Helena said.

"Are you serious?" Tam asked. "Could that mean—"

"He's here," Helena said. "Duncan is telling us he's right here."

CHAPTER FORTY

Back in the VIP lounge at launch control, Jake switched the cordless VoIP headset to his other ear to make sure he'd heard correctly. "You think he's there? In Clear Lake City?"

Across the room, Stu sat up in his chair.

"We watched it over and over, Jake," Tam said. "Helena and Jenny are convinced he's sending the message. I am too. What do we do, though?"

"I'm feeling like it might be time to get some outside help on this," Jake said. Across the room, Stu shrugged and shook his head.

"Helena's still opposed to getting any kind of law enforcement involved at any level," Tam said. "She thinks if the guys holding him get any idea the feds or anyone else is looking into it, it's all over for Duncan."

Jake hated to admit it, but he knew it was true.

"What if there's someone on the inside?"

"Is there any way you can get back to the mainland, Jake? I feel like we need you here. Can't Stewart take care of whatever's going on out there?"

"Maybe. It's probably a good idea for me to be there"—Stu scowled when he heard this—"but there are no helicopters flying tonight. My only chance is tomorrow at six a.m. There's one last passenger flight before they close the airspace for the static-fire test. I'll get things buttoned up here and catch the chopper back. How does that sound?"

"Okay."

"How's Jenny doing?"

"She's great. Focused. Once she figured out Duncan's message, she was ready for action. She wants to get out and start driving around to look for him right now."

"I'd suggest you stay put for the night. No hotel. Stay at Kingfisher."

"Obviously. We're not going anywhere."

"I know. Keep an eye on her, though."

"Understood."

"Be careful, Tam."

"You be careful too."

Jake ended the call and chewed on the news for a moment. Why would they want to make everyone believe Duncan was being held in Miami? He dropped down into one of the comfortable VIP chairs and put his feet up on a table. Even though it was nearly nine o'clock at night, the launch-control room below them was buzzing with activity.

"What's up?" Stu asked.

"They think Duncan was sending a message. They're certain he indicated Clear Lake's zip code with his fingers."

"The kid was pretty composed in the way he read the message," Stu said. "I wouldn't put something like that past him."

"He's a clever guy. And I trust Tam's take on it," Jake said. "Let's get to the mess and grab some chow. I'm starving."

"You go. I want to keep my eyes on this. Grab me a sandwich or something."

Jake left the VIP room and found his way down to the platform's cafeteria. There were a handful of people there at the late hour, and Jake found Tricia Cruz by a prepared-food case.

"Hey!" she said when she noticed Jake approaching. "How's it going? You're out here for the test?"

"Just wanted to see how things worked up close," Jake said. "You're on telem for this one?"

"She sure is," a voice behind Jake said. He turned to see Andy Lang with a pastry in one hand and a travel mug in the other. "Mrs. Nash wanted the A-Team for this launch," he said. "Only the best."

Tricia frowned. "You're not going to think I'm the best anymore if I can't keep our comms to the launch platform going for longer than five minutes."

"Untrue!" said Andy. "You've got plenty of time to work the problem. I know you'll get it ironed out."

"Thanks, boss," she said. "Jake, I'll see you on the other side."

"Good luck," Jake said. Then, "Comms dropouts?" to Andy as soon as Trish had left the room.

"I think it's interference from some drilling operation nearby. They're supposed to keep off our frequencies, but those oil guys don't give a shit about us." Andy leaned close and asked in a much lower voice, "Did you guys see anything over on the LP?"

"A little something maybe," Jake said. "We're staying the night to keep an eye on it."

"You guys need a room? We've got a hundred beds out here. It's like a hotel."

"I think we're good. Stu has his stuff arranged upstairs. But if you have any sleeping bags aboard—"

"I'll have someone run some up. Anything you need."

"Thanks," Jake said. "Hey, I know you've got a lot going on, but there's something I need to tell you." Andy nodded, and Jake leaned closer. "There are some eyes on this launch. Some weird attention."

"What do you mean? Government, or what?"

"I can't go too deeply into it, but it's important everything from here to launch day proceed as nominally as possible."

"Jake, come on, I like to keep things moving, but if I see a problem, I'm going to stop the count. I know Helena's under a lot of pressure to get this thing flying, but I'm not going to let that affect my decisions."

"I'm not telling you to pass on a scrub. On launch day, you can freeze it if you want. But up until then, I need you to keep it looking like a regular countdown with no issues, okay?"

"You're stepping on my command," Andy said. "This is messed up."

"I know it is, and after it's over, I'll explain everything. I wish I could tell you more now. Call Helena if you need to—she'll back me up."

"Fine. Whatever."

"Thank you. And, hey, if I need to get in touch with you while I'm out here, how can I do that?"

"I'm going to be pretty busy between now and the test," Andy said.

"I know. I promise, only in an emergency." Jake grabbed Andy's shoulder and gave it a shake. "Come on, man, think of all the stuff we worked at SPAWAR. Did I ever feed you bullshit then? Or get in your way?"

Andy shook his head and pulled a small spiral notepad and pen from his pocket. "This is my extension on the platform," he said, scribbling down a number. "It goes to my console, and if I'm not there, it forwards to my quarters. Maybe four people have this number." He ripped the sheet from the pad and stuffed it into Jake's hand. "Now five. Don't abuse it."

True to his word, Andy had bedding and a pair of folding cots sent to the observation room. Stu promptly dozed off, but Jake had a hard time sleeping. With the glow from the launch-control room and Stu's intermittent snoring, it was difficult for Jake to turn off his mind. If he were on land, he'd get up and go out for a run in the dark. But here on the platform, stuck on a cot, all he had were the room and his thoughts.

The few times Jake felt himself falling asleep, he was jarred awake by something. Some noise on the platform, voices in the hall, Stu rising to check on the laptop. At five in the morning the public affairs announcer began his broadcast for the day, his monotone piped into the observation lounge through speakers in the ceiling.

"Welcome to the HiPEP-D static-fire webcast here from Kingfisher launch-control operations. We are T-minus two hours and thirty minutes until our planned static-fire test of the Kingfisher Seven *in preparation for a launch scheduled less than two weeks from today. It's a beautiful morning out on the Gulf, and the vehicle's computer has begun prechilling operations in preparation for cryogenic methane and oxygen propellant fills. The HiPEP-D demonstration satellite is sitting at the very top of the stack this morning for our integrated test, and both vehicle and payload are looking healthy . . ."*

Jake got out of his cot and searched around the room for some kind of volume control or switch to turn the sound off but found nothing and gave up.

Stu sat up and rubbed his eyes. "If I wanted to listen to the webcast," he said, "I'd bring it up on my fucking computer." He raised his arms in a stretch. "I still slept pretty well, though. How about you?"

"Go to hell, Stewart."

"Not so good, huh?"

Jake went to the bathroom down the corridor, where he brushed his teeth and splashed some water on his face. He visited the now-bustling cafeteria and grabbed a couple of mugs full of black coffee, along with some muffins and tired-looking bananas. Back in the observation lounge, he found Stu on the floor doing push-ups.

"Fifty-eight . . . fifty-nine . . . sixty. Ugh." He rested flat on the floor for a moment, catching his breath.

"Show-off," Jake said.

"I need to wake myself up," Stu said, rolling over onto his back.

"This will wake you up," Jake said, giving him the coffee.

He went to the wall of glass and looked down on the scene below. Every console was occupied by headset-wearing engineers. Some typed on their keyboards or consulted stacks of documentation, and others were engaged in conversation. The mood was serious but friendly. At the back of the room, Andy Lang paced with his arms crossed, speaking to someone on his headset. At the front, critical telemetry markers were displayed on one half of the wall-size display. The other half played live video of the rocket standing clouded by vapor in the dawn light.

"Prechill procedure is nearly complete, we've passed the two-hour mark, all systems looking nominal at this time . . ."

"Look at that guy," Stu said, coming up alongside Jake. "Like he's got no cares in the world."

"He may look relaxed, but he's in high-stress mode right now. He just knows how to make it look easy."

"I don't see why you defend him like you do."

"Stewart? Shut up."

From the back of the room, there was a brief chirp.

"What is that?" Jake asked. Stu ran back to the laptop and tapped at the keyboard. "Is that your—"

"We've got data coming down the pipe," Stu said. "It just ran an automated script. In the clear too. Yep, it ran a script. Copied a big XML file. This must have taken an hour to download over Iridium."

"Let me see it," Jake said. He scrolled through the text file and frowned. "These are operational parameters for the vehicle's command systems. Everything. Launch commit, hold-down release . . . this is basically a flight profile." He furrowed his brow as he scanned over hundreds of different figures. "Inclination . . . what? I don't know what their initial frame of reference is. Maybe . . . maybe it's an unfueled simulation. Flight-termination radio system is disabled, so . . . I don't know."

"Does any of it make sense to you?" Stu asked.

"It does and it doesn't. What do these commands at the end say?"

"It's SCP in a Bash script," Stu said. "Secure copy of the XML file to some other destination. To an IP, not a host name, so I don't know what the device is. Maybe another server on the network. It's using an authentication token instead of a password, so they must have been in there before. It's got to be a trusted system they're writing it to."

"Can you print out a hard copy?"

"Stand by one."

Jake went to a VoIP handset at the far back corner of the room and pulled the crumpled paper Andy had given him from his pocket. He dialed the number, and there was no answer after ten rings. He dialed again, this time letting it go fifteen rings. He called a third time and counted the rings. Andy picked up on the twenty-second ring.

"Damn it, Jake, is this you? This had better be good, because this is not the time—"

"I need to show you something. Right now. It's urgent."

"Can it wait fifteen minutes?"

"It can't. Where can I meet you?" Across the room, the printer began to churn and spit out pages. Stu picked them up one by one.

"Level four. Meet me in the hall outside of launch control. So help me God, if you're pulling my chain—"

"There in a minute," Jake said.

Stu held up the stack of printed pages.

Jake nodded to the door, and the two of them took off at a run. They bounded down a steel staircase, two steps at a time, and entered a long corridor.

"This way," Jake said, taking off to his left. They made another turn to the right and met a dead end at a pair of doors with a security guard standing next to them. Above the doors was a sign reading **KINGFISHER LAUNCH CONTROL—BADGED ENTRY ONLY**. Below that was a digital countdown display: **T-1 HOURS 21 MINUTES 55 SECONDS**.

"Are you gentlemen lost?" the security guard asked.

"We're meeting someone here," Jake said. The doors flew open, and Andy came through, ripping his headset from his ears.

"This had better be fucking good," he snapped. "I do not have the time to be—"

Stu held out the stack of papers, forcing them into Andy's hands.

"Look at this," Jake said. "Tell us what it means."

"What do you think? It's a launch-parameters file," Andy said. "It's the configuration for the rocket. You know what this shit is—you really needed me to tell you this?"

"Look at the values, Andy. Tell us what they mean. Quickly."

Andy thumbed through the pages, squinting and scowling as he looked over the figures.

"Yeah. Funny. Hilarious. Not really. Where the fuck did you find this?"

"What is it?"

"You know what it is!" Andy said, his voice and agitation rising. He tried to hand the pages back to Stu, and a couple of sheets fell to the ground.

"I don't, Andy," Jake said. "Tell us what it means."

"Okay, great. So you've made, or someone has made, a proof of concept." He flipped through the pages, dropping another to the floor. "So what do you want to do, show me you can blow up Houston? That's what this does. It's pretty fucking clever. Launch commit, hold-down-system release, disable range-safety-signal intercept, launch inclination minus two degrees instead of thirty-three? You're going straight to Texas in this profile. East of Houston. Right to Clear Lake. What the fuck?" He nearly threw the pages to Jake, while Stu collected the sheets that had fallen to the ground. "Really funny, asshole. Now excuse me, because I have a test to run here—"

"Wait," Stu said, scanning over the pages in his hand. "Wait. This IP address. On the bottom there." He tapped the spot and thrust the paper toward Andy. "What server is that?"

Andy rolled his eyes before looking at the page. He frowned and cocked his head.

"That's not a server," he said. "That's the IP address of the primary control computer on the rocket itself. What is this, though? This SCP thing?"

Stu and Jake shared a look of alarm.

"That command copied these parameters to that IP address," Stu said. "About eleven minutes ago."

"What . . . does that *mean* . . . ?" The color had drained from Andy's face.

"That file is on board the vehicle's computer now," Jake said. "If the *Kingfisher Seven* accepted it, we aren't looking at a test anymore. The engines will keep running. The hold-down bolts are going to blow. That rocket"—he pointed to the east, toward the direction of the launch platform—"is going to launch with a radioactive payload and head straight for Texas."

CHAPTER FORTY-ONE

Tam headed westward on the Sam Houston Tollway, pushing the speed limit in her rental Volkswagen as much as she dared. The phone call at four thirty that morning had been troubling; the man on the other end spoke softly in a deep voice, filled with confidence and concern.

"Jake tells me he trusts you with his life," the man who introduced himself as Wade had said. "I think I need to trust you now. Someone's staked out at my place. Been here since yesterday around noon. Camped out in a black Escalade. Just sits there, watching the building. Sometimes he gets out and scouts around."

"Why do you think he's there for you?"

"You get a feel for these things," the man had said. "And I have a feeling right now. Also, the fact that I've heard him speaking Russian down in his car was a little bit of a red flag."

"Where are you? I can leave in ten minutes." Jenny would be safe, and Tam didn't want to move on the Duncan search until she could coordinate with Jake and Stewart.

"I'm in Sugar Land. West of Houston. Take the tollway to the interstate. Do you have firepower?"

"I can be armed, if that's what you're asking. Are you?"

"I'm armed, but not very mobile. I can't take him alone with this leg. With some help, though, I bet we can manage him. If he's actually here for me."

"Send me your address. I'll be there as soon as I can."

It took Tam less than an hour to get to Sugar Land and a few minutes to find the address Wade had given her; when she finally found the condominium complex, she orbited the parking lot and parked far away. She pulled Jake's gun from her bag and checked the chamber; the gun operated smoothly and with a comforting mechanical noise. Well maintained. In a way, it made her feel like Jake was there with her, and that gave her confidence. She opened Signal on her phone and dialed Wade's number.

"I'm here," she said.

"Where? What vehicle are you in?"

Tam felt a sudden prickle at the back of her neck; what if this was some kind of trap? Or worse, what if someone was eavesdropping on their communications?

"I parked far away," she said. "Your guy is in an Escalade?"

"Black. You can't miss it. Parked on the south side of the complex."

"Stay put," Tam said. "I'm coming to take a look."

Tam ended the call and exited the car, shouldering her bag as she stepped out onto the pavement. She'd dressed nondescriptly, jeans and a gray fleece top; her gender would keep her invisible to most as she made her way toward the complex. Around the first building to the west, she saw the car; her neck prickled again when she saw no one inside it. She walked toward the address Wade had sent her. Number 312, Unit D. The structure was made in such a way that banks of condominiums were on either side of an open corridor with staircases on the end, three stories high. She climbed the steps to the third floor, looking down the corridors as she passed each level. At the top she saw a man walking slowly, pausing at doorways. He was short, and a fresh red scar, prickly with stitches, lined the left side of his face. When he noticed Tam, he picked up his pace. She walked purposefully toward him, looking him over from behind her sunglasses as she kept her eyes pointed straight ahead. The man gave her a long look as well, then seemed to discount her completely and returned to examining the entry doors as he passed.

Tam considered drawing her gun and surprising him, but she opted for a different approach.

"Excuse me?" she said, turning back to face him. "Excuse me, but do you live here?"

The man started at the interruption, then quickly regained his icy composure.

"No," he said. "I do not." A Russian accent for sure.

"Oh, I'm sorry. I'm looking for . . . oh wait! This is Unit D? I think I'm supposed to be in Unit C. Sorry about that!" Tam made her way to the opposite staircase and trotted down to the second level and stopped. It wouldn't be smart to go to Wade's place now.

Suddenly a commotion sounded upstairs.

"Son of a bitch!" a deep voice called. "Hey!" Tam ran up the steps two at a time and back down the corridor. A door was wide open, Wade's door, and she looked in to see the Russian and a Black man scuffling on the floor. A silenced pistol rested on the tile next to them. Tam drew Jake's SIG from her bag and aimed it at the Russian's back.

"Stop!" she called, kicking the door shut behind her. She didn't want to draw unwanted attention that would bring the police. "Get off him or I'll shoot!"

The two men rolled over, the Russian's arm locked tight around Wade's neck.

"Take him out!" Wade gasped. "Shoot him!"

Tam didn't have a clear shot. "Let him go!" she yelled. "They caught your partner!" she shouted. "It's all over."

"Bullshit!" the man said as Wade struggled on top of him.

"Your partner, the other Russian, they caught him. In Clear Lake City."

"You lie," the Russian grunted. "Just now I was talking to him."

"Moments ago. They stormed your hotel room. They rescued Duncan Nash. They found him—"

"They found him?" the Russian said, incredulously. "The boy?" He let go of Wade and sat up. Wade winced and pushed himself back across the room with his arms, dragging a lame leg behind him over the floor.

"They found him in the hotel. He's on his way to the hospital now. And your partner is in federal custody."

"And the bombs?" the man asked.

"Bombs?" Tam repeated, and she flashed Wade a look of concern that was mirrored in his own expression. Before she understood what was happening, the Russian leaped up from the floor and swatted the SIG out of Tam's hand, sending it flying across the room. She felt her right arm being twisted harshly against her back, and her breathing became nearly impossible as the Russian tightened a thick forearm around her neck.

"Do you want to tell me now what is truth?"

"They got him," Tam gasped.

"Are you certain?" The man leaned back, and Tam felt her feet leaving the floor. She kicked helplessly, and her vision tunneled from a lack of oxygen. Her right arm was wrenched even tighter up into her back, and she clawed weakly at the choke hold with her free left hand. Across the room, Wade had worked his way up to his feet. He held a cell phone out in front of him.

"*Stoi*," Wade said firmly. "*Otpuskat.* Ease up, pal. Let her go. They're on the phone now."

Wade's voice was soft but assertive through the ringing in Tam's ears. The constriction around her neck loosened, just a little, and she sucked in a lurching, desperate lungful of air. Mercifully, her feet touched the floor once again to support her weight.

"She's telling the truth?"

"The CIA," Wade said. "On the phone. They want to avoid an international incident. Listen to me. She's telling the truth. *Eto pravda.* They know you're GRU, okay? They won't kill you, and they won't kill your guy. They'll let you walk, with the right conditions. Put her down and talk to this man—he can make a deal for you to get out of the country and not make a scene. You understand? *Vy ponimayete?* Your op is terminated. This is your ticket out of here." Wade held the phone out farther. The arm around Tam's neck loosened completely, and her right arm was released. The Russian slipped past her and stepped forward to take the phone from Wade.

When he looked down at the screen, Wade quickly brought the SIG from behind him, and the back of the Russian's T-shirt exploded in red. Tam yelped at the sudden noise, and the Russian fell at her feet.

"The CIA might not kill you," Wade said, limping forward and prodding the man with his toe, "but that doesn't mean *I* won't kill you." He safed the pistol and handed it back to Tam. "Nice gun."

"It's Jake's," Tam said, taking deep, trembling breaths to collect herself. "Thank you for that." She stared at the body at her feet, not quite believing that the man's life had been extinguished right in front of her.

"It was you or him," Wade said gently, touching his hand to Tam's shoulder. "I'm glad it was him. Is that the first time you've seen someone get shot?" he asked, and Tam gave a halting nod. "You're doing fine. You did great there. I owe you. Hey, you're gonna be fine. I just look calm, okay? You wouldn't believe it, but my heart's going about Mach 1 right now after putting that dude down. It never gets easy, let me tell you that."

"How did he get in?"

"I was an idiot. I heard your voice outside the door and opened up to take a look. He was right there."

"Sorry about that," Tam said.

"My fault," Wade said. "I was getting antsy. I should have just stayed put. But Jake wasn't kidding about you. Pretty badass, the way you managed that guy."

"He's not going to bother us now." Tam took a deep breath to calm herself. "What did he say about a bomb?"

“I think we need to get back to Clear Lake,” Wade said, grabbing a pair of crutches from against the kitchen table. “You calmed down now? Are you okay driving fast?”

“I mean . . . I might not be—”

Wade grinned. “Give me your keys. I’ll drive.”

CHAPTER FORTY-TWO

"These guys are coming in with me," Andy said sharply to the guard at the door of the launch-control room. The man frowned at the demand but let them pass. Jake and Stu followed him at a fast clip to his console at the back. Everyone in the room was occupied with his or her work; no one paid much attention to the pair of newcomers. Over it all at the top of the display were the words **STATIC FIRE TEST IN T-1 HOUR 15 MINUTES 07 SECONDS**. At his console, Andy slammed his body down into his chair and pulled his headset over his ears, pressing the mic close to his mouth.

"Telem, it's flight . . . hey, ah, I know this is out of procedure, but can you quickly open a secure shell to the vehicle and run a tail on master config for me? I'm . . . I'm getting an indication we may have had some corruption on the last lines of the . . . What's that? You can't access it? No, we haven't changed it . . . no, that shouldn't have changed at all." Andy leaped back to his feet and peered over the rows of consoles. His face was pale, and his hand shook when he reached to press a direct-communication button. He cupped his other hand over his microphone.

"Trish," he said quietly, "can you come back here and give that a try from my console?"

Tricia rose in her spot up at the front. She turned and made a puzzled face at the sight of Jake and Stu before trotting to the rear of the room.

"What's up, Andy?" she asked, flashing a concerned look between the three of them.

"Just give it a try, please."

Tricia took a seat in Andy's place and typed some commands on his keyboard. Jake leaned forward to see the words "Access denied" on the screen.

"Did someone change the preshared key?" she asked.

"It shouldn't be changed," Andy said.

"You can't use a password to authenticate?" Stu asked.

"No, we disable that and use an encrypted-key architecture for extra security," Andy said. "But somehow the key got . . . changed." He raised his hands and pressed his fingers to his temples.

"What does that mean, exactly?" Jake asked.

"It means we can't log into the rocket's computer," Andy said. "And we can't modify that file."

"Guys, what the hell is going on here?" Tricia asked.

"I think we need to abort," Andy said.

"You can't abort," Jake said.

"I'll abort the damn thing if I want to," Andy growled. "Trish, thank you, you can go back to your console now. We're going to abort."

"Andy, please, you can't—"

Andy leaned in close, bringing himself nearly nose to nose with Jake. "Who the hell do you think you are, talking to me like this?" he said in a low growl. Jake saw sweat beading on his forehead and upper lip. "This thing is going off the rails, and I'm going to stop it before anyone gets hurt. This is *my* command, and there's nothing you can say or do that's going to change my mind—"

"Andy!" Jake snapped. "Listen to me! Helena Nash's son has been kidnapped by Russian agents. They're behind all this. If they see the count stop, they'll kill him."

Andy shut his mouth.

Stu nodded gravely. "We're sure they're the ones who uploaded the code to your rocket," he said. "If they start to suspect we have an idea of what's going on, it's all over for the Nash kid."

"You're really not joking."

"We *need* to make them believe the count is proceeding nominally," Jake said. "We could maybe put a hold in the count for some reason to buy us some time, but we can't scrub completely."

Tricia had been following intently. "Okay," she said and took a deep breath, like she was trying to wrap her head around the situation. "So, let me think this through here. A hold wouldn't be hard. We've had glitchy comms all morning. Bad enough that I'd probably call a hold on a real launch, but I've let it slide for the test. But anyone who's been following the webcast would have heard us talking about bad comms for the past hour. Calling a hold wouldn't seem unusual, I don't think."

"That's great," Andy said sarcastically, his voice taking on a nervous, high pitch. "Just great. So we stop the clock here. Great! It doesn't halt the onboard sequencer out on the vehicle, though. It's still counting down with the bad code, and there's no way for us to stop it!"

"Get your shit together, sailor," Stu said.

The two men glared at each other for a long moment before Andy turned his gaze to the floor. "I know, I know," he said softly. "I . . . I don't know what to do."

"We need to overwrite that file somehow," Jake said.

Andy looked at the countdown clock and shook his head. "At T-minus sixty minutes, that file is read into the operations subsystem. Unless we can do it in the next twelve minutes. But without that shared key . . ."

"Fuck," Jake spit.

"Unless . . . ," Andy muttered, easing himself down into his console chair. He took a deep breath and began to work the problem. He thumbed through one of his binders for a moment before pushing it to the side and flipping through another. "Control parameters are loaded into the computer an hour before launch," he said. "But guidance parameters are read in real time, and that's from a totally different file.

Each entry in the file represents an inertial frame, read about every half second. After the launch failure, Elliot Hsu came up with an elegant trick so we could simulate activating the flight-termination system at any point during the ascent without a command from the radio. Basically for our simulations in training. It was safe because the system wasn't live, you follow? But if we could add a termination command to the *real* ascent profile on the rocket now, say, thirty seconds in . . ."

"The vehicle would be destroyed away from the platform out over the Gulf," Tricia said. "Because *we'll* activate the flight-termination system."

"Exactly," Andy said, nodding vigorously. Some color had returned to his face.

"I like it," Jake said. "But we still need to access the rocket's computer to make the change."

"We really can't get in remotely?" Stu asked. "There's no back door?"

"God, no," Andy said. "Why would we add something so insecure? We want to deny all possibilities for security breaches."

"Looks like that worked out pretty well for you," Stu said dryly. Andy scowled and began to say something, but Jake raised a hand to stop him.

"Guys," Jake said. "Enough. We need to figure out how to modify that file remotely and solve this problem, or a whole bunch of people on the mainland are going to be in real trouble."

"If they deleted our secure key," Andy said, "there's no way." He shook his head. "We need to alert the mainland. Clear Lake City should be evacuated." He spun around and looked at Jake. "I don't care what you say about this. I'm not going to have any civilian fatalities on me because I was trying to protect Helena Nash's kid."

"I understand," Jake said. "Do it."

Andy pressed another button on his console. "Houston, this is launch control," he said, pausing as he waited for a reply. "Houston, this is launch control. Please respond." Andy waited for a few seconds before hailing the mainland once more. "Come in, Houston, this is launch control." Andy shook his head and clenched his fists. "Fuck!" he spit.

He transmitted again. "Houston, this is launch control transmitting in the blind. We have reason to believe the *Kingfisher Seven* is headed for the mainland, specifically for the Clear Lake City area. Repeat, we believe the *Kingfisher Seven* has been programmed to target Clear Lake. If you can hear us, we recommend evacuating—"

"They can't hear you," Stu said. He looked to Tricia. "You said you've had communication issues?"

"Since last night," she said.

"They're jamming you," Stu said. "In case someone figured out what was going on out here and wanted to warn the mainland. I brought some VHF marine radios out, but even if they work, they won't have the range to get to shore."

"What about public affairs?" Jake asked. "Could we have the public affairs officer alert everyone on his broadcast?"

"The video feed goes out over satellite," Tricia said. "On a real launch we have a PAO out here on the rig, but for tests or sims they do commentary from a studio back at Clear Lake."

"They know there's no way we can stop it—"

"There might be a way," Tricia said, and all eyes turned to her. "The *Kingfisher Seven*'s onboard computer has pins we connect a serial cable to for plug-in testing when it's horizontal on the platform. If you used a USB-to-serial cable, you could get directly in through terminal software on a laptop—"

"And it wouldn't ask for a password," Stu said, nodding slowly.

"Exactly," Tricia said.

"But how do you do that?" Andy asked.

"You'd need physical access," Tricia said. "You would hook the cable up behind access panel two. At the base of the first stage. You'd need a ladder, but it's totally doable."

It's totally crazy, Jake thought. But the clock was ticking down with no way to stop it. He shook his head, not quite believing what was being proposed, and turned to his old friend. "Stu?" he asked. "Have you ever hacked into a rocket before?"

CHAPTER FORTY-THREE

"He's not answering," Strelka said, tossing his phone into the SUV's center console. "I don't understand why he won't pick up."

"Maybe he's still busy taking care of that man," René offered.

"It shouldn't take so long."

"Maybe his phone is dead. He could be on his way back now."

"I hope so," Strelka said. "We need a second vehicle to place the rest of these devices." They passed a large sign that read **NASA Johnson Space Center**; in the distance lay low white buildings that housed NASA's mission control and astronaut offices. The Nissan continued out along a grassy perimeter until Strelka brought it to a stop at a line of trees. He and René exited the vehicle and walked to the rear to slide out a black contractor's trash bag with a bulky shape inside. It was heavy enough that it took both of them to move it. Inside the bag were two kegs and a smaller silver tank bound together with thick windings of duct tape; at the top was a disassembled walkie-talkie, a boxy battery, and a bundle of wires. In the center of the kegs, secured by more tape, were lead-sheathed cases of plutonium and cesium.

René and Strelka quickly slid the black bundle from the rear of the Armada and down into the ditch by the road, standing it upright so the battery and wiring would remain dry inside the bag. Then they gathered tall grass and brush to camouflage the device. The assembly was nearly impossible to see, even up close, when they were finished. If anyone did manage to notice it, they'd simply think that it was trash left by the side of the road. The job had taken less than three minutes. There was one more left in the rear of the SUV, and they jumped back in to find a place to put it.

"Explain to me again how it works," Strelka said. "I want to understand in case I need to take control of the system."

"There's nothing you can do," René said, getting an uncomfortable feeling from the tone of Strelka's voice. "I thought we were going to be long gone by that time anyway."

"Just tell me, okay? I want to know."

"The system is controlled by a central radio," René said. He'd given Strelka exactly the same explanation the night before. "When the master radio picks up the rocket's carrier frequency, it sends a control tone to the radios on the devices. That causes an H-bridge circuit to send twelve volts of current to open the ball valve on the CO_2 canister. That pressurizes the system tank. A half second later, the ball valve on the propellant tank opens and the oxidizer rushes in. As soon as the two come in contact, boom. It's done."

"It will work?"

"It should work. I tested each one when the system was dry. And I used a detonation system like this once before in Ankara with concentrated hydrogen peroxide. It worked beautifully then; I have no reason to believe it will work differently now. The only thing that could go wrong—"

"What?" Strelka said. He was edgy now, agitated. "What could go wrong?"

"If for some reason the frequency of the rocket fails to be picked up by the master radio."

"That won't happen. The signal has always been strong on the other launches."

"That's the other thing," René said. "That could be a problem. If the signal is too strong, the radio could pick it up and detonate early."

"We're talking only seconds," Strelka said. "In the confusion, no one will remember that there were some explosions early."

René looked into the back at the remaining device. "So NASA will be incapacitated by this action? Kingfisher too?"

"Out of business," Strelka said. "For good. The fear of radioactive contamination from a launch failure will set the US launch industry back ten years at least. Roscosmos will be a player again, and with Grandpa gone, Vostok will own it, see? You'll have a job there, if you want. Or at Energia. You could probably run it."

"What about China? India? ESA? They have launch capabilities too."

"You don't think we have operations there as well?" Strelka smiled. "The US is the biggest threat, though. Kingfisher leads the pack. The other competitors are meaningless."

They stopped again at the far eastern side of the space-center compound, wordlessly placing and concealing a device. There were three more back at the hotel. Strelka tried Petr on the phone once again; he got no answer and gave up in disgust.

"Idiot!" he spit. "We need that other car!"

"We can fit the last three in here at the same time," René said as they turned back in the direction of the hotel.

"Fine," Strelka said. "Fine. Those are meant for SpaceX and Kingfisher. Maybe we forget about leaving one at SpaceX. Have you checked the progress of the static-fire test?"

"Not recently," René said.

"Check now. Tell me what's going on."

René browsed to Kingfisher's website on the Russian phone; the static-fire webcast was right there on the site's front page. It took a moment for the video to buffer and for the announcer's voice to be heard.

"Ten minutes now into an unscheduled hold, still no word from out on the Gulf as we're experiencing spotty communication between both the platforms and the mainland, still waiting on an update from launch control. We'll get that to you as soon as we have it . . ."

"What does he say?" Strelka said, slowing the SUV and entering the hotel parking lot. "A hold?"

"Bad communications," René said. "Is it really that, or have they figured out something's going on?"

"Actually, it's part of the plan," Strelka said, backing into a parking spot. "Vostok's people are jamming them. But Nash won't let them stop the countdown. Come. Let's get the last three devices. The hard part is nearly done."

CHAPTER FORTY-FOUR

Stu kept the inflatable boat's throttle pushed to its limit as they skimmed over the water toward launch Platform One. Jake stood back and to his side, shielding his eyes as the platform grew on the horizon.

At the base of the platform, Stu brought the boat around gently to the dock. Jake leaped up on the grated steel surface and held the boat steady as Stu threw a backpack up and followed. Stu secured the boat while Jake unlocked the gate with Andy's ring of keys. Seconds later the two men were silently running up the steps, two and three at a time. At the final landing before the platform, Jake paused at the blast shelter and propped its door open.

"I don't want to mess around if we need to get in here in a hurry," he said.

"Good thinking," Stu said, and they dashed up the final flight of stairs. They exited another steel door into the bright sun of the platform.

"Hold up," Jake said. The door to the stairs below closed behind them with a firm thud, and Jake grabbed Stu by the shoulder to stop him. "Give me one of those radios." Stu pulled a handheld VHF radio from his bag, and Jake raised it to his mouth and keyed the mic. "Launch control, we're up on the platform," he said. "How do you read?"

"Loud and garbled," came Andy's reply. "How me?"

"Same, but I understand. How's the video? You guys better not be seeing us."

"Old video is playing," Tricia Cruz's voice said. She had suggested broadcasting footage from a previous test on the webcast to make things look like a normal hold in the countdown. "Official count is holding at T-minus sixty minutes. We can't see or hear the webcast because of the jamming, but we're assuming PAO is reporting a hold."

"Roger. And where are we on the vehicle's clock?"

"T-minus twenty-eight minutes and counting."

"Rog. Give us a hack at T-minus twenty-five and every five minutes after that, please."

"Roger, Jake. Good luck."

At the center of the platform, the rocket hissed and groaned under the load of its superchilled propellants. Vapor rolled off the vehicle's sides and outward before dissipating through the open grating of the deck.

"You ready for this?" Jake asked.

"Don't think we've got much of a choice," Stu replied. "But I'm about as ready as it gets."

Andy's voice came back on the radio. "Okay, on the southern side of the integration shack, you'll find an extension ladder stored horizontally on hooks under the eaves. Do you see it?"

"Stand by one," Jake said. He took a second to get his bearings, then pointed to the low steel building off to their left. "That's it," he said, and the two of them took off for it at a run. Around the building they found an aluminum extension ladder suspended at head height.

"Got it."

Stu handed his duffel to Jake and took down the ladder.

"Okay. Access into the launch platform is going to be from the south. There's a gate in the fencing—do you see it?"

Stu took off for the gate with the ladder, and Jake followed.

"Twenty-five minutes and counting," Tricia said. "Mark."

Stu stopped at the gate and moved to the side to give Jake room to unlock it. Jake pulled the heavy ring of Andy's keys from his pocket, flipping through until he found one that looked like it would work. It didn't fit. He tried another, and that didn't fit either. He tried a third.

It slid in easily but wouldn't turn to unlock the gate. When Jake tried to remove the key, it wouldn't come out.

"What's up?" Stu asked. Jake said nothing, and Stu knew better than to press it. "It's stuck," Jake said after a moment of struggle, forcing himself to stay calm.

"Let me try," Stu said, stepping forward.

"No wait, maybe we should—"

Stu stepped forward and took the entire key ring in his hand. He gave it a grimacing twist, and his hand suddenly turned freely.

"You get it?" Jake asked. Stu frowned and shook his head, holding up the ring of keys.

"We've got a problem," Stu said. The key had sheared off in the lock from the force of his turning. "Shit!" he shouted, rattling the gate as he cursed. "Shit! Shit! Shit!"

"Forget it," Jake said. "Stu! Get over it. We need to find another way in."

"Twenty minutes," crackled Tricia's voice over the radio. "Mark."

"Come on," Jake said, starting back in the direction of the integration building.

The end of the building facing the launch platform had a roll up steel door large enough to let a rocket on its side pass in and out of the building. Over the grated deck were three sets of what looked like narrow-gage railroad tracks over which the rocket's strongback support could roll out to the launchpad. Jake followed the track to the fence. The track, cross-braced like an old trestle bridge, passed through a man-size gap under a rolling gate in the fencing, and over a twenty-foot-wide open space in the deck grate, with only a few pipes and girders between the launch level of the platform and the shimmering sea a hundred and forty feet below them.

"I know what you're thinking," Stu said, looking at the track spanning the open void in the deck, "and I don't really like it."

"I'll go first," Jake said. "You pass the ladder over the track after me; then you come across too." Stu stared at the chasm, seemingly frozen, and Jake punched him in the arm. "Come on, big guy. Snap out of it. This is our only choice."

Jake ran to the edge where the track crossed. He lay on the track, stomach down, and began to shimmy out over the steel beams. Slow and steady, pulling with his arms, pushing with his toes, staying low to get through the gap under the gate. About halfway across he paused for a breath, and he watched a drop of sweat fall from his nose and out of sight into the open air below him. Almost across. He slipped his fingers through the decking on the inside for a secure grip and pulled himself the rest of the way. He was in.

"Push the ladder to me!" Jake called, his heart still pounding from the effort and exposure. Stu got down on his knees and nudged the ladder forward, keeping it centered and straight on the track. He saw that it wasn't quite long enough for Jake to reach on the inside, so he pulled it back, extended it, and pushed it across again.

"Coming up on fifteen minutes. Mark."

Jake grabbed the closest rung with both hands and pulled the ladder toward him. In his haste he failed to keep the ladder straight, and it tipped to the right side and began to fall off the strongback track.

"Oh, shit!" Stu called. "Jake, Jesus, be careful!"

The ladder fell completely off the track, but Jake kept a tight grip on the rung. The weight of it yanked his upper body over the edge of the deck with a jerk.

CHAPTER FORTY-FIVE

Back in the room, Strelka knocked on the door to the adjoining suite.

"Mama's boy?" he called in English. "Listen, soon we will be leaving, okay? Why don't you pack your things!"

There was no reply, no moan, no cough, nothing, and Strelka turned to René.

"He must be resting," Strelka said, his eyes gleaming viciously.

"Let's hurry," René said. "We're getting tight on time. I don't want to be near these things after I arm the master radio."

"What do you mean, 'arm' it? You said nothing about arming it."

"There is a last connection I need to make. I left it open because we don't want any accidental detonation while we're—"

"Do it now," Strelka said.

"You want to be driving with those things like that?"

"I said do it now. I'll wait."

René sat at the table and pulled the back off the radio he'd been carrying in his pocket.

"You're crazy, man."

"Do it!"

It was one wire: a tiny orange twenty-two-gauge wire he'd left disconnected. He'd soldered in a screw terminal to simplify the connection. There was no reason to hesitate; if there was going to be an accidental detonation, their deaths would be instantaneous and none of this would matter. René slipped the bare end of the wire into the terminal and tightened it with a jeweler's screwdriver.

"It's done," René said, letting out a long breath.

"Give it to me," Strelka said.

"Let me carry it. I'm used to handling these things—"

"Give it to me. Now." Strelka held out his hand.

"Don't press the two buttons together at the same time," René said, giving it over. "Remote detonation. Bad news. Listen, leave it here while we move the last devices—then you can have it. I don't want you to blow us up."

Strelka looked at the toy radio in his hand. "These two buttons?"

"On the front and on the side. It's for sending Morse code. That tone activates the devices."

Strelka nodded and placed the radio next to the satphone in the kitchenette. "Come on," he said. "Let's get the last ones in the car."

The devices were encased in black trash bags, and they used a luggage cart to move them down to the Armada. Three trips and it was finished. Back in the room, Strelka pocketed the master radio.

"Be careful with that," René said.

Strelka shook his head and moved to the adjoining room's door. "Now I want you to meet our special guest," he said, looking back over his shoulder with a grin as he pulled the sliding latch aside and opened the door.

A young man stood in the doorway holding the broken leg of a chair cocked like a baseball bat. When Strelka turned to face the room, the lumber swung in a dark blur and struck his face.

"Fucker!" the man wielding the chair leg shouted as he swung. Strelka crumpled to the ground, and the wild-haired man dropped to straddle him, clubbing Strelka's face over and over.

"Fucker . . . fucker . . . fucker!" the man shouted with each swing. Each blow landed with a wet, crunching smack, and the white-painted doorjamb splattered red with flecks of blood. For a moment, Strelka tried to block the blows with his arms, but they fell limp to his sides.

“Watch his pocket,” René said. “Watch out for his pocket!”

Finally the man lurched upward, dropped his makeshift weapon, and staggered back before collapsing to the floor. His breath came in ragged gasps, both eyes were blackened, and half his face was covered in a greenish-brown bruise.

“Fucker,” he spit one last time, his chest heaving. He was slightly built with prematurely graying hair, and he was missing his top front teeth.

“Don’t move,” René said. “Stay where you are.”

Strelka lay still in the doorway, his legs askew and his face bloodied. René leaned forward and gingerly fished the radio out of the unconscious Russian’s pocket, followed by the keys to the Nissan and the pistol in his waistband. He leveled the pistol at the man on the floor.

“Are you going to kill me?” the hostage asked, staring at the gun. He grabbed the wood from the floor again, weakly raising it in the air as he panted.

“No,” René said, lowering the pistol. “Put that down.” The man dropped the splintered piece of wood and mumbled something through his ruined mouth.

“What did you say?” René asked.

“I said are you Russian?”

“No.”

“That guy on the floor is Russian,” the hostage said. “I’m pretty sure of it—”

“Shut up,” René said. “I’m trying to think.”

“It might help you to know—”

“Shut up!” René said. “Please. Just stay there. Don’t move. I won’t hurt you.” He ran his hand through his hair and turned around in place. On the counter of the kitchenette, he saw the satphone.

Vostok.

Vostok had all the information. He’d know what to do in this modified circumstance. René grabbed the phone, powered it on, and scrolled back to dial the last call in the phone's history. The call connected on the first ring.

"Strelnikov," a voice said. *Vostok.* "I hope you're on the move. I've heard nothing from Petr. Have you eliminated the Romanian bomb maker yet?"

Eliminate?

In a flash, it all came clear. He should have known. This whole time, he should have known he was expendable. The whole plan was a lie. Everything, all of it. A lie.

René said nothing.

"Strelka, are you there? I hear you—is there some kind of trouble?"

René terminated the call and dropped the phone to the floor. He went to one of the beds, grabbed a pair of pillows, and placed them on Strelka's chest. He pressed the pistol tight against the pillows and pulled the trigger so it discharged with a loud but muffled *whup*. Strelka's limbs twitched as the bullet stopped his heart. René stepped over the dead man and helped the hostage to his feet.

"Come with me," he said. "We need to get out of here."

"He deserved it," the hostage said, as if trying to comfort René for what he'd just done.

"Maybe so."

CHAPTER FORTY-SIX

Jake hung over the surface of the Gulf of Mexico twenty stories below him—while the ladder swung in his hands. Only the weight of his legs kept him from going all the way over. His palms were slick with sweat, and he grunted as his body made a small lurch forward.

"Let it go, Jake, just let it go! Drop it! Drop the ladder and get back up there!"

Jake had no intention of dropping the ladder, but a sudden roaring hiss from the rocket behind him startled him so much he nearly let go. He uncurled his left hand from the rung and brought it to his side to tightly grip the deck grate. With all his strength he pulled the ladder up with his right hand and tilted it back so he could slide it next to him. He took a breath and held it for a two count to regain his composure, then waved to Stu.

"Come on across now!" Jake called. Stu got down on his stomach and slid himself along the track. When he came to the gap beneath the fence, Stu twisted his body slightly to the side to give his pack enough room to get through. When he shimmied within arm's reach, Jake grabbed the pack straps and steadied his friend the rest of the way. Stu rolled over on his back and took a long breath with his eyes tightly shut.

"You know, there's a reason I didn't sign up for the SEALs," he said, eyes still closed.

Jake patted him in the middle of the chest. "Come on," he said, getting to his feet. "Tough part's over."

He shouldered the ladder, and they ran to the base of the rocket. It was chilly from the supercooled propellants venting from the rocket during their constant replenishment, and the humid air around them was thick with cloudy vapor.

"Watch your step," Jake said. "The deck is wide open under the rocket for the flame aperture. It's a long way down."

"Roger," Stu said. "What side are we opening up?"

Jake keyed his VHF radio. "Launch control, this is platform. We're at the base of the rocket. Which one is panel two?"

"It's the one between the fins opposite the strongback," Tricia replied. "There are eight Torx-head screws. Down at the bottom of the panel it will say 'starboard servo access panel two,' followed by a serial number."

"You set up the ladder," Stu said. "I'll get the computer ready." Jake tipped up the extension ladder, resting the ends against the corrugated titanium sheet of the rocket's base with a dull clunk. Stu dropped to his knees and began emptying his pack.

"Platform, this is launch control," Andy's voice crackled over the radio. "Jake, a heads-up: At eight minutes in the count, you're going to get heavy tank venting. Then at two minutes thirty, the strongback is going to retract. You're going to want to be as far away as you can get."

"Roger," Jake said. "Understand." Stu handed Jake an open laptop and a cable. One end of the cable had a standard USB connector, and the other end had a bundle of small wires with plastic push-in connectors.

"Hang on to those," Stu said. He clamped a screwdriver in his teeth and climbed up the ladder. Jake braced the base of the ladder with his feet and watched as Stu meticulously removed each of the screws from the panel, letting them drop one by one down through the flame aperture into the sea below. Jake did not watch them fall; he needed no reminder of how high they were.

Stu worked from top to bottom. "Two to go!" he called. A moment later, Jake felt a sharp motion through the ladder, and he looked up to see Stu bobbling the screwdriver in his hand before losing it. Jake watched it fall, tumbling, twisting, as if in slow motion. He reached for it, too late, following it with his eyes as it bounced off the side of one of the engine bells and down, down, down into the waters of the Gulf.

"I just missed it," Jake said. "Sorry."

"Don't sweat it," Stu said. "We're good." He reached up to the top of the panel and peeled it back like the lid of a sardine can. "No problem." He descended the ladder and took the laptop from Jake. "Now, if I drop that," he said wryly, "you better catch it."

"Don't drop it, then."

Stu gripped the looped cable in his teeth and held the laptop in the crook of his left arm as he climbed one handed back up the ladder. A whoosh sound came from up at the second stage, and a chilly, blinding fog washed down over them.

"Brrr!" Stu shivered.

"Hang on," Jake replied.

"I'm ready."

"Launch control, platform here. We're ready to hook up the cable."

"Okay, guys," Tricia said. "There's a small circuit board at the lower right of the access port. It should have two rows of twenty pins, numbered starting with one at the upper left."

"You get that?" Jake called.

"I got it," Stu said. "And I see the pins."

"We have visual on the pins," Jake relayed.

"Okay, good. Now on the cable, red goes to pin one, black goes to pin three, that's transmit, white goes to pin—"

"Wait up, wait up," Stu called.

"Slow down," Jake said.

"Next, white goes to pin four—that's receive," Tricia said, speaking slowly. "And green to pin five."

"We're good!" Stu called.

"Now for the terminal settings, in your emulator you're going to need eight bits, no parity, one stop bit, and 9,600 baud."

"Got it," Stu said. "Eight, N, one, and ninety-six hundred. I'm trying to connect."

"And we're at ten minutes. Mark."

"Not to add any stress here, guys," Andy chimed in, "but that propellant vent is coming up in two minutes. I'd suggest you get clear and finish up when it's done."

"Fuck that," Stu said. "We're in!"

"Stu says we're in. Now what?"

"It's a BSD operating system. Change directory to e-t-c slash trajectory. Then open the flight-params XML file."

"Okay, I'm . . . fuck!"

"What?"

"The terminal session reset itself."

"You're sixty seconds from that venting, guys."

"I'm getting in there again. What line am I editing?"

"Quick," Jake said into the radio. "What does he edit?"

"He's going to see a time at each heading. Each frame is half a second of flight time. Have him scroll down to somewhere after ten seconds into the flight. That gives it time to get away from the platform but not build up too much velocity. But you guys are running out of time on that propellant vent."

"Can we tough it out?" Jake asked.

"No! Repeat . . . negative. Get . . . of there." The signal crackled with static. "You've . . . twenty seconds. Get back . . . away . . . the vehicle!"

"Get down, Stewart. Come on."

"I've almost got it."

"I said get down! That's an order."

Stu shoved the laptop into the open access port and clambered down to the deck. Jake pulled the ladder back and laid it flat on the grating before they ran to the farthest corner of the platform. It was open to the sea, and instead of tall fencing it had a low safety rail.

"Good news," Stu said, peering over the edge. "If things get dicey and we run short of time before the launch, we can jump."

Jake peered over at the waves far below. "I think I'd rather be scorched."

A belching, rushing howl erupted from the *Kingfisher Seven*, and a dense cloud of freezing vapor washed over the two men at the edge of the platform.

"Holy shit!" Stu shouted as it passed. He rubbed his bare forearms. "They weren't kidding!"

"Platform, this is control," Andy said. "Have you observed propellant venting?"

"Yes, we just had venting. Is it over?"

"All done. You guys . . . back. Seven minutes . . . ignition. Hurry."

Jake and Stu ran back and reset the ladder. The rungs and frame were covered with a thin skin of ice, and Jake had to watch his step on the frosty decking. Looking up at the open panel as Stu clambered back up, Jake saw the laptop dangling by the USB cable. It had been knocked loose by the force of the venting fuel.

"Close one, huh?" Stu said, repositioning the computer in the access port.

"Yeah, great. Get back into that file. Hurry."

"I'm getting there. Okay, we're in. Scrolling down . . . I'm at the heading for thirteen seconds."

"Okay, he's at a good spot. What does he need to type?"

"Roger, we copy you in the file," Andy said. "Drop down two lines from the header, and indent four spaces. Then type a less-than sign, no space, followed by—"

"The terminal fucking reset again!"

"Hold, hold," Jake said. "His terminal reset. And we need you to go slow on that code. We're getting a lot of static."

"You're at six minutes. Four minutes and . . . strongback retraction."

"I'm in again," Stu said. "Okay, hurry."

"He's in, Andy; quick, give it to us."

"Okay, open bracket, no spaces, lowercase f-l-t underscore t-e-r-m, equal sign, capital D-E-T-O-N-A-T-E. That's the word 'detonate' all uppercase. Now a space and lowercase letters k-e-y, equal sign, single quote, echo, echo, zero, eight, zero, foxtrot, seven. Single quote followed by a close bracket. Now save it."

"Saving . . . it shut me out again."

"Did it save?"

"Not sure. Let me check."

"We're running out of time, Stu."

"I'm aware. No, it didn't save. Nothing was written. Have them repeat the entry, please."

"Five minutes. Mark."

"We need the command again, guys."

"What the hell . . . going on out there?" Andy asked.

"Just give me the command! We need it loud and slow."

Andy repeated the command, and Stu typed it. Stu read it out loud, and Jake repeated it over the radio for Andy to confirm.

"Saved!" he said. "I think." He descended the ladder and grabbed his pack. "Let's get down to that blast shelter."

"You're sure it saved?" Jake asked.

"I'm pretty sure."

Jake raised the handheld radio. "How much time until strongback retraction?"

"You've got two minutes," Andy said. "You aren't still up on the platform, are you?"

"Go up and check it one more time," Jake said.

Stu didn't hesitate to climb up once more. "You're kidding me," he said from the top of the ladder. "Is this thing write protected?"

"We need it one more time," Jake said. "Read it to us one more time."

"You guys need to get out of there!" Andy said.

"I'm going to try it in another part of the file," Stu said. "Give it to me. Quickly."

"One minute until . . . back retraction, guys," Tricia said, her voice very choppy through a wave of static. "Please . . . telling you . . . fast . . ."

"Give us that code now, Andy. Nice and slow."

Andy repeated the command using the phonetic alphabet. Stu let out a whoop.

"I got it! I got it." He came down the ladder as fast as he could.

"Fifteen seconds. Get clear! The engines will gimbal as soon as the strongback is out of the way. Get off the platform!"

Jake and Stu took a few steps backward, and a low humming groan could be heard in the air and felt through their feet. The clamps released, and the strongback tilted backward and away from them. Its motion stopped with a solid *thunk*, and a moment later the seven engine bells at the base of the rocket swung from side to side in unison, knocking the ladder away.

"Gimbal test," Jake said. "Let's go." He ran to the gate they'd tried to enter and stopped. There was no door latch on the inside, just another keyed lock.

"Oh, shit," Jake said, his stomach taking on a sudden hollow feeling. He shook the grating of the gate, but it remained securely latched.

"T-minus two minutes if you copy," Tricia said. "Mark."

"Any way we can climb over?" Stu asked. Jake shook his head. Without speaking, the two of them ran across the platform to where they'd waited out the propellant venting.

"We aren't far enough away from that thing, are we?" Stu asked. "Can we shimmy back under the fence?"

Jake shook his head. "Sound-suppression water's starting any second," he said. "It would knock us right off of there." He estimated they were about seventy feet from the rocket. Even if they were somehow spared the heat of the burning engines, the shock wave from their explosive ignition would probably kill them.

At least it will be fast.

"Jumping doesn't seem like such a bad choice now," Stu said before looking over the edge. "Or maybe not. Jesus, this is bad, isn't it?"

"It's pretty bad," Jake said.

"Launch platform transmitting in the blind. One minute to ignition. Mark."

"Okay, Stu, at fifteen seconds, let's hang over the side. Maybe the edge of the platform will be enough to shield us from the blast."

Stu laughed at this. "You're just coming up with shit to keep us busy while we're dying, right?"

Jake nodded. "Pretty much," he said. "We'll try it anyway. Here, get down and get ready. We'll swing over the edge and hang at my call."

"We're not going to be able to hang on too well if our damn fingers are being burned off, are we?"

"You have a better idea?"

"Launch platform in the blind, thirty seconds to ignition."

A pulsing, rushing sound began as the *Kingfisher Seven*'s turbo pumps started to spin up. It was a sound Jake had listened to a hundred times before. Never this close, though. And now it would be one of the last things he ever heard. He closed his eyes for a moment and focused on the sound. Something was wrong: a vibration, a pounding. Something was off. The pumps were assembled with the precision of a fine watch, and they shouldn't sound like this. If a bearing race had cracked or a turbofan blade had broken free, the rocket should be smart enough to detect the fault and self-abort. The ragged thumping got louder, and Jake tried to hold his breath.

"Fifteen sec . . . till ignition."

"We might be in luck," Jake shouted from his crouch at the edge of the platform. The pounding sound was almost overpowering now.

Abort, you fucker! Abort!

"Come on!" Jake said through clenched teeth.

Stu grabbed his arm. "Turn around, Jake!"

"I'm going to watch it."

Abort!

"Jake, turn around!"

A deafening rush like Niagara Falls sounded over the platform as thousands of gallons of water began to flow into the flame aperture, and a torrent of chilled fuel rushed from the seven engine bells as they prepared for ignition. Jake's hair was whipped by a gust of wind. Over the cacophony, Jake heard Tricia Cruz's voice.

"T-minus ten seconds . . . nine . . ."

"Jake, I'm serious, look!"

The wind and noise were almost too much, but Jake allowed himself to be twisted outward by Stu to face the sea. There, hovering fifteen feet in front of him, was a Robinson R44 four-seat helicopter with its door wide open.

CHAPTER FORTY-SEVEN

René drove along the road where they'd dumped the transfer tanks the day before; he saw them gleaming in the ditch as they passed. The hostage sat in the back seat.

"My mother owns this facility," he said. "If you take me there, I'll make sure they understand you aren't responsible for anything that happened to me. There's probably a reward for my return."

René pondered it for a moment. He'd left too much of a trail. The dead men on the boat in Florida, the purchases for the bombs, the bombs themselves . . . there was no way he'd be able to explain any of that and get away. But away to where, exactly?

René turned at the same gatehouse they'd come through to get the chemicals. It was unmanned again. Inside the perimeter, he could buy some time to plan his next move.

"The main entrance is less than a mile down the road—"

"You need to shut up!" René said. "Now hang on."

He backed up the Nissan and floored the accelerator, tearing the gate off its hinges as he smashed through it. He swung the vehicle from side to side to shake the twisted chain link from atop the vehicle, then pressed forward toward the fueling complex. In his side mirror, René saw a flashing yellow light atop a white pickup truck that had begun to follow him.

"There wasn't supposed to be anyone here!" René said, bringing the SUV to a halt.

"There's generally elevated security during launch and test operations," the hostage said.

"Be quiet," René said. As the pursuing vehicle tried to pull alongside, he thrust the pistol out his window and emptied the clip over the truck.

"Stay back!" he shouted. "I have explosives in here! Give me room, five hundred meters! Anything closer and this whole place goes up!"

The truck turned back and returned to the open gate.

René pressed forward.

CHAPTER FORTY-EIGHT

Denny Wade was at the controls of the hovering helicopter.

"Eight . . . seven . . ."

Wade guided the chopper so its skid kissed the guardrail at the edge of the platform. Stu leaped onto the skid, and before Jake could even react, his friend grabbed a handful of Jake's shirt and yanked him aboard.

"Five . . . four . . ."

Wade dipped the Robinson forward, down toward the Gulf's surface, accelerating away from the platform like a roller coaster car diving off the crest of a rise. Kneeling on the cabin floor, Jake wrapped an arm around one of the rear seats to keep himself from tumbling out of the aircraft.

"Three . . . two . . . one."

Through the chopper's open door, Jake saw a brilliant flash and a jet like a massive blowtorch down through the structure of the launch platform. The surface of the water roiled and flashed to steam from the intense heat. A half second later they were shaken by a sound louder than a thunderclap, followed by the roar of combustion as the *Kingfisher Seven* slowly climbed into the air. Jake pulled himself up onto the seat and threw a pair of headphones over his ears.

"Follow that thing!" he said. "We need to keep visual on it."

Wade nodded and threw the speedy helicopter forward, climbing gradually as the rocket accelerated away to the north. He fought the controls as they were buffeted by the shock waves from the rocket's blasts, and Stu pressed a hand against the cabin headliner to keep himself in place as they were bounced around.

"Where did you put the second detonate command?" Jake asked. "What time in the file?"

"Two additional frames," Stu said, still bracing himself with one hand as he adjusted his microphone with the other. "Just to be sure it saved. First one was at thirteen seconds, with Andy on the line. Next I put it around fifteen, and the next after that was eighteen-ish."

Jake looked at his watch. Five seconds to go, and their ride calmed as the rocket built speed and pulled away from them.

"Coming up on thirteen," Jake said.

He mentally calculated the velocity of the rocket. At thirteen seconds, it would be going roughly fifty meters per second, a little more than a hundred miles per hour. The Robinson maxed out at 140 miles per hour. He glanced at his watch. Thirteen seconds had passed, and still the exhaust plume glowed steady ahead of them. It was surreal to see it moving low and level with the surface of the earth rather than climbing away on an orbital trajectory.

"Now fifteen seconds," he said. The rocket would be going maybe a hundred and thirty miles per hour now. At the same rate of acceleration, the *Kingfisher Seven* would reach Clear Lake in less than three minutes. Even if Wade pushed the Robinson to max speed, they'd be arriving minutes late to a smoldering hole in the ground.

"Passing eighteen," Jake said. "Wade, maybe climb up so we can alert them by radio—"

Jake was suddenly blinded by a fireball brighter than the sun. It lasted for half a second before it faded to a glowing red ball framed by black. In less than two seconds, it had mostly burned out, leaving a black cloud in the sky and multiple arcing trails of tumbling debris.

"Fuck yeah!" Stu shouted.

Wade threw the chopper into a hard left turn. "Hang on," he said calmly. "Shock wave."

The Robinson lurched with such force Jake worried it might be broken apart. The concussion knocked the air from his lungs and sent a squeal through his headset, and when he blinked and shook away the shock of it, he saw one of the doors hanging askew and a series of cracks running through the bubble canopy.

Wade turned back to the north, completely unfazed.

"You guys want to tell me what that was all about?"

"Long story," Jake said. "But how the hell did you know we were out here?" He unplugged his headset and wiggled up into the front left seat. "Nice to see you, by the way. How's the leg?" They clasped hands, and Wade grinned.

"Good enough to manage a rudder pedal. Who's the passenger?"

"That's my partner, Stu Gallagher," Jake said. "He's navy."

"Figures."

"Seriously, how did you end up saving our asses?"

"Funny thing," Wade said. "You gave me the number of your associate in case things got weird. Yesterday, things got weird. Russian visitor casing the place. I called your friend Tamara for some backup."

"How did that go?"

"My brother-in-law's not going to be too pleased about the mess we left him in his condo. But the problem is eliminated."

"Damn," Jake said. "And Tam's okay?"

"A little rattled when the shit went down, but she's good now," Wade said. "We picked up some intel when the Russian came for me, so I made the trip out to control to pass it on to you. Andy Lang told me you were out at the launch platform, so I headed over. Guess I showed up at just the right time."

"Can't thank you enough," Jake said. "What's the intel?"

"So this rocket we just followed, it was capped by a radioactive generator, right? And you guys stopped it?"

"Thank fucking God," Stu said.

Wade raised an eyebrow. "I would agree." A puzzled look came over his face, and he reached into his pocket to pull out a phone. He unlocked it and read a message before passing it over to Jake.

"We're close enough to get LTE," he said. "Your friend sent a Signal message."

If you've connected with Jake, Tam's message said, tell him we have reports of shots fired at Kingfisher at propellant loading complex.

"You mind if I reply?" Jake asked.

"Go right ahead."

Jake tapped out a response as fast as he could. It's Jake. Rocket destroyed. Are you safe?

I'm safe, came a nearly instantaneous reply. But we have dirty bombs here. They found one by JSC. Another here. Kingfisher campus on lockdown.

"Oh, shit," Jake said aloud, hit by a sudden understanding. "To be distributed in the area and set up to detonate when the rocket came in. To maximize the effect in case nothing was released from the RTG."

"This is fucked up," Stu said.

Try to keep law enforcement away, Jake wrote. Tell them propellants are explosive and they need to keep back. Do whatever you can to keep them off the perimeter. Lie and say it was a propellant issue if you need to.

I'll do what I can.

Jake leaned to his side and saw the surface of the water below them covered with flaming, smoldering debris. He hoped the RTG had held together.

"Wade," Jake asked, "can you patch me into Kingfisher comms?"

"Stand by one," Wade said, turning a knob on the helo's console. "You're on. Go."

"Kingfisher control, this is Jake Moran inbound for Clear Lake City. Do you read?"

"Go ahead, we read you loud and clear," a male voice replied. "Do you know what happened out there?"

"The *Kingfisher Seven* has been destroyed roughly ten miles south of Galveston Island. We have visual on the debris field—"

"Jake," a female voice interrupted. "This is Helena. They've patched me in—do you read me?"

"Loud and clear, go ahead."

"To confirm, the *Seven* left the pad? Are you saying it *launched*?"

Jake thought for a moment. The frequency he was speaking on was wide open; anyone could be monitoring it.

Fuck it, he thought. The truth needed to get out there.

"That's affirm. The flight profile was sabotaged in a way that allowed a launch . . . with a nonstandard trajectory. We were able to overwrite the profile . . ." He thought for a moment about how best to phrase it. "We modified the profile to ensure detonation of the range-safety system away from Kingfisher assets or interests on the mainland. The vehicle and payload were destroyed ten miles south of Galveston Island."

There was a long pause over the air. Long enough that Jake wondered if the radio link had gone dead. Either that, or Helena was furious over the information he'd just divulged on an open frequency.

"Thank you, Jake," she finally said. "We are grateful." She paused again. "You should know the facility here is locked down at the perimeter per Tamara's instructions—"

"I am aware. Stay put and keep it that way as long as you can. We have some business to wrap up at the propellant complex. Can you put Tam on, please?"

"She's not in my office now, Jake. She told me she had a hunch she needed to look into."

A hunch? "If you see her, will you tell her to stay put and contact me so we can coordinate? I'll be on the ground in five minutes. Moran, out."

Just then they passed over the shoreline, and Jake saw emergency vehicles with flashing lights lined along Seawall Boulevard.

“That explosion must have been a hell of a sight from Galveston,” Wade said. Jake drew his phone from his pocket and typed out a message to Tam.

I'll be there in minutes. Meet me on the ground.

The indicator showed the message was received, but not read.

The streets of Galveston Island flashed below them, followed by the tanks and ships and refineries of Galveston Harbor. A Coast Guard cutter rounded the eastern tip of the island, no doubt headed out to investigate the explosion. Ahead of them the sun glinted off murky ripples on the surface of Clear Lake.

Jake glanced at Wade. “You know where that propellant complex is?” he asked.

“I do, but are you sure you want to come in from above? Kind of kills any element of surprise.”

“Good point,” Jake said. “Let's go to the helipad.”

“No,” Stu said, leaning forward. “Take us to the parking lot.” The main Kingfisher building was ahead of them now, the flashing lights of police cars at the entrance. “See that Sprinter van? Put us down right next to her.”

CHAPTER FORTY-NINE

The chopper's rotor blades were still spinning down as Stu jumped into the back of his van and began digging through bins. Jake and Wade stood outside the open doors.

"If you guys need air support," Wade said. "I'll be standing by."

Stu came to where they were waiting and handed each an earpiece wired to a clip-on radio the size of a deck of cards.

"Voice activated," he said.

Jake looked over the radio and inserted the earpiece. "Wade," he said, "you monitor the situation. Keep us posted on what's going on back here. You need a weapon?"

"I'm stocked up," Wade said, thumbing back at the Robinson.

"Figures." Jake gazed around the area and quickly checked his phone. There was no reply and no time to waste. "Ping Tam again. Hopefully she can keep law enforcement out of the complex." There were no signs yet of flashing lights or sirens at the perimeter of the property. "Stu, you ready to do a little off roading?"

"Always ready."

Jake grabbed Wade by the shoulder and gave him a shake. "You saved our asses, man. Thank you."

"It was the least I could do," Wade said with a grin. "You guys be careful. Propellant depot is to the north with the big tanks. The property is bisected by a canal, so you'll want to keep to the east service road. There's a lift bridge you'll have to go over. You can't miss it."

"We'll keep you posted," Jake said.

He jumped up into the van and pulled the doors shut behind him. Stu had already made his way to the driver's seat.

"Lift bridge," Stu said, starting across the parking lot. "To the east." He drove off the pavement and straight over a landscaped berm into a manicured lawn. "Field glasses are in there," he said, pointing to the glove box.

Jake popped it open and took out a pair of folding binoculars. Stu plowed ahead, out of the landscaped area and into some tall grass. Jake adjusted the binoculars and looked out ahead through them, the jouncing of the van amplified through the lenses. They crossed the lift bridge, and the brush became thicker, more tangled, whipping at the sides of the Sprinter as they passed through. Jake heard a far-off siren; to his right, nearly a mile away at the property's fenced perimeter, he saw an emergency vehicle speeding down the road.

"You said Tam's keeping responders off the compound?" Stu said.

"Let's hope," Jake said. "Go for that line of brush. There's a break about three hundred meters ahead."

"I see it," Stu said. They continued forward and up onto a dirt utility trail that looked more like it was used by off-road four-wheelers than full-size vehicles. Stu eased the van through the tight gap in the brush, immediately stopping the vehicle as the branches swung clear from the windshield. A hundred and fifty meters ahead of them, next to a tall cryogenic propellant tank, a large white SUV was parked in the grass.

"If I was a betting man," Stu said, "I'd say that's the fucker we're looking for. Despite the new ride."

Jake lifted the binoculars and brought the SUV into focus. It was parked next to a concrete pad beneath a spherical tank held high on four girdered support pillars. A sign on one of the pillars read: **LIQUID OXYGEN: –218°C/–361°F—FREEZE DANGER—COMBUSTION DANGER—NO SMOKING.**

Jake looked at the SUV again. Its tires were mud spattered, and the driver's side front wheel had sunk into the muck.

"And if I was a betting man," Jake said, "I'd put some money on that shitbox being stuck."

"Oh, fuck," Stu said. "Jake, quick, a hundred meters to your left."

Jake swung the binoculars back toward the Kingfisher complex, and his blood went cold.

Tamara Rinaldi, with Jake's SIG gripped in both hands, was walking toward the tank.

"No, no, no, Tam," Jake said out loud. "Get back, get back, get out of there, Tam!" He pressed the earpiece in his right ear. "Wade, do you hear me? Message Tam, call her, tell her to stop and get out of there."

"Roger," Wade said. "She hasn't answered my—"

"Just do it!" Jake raised the glasses again. He could see Tam's mouth moving, like she was shouting something. He turned back to the SUV. Visible through the driver's side back window was a silhouette—maybe a headrest, maybe a person? There was a movement below the rear passenger-side bumper. The barest movement, a shoe? He turned the binoculars back to Tam. She moved slowly now, in a tactical crouch, shouting toward the white SUV.

"Stay here," Jake said. "Set up on the roof. Look for a shot, but don't take anything until I say." He opened the passenger door of the van.

"Give me a sec to get you a sidearm," Stu said.

"You're my sidearm. No time. I need to get out there."

"Tam kind of looks like she's got the situation under—"

Jake was already out of the Sprinter and moving to the edge of the ditch. He waved his arms to get Tam's attention, but she was locked in, creeping forward and shouting at the unseen person behind the vehicle. Her voice barely carried over the distance.

"Freeze!" she shouted. "Don't move! Put the gun down at your feet and keep your hands in the air!"

Jake leaped over the ditch and started toward Tam at a jog. She was about fifty meters from the tank now. Jake swung wide to the right to keep the white SUV between him and the unseen man.

Stu's voice came over the earpiece. "I've got one person in the back seat," he said. "Got him in the scope."

"Is he armed?" Jake said in a low voice.

"Not moving. Seat looks reclined. Anything fast, though, and I'm taking him out."

"Negative, negative. Hold your fire. If you see anything, tell me first."

Across the field, Jake saw that Tam noticed him. He waved his hand low, hoping she would understand not to acknowledge his presence. She kept her gaze focused on the person behind the white SUV.

"Put the gun down!" she shouted.

"It's not a gun!" a voice called back. "This will send a radio signal! There are bombs all over this city! Radioactive bombs! One signal from this and they all explode!"

"Stu, did you get that?" Jake whispered.

"Negative, repeat."

"He says there are dirty bombs spread around. He has a detonator. Are you seeing him at all?"

"Just glimpses. No clear shot."

"I have more in the car!" the voice called. "And a hostage. Someone you have been looking for!"

"It's Duncan in the car," Jake told Stu.

"Roger. I'm watching."

"Hold it up!" Tam shouted. She was only ten meters away from the tank now. "Show me that's not a gun!"

"Why should I show you anything? But look, here!"

Over the car, Jake saw the man's hand rise in the air with a black-and-orange object.

"It's a radio," Stu said. "Consumer walkie-talkie."

"Can you take it out?"

"He's moving too much."

"Tell me if you get a clear shot on any part of him."

"Rog."

Jake forced himself low and slipped behind the rear of the SUV.

"You see?" the man said. "It is a child's toy! But I've made it very dangerous. If I let go of this button, it's all over! For all of us here. And the city will be in a panic."

"I heard him," Stu said. "He's twitchy. Cornered. Stay quiet there. You're too close. That's no dead man's switch. He's bluffing."

Jake wanted to suggest they not take any chances, but he kept his mouth shut.

"Fine," Tam said. "Here." She put the SIG down on the ground at her feet and took a step closer. "You want to get out of here. I understand. Maybe we could make a deal."

"There are no deals to be made! I am the one with all the options! I'm telling you, go away from here or we all will die!"

"You might be out of options," she countered, "but I have an idea."

Jake watched Tam projecting supreme confidence, her eyes completely focused on the man.

"I've got a clear shot," Stu said. "Wait, negative, he's behind the car again. Come on out of there, you little fucker. Come on out and meet—"

"Here's my idea," Tam said softly. "You let the person in the car go, and I'll go with you instead."

No, Tam! No!

There was a pause, and Jake could tell the man was considering it.

"Why would I do that?"

"Because I am important," Tam said. "I am in the news all the time. People recognize me. If you have me, you'll have great bargaining power."

"Where is she getting this shit?" Stu said.

"Not the time, Stewart."

"How do I know you're more important than the man I have here?"

"You just need to believe me."

"How . . . how would we arrange it? This car is stuck. We would need transportation. I think you're not telling the truth! You're nobody."

He wants to deal. There's a chink in his armor.

You can't take Tam, though. No way in hell you take Tam.

Jake looked up to the sky, the high clouds, the tank looming over them. Suddenly, he knew exactly what to do.

"Cover me, Stu," he said, and he got to his feet.

"What are you doing, Jake? Don't give up your position! Stay down, stay down!"

Jake stepped around the white Nissan Armada with his hands in the air. The man behind it was small and wiry, clad in black, with dark eyes and a deep scowl. Eyes that suddenly flashed with recognition. "It's you," the man said. "The one who murdered my men in Africa."

"Jake," Tam said, glaring with exasperation.

"There's no deal here," Jake called out. "She's bullshitting you. She's nobody. Just a cop."

"Jake."

"You're the one," the man said, his expression hardening.

The realization of who he was facing hit Jake all at once. How this man had survived the blast in Mali didn't matter—none of it mattered while they still had Duncan.

"Maybe I am," he said. "That man you have there, though, is the son of the woman who owns this company. He has great value." Jake stepped closer, felt Tam silently seething.

The small man's eyes narrowed. He quickly looked from the car, to Tam, and back to Jake, fingering the detonator.

"What I suggest," Jake said as calmly as he could, "is that we let this thing between us pass." He held out his hands away from his body. "I'm not armed. The cop wants your hostage back, but I only care about the bombs. I don't care about you, or her, or the guy in the car. If you put the detonator down, you and the hostage can leave and arrange a ransom with the mother separately."

"Leave," the man scoffed, looking around them.

"That's right," said Jake. "I'll call a helicopter right now. All I ask is that you put the detonator down."

"You lie about the helicopter."

"Watch." Jake raised his hand to his earpiece. "Wade, will you come up and hold station by the northernmost tank? Stay about five hundred feet off the deck."

A moment later the far-off sound of a helicopter's rotors thumped over the landscape.

"You hear that?" Jake said.

The Robinson appeared overhead, its rotor wash shaking the puddles and grass around them.

"So now, here's what we do!" Jake shouted over the noise of the chopper. "I'll step back with the cop to give you room. We'll go back about fifty meters. When you feel safe, put down the detonator. Then the chopper lands. Okay?"

The man stared at Jake with narrowed eyes, saying nothing. Jake took Tam by the elbow and began to step back. Tam yanked her arm from Jake's grip.

"What. The fuck. Are you doing?" she asked, stepping back with him.

"Trust me," he told her.

"I had it under control! Now you're giving Duncan away?"

"Trust me."

Fifty meters or so away, Jake stopped.

"If you're thinking I've got a shot on this guy," Stu said, "think again. I've got nothing."

"Stu, do you see the valve at the bottom of the tank?"

"I see it."

Jake nodded, then signaled for the man to place the detonator on the ground.

Slowly, eyes up, the man knelt and left the walkie-talkie on the concrete slab.

Jake brought a hand to his earpiece. "Shoot the valve, Stewart. Take it out."

A sharp *crack!* sounded over the noise of the chopper, followed by a nearly simultaneous *ping!* and a rushing, glugging sound like water. The man looked up in surprise and horror from the base of the tank before disappearing in a blooming cloud of frozen fog that roiled and pulsed around him as the tank spilled supercooled liquid oxygen onto the slab.

"Oh my God," Tam said, clapping a hand over her mouth.

The tank ran for thirty seconds before emptying, sending a cloud of white vapor into the chopper's rotor wash.

Stu came running from the direction of the Sprinter. "I had no idea where you were going with that!" he said, shaking Jake by the shoulders. "No idea at all! That was fucking perfect, Jake! Brilliant!" He took off at a run toward the tank.

Jake turned to the helicopter and pressed his earpiece. "Wade, if you're receiving me, can you get on any law enforcement frequencies? We could use an ambulance over here."

A moment passed before Wade replied. "No joy," he said. "I'll set down back at the main lot and send someone over. From up here I can see at least seven emergency vehicles lining up at the main entrance."

Wade wheeled the chopper away.

Jake and Tam walked toward the tank. The ground shone with ice; the air was filled with a crackling sound like shattering glass as the leaves and blades of grass around them fractured under their own weight. At the corner of the concrete pad, Stu stood over the small man frozen solid in a twisted pose of agony.

Jake stepped carefully to the Nissan, which was covered with frost. The rear driver's side door handle was so cold it nearly burned, and Jake covered his hand with his sleeve to open it. Inside, Duncan Nash turned his head and blinked.

"I know you," Duncan said weakly.

"We met before," Jake said. "You helped me out after that helicopter crash. My turn to return the favor." He offered his hand, and Duncan shook it. "I'm Jake Moran. And I know someone who's going to be very happy to see you."

Duncan closed his blackened eyes and nodded. "Thank you," he said.

"Sit tight. We'll get some help here in a minute."

Tam had stepped back into an area of drier grass and stood with her arms crossed and an unreadable expression on her face. Jake walked slowly to join her.

"I . . ." A voice sounded in Jake's earpiece, and he shook his head.

"Jake, it's Wade back at the main parking lot, you read?"

"Just a second," Jake said. "Moran here, what's up?"

"Help is on the way, but can you give me a status on the Nash kid? They're trying to patch Helena in to speak with you, but we've got incompatible comms, looks like."

"He's pretty beat up, but alert—" A siren wailed as an ambulance crept over the canal lift bridge. "Wade, stand by one," Jake said before waving to Stu. "Stewart! *Stewart!* Stop those guys before they get stuck!"

Stu understood immediately and took off at a run toward the ambulance, waving his hands in warning.

Jake raised his fingers to his earpiece. "Wade, sit tight, let Helena know we'll be right there." He gestured for Tam to follow him to Stu's van. Fortunately, the keys were left in the ignition, and Jake started up the Sprinter and looped around the ambulance.

Stu, assisting in pulling a gurney from the back of it, glanced over with a look of surprise as his van passed by.

Jake and Tam were silent as they drove over the lift bridge and through the tall grass back to the parking lot. Tam shook her head and pursed her lips like she was trying not to smile.

"I wasn't some damsel in distress, you know," she said, looking forward. "I really did have things under control."

"You did," Jake said. "I know you did. I'm sorry I got in the way of that. I just didn't know—"

"Didn't know what?"

"Hold on," Jake said. They were back in the parking lot now, and Wade waved to them from the far side, where the Robinson chopper sat still. Helena stood—much smaller—at his side and stepped forward to pull open the van's door once Jake rolled to a stop.

"You've seen him?" Helena asked firmly. "He's alive?"

"He is," Jake said, stepping down to the pavement. "I think he's going to be okay."

Helena's eyes shone for a moment; then she blinked and nodded firmly, touching her hand to Jake's shoulder. "You saved my son," she said. "You saved him. And"—she looked to the Kingfisher building and nodded again—"you saved so much more. I'll never be able to thank you enough."

Jake grinned. "Well, if I ever need something launched into orbit," he said, "I'll know who to call."

Tam joined them, and Helena reached to grasp her hand.

"Anything," Helena said. "Anything I can do."

More sirens sounded at the front gate, and Wade raised his hand to shield his eyes from the sun as he surveyed the scene. "Helena, I think we've got some people knocking at the door who are going to want to speak with you. You want to do that out here, or . . . ?"

"I think you raise a very good point, Mr. Wade," Helena said, peering off toward the gate now too.

"Let's get inside," Wade said. "You guys too. Might as well be comfortable while we make our statements, you know?"

"We'll be right there," Tam said. "Give us a minute."

Helena and Wade started toward the front entrance of the main Kingfisher building, and Tam squared herself in front of Jake with her hands on her hips.

"So what didn't you know?" she asked.

"Excuse me?"

Tam rolled her eyes. "In the van. You said you were sorry. You said you didn't know . . . something. What didn't you know?"

Jake looked to the sky for a moment to collect his thoughts. "I didn't know what was going to happen. Where things might have gone if that guy accepted your offer. The thought of him taking you . . . I don't know." He glanced over his shoulder at the emergency vehicles lining up at the entrance gate before meeting Tam's eyes again. "I should have stayed back, but I guess I couldn't handle it." He shook his head. "If he took you, I don't know what I would have done, okay?"

"You would have figured something out," Tam said. "You seem to have a knack for it."

Jake shrugged. "Whatever your plan was, though, you obviously had things under control."

"I guess I was making it up as I went along."

Jake nodded. "Story of my life," he said, but Tam didn't laugh.

"I suppose it could have ended quite badly," she admitted.

Jake said nothing. The sirens grew louder, and the two looked at each other for a long time without speaking.

"But," she finally said, "your way worked. It worked very well. Thank you."

"We took care of it together."

"We did, Moran. We certainly did. I'd say we even make a pretty decent team."

Jake wanted to say something funny, a joke to break the tension. Instead, he shook his head, stepped forward, and held Tam in a close embrace.

"We do," he said, holding her as tightly as he could. "We really, really do."

ACKNOWLEDGMENTS

This book would have died with Shawn without the love and support of Julie Klomparens, Abigail Koons, and Kerri Buckley. Shawn's family would like to thank Ed Stackler and Megha Parekh and the staff at Amazon Publishing.

ABOUT THE AUTHOR

Photo © 2014 David Swift

Shawn Klomparens is the author of *Jessica Z.* and *Two Years, No Rain*, as well as *The Banks of Certain Rivers*, written under the pen name Jon Harrison. In 2014, Klomparens received a Creative Writing Fellowship from the Wyoming Arts Council. He lived and wrote in Jackson, Wyoming, with his wife and two children until July 2024, when he died of a terminal illness.